I0612081

IMPROBABLE
Male Love Stories

PETER MELILLO

Copyright © 2020 by Peter Melillo

Cover design by Linda Kosarin/The Art Department
Typeset by Raymond Luczak
Cover photo by Judy Clarke

All rights reserved, including the right of reproduction in whole or in part in any form.

Published by Querelle Independent, a division of Querelle Press LLC
2808 Broadway #4
New York, NY 10025

www.querellepress.com

ISBN: 978-1-7335980-2-6, paper edition
ISBN: 978-1-7335980-3-3, e-book edition

Distributed by Ingram Content Group
Printed in the United States

First edition 2020

Published by Querelle Independent,
an author publishing service division of Querelle Press

For Robert W. Imlah
1946-2012

CONTENTS

Preface

Improbable: Male Love Stories is a collection of twelve gay-affirming short fictions. A more descriptive title would be *Unlikely: Man to Man Adventures of the Heart on or about Holidays and Bicycles*. Clearly the most accurate title is too long. To prevent sexual orientation confusion, same-sex sex or sex talk is present in many of these stories.

It is acknowledged there are more than twelve holidays each year; some more esoteric than others. This holiday sampler is a random assortment of new and old special days. The collection is fiction; any similarity to non-historical persons, places, events, bikes, bicycles, derailleur, bike-shop-gay-bar, velodrome, jockstraps, or playing cards is coincidental.

In the story "New Year," Maximillian Foreaux is rescued from a potentially lethal New Year's Eve. Two strangers bring in the New Year having overly long, drawn-out sex. Then complications are uncovered, look impossible, and move on from unlikely to possible with conditions."

"Valentines," mentions; after midnight, public park cruising for sex in the age of social media hookup apps using GPS, queer bashing, homophobia, a transsexual psychiatrist, a gay hotline, deformed penis, a telephoned bomb threat, and the gay community's relationship with their police department.

For this "Earth Day" short story: the color is pink, boys can wear dresses, and meeting a match can radically change plans. A deluge pours rain continuously from March twentieth, Spring Equinox, to April twenty-second; "Earth Day." Meanwhile human habitation on planet Earth slides toward extinction. A bicycle accident precipitates an effeminate top topping a macho top, and for that there is a consequence.

"Finals" is about an end of semester blind student's reader and unanticipated events. A reference to Paul Goodman's legacy and Helen Keller's wisdom is mentioned, as well as Delayed Action for Childhood Arrival (DACA).

In "Memorial" the United States of America's historical baked-in domestic conflicts are exposed to understand how the country was lost to Mother Russia's New Soviet Union without a shot fired. Al and Noland do what persecuted homosexuals always have; made the best of a bad situation.

Christopher Street Liberation Day – "CSLD" is about an uncle relating his first-hand experience of the Stonewall Rebellion, and one year later, the first New York City Gay Pride march, to his nephew and nephew's intended. Historical context sets up the three-day rebellion in this telling of events. The revolt mentioned in "CSLD" is as this writer remembers experiencing the second of three nights of rioting in Greenwich Village, on June twenty-eighth, nineteen sixty-nine.

In "Independence," nonfiction style is wrapped around fiction to set context. Readers put-off mixing nonfiction with fiction should skip the first three and last two pages of this story. Mentioned in this story are: consequences of interfering with children's bodies and minds during developmental stages. Also mentioned, peculiar mother love, pediatrician child sex abuse, boy scout camping, thumb sucking, and perceived divine relations related to biological maturation.

Neither the first Monday in September or Labor Day are mentioned in this "Labor" story. A Native-American bakery night-foreman day-college student and two hearing-impaired baker's apprentices interact in opposite ways in this short fiction. Some readers may take issue with sex in the workplace and might want to skip this story. Other topics touched on are yeast versus baking-powder-soda-eggs as leavening, cochlear implants, building a relationship, and Wayne Griffiths' NORM. A much earlier, less developed version of this story was published online as "Bench Hands."

In "Halloween" Jeremy Long lived his last eleven years through a fog filter. He never believed in ghosts and thinks at age twenty-two is too old to start. When pressed for an explanation of parapsychological goings on in his new home, he decides he's gone bonkers. But Jeremy has no clinical symptoms to support his self-diagnosis of insanity. Ultimately, he relies on Albert Einstein for a rationalization. An early version of "Halloween" was published on line as "Haunted Property."

"Thanks" reveals a family's rocky present and disturbing past while eating an elegant Thanksgiving meal. They don't have to love or even like each other. But the matriarch demands they behave like her idea of a family. She holds the purse strings and will even from the grave.

"World AIDS Day" explores the question, "Is HIV-AIDS a terrible new *gay* disease deserving little or no public health response? Or is it a mutated retrovirus without sexual orientation? Silence equaled thousands of unnecessary or premature deaths due to a malicious U.S. President's homophobia. In 1987, after 50,000 U.S. citizens had died from AIDS complications, Europeans with the United Nations declared December first, nineteen eighty-eight, World AIDS Day. President Ronald Reagan explained he never uttered AIDS in eight years as President because, "Gays want special treatment, and I refuse to give it to them." In the meantime, worldwide 41 million people have died from a disease President Reagan refused to mention.

Two mama's boys and a fireman address the emotional aftermath of a Christmas Eve home burnout. Mothers and other deities often teach, "When one door closes, another opens." "Christmas" deals with middle-age bisexuality, ménage-de-trios, values, 9/11, and the Boston Marathon bombing. A much less developed version of "Christmas" was published online as "Christmas Spirit."

It is hoped these twelve-short sort of love stories will show gay men having the same foibles, wants, and needs as the heterosexuals who created us.

New Year

Always too busy, punctuated by flurries of frenetic invention, I've created much more wealth than most people my age and then some. It's true, when younger, I was either full out whirlwind of creative output or dead in the water at full stop. Then, just before turning twenty-three, with ongoing pharmaceutical intervention, I jettisoned the stops to become fulltime arrogantly productive. It's better living through chemistry, and includes as much sex as I want. Consequently, I have little time or interest in messy after-sex complications. I'm not that kind of guy.

My most recent invention, a carbon fiber autonomous electric recumbent bicycle with discrete direct satellite GPS guidance. The new bike is not for anyone not thinking ahead of their time. Plus, the cost is extravagant, with a long waiting list to buy, and the factory is working three shifts at full capacity. Like most of my commercial ventures, the bike is earning me better than expected. So, I'll soon be selling that company and rights. I enjoy passing on my successes to others, at a profit. For me it's ever onward and upward.

Looking ahead, I've stepped away from my engineering background to make art. My latest passion is putting oil paint on stretched-canvas. Now that my work is selling well, I may open a gallery to increase profits. At age thirty-three, I look better than I did at twenty-three, with a libido to match. Even though I stand five-feet, four-inches at 127 pounds, I possess the energy of a giant. My new hair style accents eye color and projects a dynamo with a big dick? Simply said and not bragging, I'm rich, good looking, and very good sex in bed.

As the New Year approaches, I desire something out of the ordinary to bring in another prosperous twelve months. Elusive rumors of an exclusive party cloaked in mystery have drifted my way. Shouldn't a New Year's Eve party be a little crazy to be fun? Based on my lifestyle, the farther out from normal the more rewarding the experience, up to the point of death or worse incarceration.

Exactly how I wrangled an invitation to the esoteric New Year's Eve party at the luxurious Triumph Palace in midtown Manhattan, discretion forbids telling fully. But the bribes were sizeable. Often oblivious making paintings, I didn't anticipate what I was getting into when a uniformed messenger appeared. He insisted I sign for a fancy handmade gilded invitation. As I scribbled my name, the messenger addressed me with condescension. "You will *dress down,* or not be admitted, with or without this invitation."

My assistant, Matty's research indicated an older male couple was hosting the party in their 10,000-square-foot midtown Manhattan apartment. The couple owns the building, most of the adjacent neighborhood, and is wealthier than a medium size developed country. Sounds like my kind of folks. Reportedly, they don't flaunt their prosperity. I don't show off either. My inquisitiveness was roused, when Matty couldn't find the source of their riches.

Marty helped dressed me down, as the party required. He shopped at one of the better church thrift store for worn-out, once expensive, homeless looking clothes. There are many superstitions portending to start a new year auspiciously. I'd not heard of old clothes being one. But far be it for me to question the party host's foibles.

* * * *

To say the party place was grandly stylish would be grossly inadequate. The elevator opened inside a palace-like opulence, containing a mix of wall-to-wall people. I was immediately greeted by a handsome, tall, young gym bunny. He took my invitation, crossed my name off a list, and motioned to one of two stunningly beautiful young men holding trays of Champagne flutes. Both men standing above me were well-built, very tall, and nude except for formal black silk socks held up by black garters and formal black bow ties. It was a theme I noticed repeated among severs and their handlers.

My greeter handed me a flute of Champagne off the other man's tray and said, "At midnight, peel off the symbol on the bottom of your glass and place it on your forehead. There is a game to start the New Year."

I wanted to ask details about the contest but was well out of my comfort zone, craning my neck looking up. In addition, I was clothed, and they were not. Anyway, the height imbalance was giving me a crick, and it would have been rude to do a closer inspection at eye, I mean crotch, level. So, I attempted to mingle, not something I do well.

Looking around the crowded party, I didn't see anyone I knew or celebrities and notables I'd anticipated meeting. I did notice other party-goer wearing artistically interesting, obviously old, well-worn thrift shop togs. I did a fast empirical calculation of the room. Seventy percent of attendees wore high-end custom-made for them formalwear, twenty percent present wore second-hand homeless-like garb, and the last ten percent present were servers and their supervisors walking around nude.

The servers offered trays of Champagne, white powder neatly cut into lines, and indescribably delicious, exotic finger foods. The party hosts must have depleted every professional model agency providing tall, nude male servers between the ages of eighteen and twenty-five.

Despite my controlled hypomania, I am not a party person. So, after a time standing in a corner, comparing servers' usually hidden attributes, for future fantasy tableaus, I finally got bored. And I decided the party was a bust and to go home and welcome the New Year with a hand job before working on my latest large painting.

Just then, a man my height, whom I'd not noticed among the throng of party guests, walked over and conspicuously looked me up and down. "Hi, I'm Josh. You are the most attractive man dressed in old clothes at this shindig."

"Let me suggest you visit an optometrist. You'll be surprised how your vision improves with corrective eyewear."

"Don't be rude, I am being nice, and you look in need of a friend."

"I'm just leaving."

"You *are* the most attractive man our size here, and for your information, I have twenty-twenty uncorrected vision."

"Good for you."

"Let's cut the small talk. You are the size I like and want to bed you to welcome the New Year."

"Have you looked in the mirror? We appear the same age, weight, height, eye and hair color, and even dress. Except I'm over thirty and you are not. We are too much alike to make for an interesting hookup."

"Dwell on our difference, I'm a well-trained bottom, and you carry yourself like a top. I can take all you got and more to bring in a New Year to remember. Age is irrelevant, if you can keep up."

"Ho hum, really? A change of topic, my good man. What do you know about this party's midnight games?"

"I will tell you for a lay."

"Tell me now, if you remotely hope for a rump hump from me."

"Oh bother … as you wish kind sir. Not all guests received a symbol under their glass, like we did. The doorman makes the connection from our old clothes, and summons over the server with the stick-on. Formally dressed penguins watch us put-on a show."

"What's the show?"

"How suicidal are you?"

"It's not my usual mood."

"According to my information, after the stroke of midnight's shouting, horn blowing, and confetti tossing, those with self-stick symbols are herded into a room, and squeamish guests leave. Next, big nude bruisers match-up our symbols, strip us naked in pairs. Then our hosts and other penguins do some unsolicited crotch groping and ass probing to set the order of matches. The gladiator-like game is to stick your forehead symbol on your opponents' ball sack while not getting his on yours. I'll let you imagine how all that wriggling, punching, kicking, and slapping looks and feels."

"Sounds like an orgy. Are there prizes beyond slap and tickle?"

"I've heard the prizes can be extravagant for the thumbs up participants."

"Do the thumbs down get consolation prizes?

"They get an involuntary injection and taken to a guest holding pen for party losers."

"How do you know this?"

"A friend of a friend arranged my invitation. I was told what to expect and consequences for not playing along with great flourish and gusto."

"That's it, I'm out a here, see yah."

"They just locked the elevator, you can't leave the way you came."

"What the hell!"

"You didn't let me finish telling you about the late after-party, party, in the kitchen. It happens after most formal guests and staff left."

"New friend, please elucidate?"

"The after-party party is to get rid of thumbs-down, drugged or drunk party pooper guests. They get more or less snuffed, in unusual ways for arcane entertainment. Guests count out load as humane remains slowly disappear in a supersize industrial garbage disposal. After the last body goes in, their old clothes follow into the disposal. They're all ground up together and sluiced directly to the City's sewage system."

"What do you mean more or less snuffed? I thought that was either-or?"

"I've heard some folks go into the disposal's whirling blades while still moving. That's why you must put on a good show, for our illustrious hosts, to keep from disappearing into sewage."

"Is what you say true?"

"Stay and see. Did you notice we are the only ones here our size? I guess it is you or me and the garbage eating machine."

The elevators were locked, and there were no other exits visible. "Do you know a way out of here?"

"Yes, but first, your place or mine? I live in Jersey."

"Brooklyn, is closer."

"Follow me ... there are fire exit stairs by the staff bathrooms."

"How do you know that?"

"I'd heard rumors about this party. To be safe, I looked up the floor plans for this place. Call me paranoid. Just don't call me Shorty."

"I'll call you what I want. I always get my way."

"Well, we'll have to see about that?"

I wish I'd done more research myself. "Before we met, were you going to play this to the end?"

"I was thinking if nothing more interesting happened, I might see how crazy it got. Then you came along. I'd rather make love with you than fight you to stay alive."

"Uh ha, I see, okay ... get me out of here and I'll throw you a fuck."

"Just so we understand each other, I want a long ride on your dick to screw in the New Year properly, promise not to disappoint me."

"Or what, you'll beat me up and feed me to the sewer?"

"No, I'll be sad."

Josh is exactly my stature and all his parts fit together attractively, only he isn't the size I usually bed. During our escape down the fire-stairs, I asked how he got to the party from New Jersey. He had taken his touring-bicycle on the New Jersey Path train, and then rode it uptown from the Christopher Street stop in the village.

Once outside the party building, a promise is a promise, we biked downtown, then over the Brooklyn Bridge to the loft building I own in Crown Heights. Normally I'd take a trick uptown to my fancy six-room apartment, on the upper Eastside. But Josh was a stranger from strange circumstances. I didn't want his karma tainting my home. Plus, I needed to get as far away from that lethal party as possible. My living-work loft space fit the bill perfectly.

Bike riding in New York City is for all seasons. The freedom to move fast through stopped traffic-jams, and pedestrian clogged-sidewalks, while looking down from a bicycle seat at stuck masses, was invigorating. New Year's Eve's weather was brisk but not cold for bike riding. There was no breeze, and the moon was full and bright. With no traffic on the bridge, we got to my Brooklyn place before midnight.

I had a case of Prosecco stashed in the loft for special occasions. We drank from a bottle, leaving a trail of outer then inner garments as we stripped each other headed to the sleeping area. He was more than an eyeful nude. His body parts all fit together perfectly. in just the right proportion. He had sparsely haired legs and calves well defined from bike-riding. His pretty butt was hairless, supple yet firm. I'd watched it with interest when he bicycled ahead of me to the loft.

The New Year arrived, complete with near and far fireworks' sounds, to accompany our mouths and hands getting busy with exploration. His cock and balls looked similar to mine, but slightly smaller. He was hot we were hard, and we'd just escaped having to kill each other at a lethal party. It was time to clear our heads, get down and busy.

Something new occurred, I allowed him to be active. He got extremely animated pleasuring me. At first, his body felt odd in my hands. I have always preferred much bigger than me men, to overpower and conquer anally. But Josh's adoration made me feel big. To focus on his love making repertoire, I turned off the lights. Without visuals, my tactile pleasure was measurably enhanced and I wasn't distracted.

When I took charge, my enjoyment was boosted higher. His aural feedback demonstrated how much he liked being dominated. My toothy-nipping got the loudest response. He was hot, and I adored being worshiped and flattered by a submissive. We intuitively switched back and forth without discussion or resistance. Active, passive, flowed back and forth between us to keep the energy fluid. It was almost like we read each other's minds.

In my experience, foreplay is either too short or goes on well beyond my cock's boredom quotient. Josh got it just right, like he knew where I was, and how to keep me fully aroused. Then at precisely the right instant, he pushed me flat on my back, rose up and slid me into his tight ass. He swallowed my cock to the hilt in one smooth motion. Then it got hotter as he rode me, going up and down, impaled on my most-interested throbbing cock. As best as I could see in the dark, it looked like he rode a merry-go-round horse, ecstatically gliding up and down my pride and joy.

"Wait, stop, I need to put on a condom."

"Don't worry, I've got you covered. I'm negative."

"How do you know I am?"

"You wouldn't have been at the party if you weren't. Powerful people have ways of knowing things they shouldn't."

I was most definitely negative, and the greater danger came being anal receptive. Still in all, bareback riding is an antiquated, foolish, risky vice. Then he got me distracted, gliding up and down my dick, doing a little hula-hoop twist as his bottom reached my pubes. He followed that immediately with a cha-cha-cha motion when he contacted my nuts. At slow speed, what he was doing was erotically delicious. As he increased the pace, sexy feelings increased to *full on fabulous,* beyond words. My crotch went from interested arousal, to stoking fire toward full rolling boil.

Josh continued to ride my cock carousel-style, right up to the edge of a big cum blasting, welcome to the New Year orgasm. Then he froze a microsecond short of getting my nut. He wasn't moving a hair, just before I pulled the trigger. At the exact moment, I expected to plunge over the edge into bliss, he was frozen like a stone statue. We were panting in unison ready to go. My eyes questioned his in the dark. He looked back in wily triumph.

Then I noticed his hands pinned my shoulders, and his feet locked my knees tight. His body weight controlled me, immobile. In that instant I knew what it felt like to be under another's control, and I didn't like it. Who was top who was bottom now? I built my life and fortunes being on top.

Just as I felt my face register frustration and my cock start to flag, he began kissing me with renewed energy. He was more attuned to my needs than anyone I'd known. I kissed back, I like kissing. What else could I do stationary? I became aware my breathing was back to normal. My cock was alert from the kissing, but no longer on hair trigger, fire command. Again, he caught my attention, sliding up and down my dick. This time he used a lighter ass grip.

The second time he brought me right to the brim of a huge blasting climax, it happened much faster. Again, I was immobilized just before blasting bliss. *What was his game?* I could just make out his smiling eyes. In concession, I smiled back. At the party, he'd said he wanted a long ride. *Was this a contest?* As I was about to ask, he folded his head down and licked my nipples. The luscious sensation drew enough attention to distract me. On male principal, I tried to twist and turn to gain control to shoot my rocks off. In response, he sucked my nipples harder. It felt exquisite, so, made me stop squirming.

He started riding my cock again, once I'd stopped moving. *I wondered, was there a chance of having an accidental discharge? No, he moved too slow and easy.* I needed more friction. He seemed to know that, and rode slower-slacker. When my cock started to wilt, requiring more stimulation, he squeezed tighter and moved faster. Fulfilling my want, just as it arrived. He was magnificent. I'd never been so sexually aroused, simmered-down, and then keyed up again, and again. Concentrating on our friction-speed interplay drew my focus off the primary, cumming, until that thought brought it back. At each apex, beyond my usual turned on state, my guts went into turmoil, twisting. *What was pleasure; what was pain. When did I surrender to his control?* Once more he pinned me before I could push through the last second to a well-deserved, much anticipated finish. *Could he somehow know my thoughts? No.*

Josh's eyes glowed with delight in the dark, he was enjoying himself. It wasn't about just teasing my body anymore he was in my head too. My face showed what I was thinking, *I'm the top, I know I am. At the party, he said he wanted to be topped by me. Should I put a stop to his teasing? I didn't sign on for weird.*

While I was lost in thought, he moved his hands, braced himself, and swiveled around 180 degrees, still with my cock pegging him in place. The movement caused new sensations in my crotch that distracted my cognition back to present tense. Full focus arrived just as Josh fingered my toes, first one foot then the other. Delighted, my toes found his finger play tantalizing, overpowering really. And my mind began flying red flags. *Were we building toward aching blue balls to start the New Year? Blue balls came from not discharging after too much buildup. A man needs to release his pent-up sperm. Didn't he need to cum too?*

Alarmed, I tried to wiggle and writhe to finish by shooting spunk. In response to my effort, he leaned back, moved his hands behind, and pressed my chest into the bed. I couldn't move. To gain control of something, I concentrated on taking slow deep breaths, and ruminated, *We should have talked, set ground rules before starting, my bad. Was I getting pissed at him or me? From the start, he had been anticipating my moves, wasn't that invading my privacy? Yet I was sharing pleasure on a level I'd never known, or knew existed. I needed to figure out what I wanted. Win his game by overpowering him like a brute, or lay back and enjoy being powerless over his power-bottom skills.*

Watching my face, maybe reading my thoughts, he began shimmying up and down my pole again. Slowly and loosely at first, and then by measured increments, he squeezed tighter and increased speed. We'd been there before. What should I do about it? Nothing?

I hatched a plan. Just when I anticipated his stopping, I'd roll him onto his side and thrust hard and fast and finish, done! The thought was thrilling, it wouldn't take much in and out to get my debt to him paid. I'd make my move quickly, at precisely the right instant. Then the moment came, and he thwarted me. Josh was ready when I made my move. He pushed back hard. I almost got there, just not quite enough movement to finish. *How could he have known what and when?*

My mind stewed on my immobilized circumstance, searching for another way to climax. Then it occurred to me, *I don't know the rules for domination, bondage and all that other esoteric sex crap. Could it be Josh likes to top-tops, the way I enjoy topping much bigger than me. Does he think I should just lay back and let him do as he pleases? Maybe he thinks my not speaking gives him consent to his whims?* Josh brought my attention back to him tickling the bottoms of my feet.

Then he got me back to the edge of cumming, quickly, again, and again, and yet again. Each time the intensity of my need to blast cum increased, just beyond my pleasure pain limit. And each time he'd stop just short of my bliss. Obviously, I didn't know the rules of the game, *Still, how could he toy with me, like he knew me so well!*

Josh rotated back around, still sitting on my cock, eyes on fire we made lusty-eye contact in the dark. He *was* definitely in my head. So, I projected what I was thinking, *If my cock loses interest, it will shrivel, and we'll both be very sorry.*

He nodded yes and began to fiddle thumbs and forefingers on my nipples hard. The next time we locked eyes, I spoke for the first time since we started sexing. "I've had too much fun I need to cum, right now!"

"It will happen when I say so."

"Now, I want to cum now!"

"Huh, or what do you suppose?"

"I'll burst."

"Oh, okay then, you may cum when you feel the first salvo of my spunk hit your face, not before."

The idea relief was seconds away shot hope to every stoma. Josh's hand started sensually stroking his half-interested cock. Then hard, he pointed it at my face, and his active hand turned into a blurry fist. Determination written on his face, he was pulling and pushing back and forth faster and faster. Out of breath he demanded, "Close your eyes and keep them shut."

At that point, his attention was off me. I could have taken over and forced my orgasm into him. But anticipation had switched my focus to *his* approaching detonation. My eagerness for release had gone well beyond nerve wracking, to be supplanted by vicariously panting his. So, eyes closed, hearing him get ready to get off, in a weird way it added another element to my promised impending ecstasy?

Eyes closed I sensed his self-pleasure build to its peak. He was still gyrating on my prick. I felt his urgency abruptly stop with a grunt and prolonged-shudder. After a silent anticipating void, he uttered, "Oomph!" Then a hot ribbon of cum hit my left ear lobe, and draped down my cheek to chin. It was immediately followed by a second salvo that streaked down the right side of my face, nose to jowl. Each of his first three hot jizz fusillades was propelled with a grunt. I lost track of the number of his cum blasts because of the smell of his testosterone in my nostrils.

Then abruptly, I was floating-weightless-mindless in joyous bliss beyond any issue I ever experienced. In half-twilight-awareness, Josh finished spurting facial cream vigorously riding up and down my dick, squeezing his sphincter hard. With so many build ups and blocked finishes, having my eyes closed enhanced rapture, beyond imaginable. Then after an interval of serene euphoria, I was gloriously whitewashing Josh's insides. Finally done, it *was* worth the torture to get there. I'd never reached that height of elation before.

Panting, heart racing from prolonged ecstasy, Josh leaned forward, up off my cock and we kissed deeply. Then he slid his lips sideways to slowly lick his cum off my face. Finished, he said, "Now it's safe to open your eyes."

Before I could formulate what to say or even speak, he was all kissy face again. Josh was very attentive after sex. Given my confusion during the deed, his after-play was grounding, reassuring. The next thing I knew, he was contentedly sleeping in my arms, his mouth glued on mine.

I took a moment to reflect on what just happened, with a stranger, in my bed, and why and how we were there. It was too much, so, I got disentangled and headed to the bathroom to pee. Before I came, my insides were in mixed-up in turmoil. I needed to know I was back to normal down in that department.

Surprise, surprise, I was wearing an over full condom. *How come I didn't know this before we fucked?* He must have rolled it on with his mouth during foreplay, before he mounted my cock. *Was I so turned on I didn't notice, obviously!Strange occurrences were accumulating, mostly out of sight.*

When I returned to the sleeping area, my plan was to snuggle up next to Josh, cuddle him and Morpheus. Then I noticed I'd forgotten the bathroom light on. As I moved to turn it off, I noticed the bedside clock. We'd been sexing for hours, it was sunrise. *With that much time fucking, was his bottom sphincter-ring retracted back in tight, or had it puffed out the way they show in some pornos?*

I was sure he wouldn't mind my looking. Given the degree of intimacy we had just shared. So, I gently rolled him over and spread his cheeks. His tight little pucker was tucked back in, snug. But the area around it looked well exercised to a blushing pink. Then I glimpsed something black inside his inner thigh near where it became his groin. Maybe it was a birth mark or mole. I was feeling this guy as a keeper. He'd taken me to new places, and worked hard to get me there. I wanted to know everything about him. So, I rolled deep-sleeping Josh back over, his pretty cock was half-hard in sleep. I couldn't make out what the black was, until I pulled his loose-scrotum to one side.

Flabbergasted, I felt like I'd been punched in the gut. I stared open mouth at a small black swastika tattoo, hidden by his balls. All my warm, cuddly, nesting feeling for Josh turned to ice. He was no keeper, there was no place for a hate symbol and what it represented in my busy productive life.

I went back into the bathroom to think, *Kick him out now, or kick him out when he wakes.*I took a long shower and tried to scrub Josh's touch off my body with a loofah and lots of body wash lather. The man had gotten under my skin and wouldn't scrub away. *People are never what they seem, and that was always disappointing.*

After drying, I yanked on a new pair of green flannel gym shorts and a new white t-shirt. It was one of my quirks, to start the New Year wearing new clothes. I headed to the kitchen area and brewed a pot of coffee, the hidden swastika rattling around between my ears. *Why didn't I pick up some clue, a warning vibe?*

I escorted a mug of coffee to my work area and stood before the half-done, large canvas that needed finishing. I tried to focus on the canvas and bright happy colors to add. That failed, so I tried to think about my new venture opening a gallery to sell my art. That failed too.

My mind wouldn't leave what that damn swastika represented. I don't do well going from one extreme to another. We had had amazing sex and now I was feeling awful, tricked by a New Year surprise. There was no room for Josh, and hate … forgetting him became my plan.

Coffee and meditation usually don't go together for me. But I had to gain control over my thoughts, so I unrolled a mat and assumed the position. With stern determination, I finally cleared my thoughts to stare into the abyss, and as Nietzsche said, 'It started back.'

Then the next thing to enter my consciousness was freshly-showered Josh wafting clean- smelling body wash aroma. Standing over me, he said, "Happy New Year, may I help myself to coffee?"

I shrugged back to consciousness, and nodded my head in the coffee's direction. "There are clean mugs in the dish drainer, milk in the fridge, sugar on the counter, spoons in the draw, and your bike by the door."

"What's up? Am I picking up negative vibes?"

"Yeah, about that, let's skip breakfast. After your coffee, please leave."

"Today is a holiday. After last night, I thought you'd want more fun and games."

"Thanks, but no thanks."

"Did I do something to offend?"

"I intend to finish that painting today, without you present."

After scrutinizing the painting, Josh walked over to a rack of finished oil paintings and studied each. "Okay something happened, what? Last night you were a volcano and now you're an iceberg. What's up with that?"

"I don't want to talk about it. Just drink your coffee, get your bike, and the door swings out."

"Huh, last night I thought we started something special. What happened?"

"I'm not feeling talkative today."

"Last night was unique, I want more of that."

"Take a hint. Drink your coffee and go."

"Oh wait, mood change, I got it."

"Finish your coffee before it gets cold and split."

"Did you take your meds today?"

"What's that to you?"

"After my shower, I peeked in your medicine cabinet, looking for a razor. I'm familiar with most of your medications,"

"Were you looking to steal my drugs?"

First looking insulted, then Josh laughed. "No, I wanted to know as much as possible about the guy I'm beginning to fall for. Last night was a test, you passed."

"Do you even know who I am?"

Grinning, Josh shook his head no. "You didn't introduce yourself last night. I know you know, I am Joshua Middlebrooks, new MBA at Acme and associates Financial Planners? Don't look nonplus, I know you know because you went through my wallet while I slept and returned it upside-down."

I was caught and rattled for invading *his* privacy. "I wanted to know who was sleeping in my bed is all. Were you prescribed the same meds as me?"

"My favorite cousin, Randy, took most of them and some others but in higher dosages."

"How's that working for him?"

"Randy killed himself last summer."

"Sorry for your loss ... you still have to leave."

"He was the only *out* person in my family when I came of age. My parents loathed him and then me for being gay."

"Did that cause his suicide?"

"No, he was the *one* of every four bipolar-I people, you know, who kill themselves."

"I didn't know. My meds are working just fine, thank you for asking."

After a long pause, Josh walked back to the kitchen area, retrieved his mug of coffee, and splashed milk in it. "What *is* your name? I can tell a lot about you from last night and now seeing your paintings."

"Maximillian Foreaux, it is printed on my medicine bottles and signed at the bottom of the paintings. Okay, that's enough familiarity, now you have to go."

"I wasn't sure they were your meds, it doesn't look like anyone lives here full-time."

"Discussion over, I want you to leave."

Still not tasting his coffee, Josh appeared to be thinking. Then, laser-like, he made eye contact. "Just so you know, three out of four don't commit suicide. Although, I suppose everyone has thought about it, one time or another. I did when my folks threw me out."

"How did you decide I'm not the next suicide?"

"I didn't, I just want to go deeper with you. I think you're hot to look at and in bed, so don't off yourself, okay?"

Why won't he leave? Why am I having this pointless conversation? But I do like how he looks, tastes, and feels ... the fucking fascist. "There is a lot of space between having a thought and taking drastic action. Don't worry about me just go on about your business, out that door."

"I really like you."

"Are you bipolar too?"

"No, but it runs in my family. For the record, I'm twenty-seven and very vigilant about mental health symptoms. I'd be onboard helping you manage yours."

"Drink your coffee and out you go, I don't need help."

"Come on, last night we were into each other. This morning you're kicking me out. Is it bipolar or did I offend you? I'd still love to kiss you."

"It's too early for kissing."

"Remember you're negotiating with a fresh, new MBA."

"What can you tell from my paintings, Mr. MBA? Here's a chance to be totally honest, before you go out the door."

"You have discipline, integrity, and something new to say with your art. Some of that was confirmed in bed last night."

Blushing slightly, I stood and stared at the unfinished painting. "I'm a sucker for flattery … it is a weakness. So, I guess we can talk a little, while you finish your coffee inflating my head."

"What's up this morning?"

"Since you insist, I found the Buddhist symbol the Nazis' stole, tattooed near your nuts. I hate the hate it represents."

"You're good. Usually it takes three or four dates before discovery. What exactly does it mean to you?"

"Dehumanized intolerance, genocide, unbridled evil, shall I go on?"

"Those are strong words. For me it's a tattoo with no meaning, beyond it wasn't my idea or choice. I couldn't prevent it and survived."

"I want to see tattoo and you on your touring bicycle, pedaling back to New Jersey. I'll draw you a map if necessary."

"At least let me explain."

"No explanation necessary, you stopped being welcome when I found your swastika."

"How about an exchange, you tell me about being bipolar and I tell you about my tattoo?"

"Why waste time? My reaction was immediate and gut wrenching, I wanted to throw up."

"But you didn't, I would've heard."

"I showed restraint, letting you finish sleeping and offering coffee. You should have given me a hate symbol spoiler-alert last night. We could have avoided this morning's unpleasantness."

"Oh, I see, you're feeling guilty because you pried my legs apart and lifted my nut sack and found something you weren't expecting. Just what were you looking for between my legs? *Did you lose something?*" Josh leaned back against the kitchen counter and brought the coffee mug up for a sip.

"You can be sure it was not what I found."

"Be fair, let me explain. Last night was special on several levels, *and* you didn't take any money or credit cards from my wallet when you looked inside."

"Fair? Ridiculous, you think a swastika represents fairness? Wait, don't answer that. I don't want to hear your response. I just want you gone."

"Max, give me half a chance. I deserve that." This was said with volume turned-up, and body language rigid.

After a nonresponsive pause, while we sipped coffee, I made unsympathetic eye contact. "You're right, I owe you for getting me out of that party last night. You got a quarter ... okay flip it. I call tails."

"It is heads ... see? So, I want to know your symptoms, when you were diagnosed, meds, and side effects. Are you Bipolar I or II, and how are you doing with it?"

"I wonder, are you a mental illness freak? Only my psychiatrist and psychopharmacologic guy require that information. Is bipolar your fetish or what?"

"No, it is you I'm interested in. The best-looking man my size at the party, remember? I suspect being bipolar takes a lot of time. I may want a portion of your leftovers."

"Hence, you see our chatting as an interview, not a swan song? This Bipolar II doesn't do well pressured. You need to go court a different guy."

"No pressure, I want to know everything about you. Based on last night, I'm considering a future marriage proposal."

His future marriage proposal was dismissed before the fact. "All right, I'll humor your flattery with the twenty-five-cent version of my crazy. As a teenager, I had high and low symptoms that were more than, but close to normal adolescents."

"Like how, tell me?"

"I'd get way overly enthusiastic about something, anything, and then feel too low when the interest waned. In College, with an engineering major, manic behavior was the norm. It was expected before midterms and finals, and nobody thought anything about crashing after a big flurry of activity to keep your GPA up. I suspected something was up with me. But hid it, and I worked extra hard not to appear too crazy."

"Were you ever hospitalized?"

"Appendix and tonsils at twelve, not for bipolar, but a psychotic episode could still happen. After high school my primary care physician couldn't figuring out why antidepressants didn't work. In the end, he sent me to a psychotherapist who referred me to a good psychopharmacologist who knew her stuff."

"What are your triggers?"

Most people couldn't care less about Josh's interest, or was it more flattery? "Insomnia is my trigger. Once we got that figured out, regular life became manageable. You sure you don't know who I am?"

"You said you are Maximillian Foreaux, artist."

"So far, since I've eliminated the bipolar lows, and trimmed the highs, my life has been a financial success. I've no need to steal from your wallet. I could easily buy the company you work for without a thought."

"Did I touch a nerve, about my wallet?"

"You know I'll be on medication for life. It's potent and no doubt will shorten my time walking around. I'm cautious about emotional attachments, I don't do them well."

"Me too, I am usually cautious with strangers. But there is something about you last night."

"What?"

"Frankness of your paintings, how well we fit together. We get each other, and just met."

"Why did you talk to me at the party?"

"The best-looking man at the party looked unapproachably uncomfortable, standing by himself in a corner. You were an enigma."

"There was no one there I knew or wanted to know. I *was* uncomfortable with the nudity and expensive formal attire, in ridiculous contrast to what we wore."

"The first thing I said to you was my name."

"So, what, you wanted a formal introduction or something?"

"No, but it is civil to be acknowledged by one's name. Maybe even like hearing your name spoken. Were you being bipolar, rude?"

"You may leave, the door is there, scoot."

"Hold on, I heard your story. Return the courtesy."

"Grow up, there is no reason to continue this conversation? I told you what I think of your swastika and you just called me rude. I'm not rude, but *do* take offense at the accusation."

"Hold on, I will truthfully answer anything you ask. I can't leave without explaining what has upset you."

"Fine, fair is fair. I'll listen, just don't expect to change my thinking, it's made up. Mind if I paint while you talk?"

"See, now *that's* rude. Are you trying to hurt my feelings or what?"

"You sipped coffee when I spoke."

"I didn't bring a toothbrush, this morning I have cum breath. Remember, last night I licked cum off your face? As I recall, you showed appreciation with kisses."

Do I need this? If he'd leave, I could paint, meditate, or nap in peace. Why am I indulging this man? "True, it felt good after climaxing, but then your swastika canceled everything. You might not think so, but I'm trying to be fair. If I wanted to be rude, you'd already be on your bike headed out."

"All right, paint, I'll talk you listen."

I went over to my work area, squeezed tubes of paint onto my paint pallet, mixed them and stood back, brush at the ready. I looked over at Josh who was watching me and gave him a nod to speak. Despite his tattoo, he was easy on my eyes, and reminded me of our extreme passion in bed. *What was he waiting for, an engraved invitation?* "So, what's your story?"

Josh told me that when he was fifteen, his mother spring cleaning his bedroom found male nudist magazines his gay cousin Randy had loaned him, hidden under his mattress. When he came home from school that day, his fanatically religious parents were waiting, made him kneel, and prayed over him. Then they handed him a plastic garbage bag containing his clothes. They said his soul was lost to hell and he should never darken their door again.

After sleeping rough on the street for a week, a degenerate older man brought Josh home, wet, cold, smelly, and hungry. The man, forcibly taught Josh to be a sex slave, as a hobby and then to pass around to his friends for their amusement. Josh credits During this time he learned to give maximum sexual satisfaction for his survival.

When sex got too rough and Josh complained, he was promptly sold to a pimp named Dangitdingle. He learned fast to adapt to his new master's ever-changing ways, or be killed. Dangitdingle preferred pimping females. He used Josh as part of a trio, two girls and a boy, and as a janitor.

Depending on the police, the economy, and weather, the prostitution business was unpredictable. Dangitdingle had to run drugs and commit other nefarious acts when prostitution wasn't covering his expenses. One slow business cycle, Josh was sent by cab to accompany a large suitcase. When he got to the designated location the police were waiting with handcuffs. Dangitdingle and his buyer Big Bruce, aka BB, had been under law enforcement surveillance. By then Josh turned sixteen, and the quantity of white powder in the suitcase warranted his trial as an adult. Mandatory sentencing for the drug weight carried was twenty-five years in an adult maximum-security prison.

The day after new prisoner orientation, Josh was jumped. He was about to be gang rapped by unaffiliated senior citizen inmates, when suddenly two huge, middle aged, white southern "crackers," covered in Nazi tattoos broke up the rape party with fast swinging fists and hard kicking feet. After Josh was dressed, the rednecks dragged him to their leader. He was given a choice: join the Aryan Brotherhood and get a swastika tattooed on his forehead, or fend for himself as a new little fish in a general prison population of big, bad sharks.

Josh's other problem at that time was figuring out who he was; a family discard tossed out like trash, a homeless teen sex slave, a low-level drug mule, or an incarcerated felon for the next twenty-five years. All the above, was not an acceptable answer for self-esteem. The idea of wearing any tattoo on his face seemed antithetical to finding any positive self-image. It was beyond frightening for a floundering queer teen to consider any facial tattoo.

Without thinking Josh spoke in a rush, too loudly. "Can I have the tattoo somewhere it doesn't show, and still get your protection?"

The leader took the boy's request as a challenge to his authority. "Of course, you can," the Aryan leader sneered, "as soon as you beat down the two men who rescued your puny pussy ass from the old farts' dicks. But when you lose the fight, and you will lose, then you are no longer welcome in the Aryan Brotherhood. Not to worry, as a parting gift we will give you big black swastikas tattooed on each of your four cheeks and a chin one for good measure. But no forehead tattoo for you."

Before he knew what was happening, the two big rescue-lugs were rushing toward him. With no fighting skills and figuring he was dead already, Josh did what was taught in high school P.E. football; tucked and rolled forward. The attackers tripped on Josh's small body as it rolled toward their rushing feet. Being big, heavy men, they fell-down hard. Little Josh instantly sprang to his feet as the two brutes were struggling to regain balance to stand. Releasing queer-rage that had been fermenting for years, Josh grabbed the right ear of one and the left ear of the other and repeatedly slammed the lugs heads together. It looked like he was playing cymbals with the goons' heads. Josh was running on pure adrenalin. Three other large Aryans had to pull him off the downed, bloody, unconscious bullies.

The Aryan leader looked surprised, then resigned, and told some mousey guy, "Take this new Aryan, Josh, to your cell, rim him good, and then give him a tattoo where the sun-don't-shine but your tongues did."

"You saw the result of my prison experience between my legs this morning."

How could I not feel for this guy? "Your life is so different from mine, I thought I'd been dealt a bad hand. How long were you in prison?"

"Before I could adapt or even understand Aryan Brotherhood life, I was taken back to jail. It seems the over eager District Attorney moved too fast to lock me up and acted on inconclusive lab evidence. When the police finally cleared their lab backlog, the *drugs I was carrying* turned out to be baking soda mixed with baby laxative. It is not a crime to carry quantities of that mix to a drug bust. Since I had no previous criminal record, my lawyer sued for unlawful incarceration and we were given a large financial settlement. The lawyer took half and my half allowed me to finish high school as an emancipated minor. The rest was invested for college and graduate school."

"Lucky, you turned lemons to lemonade."

"I guess so. If I had completed the delivery as planned, I would have been killed for ripping off BB. That's the story of why I have a swastika tattoo. I didn't ask for it, never wanted it, and it can't get removed safely."

I needed a moment to digest what he said. So, I made small talk. "You could write a memoir, or make a movie about your life, right? Nevertheless, I wanted to vomit when I saw your swastika."

"You're fixated on a symbol, not me. I'm a person, who got a tattoo against his will."

"I *am* trying to understand."

"Max, I escaped a horrible fate having facial swastika tattoos and regular gang rapes. But that is not what you want to hear … is it?"

"Indulge me."

"I'd rather skip the swastika's history; it isn't about me or what I believe. I didn't even know its Buddhist origins before you told me."

Could he really be that naive? "What *do* you believe? Did you find out who *you* are?"

"What I believe is, good and bad come in every race, culture, and creed. All of us deserves a shot at a full, happy life and that includes, women, all races, queers like us, the handicapped, and every age group. It's on me to have a quality life; I'm working on it despite an unwanted tattoo and a rough start."

Asking too many questions, and not knowing when to stop, is where I've screwed up in the past. "That's it, finished, Mr. Liberal Banker?"

"Not quite. I fight my conservative colleagues who demand First Amendment rights to spew homophobia and other hateful bigotry but won't listen to my point of view. I give as good as I get!"

"Done now, *finito*?"

"Each of us deserves to be acknowledged, liked, even loved, and usually that starts with speaking our name; *Maximillian*. If we don't stand up, out and proud ready to fight, we facilitate our oppression."

"Gosh, you are political too."

"When necessary, I can be."

"Jeez, what a pair of short guys, I'm a certified crazy rich guy, and you are an exonerated felon with a Nazi tattoo who fights bigots."

"Sounds like a match. I prefer men of diminutive stature to dominate me, when I want to be dominated."

My storm clouds were clearing as we talked. "I prefer big men, but you are growing on me. Don't get me wrong, I still find your swastika upsetting-offensive."

"I get your problem, but it saved me from a life worse than death. Do you think we can find a middle ground?"

"Come back to reality. We shared one night. Why push it? I'm sure there is a white supremacist somewhere salivating to connect with your adornment. Make that man happy."

"You're the man I want. Let's forget about this morning's surprise and reset back to last night."

"Why do that?"

"We bonded almost instantly without knowing each other. I saw what I was feeling returned from you; at the party and in bed in the dark. That's never happened before."

"You're right, we had an unusual ... no, strange, but beautiful first time."

"Before sex, we didn't speak on the bicycle ride from Manhattan to Brooklyn, and yet we got in each other's heads. Did you notice?"

"Remind me?"

"When I pedaled ahead of you, I rode directly up to this building. I've never been here before. It was like you were in my head guiding me."

"Right, that was uncanny."

"For the most part I knew what you were thinking during sex, even when it wasn't about sex."

"What was I thinking besides sex?"

"Was it smart to bring someone you just met to your loft instead of your doorman apartment?"

"Why?"

"You were robbed in your home, by a trick, two years ago."

"Wow you're a mind reader. That's eerie, but no stranger than your tattoo upsetting my chemically stabilized equilibrium."

"What was on my mind last night besides keeping you on the edge of an orgasm?"

"This is crazy to say, but you were thinking Brooklyn is far from New Jersey, and you might get lost going home. At the time, I thought it was my feelings, not your thoughts."

"Go deeper, I felt you in my head."

"… Could you borrow my recumbent bicycle's GPS?"

"Look at that, we could have conversations without speaking and take intimacy to a new place. Last night, I think our minds melded when we came. That's unheard of!"

"Okay, you turn off reading my mind, and we try to communicate like normal people."

"As you wish."

"Look me in the eyes. Can I trust you?"

"Yes, I'm trustworthy and fully bonded at work."

"I know this will sound odd, but let's say … strictly as an experiment ….we explore being together. After getting your tattoo altered?"

"Altered how? The doctors say it's too close to a major artery to safely remove. None of them would risk it."

"I have some ideas that might become clearer once my face is more familiar with that part of your anatomy."

"You're thinking more ink."

"I could design an overlay that would alter the message without a lot of new pigment."

"There you go again."

"What?"

"So far today you've gone from absolute banishment, to solving your problem with me, without *me*. Hey, what about *me*? It's my body you want to redecorate."

"You're right. Let's forget the whole thing."

"I guess if I want to be with you, I have to accept Bipolar II ultimatums."

"Ah ha, back to that, are we? Then what's *your* solution Mr. Wisenheimer?"

"How about we start dating like ordinary people. And if we want to make love, I put duct tape over the tattoo."

"Duct tape is tacky. I'm older and richer than you. I prefer quality."

"Quality is in the love making, not the tape."

"I wonder if I'm falling in love with you, after all this turmoil and blah, blah, blah? *But* I won't allow a Nazi anything showing in my bed."

"What about after a fair trial? If we decide to take dating to the next level, you show me your tattoo redesigns. We talk them over, and maybe make changes. Then apply a mutually acceptable design to my crotch-ink, as my sign of commitment to you. And you get a compatible tattoo as commitment to me."

"I'm not allowing a swastika anything on my body, no way, no how!"

"That's why I said compatible not matching."

"Huh, agreement on something besides sex ... how about that?"

"Happy New Year!"

Valentine

What happened was, I got restless. I was still energized after clearing a huge backlog of projects, working from home and emailing the results to the office. Another Valentine's Day had found me home alone at night with no honey to cuddle. To clear my head and cut the doldrums' poor-me, I went for a walk. With no destination in mind I arrived at High Park on Hemlock Street, unaware of the time. I often visit the park at different hours to stretch my legs and breathe oxygen-rich park air thanks to the trees. The park was a short distance from home.

Mornings in good weather, retirees read newspapers, sipping coffee from throwaway cups. Others practice Tai Chi, and some even chat walking their dogs in the pastoral scene. All kinds of workers eat their brown bag lunches and kibitz on the park's benches at noontime like in early Americana paintings. After work hours, furtive couples make out, enjoying extracurricular romance before going home to waiting spouses and domestic disorder. After midnight, the denser park vegetation gets busy with men looking for anonymous sex with other men, no questions asked.

I realized it must be after midnight when I noticed moon shadows moving between the trees deep inside the park. I watched the ghostly images for a few minutes. Thoughts collided head-on in my brain, *Isn't that quaint, what they're doing is centuries old-fashioned. And, what an inefficient time waster in the age of hookup apps with GPS for close proximity quickie sex. On the other hand, in the dark park, politically-straight-identified and sexually-indeterminate guys can consort with closet queens, screaming queens, and the shouting-proud out crowd. These men can give each other sexual relief without reprisals or even speaking.* Then a common Internet practice cleared my mind, giving cause and effect to what I was watching, *"No face photo – I'm speechless."* Thinking about sexual politics made me tired, the walk had served its purpose. It was time to go home and sleep.

From who knows where, without warning, a gang of eight adult-size kids on BMX bikes surrounded me. They were shouting homophobic taunts. The next thing that happened, some teens were off their small-bikes, punching and kicking me. I hadn't done or said anything, the attack was without provocation. Then all the teens were off their bikes and I saw brass knuckles and knives glint with moonlight. Just then a car horn started blaring. I decided I was done for, so repeated the Lord's Prayer under my breath as I was pummeled to the ground. The honking car's driver shouted,

"I've called the police, they're on the way!"

I lost consciousness to wailing siren sounds. Then I was in a hospital emergency room, confused, naked on a table, attached to IV bags. Several medical people were standing around talking. I passed out again when one of them gave an injection to stop me from shouting what happened over their incoherent babbling. I woke again in another pace. I was wearing a hospital gown, tucked in a bed, and attached to an alarm beeping IV machine. Groggily, I pushed the bedside help button.

"Welcome back to the land of the living. This machine will beep from time to time, it's old and cranky."

"Where am I?"

"This is the Public Hospital, and you, young fellow, should not go prowling around late at night in dangerous places. You obviously found the trouble you were looking for."

"Can I go home?"

"No, you are on twelve-hour observation, and the police want to talk with you."

"Where are my clothes?"

"Don't know, you were brought to this floor wearing what you are wearing."

"Could you find my clothes please, I want to leave."

"I'll call the doctor."

The nurse left and I did an inventory of my injuries. As I was about to peel the largest bandage back, a sleepy-eyed guy in a wrinkled lab coat walked-in. "Hi, I'm doctor Childer, do you know your name?"

"Joseph Grimaldi, I want to go home."

"Sorry, you're on observation protocol. Do you have a headache, double or fuzzy vision, feel nauseous?"

"No headache, I see fine, I do have pain everywhere I see a bandage."

"I'm writing something on this piece of paper, please read it?"

"You wrote my birthday. How do you know my birth date?"

"It was in your wallet."

"May I have my wallet?"

"When you are discharged."

"Where are my clothes? I'd like my clothes, please"

"Anyone brought to the ER unconscious, has their clothing cutoff them, so injuries can be examined. You lost a lot of blood. The IV is replacing it with a saline-dextrose solution. I'll increase your morphine drip."

"What about my shoes, cell phone, keys? You have my wallet."

"If there was blood on your shoes, they were burned. You'll get your pockets' contents at discharge. What were you thinking going to a queer park after midnight? Are you feeling suicidal?"

"No, I needed to stretch my legs."

Sleep came immediately after the doctor left, along with terrible nightmares. In sleep I fought attackers. Then an eerie awareness dawned me into morphine fogged-consciousness. Two rumpled looking middle-aged strangers staring from the side of my bed. I pulled down the hospital gown it was bunched up around my arm pits.

"I'm Sergeant Martha Shanahan and this is my partner, Detective Lloyd Klutzinbean. Can you tell us what happened last night?"

I repeated my story to the skeptical cops ... I heard a car horn and woke up here."

"Here is my card, call me to set up an appointment to look through mug books." With that said the two cops ambled out of the room.

I was naked under the thin hospital gown, so pushed the call button to summon the nurse. When she arrived, I said, "May I have my cell phone to call someone to bring me clothes?"

"Use the bedside phone dial nine to get an outside line."

"All the numbers I need are in my cell phone."

"You must follow hospital procedures."

The only phone number I knew by heart was my ex-lover, Clark, and he hated me. "Hello Clark, I desperately need a favor. Wait! Please don't hang up I'm in the Public Hospitals. The apartment door key is still under the doormat. I need you to bring underwear, socks, shoes, pants, shirt and a jacket. I'll forever be in your debt ... A blow job ... okay if you insist, whatever you think is a fair price for disturbing 'your peace and tranquility.'"

I channel surfed mind-numbing daytime television, between dozing on and off waiting. Then Clark arrived, didn't say a word handing me a shopping bag with my clothes and shoes. After I dressed, Clark and I coldly-stared at each other. He didn't even ask what happened, or why this hospital? And I didn't feel like saying, "I'm the victim and everyone thinks it's my fault."

"Knock, knock, Hi I'm Malcolm the social work intern. Judging by your clothes, you aren't indigent, so, why are you in the Public Hospital for the down and out?"

"It wasn't my idea, I was unconscious on the sidewalk. May I go home?"

"I have your discharge plan and this envelope contains the contents of your pockets, but first I need to verify this is your insurance card. What is your name, and birth date?"

"Joseph Grimaldi, 9/9/91, and that card was in my wallet; which hopefully you have in that manila envelope."

After signing forms, Malcolm handed over the envelope with a slight smile.I opened it in a hurry, wallet and its contents were there, along with my Rolex watch, keys and pocket change.

"Thank you, Malcolm, you are the first friendly face, I've seen here. Oh, this is Clark, my-ex, he brought my clothes. His face is stuck in that scowl for life."

"The scuttlebutt here is you were queer-bashed, and as you may have noticed this hospital doesn't treat gays well."

"Does my hospital record say I was queer-bashed?" Out of the corner of my eye I saw Clark sit up straight at my words.

"No, not yet, it depends if you make it a hate crime with the police. They haven't given us copies of their paperwork, all the records are supposed to match. A hate crime requires a lot of extra paper."

"Why did you assume I was gay? Is it written on my forehead?"

"Relax you've been through a trauma. It's a tribal thing, it takes one to know one."

"Bless you, your colleagues' consensus was I brought the assault on myself and got what I deserve."

"That's them being self-protective."

"They almost had me believing victimizing the victim is approved medical practice. Where I was, when I was there, or what I was wearing does not make being slashed, beaten, and stabbed my fault, no matter what they think." This was said reassessing pain from various swollen punctures, cuts, bruises, and scrapes.

"Clark spoke up for the first time since arriving. "Malcolm, would you be willing to go on record this hospital discriminates against homosexuals?"

Malcolm looked from one to the other of us shaking his head no. "I'm a second-year graduate student. This is my final semester field placement to complete a master's degree. You're asking me to commit professional suicide before I graduate."

Clark gave Malcolm a beseeching look and said, "I am a civil rights attorney if you help me maybe I can improve conditions for patients and staff."

"I need to graduate and get a job. It should be easy for you to find out why this hospital always has job openings and chronically runs short staffed. An ad in the newspaper should get you plenty of former employees and patients willing to testify."

"A list of patients discriminated against, would help."

"That would be unethical."

"It is not ethical for this hospital to discriminate against gay people? Even if he is my ex and deserved it."

"I wrote a paper documenting what's going on here, and received positive feedback from my professor. Then he said off the record, I should keep my head down and my mouth shut to survive professionally."

"Can I have that professor's name and number?"

"Sure, but our names can't be involved."

"Here's my card, stay in touch Malcolm."

"Now for you Mr. Grimaldi, your discharge plan is to go home and rest for at least two weeks. In five days come back and have the stitches and staples removed at our walk-in clinic. Ask to see Dr. Sonabend, he is the best resident and worth waiting for. Then seek outside counseling, all the shrinks here are major homophobes. Finally, if you sign here and here and initial there you are free to leave."

"I don't believe in shrinks, I'm into independent self-reliance. I'm a Conservative Gay Republican and know how to successfully handle life on my terms."

"Didn't you just tell me and your boyfriend you were victimized twice? Once out on the street and then here in the hospital? Get over yourself, you require professional help to heal from two traumas."

"Don't worry Malcolm, I'll scrounge up his old dog collar and lead him to a shrink, on a leash if necessary."

"Clark is no longer my boyfriend. I loved him once, now he has a new younger version of me about to be his legal spouse. And yet he wants a blow job in return for bringing me my clothes, can you imagine that?"

"Malcolm, doesn't he have pretty lips? Just imagine them sucking your cock, and he has mad suction skills. I can attest much better than average."

"Uh okay, I already have a boyfriend and you two obviously have issues to work through, so I'll leave you to it. Nice meeting you both, bye, play nice."

I went back to work two days after hospital discharge. When the detectives phoned, I said I wouldn't be able to recognize my assailants. It had happened so fast, late at night, and I was tired.

Dr. Sonabend was cute, nice, and had gentle hands removing staples. I got hard, and was embarrassed by it. So, I was ready to leave in a hurry when he said, "Your chart says you were also injured on the backside."

"I was hoping to get away without exposing myself."

"I'm a doctor little shocks me or escapes examination. Have you always felt shy about your body?"

"No not usually, but my first memory in this hospital's emergency room was laying on a table naked and all these strangers standing around staring at me. Then that scene was sort of repeated by two cops. I have an okay crotch, but nothing out of the ordinary."

"Relax, I don't need to see your precious privates, unless they were injured. But I do need to see your butt if I'm going to sign off on your insurance forms. Go stand against that table, bend over and drop your draws. I promise to only look at recent lacerations."

I did as I was told with dread, my erection wouldn't go down.

"Interesting, you have a Greek letter carved into your left ass cheek. It's just deep enough to leave a scare but not damage the muscle, so, the assailant must have been left handed. The good news is the stitches have dissolved, the scare will fade but leave a permanent mark. Okay you can pull your clothes up."

"You are kind, I don't see that much."

"So, you were queer-bashed?"

"Why not say I was mugged, or it was an unprovoked assault?"

"The hospital record says no property was stolen."

"That's because they were scared off by a car horn."

"All your physical wounds are healing nicely. I'd advise you wait six months before consulting a plastic surgeon if you want to remove the lambda. Be aware your insurance won't cover cosmetic procedures. The crime victims fund might pay for removal if you report it as a hate crime. Do you know what lambda stands for?"

"It's a gay liberation symbol."

"Are you gay?"

Something boiled over inside me and I raised my voice in anger. "I thought it was obvious! The hospital staff said they came to that conclusion because of where and when I was attacked. What's the problem am I not gay enough, you have to ask?"

"Chill out dude, we both sings in the same choir."

"Sorry, I seem to be losing my temper a lot, lately, for no reason."

"Before the lambda was adopted as a gay liberation symbol, it was and is an indicator of unlimited energy in nuclear physics equations. Yours doesn't have to be gay if you don't want that. Which therapist are you seeing; I'll follow-up with her/ him?"

"I'm handling what happened as a responsible adult, on my own. Do I seem crazy to you?"

"Don't be a jerk; you experienced physical and mental trauma. You didn't cause these injuries, so get beyond them with help. I've done what I can for you, now you need to talk it out with a professional."

"I wouldn't even know how to shop for a therapist. I'm sure the ones my insurance company lists are all Liberal Democrats who work cheap. I doubt we even speak the same language. You know, I heard Democrats eat their young."

"Hmm, I think I know the perfect person for you, if your insurance allows going out of network." Rummaging around in a backpack extracted from a lower desk draw he said, "I have a bunch of cards someplace, oh here, take this one and set up an intake interview. Okay, we are done, make peace with what happened and take care."

Dr. Sonabend M.D. referred me to Dr. Rothblatt, who didn't look like a psychiatrist, whatever they look like. He was about my height, but much older. His tight black T-shirt showed bulging muscles under an oversize well-groomed handlebar mustache. Biker tattoos ran down both his arms, and he was wearing black leather riding-pants and motorcycle boots. He strode the room ready for combat. I was intimidated. And also, the only one wearing an expensive suit and imported silk tie.

Photos on one office wall were of expensive Italian motorcycles, either he was riding some or his younger sister sat astride older models. After a neutral greeting, to break the ice I said, "I definitely see a family resemblance between you and your sister."

"I don't have a sister."

"Who's that?"

"Me, before the transition."

I felt like I'd been punched in the gut, and probably looked ridiculous with my mouth dropping open. I plopped down, a chair was right there, and then he sat in a matching chair facing me. His eyes never left mine.

"Before and after photos can be a surprise."

Breathing deep through my mouth to recover from shock, I said, "I don't know anything about transsexuals."

"Is that why you are here, to learn about transitioning?"

"No, professionals and friends strongly suggested I talk to a trained professional."

"Let's save each other sometime. I only work with patients who desire change and are ready to work hard to achieve it. Nice meeting you, I won't charge for this consultation, goodbye and good luck." He stood and headed toward the door.

Normally I would have just left in a huff. But lately my nerves were frayed. I stayed seated and said, "You are brushing me off, just like that? It wasn't my idea to come here, but I refused to be dismissed out of hand like a child. Behave like a professional, you certainly don't dress like one." Maybe I was deflecting or maybe I didn't know what I was doing. But first his attitude intimidated me, then it pissed me off.

The doctor gave me an inquisitive look, turned around and took the seat he'd just vacated. "I'm listening."

"My life changed in bad ways since I was queer-bashed. I don't know if outside help will make a difference, or if getting my old life back is possible."

"Sounds like you could use some psychotherapy. Since it appears you are not leaving, why don't you tell me why you *are* here?"

"Is that how it works, you expect me to talk and you just listen?"

"Basically, if appropriate I might see a need to comment or ask a question. We are also allowed to sit in silence."

"I don't want to be psychoanalyzed over the rest of my life, and I won't take any mind dulling drugs. I need my wits to earn a living."

"I'm not a psychoanalyst and prefer short-term talk therapy. We can agree to disagree on most things, but if I strongly believe you will be best served on medication. If you refuse meds, I will refer you to a different professional. Now tell me what brought you here, or leave and think about what I said, and then get back to me, or not."

"I like that you stood up to me. Since I was attacked, I've not been myself. Without intending to, I'm rough or gruff with people and for the most part they just wilt. It is not like me to be uncivil, but I am a lot lately."

"Normally for a first appointment, I ask intake questions, demographics and personal, for the forty-five minutes. Then we start talk therapy the next session. However, in the time we have left, why don't you tell me what's going on? I'll give you my intake form as homework, bring it back next week. If there will be a session next week. Self-reporting may demystify the process for you. If I have any questions after reading your intake, I'll ask. Do you want to start?"

I told the psychiatrist what had happened. How I was okay being gay, until the insults punctuated with violence, and then people saying it was my fault. In the short time, I was in his office, I spoke of how I felt my core-self torn-apart in how I was in the world. I'd never put those words together like that, but they captured my dilemma.

On our second meeting, Dr. Rothblatt perused my take-home intake form not saying anything and then asked me to tell him my story from earliest recollection to the present. He listened without comment but occasionally asked questions for clarification. At the end of the session, he asked me to keep a bedside journal, to revisit the scene of the crime at high noon, preferably on a sunny day, and made an appointment to see me the next week.

I don't know why, because I did all the talking, but I felt better after our meeting. Resistance to the process of therapy was replaced with a slight glimmer of hope that I might get back some of my old self. My anger at the world and acting-out diminished a notch or two right away. The doctor explained the psychotherapy process and invited me to explore it on the Internet or at the library. For example, his asking me to tell my history from earliest remembrance and nightmares was called psychodynamic therapy. Exploring my feelings about what happened was object relations, and homework exercises he gave, like going to where I was stabbed and beaten, was cognitive behavior therapy.

One exercise was to stand in front of a mirror and call myself the same homophobic epithets the bashers used. Then take a breath and ask, "Is any of it true?" It was difficult to start, but by the end of the exercise, I was shouting, and it felt good to get the venom out. It occurred to me that seeing a shrink wasn't a cop out after all and could have helped during other difficult times. But I learned from my therapist dwelling on the past obscures a full view of the present.

Going to the scene of the crime was difficult, I went at noon, and it brought the experience back. But I survived it, and that proved I wasn't a wimp. After we talked about how it felt to revisit the place, he sent me back to the park at six o'clock, and then again, a week later at ten. Going at midnight two weeks later took all my intestinal fortitude. I did it, so Rothblatt wouldn't accuse me of being weak. I handled it better than I expected and felt strong facing down my fears. As a bonus, I reclaimed my neighborhood park.

Out of the blue, just when I figured out what therapy was about and looked forward to going every week, the doctor asked, "Have we accomplished what you came here for?"

I gave his question thought before answering. "I'm not getting mad for no reason, and I accept I'll never be who I had been before the attack. Yes, I guess we did."

"Then I suggest we wean you off therapy. Come every other week three times, and then once a month after that. This is on condition you do volunteer work to reinforce what we accomplished."

I'm a conservative Log Cabin Republican and believe people should be responsible for themselves, no free hand outs, ever. Making people dependent is bad for them. "Sorry, Dr. Rothblatt, I'm not the volunteering type, work must be paid."

"It is required to reinforce your therapy. You need to share what you learned."

"I'm against free lunches and we must be remunerated for labor. Otherwise it's Communist slavery."

"Reward isn't always measured in cash."

"What if I don't want to volunteer, and just stop therapy?"

"It's a free country."

"Huh, that was glib, sometimes I don't get you. On the other hand, you haven't steered me wrong so far."

"Here is a telephone number, they always need volunteers. I consult with them from time to time, pro bono. When I see you again in two weeks, tell me about your new adventure helping others get through what you did." We stood and shook hands and I was off on another jaunt I had reservations about.

I telephoned the gay hotline and asked, "What are your requirements for new volunteers, how much commitment is involved, and how long is the wait for a training class?"

"Be at 323 East Twentieth Street, fourth floor at three thirty on Saturday. Hold on a minute ...Okay ask for Manny," and he hung up. I had plans for Saturday afternoon to go on a fifty-mile bike ride with Clark and his new husband. Already I did not like the casualness of the gay hotline. My instinct was don't go, but challenging Dr. Rothblatt and losing *again* was not an option my new ego would allow.

The sign indicating the fourth-floor office suite said, "Hotline." The door was unlocked so I entered a large windowless, empty waiting-conference room combination, with lots of chairs stacked against one wall. The inside door to the hotline room was open and spilled light out.

When I stuck my head in, a good-looking young man was discarding and replacing pages from three, three-ring binders. He looked up when I said, "Hello, is Manny around?"

"I'm Manny, how can I help you?"

"I'm here for the new volunteer orientation. Am I the first to arrive?"

He handed me a blank three by five card and a pen. "I'll be through updating these pages in a minute, and then we'll talk. In the meantime, write today's date, your name, address, occupation, and all the telephone numbers we can reach you at."

When finished, I said, "Here you go," and thought too casual for my tastes.

"Okay then, what questions do you have about the hotline?"

"What are the requirements to volunteer, how much time is required, what is your title and what is the structure and affiliations of the organization?"

"If you are breathing, you qualify. The hotline requires a minimum of one four-hour shift each month, but most of us work one a week, it's easier to remember. If you work less than once a month or have two, no shows, you're out. Did I answer your questions?"

"What is your title, the structure and affiliations?"

"I'm a volunteer just like you, we are just ordinary gay people speaking to telephone callers. Volunteers come and go and come back, a few of us have nothing better to do than stick around and see to it the organization survives."

"Huh, that sounds unstructured?"

"We are run by consensus at a monthly business meeting. All volunteers who show up have a right to vote and speak. We are a leaderless by design. At the monthly meeting, someone volunteers to facilitate but isn't allowed to lead two consecutive meetings. Any business that can't wait for the next month's meeting is handled by an emergency committee that dissolves when their task is accomplished. We have fund raisers thrice a year for rent, the phone bills, and small advertising budget."

"Don't you have sponsors?"

"Being affiliated with another organization, or beholden to benefactors, goes against our founding principles. That said, we are an active resource for the gay community as a voluntary service organization. Does that answer your question?"

"Why in the world would you choose consensus? It is the least efficient system known to man."

"It's democracy in its purest form. That's how the ancient Athenians governed, and the founding fathers of the United States modified."

"Why go leaderless?"

"You sure you want to volunteer?"

"I think so, please answer my question?"

"After the Stonewall Inn riots in June 1969, the four main homosexual liberation organizations' had a planning meeting to forecast a future gay community."

"Interesting, I didn't know ... should I take notes?"

"Just listen, the gay groups at that time were the Mattachine Society, the East Coast Homophile Organization in Philadelphia, the Gay Activist Alliance, and the Gay Liberation Front. Politically, the four couldn't have been more different."

"How so?"

"Mattachine was an apologist group of mostly older men with money and influence, the homophiles were a casual-social west coast transplant, GAA was strict Robert's Rules of Order taken to an extreme, and the Gay Liberation Front was kind of the gay arm of the Weather Underground."

"Weren't *they* subversives or something?"

"During the Vietnam War, so the books say, America was divided in half. One side was pro-war, 'My Country Right or Wrong.' They had fanatics shooting down college students protesting the war. On the ant-war side, 'Give Peace a Chance,' people included the Weather-Underground, who blew up military induction centers for peace. This country was on the brink of its own civil war over the Vietnam Civil War."

"When will I be tested on this information?"

"No test, our gay parent organizations were adamant that the emerging gay community be nonpolitical. They also agreed each service group had to be self-sustaining independent. With so many assassinations of national leaders around that time, leaderless made sense."

"So, the hotline was a product of that original planning meeting?"

"Not exactly, we were supposed to be the Lesbian and Gay Information Exchange. Unfortunately, the telephone women and men couldn't get along, so now there is a lesbian switchboard and this gay hotline."

"Thank you for explaining that. How do day to day operations work without someone in charge?"

"You see before you three office chairs and three telephones on a long counter. Each with one of these ring binders and box of index cards, on three walls are bulletin boards covered in information. We have two shifts every workday, four to eight and eight to midnight. For the weekends and holidays, we add extra shifts to handle caller overflow. The first Saturday of the month, we have a business meeting from two to four out in the waiting room. Any questions?"

"Jeez, I have trouble getting out of my office by seven most days, how do your people get here at four o'clock?"

"Some volunteers cycle through between jobs, some work from home. Our older, retired volunteers gravitate to the early shifts. You could volunteer for the late shift or weekends."

"Huh, are early shift calls different than late night ones?"

"We get three basic types of calls. Here, look at yesterday's log sheet, the short duration calls say information or hang up, or jerk offs. These longer calls say raps, and there is no suicide call listed last night. Suicides take the most time."

"Once I learn where information is located, I'm sure I can handle that. I don't know what a rap is, and I know for sure I'm not qualified to handle a suicide phone call."

"A rap call is from someone who needs to talk, and you mostly listen. Keep your opinions to yourself and anything you say is to reassure the caller, 'this too shall pass.'"

"Won't I need special training?"

"Most rap calls are about someone's struggle with being gay. The early shift gets more latchkey kids after school, and the late shift has more lonely older adults. But it's not carved in stone, younger ones call late and older ones call early."

"Huh, just people to people ... but what about those suicides?"

"Don't worry, I'll show you how to handle suicides. We have a helpful book over there. You should read it when your call volume is low."

"I wonder if I have enough empathy to volunteer. Some of my friends say my rightwing politics proves a lack of compassion."

"I wouldn't worry about that. The callers guide us. Anyway, I don't get a psychopathic vibe off you. Your proof is you were concerned enough to bring up the subject."

"But I've had no training beyond this pleasant conversation with you."

"If you're gay, that's enough training for our callers. If you work the same shift every week, you'll cultivate some regular callers. They will ask to speak to you. Callers select us, based on tone of voice and degree of sympathetic responses."

"That's interesting, they pick us."

"Keep in mind, no matter how much personal information gets shared, you are both nothing more than disembodied voices, like ghosts. Under no circumstance may a volunteer meet or date a caller. If you do, you are expelled immediately and may never come back."

"No dating, ever, sounds like a rule."

"Dating callers is dangerous and illegal and puts the hotline at risk, understand?"

"Understood. So, my rule is, I don't want to talk to queer-bashers!"

"Remember I mentioned a lot of raps are from people struggling to be gay. For some, the struggle is to come out to themselves. Most queer-bashers end up being homosexual after they stop trying to destroy the part of themselves they've been taught to hate, and we represent."

"Are you serious."

"For a few callers, it's either suicide or kill us, and by our listening, they find other options. Don't worry, by the time a basher calls us, their homophobia is on the decline. Like it or not, we become a life line to their better self. But hold on tight, it can be a bumpy ride to self-acceptance for some."

"I don't want to talk to bloodthirsty thugs and try to convince them they have a right to be gay. What if I refuse to talk to a caller?"

"Hand the call off to another volunteer. If your coworkers are busy, tell the caller to phone back on the next shift. You'll do fine, don't overthink it. Oh gosh, look at the time, I got to go."

"Is that it?"

Speaking while putting on his mackintosh, Manny said, "Hotline isn't for everybody. There is no shame in self-selecting out. If you want to give us a try, sign up for three training shifts. Put a T in brackets in front of your name. I'll make sure you work with a different experienced volunteer each time. We call it "monkey see monkey do" training. Chose shifts on a day and time that suits your schedule. If I don't catch you again, ask the volunteers you work with to explain our suicide protocol. Nice meeting you. I got to rush, welcome aboard and good luck."

As Manny left, I was wondering if I wanted to deal with the hotline's lackadaisical non-structure. Then I reminded myself it wasn't my idea to be there. While I was thinking it over, two hotline volunteers arrived to work their shift. They were Todd and John, who peeled out of their coats and then turned off an answering machine. I introduced myself as a new volunteer and asked if I could observe.

Todd patted the empty chair between them. "We'll do you one better, you can answer the phones and we'll guide you. If a call gets heavy, just hand it to one of us."

Like therapy, my initial apprehension about volunteering was an ignorant overreaction. The way therapy was all about me, the hotline was all about the caller. It became clear what my therapist was doing, and I learned my rough patches were nothing compared to some folks' suffering. My innate arrogance learned humility from other's pain, and I got balanced in the process. Once over my apprehension, I liked volunteering. I thought about doing a second four-hour shift every week. But other volunteers and Dr. Rothblatt said more than once a week was a ticket to burn out.

By volunteering the same day and time, Tuesdays from eight to midnight, I developed regular callers. Like Manny said, they came and went like ghosts, depending on their need for a disembodied supportive voice to listen on the telephone and be there for them.

The down side of rap calls was the occasional guy talking away and suddenly hanging up midsentence for apparently no reason. Experienced volunteers explained those were stealth jerk off calls. It was hard not to feel taken advantage of, used. The hotline jack-off policy was to give the caller the phone numbers of sex lines or hookup apps and log it as an information call. When a caller insisted, we were the only one they wanted to fantasize about while pleasuring themselves, we hung up and logged it as a hang-up.

The worst of the sex-driven calls wanted a date. They'd try to sound seductive, or offer bribes, or even make threats. The few I wasted time with had created elaborate fantasies about my looks based on the sound of my voice. They usually had definite plans to use all my orifices for their fullest enjoyment, like a blowup sex doll. I wasn't included in the fun.

Being exposed to callers' sexual needs got me thinking about what I *believed* versus what I *knew* about sex and love. Online, the nature of male desire was explained by endocrinology; glands hormonal discharges leading to wet-friction leading to orgasm and ejaculation *whoopee doo*. That information was not helpful. It was too clinical, and not suited for our caller's self-sexual-repression and unrealistic romance-fantasy tableau of us, the result of their oppression.

What got me into deep thinking about the nature of desire were the straight boys who called the hotline in a panic, petrified they might have turned queer. Some kids had experimented with same-sex sex and liked it. Most only got extra turned-on during a masturbation fantasy and then felt extreme guilt afterward. Reassuring most of these boys was easy. For the difficult cases, I suggested bisexuality as a legitimate means of assuaging homosexual panic's recrimination. Most bisexuals I knew in college were curious straight guys, or gays not ready to come out.

So, what was my problem with the old farts? Then it hit me, the middle-aged and older men, who desperately lusted after constant sex for sex's sake, no strings attached, wanted the adolescence they missed while hiding in the closet. Apparently, trying to be someone you're not interferers with normal adolescence development. Once I figured out why these older men were sounding like perpetually horny sixteen-year-olds, they stop being annoying.

Like it or not, volunteering at the hotline opened my mind to possibilities I'd not wanted to consider. Before the queer bashing, I had my life figured out and gladly accepted a birthright of educated white male privilege. Issues I encountered in life were neatly placed in tidy boxes labeled, "worthy" or "unworthy."

After two years volunteering, my values had changed. I was no longer a hardcore rightwing gay Republican, dividing my fellow humans by worthiness. If pushed, I'd be forced to say I'd become-a-moderate who believes most people have a right to be here and their simple basic needs met, at public expense if necessary.

My few real friends adapted to my expanding horizons. My many politically conservative acquaintances wrote me off as brainwashed by the bleeding-heart, liberal mass media false news conspiracy machine of the deep-state. For the most part, renovations to my personal values came from exposure to hotline callers' desperate needs and wants beyond my wildest imagining.

A new friend, Eugene, a middle-aged architect, had been working the Tuesday eight to midnight shift alone before I joined the hotline. Like Manny and John and Todd, Eugene was a volunteer of many years' service. Ours had to be a Platonic friendship, since Eugene was in a committed long-term relationship with Jeff. Occasionally they invited me along to be a third wheel for going to the opera, and they gave the best parties.

Two years after being attacked outside a park, Valentine's Day fell on my hotline shift. I was running late due to an unavoidably over-long staff meeting at work. When I hurried into the hotline office, Eugene looked at his watch, smirked, tapped it, and wagged a scolding finger. "You are forgiven this time, but not next. Oh, and there is someone to see you in the waiting room."

"Huh, that never happened before."

"I don't know who or why or what, but the phones are jumping off the hook, so *mach sneller.*"

Flapping out of my overcoat, then heading to the waiting room, I said, "Sorry I'm late, be back in a second."

"I'll hold you to that."

"Hi, are you waiting to see me?"

A stranger stood and threw his arms around me, and planted a big wet kiss on my mouth.

"Wow fella … what did I do to deserve that?"

"Happy Valentine's Day Joseph, I'm Adam. You have been listening to my tales of woe for over eight months. I want to thank you in person for helping me find myself, and stop beating-up fags."

Adam was better looking than I imagined. His rough deep voice disguised looking much younger than his eighteen years. He was slightly taller than me, thin for his height with bright sparkling light-brown eyes. His medium-brown mop of hair could use a trim, otherwise he appeared presentable, but nothing like I imagined.

"Adam, thank you, but I've explained more than once on the phone, volunteers cannot meet callers. It's a strictly enforced rule."

"I know, that's why I volunteered for the hotline. I've already had two training shifts. Volunteers see each other, right?"

"Wait a minute, except for wailing on gays, you've got no gay experience."

"Trust me I can handle talking on the phone. You and I did it for more than half a year. Anyway, I want my first man to man sex to be with you, and this is a legit way to get that. We got so close on the phone, laughing and crying, you are the logical one to deflower me."

"Hold on, Adam. Now that I know what your sexual wants are, where am I in this picture?"

"I read someplace that first sex should be memorable. You know so much about me and my struggles to face facts. I want you to do me, and then as a reward, I'll do whatever you ask. I feel safe with you. That's fair; isn't it?"

"Reality check, it won't be your first time. You've had sex with females."

"That was different. You used to say on the phone there is nothing worse than bad sex. Me and women was wrong and resulted in bad sex."

"No thanks Adam but thank you for asking."

"Don't chuck me away, I came here to give myself to you. I trust you."

"Look, showing up to say thank you is really sweet. But we never talked about *this* on the phone."

"Because you said we could never meet. Don't make me mad, I need your help to catch up on what I've missed."

"We've been talking about that on the phone."

"I just turned eighteen, that's how I could be a hotline volunteer. Oh shit, that's it, now you see me, you are turned off. So, that's why you don't want me."

"I didn't say that."

"Then you think my not having experience will be bad sex and bad for the hotline."

"Stop, you have as much to contribute as any of us. The hotline is just gay folks talking to callers. But sex is another matter."

"I thought since you know me so well, you'd say lack of knowledge disqualified me. That's why I didn't tell you I volunteered. And I was afraid you wouldn't sleep with me if you knew my plan."

"From our long conversations, you know I care about you. The last thing I want is for you to be hurt. I need time to think this over."

"You are who I want to give my virginity. Where's the problem with that?"

"No problem, only you waited this long, why rush it? You wouldn't buy a car on a whim."

"This is not a whim, I've been getting ready for eight months. Let's make this a special Valentine's Day."

"What I never told you is, I volunteer because I was queer bashed. I'm trying to get my head around sleeping with you, a queer-basher. Talking on the phone was therapeutic, but can I perform in the flesh? I don't know?"

"Oh, my God … but I didn't bash you! You know I don't do that anymore. Let me make it up to you."

"You make a convincing case for trying firsts, for both of us. Do you have a place in mind for this experiment?"

"You have a place."

"How about we get used to how the other looks, visuals are a big part of getting turned on."

"Looking at you makes my dick hard. I can see you are thinking about taking my cherry, aren't you? That's the Valentine I want."

"It wouldn't be right to leave Eugene to work Valentine's Day by himself. We get some heavy calls on holidays, and after my shift it won't be Valentines."

"Remember you always said find compromises rather than collect disappointments?"

"Yes."

"How about I work the shift with you two?"

"If Eugene is agreeable, okay."

"So, that guy in there is Eugene, I've talked with him when you weren't here. I'm mostly copycat trained and eager."

"Will it be okay to discuss your sex request with Eugene?"

"I don't know about that, sounds embarrassing. And I am not ready for a threesome. I've not even done it with you yet."

"Eugene and his husband are sexually exclusive. Getting a second opinion for something important is a good idea. I care about you and I care about the hotline, and suddenly I'm feeling on thin ice with both."

"It feels weird bringing Eugene into my first time with a guy."

"It is embarrassing for me too. I don't like making my personal business public. And I'm not leaving Eugene to man the phones alone. That's my ultimatum, you decide?"

"I want your body tonight. Let's get Eugene's permission."

Back inside the hotline office, I introduced Adam to Eugene and indicated the middle chair for Adam. Eugene had no objection to extra help. He was clearly fielding a heavy call. The telephones were all lit up with lonely hearts needing assurance tomorrow would be better. Considering, until recently Adam beat-up "fags," to fight his fear of being one, he proved to be a kind, considerate listener to callers.

At ten o'clock, I switched on the answering machine for a quick break and with some unease told Eugene about Adam's sex wants with my body.

"And you are expecting me to say don't do it, and quote some obscure hotline rule, right? I can't, there is no such statute. Volunteers have dated each other from the beginning." Then he took a long look at Adam. "It always takes me a little time to put a face with a voice I know from these phones. Honey, are you sure you want to take an irrevocable step with Joseph? Physically you just met."

"Yes, it's been my dream for a year. I've been having disaster sex with girls since thirteen. I'm ready for man to man sex, and I want this guy to deflower me and take my maidenhead."

"You my two-fisted boy are no blushing virgin living in the nineteenth century. Do you read Jane Austin?"

"Are you making fun of me?" Anger flashed across Adam's smooth young face, his cheeks flushed and his hands balled-up into fist.

"When warranted, you can count on it dear."

I put my hand on Adam's shoulder, and rubbed it. "Eugene has a collection of black belts he's earned in different martial arts, and he's one of the good guy." At the sound of my voice and touch, Adam's anger left as quickly as it arrived.

"Don't say I'm too young and confused, I'm not. I know what I want, and this older guy has taught me a lot."

"Uhm hah, let me see. I've talked to you, Adam, when Grimaldi wasn't working. I know you care for Joseph. I've overheard Joe's end of conversations with Adam, and he light up talking. Okay, so, what are the plans, girls?"

"How about, instead of staying late as planned, I leave early. We'll log-in more calls than usual with Adam helping."

"If you ladies don't mind my getting in your bedroom business, what's the plan for when you get naughty?"

Blushing, Adam swiveled his chair to face Eugene. "I want him to finish driving-out my gay-hate demons. My biggest homo-terror was to be used like a woman. Once I accomplish that, I should be clean of self-hate."

"No, no, no, bad plan sweetheart, *bad, don't do that.*"

"Why not, it's my plan."

"If you only want one sweaty night as a one-off, then it's fine. But if you took a year to get this far, what's the hurry girl?"

"Okay Dr. Ruth, what is Cupid's advice for our Valentine's Day tryst?"

"Joseph, for the first several times you make *wind and rain,* only use fingers and hands to bring on the storm. Whatever you do ladies, don't try to cum together, take turns giving and receiving. It's so much easier and better sex."

"How are you defining several times?"

"Five or six or more Adam, you'll know when you've taken manual manipulation to your limits ..."

Adam jumped in with eagerness again, cutting Eugene off. "When do we get to screwing out my demon?"

"Patience, is necessary for memorable sex, you have to build it in layers, honey. Add licking and nibbling to fingers and hands but absolutely no sucking."

"What makes you so smart? Are you one of Dr. Ruth's imps?"

"Hey Joe, don't pick on Eugene. I'm learning how to have spectacular gay sex from an Architect. He's a builder with black belts for fighting."

"Sweetheart, since you want spectacular, when Jeff and I first got together decades ago, he gave me a book called *Sensate Sex*. Even now, whenever we feel our sex life is getting mundane, we open that book for inspiration."

"Tell us more, mighty sex master?"

"If you insist, most people try too hard and then fail to climax together. Then they continue having disappointing sex, trying to realize the impossible. But if they take turns giving and receiving pleasure, the best part of sex lasts longer. Both fully enjoy it, and the climaxes are spectacular."

"Break over, let's get back to work. I'm anxious to start practicing what you're preaching Eugene."

"Then why don't you girls leave now. I'll tell the callers I'm working alone, and to keep it short. You two go forth and multiply or at least make the motions."

"Thanks."

"Good bye, Eugene."

Driving to my place Adam said, "On the phone Eugene sounded so masculine, in person he's not."

"He's like that. I go to the opera with him and his husband Jeff, their camp show is often more entertaining than what's on stage. Jeff was a Navy Seal."

Then we were silent. Not an anxious silence, it felt deeper, like earned acquiescence. We were strangers who knew each other's inner-life for eight months. I expected once we were in my apartment, we'd be all over each other. Instead, feeling awkward, I plopped down in my reading chair. Adam took the sofa across from me, and we stared at each other. When it dawned on me I was trying to meld his good-looking body with eight months of disembodied emotional content, I stood up and so did he.

Without violin music swelling, like two masculine men we flowed into each other's arms and penetrated lips with tongues. Then it got all tactile fuzzy.

Clear focus returned when Adam's cock swelled even larger and then gushed cum in my mouth. Somehow, we were on my bed, naked and had not followed Eugene's recipe for success. I scooted up to Adam and we lip locked again. Then he took me in hand. I came a lot while he was tongue fucking my mouth.

"Joseph, this was the best sex ever, it was great!"

"I agree, it was a special valentine."

As we cuddled, I took note of Adam's deflating cock. In my travels, most cocks have a fireman's helmet shaped dickhead on the business end. Adam's looked more like a World War I infantry man's helmet. My old overly judgmental self would have been turned off he didn't have a perfect cock. Since he wasn't self-conscious having me checking out his deformed dickhead, why should it matter to me? On deep think, size and shape didn't matter to the new and improved, politically moderate me. So, I resolved to make it my business he receive the most pleasure possible from his fuck stick. He was so much more than just a dick.

At first it didn't sink in I'd just had sex with an ex-gay basher, and then shrugged the thought away when it resurfaced. Getting my head shrunk and volunteering had led me to new insights. Giving is good as or better than taking, love should be easy, and loving Adam meant including his past.

Adam's parents were permissive about when he came home but expected him to be in his bed for breakfast wakeup call. They were a family that talked over breakfast. So, I drove him home, his head on my shoulder. The image of reformed queer basher Adam snuggling on my shoulder, confirmed I'd gotten well beyond my bashing to a new and better place.

Adam was a second semester, first-year student at the community college with an undeclared major and part-time job as a barista at Coffee-X-Us. I still worked too much, but we both found time to be together once or twice a week and work a shift at the hotline. When falling in love, everything is doable.

With computerized help, I located the book Eugene referenced. It was out of print, but I found a used copy in a dusty old used bookshop. The book's actual title, *Sensate focus to Better Sex*, was written for straight cisgender people. But Adam and I had no trouble modifying it for our purpose. We took Eugene's suggestions and let *Sensate Focus* direct us, slowly following the program, in tune to each other exploring sensual places, without performance anxiety failures. It was fun.

Without noticing, we went from mid-February to early May, completing a third of the *Sensate Focus*. As the end of Adam's school semester loomed and our passions continued to blaze, we made plans to spend July and August at my country cabin. But best laid plans and all that, Adam lucked into a paid summer internship with a robotics update project. The internship involved traveling with a team of professionals and other students, inspecting new developments in robots, and compiling a report. The report was due just before his next school semester started at the end of August. In four months, our relationship had deepened to the point we could be sad our summer plans were for naught *and* be happy over his good fortune. With the sensate exercises, Adam learned to slow down, relax, and even sometimes be still under my subtle sensual touch. I learned to be authentic for him.

"Summertime is when people's juices go berserk. Think you can be faithful and wait for me?"

"You didn't need to ask."

"Then I'll be …"

I put a finger against his lips. "Don't say it. I want you to explore any safe opportunity that catches your interest."

"I thought you loved me, how can you say that?"

"Adam, I do love you, more than you can imagine, and I show you."

"Then I don't understand?"

"I choose to wait for you. And give you the freedom to have adventures or not if you like."

"What if I find someone I like better than you?"

"I'll be sad for me and happy for you. Don't make this into a big deal. I will be here for you when summer is over; if you want."

"Oh, I get it, you read that bumper sticker; 'If you love someone, set them free, and if they don't come back, kill them.' That's it, right?"

"Not right, I could never kill you or anyone. My self-acceptance came early. At this point, I've sampled most gay configurations that interested me. You on the other hand are just finding your feet. Explore new experiences if they arise. Don't regret a missed opportunity."

"Okay, but even if I take your suggestion, I'm saving my grand opening for you. *And that's a promise.*"

"Whatever you say, we still have two thirds of the sensate book if we don't get distracted."

"Would you like me to tell you about any extracurricular sexual adventures, I might have?"

"You've been working the hotline long enough to know my answer. If it will make you feel better, do. If not, it's private."

"Got it, you'd rather not hear about me snogging another guy, but if I'm bummed out, you want to know why, right?"

"Fascinating, in only four months you have me figured out."

When Adam returned from his summer internship, he looked more like the man he was becoming than the boy who beat queers to act straight with his friends. His outlook had matured to match physical changes, he walked and talked with adult assurance.

"Adam, welcome back, you're a sight for sore eyes."

"I missed you, let's skip the small talk and get to what I've been starving for. Your mouth sucking mine."

First time sex play after the hiatus was urgent, and at the culmination we pumped out much more cream than ever before. "Let me grab a washcloth and clean us up, then I want to hear about the internship…"

"What's important is, I've decided to major in robotics. I guess that's no surprise after the internship."

"What's the plan?"

"Let me speak to my advisor at school. Now having a major, I don't know what classes I'll need."

Driving Adam to his parent's home, he finished sharing the high points of his trip to robot enthusiasm. What I know for sure is, Adam and I were compatible and had great sex. But we were brought together due to improbable circumstance, hotline caller talking to a hotline volunteer.It's the underlying connection that made me pause, reformed queer basher in the arms of recovered queer bashee. Were the contradictory dynamics driving us, or was it a waste of time to wonder?

By the Christmas holiday, we had finished all the exercises in the sensate book. I couldn't postpone his objective any longer. I mounted a willing, eager Adam for the first time on Christmas Eve, in front of the tree we decorated and toasty banked fireplace. It was Christmas card perfect. I placed him on all fours and took him from behind. Ten months into being intimate, we knew each other's body like our own. When he was well lubricated, I pushed in with minimal resistance. He pushed back in eager acceptance. I had to bring myself back from the edge till finally I couldn't stop the ultimate blossoming ecstasy. Just before my zenith, I reached under and stroked his hard cock in rhythm with my thrusting. As I went into bliss, Adam's body started pulsating then went into a contained frenzy, finally going breathless with delight. Despite *Sensate focus* advising otherwise, we came together.

"Did we exorcise your demon?"

"Yes, we got it good. Just like I hoped we would. We screwed that demon down and then I expelled it out of my cock, I'm demon free."

"Why are you crying?"

"You wouldn't understand."

"Try me."

"Nobody could understand how hard it was for me to get this fear finally done and finished."

"You've told me some of your journey. When you're ready I'd gladly listen to the rest."

"Thank you for an unforgettable first time. No more pretend or hiding or dread of being found out to be a liar and fraud."

"Congratulations, good for us."

"Before I started talking to you on the hotline, I would have rather killed myself than do what we just did."

"I remember, you told me."

"You just unlocked the door to escape my false phony-self. What a long hard way it was."

"I think I know how it works, my demon was rightwing conservative arrogance. And I didn't even know I was deluding myself until almost killed by teenagers."

After Adam's deflowering our time together lightened, pressure-off, and we grew closer and more comfortable as a couple. I noticed we were smiling or laughing more. He began talking about coming out to his family. Then one day out of the blue he said, "Let me ask you something."

"Shoot?"

"Do you ever think about taking revenge on the guy who cut that Greek letter on your ass cheek?"

"Right after it happened I dwelled on vengeance. I even considered getting a concealed carry pistol permit, but I've evolved. Why do you ask?"

"I've found the guy … he brags how many lambdas he's carved, leaving his mark like Zorro. I could hurt him for you."

"No, don't do that!"

"Why not? You'll have that scare the rest of your life. Let me give him something to remember too."

"First off, I care about you. He and his friends carry knives and know how to use them. Second, I never let anyone fight my fights, it is a point of honor. Lastly, the way I knew I was healed from that trauma was when I realized in my heart, I had forgiven the kids who bashed me."

"Don't worry about me, I can handle myself. But I understand not letting someone else fight your battles. I'm the same way."

"Ever notice some hotline volunteers get a lot of suicide calls? I've never had one. But for some reason I get more than my share of calls from gay bashers, and not just the ones ready to face themselves like you were."

"You were my salvation, when I needed it."

"My most rewarding calls are angry, overflowing with hate, shouting insults, calling me every name they can think of. Those calls give me satisfaction, because I don't hang up on them, even though I'd like to. When the caller runs down I ask, 'do you feel better now?' More often than not, I get a yes and move from being an object to hate to a person. Some of these guys go through hell to get to self-acceptance, and you know some of that."

"So, that's what you are doing when you hold the handset away from your ear for long periods of time. I hang up on those creeps and so does Eugene."

"Hey, I don't judge you, don't judge me."

"Still, I want to hurt the guy that hurt you. I owe it to you."

"No, you don't, sooner or later he will have to face his demons, like we all do. I want your promise you'll leave him alone and not mess-up your future and chances at getting into a decent four-year college."

"Speaking of which, next month the college applications for the fall are due. Do you think you could check over mine?"

"Sure, it will be a privilege."

Adam hit his final semester at the community college with renewed enthusiasm. Our sex life added a homework-tutoring extension, for after making *wind and the rain*. Life was good, we were happy, and the future looked bright. Then in early April, something unexpected happened on our regular Tuesday shift at the hotline.

"Damn what happened? Adam, you look white as a sheet."

"My last call was a bomb threat."

"Grab your stuff, let's get out of here!"

"Not us, Eugene, the caller said a suicide bomber is going to detonate at the

School Bus Museum and Picnic Grounds at noon tomorrow. He said it will be full of children on field trips. What should I do?"

"What's the hotline handbook say under bomb threat? It's right there."

"Okay, okay here … if the bomb scare is at us, leave fast and call for help from outside. If the threat is for another location, call 911. When logging calls coming and going about a bomb, log everything said. Also, write up an emergency incident sheet with the caller's exact words and attach to the log. It says if you can't get through to 911, phone the FBI, their number is here, and if that fails call the local police precinct. Okay I'll write down everything he said, verbatim. You call 911 and you call the FBI if it's busy, okay?"

"Mary, who died to make him Queen?"

"Eugene, be nice, we are having a bomb threat, that's not usual, let him rein. Please call 911."

Eugene's voice quickly went from frustrated to mad talking to the emergency number. "911 will only take right-now emergencies. I gave the supervisor my name and this number. She said someone would phone back when they have a minute. In case you wonder why, the poor service, they are busy."

"Good luck with that. Look, our phone lines all lit up when I clicked on the answering machine. We are too busy too, 911 will think we are cranks if they try to call back and get constant busy signals. What should we do?"

Telephoning the FBI was like going into a labyrinth of computer voices demanding extension numbers or offering a staff directory, giving business hours, and website addresses. So, I left my name and the hotline telephone number at each juncture that beeped, finally throwing my hands up in frustration when I realized I'd been run around and completed a circle.

"What do we do?"

"Adam, read us what the caller said?"

"The caller sounded young, and said, 'Tomorrow at noon a suicide bomber will blow himself up at the School Bus Museum.' I asked how he knew that. He said, 'The bomber is my neighbor and we get high sometimes. Lately the bomber joined a weird religious cult and acts different than before.' I asked for his name, or what to call him. Then he said, 'I don't want to get into trouble,' and he hung up.'"

"You think he was for real."

"I don't know, but wouldn't want to bet lives on a few seconds of conversation."

"Right, let me call the local police precinct, they're not far away. 'Hello, I'm calling from the gay hotline …' He hung up."

"Let me try, I won't say gay. 'Hello, I'm calling about a bomb threat.' Yes, your read out is correct this is the gay hotline.' She hung up."

"Now what do we do?"

"I'll try them, that way we all tried. Maybe I'll get through. Hello this is an emergency, a bomb threat … He hung up."

We swiveled our chairs around and looked at each other, exasperated. Then Eugene said, "Hand me that index card box marked inactive volunteers … thanks. We had a volunteer a while back who went to the police academy. He might be a cop and can recommend something. Otherwise I think we have a big problem. Here it is, let's hope he's home. Hello is Owen there? Okay, do you have a number where he can be reached? Thank you … Hi, may I speak to Owen, this is an emergency. Okay, then can you get him a message right away? Tell him I'm calling from the hotline and it is life and death urgent. My name is Eugene, he knows me. Thank you."

"Unless someone has a better idea, I think we should answer the phones. So, Owen can call you back."

"Yeah, the FBI or 911 or your caller with more info on the bomb might be trying to get through too."

"Good, doing something is better than doing nothing."

"Damn straight, we need to stop a tragedy."

"Chill dude, it might be a hoax."

After twenty minutes trying to sound normal, keeping regular hotline calls short, there was a loud banging on the outer door to the office suite. We keep it locked for safety sake on the late shift. Adam went and answered the door. Then seconds later, two uniformed police patrol officers entered the hotline office with Adam.

"Hey, Owen, we are glad to see you."

"What's the problem Eugene?"

Adam handed Owen his incident write-up of a bomb threat and the clipboard with the log sheet showing our failed attempts contacting 911, FBI, and the local precinct three times. Owen handed the papers to his partner, turned on his radio and requested a sergeant to respond to the hotline address as soon as possible. Turning back to us, he said, "Still no copier at the hotline? When are you guys going to catch up with this century?"

"It's about money, you remember how it is. Anyway, the lawyers let us use their copier in a pinch."

"You got the key to their office?"

"It's in the lockbox, and yes I know the combination." That said Eugene reached over took the locked box down and opened it, picked up the log sheet and Adam's write-up and went to the lawyers' office next door. Just as he returned with the photocopies a sergeant and another uniformed officer arrived. Eugene handed the copies to Owen who passed them to the Sargent and the four cops went into the waiting room for a confab.

As the police were leaving, Owen turned back into the hotline. "We got this, you guys can stand down. But if you get another call about this bomb, let me know. In the future, if you can't get me call GOAL, they have a phone tree, and you can talk to a gay cop fast. At the next hotline monthly meeting, you might want to suggest a formal linkage with GOAL. We can help in a lot of situations."

"Thanks, Owen."

"Thank you, I'll let you guys know how this shakes out." That said, he was out the door and going through the waiting room.

"What goal?"

"GOAL stands for Gay Officers Action League, it's a group for gay cops."

The police sergeant came back and stuck her head in the door. "I want to thank you men for your effort to avoid a calamity, and to let you know whoever hung up on you at the precinct will be severely disciplined. I didn't know the hotline was here."

"We were set up after the Stonewall Riots."

"Do a lot of gay kids call?"

"Many of our coming-of-age calls are from straight kids of both genders looking for reassurance they are normal heterosexuals. It is hard to be a teenager."

"I had no idea about your work. We need to mention the hotline at police academy trainings."

Adam raised his hand like a student in school. "Since you brought it up, may I make a suggestion? Rather than punish those who hung up on us, it would be better if we could sit down with them and do consciousness raising."

Eugene, still keyed up, couldn't contain himself. "Consciousness raising now that's an antique concept sweetie."

"See what happens when you teach them to read?"

"Hey, don't you guys pick on him! Now young man, before you tell me about consciousness raising be aware GOAL does a sensitivity training for new recruits."

"That sounds like cops talking to cops. What I had in mind is like the hotline, ordinary gay citizens talking, person to person to your people. Cops want respect from the public but don't always give it."

"I'm listening."

"Maybe this is off track, but I used to be a homophobe who regularly bashed fags until I accepted myself as one. During my thug days, the police often encouraged me to beat up queers. Not in so many words, but with a wink and a nod. If not for the hotline, I might have killed somebody. If I had committed murder, the police would have arrested me to be punished for a terrible crime they were partially culpable for with a wink and a nod. Can you imagine how confusing that is to understand?"

"I hear you, but a dialogue would have to go both ways. Are you aware we sustain more injuries responding to domestic calls than chasing criminals with weapons? And if the domestic trouble is between two men or two women the probability of my officers being hurt goes up tenfold."

"I'd be open to hearing their problems in exchange for them hearing ours."

"Tell you what, I'll run your request up the flag-pole and if any boss salutes I'll follow through, and let you know."

"Thank you for listening."

"Hey, no matter what happens tomorrow with that bomb threat, you boys are my heroes tonight."

Earth Day

Spring rain had been pouring nonstop for a month, its chilly, damp dreariness soaked everything to squishy over-saturation. Work on Earth Day eve was harder than usual, rearranging electricity from the grid here, to supply it there. The second shift at the power station was all about circumventing a brownout to avoid a major blackout's nightmare chaos. Using chicanery, we dodged a bullet. At shift's end, every customer had juice flowing.

Wrung out tired to the bone, I sloshed my restored, rose-petal pink 1936 Studebaker pickup truck toward home. It was 12:10 AM on Earth Day, not a happy holiday for a dying earth. Traffic on the highway was only me amidst the heavy precipitation, then a bicycle rider appeared in my high-beam headlights. He was moving fast, the wet asphalt on the road's shoulder offered his narrow tires no resistance. I sped up for a closer look. In my youth, I'd been an avid cyclist. So, I wasn't surprised to see someone training after midnight in pouring rain. I thought, *Yes, I too was once that crazy.*

Then abruptly it was like watching a slow-motion scene in a movie. Suddenly, the cyclist was catapulted skyward, flying head over heels out of his toe clips, up off the cycle, airborne seconds, he completed an arc as he tumbled back to earth. He landed a good distance from launch. It looked like he'd been shot out of a cannon, and its trajectory had sprawled him out on the pavement. The bike's front wheel must have dropped into a water-filled pothole. I'd never been that close to an accident, its suddenness was heart stopping.

Once the fast-moving, bright blue bicycle dropped into the hole, it seemed to freeze a crazy instant while ejecting its rider. Then it somersaulted forward, flipped around wildly, looking alive, and finally stopped *directly in my path.*

White knuckled, I realized I'd been pumping the brake pedal to no effect. The wet, old-fashioned brake pads wouldn't dry enough to grab hold, and the road surface was slick as greased glass. I swerved sharply to avoid the bicycle and my antique pickup went into a skid. Breathless, I eased the steering wheel in the direction of the sideways slide and recovered from the spinout just as I went off the road. The brakes finally grabbed, tires held, and the Studebaker stopped dangerously close to the downed bicyclist lying like a heap of old wet clothes on the road's shoulder. Shaking in my boots, I thought, *Hell, I hadn't been going fast enough to lose control, was I?*

As my racing heart and breathing slowed, I climbed out of the truck. The downed rider had sat up, surrounded by eddies of runoff rainwater. He looked dazed. As if the situation wasn't bad enough, out of the corner of my eye I saw a behemoth tractor trailer rig roaring out of the heavy sheets of rain. It was headed straight at the disabled bicycle lying on the highway. The truck driver wasn't slowing down. Without forethought, I ran back and snatched the damaged bike out of the path of the speeding giant. The dirty wake from the mammoth thoroughly redrenched me as it flew by, its air horn blasting.

Slogging back, I leaned the wrecked bicycle against my truck's front bumper. Cursing wet, I trudged over to the cyclist. "Are you hurt? Should I call for medical help?"

Pulling his scraped, dented helmet off, the rider mumbled, "I'm all right."

Other than confused, he looked okay. I was surprised to see he was Asian. We usually only see other rednecks this far out in rural America.

With my truck's high beams behind me, shaking rain off my face made the water fly out of my long gray hair in halo like sprays. "Can you move your arms and legs?" He complied, cautiously checking his extremities one by one.

"By the way, I'm called Chet."

"I am Chu Ke Tsai, and you look like an angel with a halo," He said while carefully examining injuries, like he knew what he was doing.

"Trust me, I'm no angel, honey. Do you have a headache or double vision?"

His tone changed. It became louder, sharper, authoritarian. "I'll be fine, are you a medical practitioner or something?"

On guard, I said, "No, and I don't want to be sued for practicing without a license. You'd think at my age I'd know enough to mind my own business, wouldn't you?"

Reeling ire back in, he looked contrite. "Why would I sue an angel who stopped to help?"

"Beats me, maybe we live in paranoid times. If you're all right, I'm on my way."

In another sudden mood, shift he stared at his bike leaning against my truck's bumper, then at me. "Did you hit me with your truck? I have no recall of what happened?"

Reflectively, my hands balled into hard fists as rage surged through my veins roiling my already dark mood. I stood there, rain pouring off me by the bucketful, getting chilled, and I glowered at him. "No dear, I didn't, but this Good Samaritan shit is overrated. I'll know better next time." Reaching down, I yanked him to his feet by an elbow. He grimaced, and I felt a low voltage electrical vibration when we touched skin to skin. Was it my imagination … it distracted me for an instant. Nevertheless, I unceremoniously elbow-guided him to the front of my pickup's pristine pretty-pink chromed bumper. "Do you see evidence of a collision?"

Grimly he said, "No, there is no damage. Is this your wife's truck?"

I dropped his elbow and grabbed up his bicycle and handed it to him. The destroyed front wheel and blown-out tire were mute testament he'd not been rear ended. "I never had a wife, and you just proved something I already knew, 'The road to hell *is* paved with good intentions.' I'm out-ta-here. And by the way, you're welcome."

Eyes lowered, voice apologetic, he said, "Wait, don't go. I'm sorry … ugh why is it pink?"

"What's wrong with pink?"

"Nothing, sorry I'm all screwed up … what happened?"

"What do you remember?"

"One minute I was pedaling fast, flying in highest gear, and the next I am spread out on the pavement like road kill. Did you see it happened?"

His jumbled, apologetic manner calmed me down a tad. "It looked like your front wheel dropped into an underwater pothole. Look at that wheel. It's destroyed, no way can it be salvaged. Your bike frame looks bent too. If it were me, I'd junk 'em."

"I will. But right now, I'm in a predicament. Miles from anywhere, in the middle of the night during a storm, with a disabled bicycle."

His cognition seemed okay. One way I've learned to control my too fast to fists is by using objectivity. "And you have no broken bones *and* are alive."

"I like you, you're a realist. Is Chet short for Chester?"

"It is, and for asking, I'll drive you to that all night diner off the interchange. It's about fifteen minutes that way. You can call for a ride from there, get out of this downpour, and have a hot drink."

"Chet, I am sorry I accused you of causing the accident. Would you mind driving me home? I'll pay you well for your trouble. My place is over by Millard State Park."

"That is forty miles in the opposite direction from where I'm headed, it's late, and I'm wet, cold, and cranky. Not tonight, new friend, some other time. Call a taxi from the diner."

Showing a smidgen of self-pity, Chu Ke Tsai sulked, then mumbled. "The problem is there are no all-night taxis out here and I don't have anyone local to call."

"Why is that?"

"I moved here last year after trying too hard for too long to save the planet. I telecommute to work back in the city. I live alone, work a lot to keep my mind off … you know. I haven't met any friendly people out here. You would not believe the way the locals and especially their children stare at me on the street and in stores."

"Oh, I can imagine. Diversity is not one of our strengths. They don't like pink either."

"Will you rescue me? I can make it worth your while, name your price."

"Like I said, I'm worn out from work and waterlogged cold. There is a no-tell motel a few miles down the road from that diner. I'll take you there. Tomorrow you can sort it all out, the cabs will be running, and if I'm not mistaken, that diner delivers. You'll feel better after a hot shower. I know I will."

Chu Ke Tsai didn't say anything more but looked miserable. After several minutes driving, a new thought popped up. *He must be as wet and cold as me and probably hurting from his tumble on asphalt.* I took a long apprising look, even wet and discombobulated he was hot. His Spandex bike riding singlet showed most of everything. He was well muscled in the right proportions, with a nice size basket and killer ass. I liked what I saw all the way down into my panties.

"Tell you what, Mr. Tsai, that motel is out of my way home, the closest place to right here, right now is mine. I've got a spare room. It's not fancy, I don't live elaborately, but it's warm and dry. Tomorrow I could drive you home on my way back to work. But just in case you couldn't tell, I'm gay and pink is my color. You got a problem with that, big fella?"

His mood lightened, and he responded with a beautiful smile that lit up his face. "No problem, I am Taiwanese-American. Thank you for stopping and helping." Spontaneously we exchanged a brief "hello stranger" handshake. *Damn, I felt that slight electrical pulse-quiver again when we shook hands.*

I said, "I get first dibs for the shower."

"What kind of work do you do at night, Chet?"

"My job title is supervising electrical engineer, second shift at Regional Power. We operate around the clock to keep electricity flowing by drawing juice off grids. But this unrelenting weather strains the system with constant short outs and downed lines. Tonight, I had all our emergency crews out and was switching power from all over everywhere, including Canada to keep people's lights on. We came close to a total blackout twice. I was like a juggler with too many balls … listen to me blabbing away … sorry you asked?"

"No, it sounds like exciting work."

"Why are you training in the rain, other than the sheer delight of no resistance from the wet road?"

"The Race-Across-America this summer is keeping my mind off the end of the world, due to global warming. I am training every free hour I get. It's a rain or shine, twenty-four hours a day, seven-day race. I hope to at least finish."

"Damn, I've heard that's a killer race. It's even crippled some riders, right?'

"Right, but with global warming ending everything, this will be the last race."

"I know we only just met an all, but I say don't do it."

"Thanks for the advice. What's your opinion on this manmade climate catastrophe?"

"I can see why you haven't made any friends out here. Rural people don't buy climate change, and not manmade."

"In the urban world I recently left, they'd be called climate deniers. What's your position?"

"It's complicated, late, and I don't like politics."

We didn't speak after that exchange. Chu Ke Tsai's silence probably came from the shock of his crash, not being able to get home to his own bed, the fact that I just told him not to do something he was training for every day, and how creepy I might turn out. He had a lot to think about.

Silence was fine with me. I was uncomfortably wet and cold, tired, and the power might still go down over night, then all hell would break loose as a result. The third-shift crew that relives my team was our least good, but since overtime pay is verboten these days, I and my gals and guys had to go home, like it or not. Road conditions ahead in the direction of my house were dangerously slippery for my old lady Studebaker. So, the situation was not conducive to chit-chat with the macho stranger sitting next to me.

Then in my head, accusations started beating on me. *Did I cover all the bases before leaving work? Stopping to help was stupid and I risked my health in this unforgiving weather. It was dangerous inviting a stranger home. I was acting out of character and should know better.*

Just then to sidetrack my thinking, the rain increased, banging down in thicker sheets as a ferocious wind violently blew up to shake the trees as lightning frisked instantaneously into and out of view on the horizon. As the storm intensified, I pulled off the state route onto the narrow twisting back-country, unpaved road that leads home.

Ten miles from work, perched high in the foothills, my little house was surrounded by big old growth hardwood trees that hid it from any traveling eyes on my isolated road. I parked the pickup in its usual space, next to my other restored vintage pink vehicles garaged under low hanging conifer branches. Around us the big trees danced pugnaciously in the fierce wind. Lightning and deep, rumbling thunder traveled swiftly from the horizon to directly overhead.

We climbed down from the pretty-pink pickup without exchanging a word and sprinted through the cold driving rain toward the house. Chu Ke Tsai ran beside me, both of us fighting to remain upright in the wild wind. Lightning crackled around us like photographers' strobe lights popping, causing eerie landscapes to flash alive then instantly extinguished. All the while thunder assaulted our ears and shook us like concussion grenades detonating near our feet.

I dashed up the porch steps to fumble a slippery wet key into a dripping lock. The door swung open and we rushed inside the mud room. We were sopping wet, cold to the bone, feet squishing, and teeth chattering. I kicked out of my boots, peeled off water logged clothes, leaving them in a pile to puddle on the flagstone floor. Naked, I made a mad dash through the house and got a hot, steamy shower running.

After a hesitation, Chu Ke Tsai must have mirrored my actions because he was in the shower with me, scant seconds later. Showering together was not my plan. He was three or four inches taller, maybe twenty-five pounds heavier, and a few years younger than me. I liked what I saw and wondered if he always got a hard-on showering with a lady-man. He had a nice set of genitals and an ass that made my mouth water, 'Happy Earth Day.'

The steamy, hot water and nearness of his erection helped me to relax and feel friendly enough to reach out and soap Chu Ke Tsai, all over. Once again, I felt that low-voltage electrical pulse surge where I touched his skin.When I finished soaping him, without a word he returned the favor, soaping me thoroughly, especially my pits. After lathering, shampooing, and rinsing off, we took turns drying each other.

It all felt natural, except we'd skipped a couple of steps going from complete strangers to unselfconscious touching the other's nude body. Also, our dicks looked similar and even matched size-wise. The big mystery was when we made skin to skin contact, I got a buzz. Not wanting to break the flow of stress-reducing activities, the hospitality offers of food and hot drinks would have to wait. It was late.

When we were buffed dry, I pointed Chu Ke Tsai toward my bedroom. My intention was to loan him a bath robe and then direct him to the guestroom across the hall. But somehow, we weren't ready to cover-up and instead toppled onto my bed in a tangle of arms and legs. Then our mouths found each other hungrily, and we did extensive exploration with fluttering tongues. The oral searching expanded to include mouthing other body parts, then kneading fingers and stoking palms joined the party.

He was driven by a lust I easily reciprocated. But neither of us had given the slightest hint, by look or gesture before the shower our hormones were bordering on ravenous. *Oh, wait Mary, maybe the straining erections in the shower were a clue?*

Then the electricity mystery expanded. Full-body contact skin against skin felt like being encased in a low voltage, vibrating electrical cocoon. It wasn't unpleasant but defied my knowledge of electrical energy. On the road or in the shower, I felt contact points of voltage. But now it was a live current encasing two adult bodies squirming with desire. *Where's the source? How to measure it?*

"Why didn't you mention being gay when I told you I was?"

"I'm not gay. For me, any warm, wet, willing hole has sufficed. Gender has never been an issue." Then he grabbed me and began enthusiastic kissing again.

After what seemed like a long time energetically sucking mouth, he pulled away panting hard and rolled onto his stomach. My eyes savored the beauty of his perfectly shaped, bicycle seat-hardened, hairless, well-muscled butt. I couldn't keep my hands off. They touched, caressed, patted, and massaged. As my hands and fingers physically manipulated his splendid physique, Chu Ke Tsai's breathing returned to normal and relaxed, yielding under my fingers.

As my eyes feasted on of his perfectly sculpted body, my racing mind was slow to catch up. Finally, it asked, *What's going on? This wasn't the plan, and he gave no verbal consent. Have I lost my way letting lust go unrestrained? I'm an engineer, I make careful calculations. Am I taking advantage of this guy's troubles? Doubt it. He is matching me lust for lust and it feels damn good and I am overdue for a little dalliance.*

Going counter to my chastising mind, without prudence I spit into his ass crack. Then in a slow rotating motion, I gently inserted one spit-slick finger into his very tight bung hole. Experiencing resistance, I scooted down his back and sniffed my finger. And only found male musk scent. So, I dove in with a fluttering tongue, Chu Ke Tsai had been clenching. But bit by bit, he opened to gentle, wet pulsating incursion. When he sighed and wiggled side to side, my tongue pushed in as deep as it could reach. To augment his demonstrated appreciation of depth, I removed tongue and inserted two fingers. He increased dynamic, nonverbal physical reply to my digits dance. Reaching a peak, he hoarsely whispered, "Deeper."

I let my thumb caress outside of the same area my finger stretched out deeper to massage. "You ready for a ride?"

He nodded to the affirmative saying, "Yes!"

I withdrew my fingers and slipped on a condom. I moved up over him and pressed my cock into his spit-slick outer sphincter. His body tensed, and his upper torso reared back. I stopped moving, then after a pause slowly massaged the small of his back, those muscles were tight. When his tightness loosened under my pulsating fingers, I moved the massage up his back to his wide manly shoulders, and then back down to a narrow waist. When he relaxed enough, I pushed my cock in further and he reflexively tensed. *He was too old to be a virgin. It must be the idea of being womanized.*

"When you are ready, push back and take me at your speed. I'll wait."

Then he seemed to focus, gathered himself and warily pushed up and back. When my cock touched his inner sphincter, he stiffened but didn't squeeze me out. *I'm in limbo half in, half out. Maybe it's time to stop and do something less invasive.* And yet the electrical current vibrates with increased intensity the deeper I'm in.

Reaching between us, my hands found and lightly fondled his lovely muscled ass cheeks and thick biker's thighs. Then for no conscious reason, I stretched up and nibbled and sucked his ears, nipping, licking, and slurping down his neck to the tops of his shoulders. The electrical energy didn't change.

Of its own accord, my left hand moved deftly under him, first fondling his inner thighs and then aroused cock, and finally cupping his balls. I liked the feel of manipulating his weighty nuts in their silk soft bag. What lady-man wouldn't like that?

Based on his murmurings, he liked what my hands were doing down under. I could imagine on another occasion mouthing his egg-shaped nuts to distraction. At least until they were ready to pop a load in appreciation. As if reading my mind, his squirming reached another peak.

I froze all movement to let him draw back from an inadvertent orgasm. After that expectant ready to cum instant, he became tranquil by degrees. Then my hands down under reanimated to travel up to his pretty dark nipples. Playing first with the right, then switching back and forth between the two to gage sensitivity. The left nipple won, so I rewarded it with extra attention and added light counterpoint accompaniment to the right creating a duet.

Proof he liked the tit play was his hole opened and resistance melted around my straining cock. He decisively pushed up, taking me in all the way to the pubes. We both breathed a satisfied sigh as we felt my cock stretch-out inside his love tunnel. Finally, we were arranged properly for a primordial horizontal dance. The same as choreographed by prehistoric cavemen depicted on cave walls.

I pulled his hips up and back, bringing him up onto his knees while squatting back on my heels. Then, using easy strokes, we began a slow boogie. Chu Ke Tsai caught the rhythm and imitated my movements in reverse. First using short back and forth movements, then we got into sync. The rhythm's cadence became adamant and my strokes longer, stronger, faster, and more insistent and we matched each other's energy.

Before long he rode the full length of my cock with relish, so I stopped moving and let him drive. My mind traveled back, watching through my pickup truck's windshield, his ass encased in Spandex flexing as he pumped bicycle pedals. In front of me was my fantasy come to life. Real or imagined, gentle blue electrical sparks were flying around us the faster we fucked, push-pulling me to a climax.

My fantasy focus got preoccupied when I caught sight of my rapidly moving dickhead just about to exit his thrusting ass ring. Its condom encased loose sensitive skin bunched *forward* to cover dick's head moving in *opposition* to exit. When his movement reversed, the latex sandwich opened to show dick's head again. Then as it slipped back in his ass, the loose skin unbunched and smoothed flat on the shaft. Unbelievable, my dick moved in two directions at once. The size of these counter actions was made more obvious and bigger by the condom. The latex sleek-flat covering going in, was double covered in reverse coming almost out. These visuals added another element, to my already intense stimulation.

Along with everything else going on, watching what I was feeling as he rode the full length of my cock, shoveled heaps more pleasure on enflamed desire. At just the right instant, instinctively I grabbed his hips and took control, driving in and out of his ass with mounting potency. I quickly hit my stride fucking hard and that brought me to the edge. Then like my antique pink pickup going into a wild skid, I slammed into a noisy orgasm that blasted me into a serene outer space like swirling, high-energy vortex of ecstasy.

On a semiconscious plane, I experienced Chu Ke Tsai's insides and then outside churning out his orgasm fuel just as I finished. His prostate jumped in climax against my still-hard cock. His anal muscles grabbed, squeezed, and released with each forceful cum blast. Through ragged, heavy breathing, he made short soft grunts to propel his ejaculations. Our electrical field seemed to intensify during the orgasms and then a rheostat dimmed the electrical sparks as we went into the low-voltage caressing of after play, still cock docked.

Smiling over his shoulder, short of breath Chu Ke Tsai said, "Happy last Earth Day Chet."

"Yeah back at yah, new friend, good fuck."

As our breathing slowed to normal, I pulled out, and he rolled over for renewed suck-face. Soon Chu Ke Tsai was asleep, our arms entwined, holding each other. Used to sleeping alone, I dozed on and off, fitful but sexually content. He slept deeply snuggled in my arms. I thought, *We fit together so well, like two perfectly crafted halves of something inimitable. How is that possible?*

Wake-up time came too soon. I pried myself out of Chu Ke's strong grip, and he half woke. "Do you need to check in with your job?"

Half asleep, he took the offered bedside cell phone. I headed for a quick shower. After drying off, I pulled on an old flowery pink housecoat. Glancing in my bedroom, Chu Ke Tsai was back asleep hugging my pillow. He looked adorable. It sounded like the intensity of rain on the metal roof was slowing down a smidgen ... first time in too long.

To chase the chill, I started a hickory wood fire in the front room's cast iron wood stove and another in the kitchen's cook stove. Next, I got the coffee ground, grits, and biscuits going. After slipping on a pair of mud boots, rubber slicker, and hat, I went out to feed the chickens and other critters and collected eggs. Back inside, I kicked out of the rain gear, gathered our wet clothes from the previous night, and then mopped up rainwater puddled on the mud room floor. A lady-man's work is never done.

Finally, a big mug of steaming coffee in hand, I sat at the kitchen table and replayed last night's after-work events, in my head. I got extra hard when it came to the sex and wanted to play some more, but common sense said no. Chu Ke Tsai had to be sore this morning. He'd been through a lot last night.

Just then, Chu Ke Tsai walked into the kitchen. He was nude, his straight, black hair damp from another shower, and he looked even more handsome than in bed. His cock, looking very familiar, was half hard under a bush of almost straight pubic hair. I stood, poured, then handed him a mug of coffee and put bacon in the big black skillet.

"I couldn't find my clothes, I hope you don't mind me walking around naked. I would wrap myself in a towel, but all I could find were cold and wet."

"You want to borrow a robe? I have a few one-size-fits-all that were gifts I never used."

"If you don't mind, I feel free and natural like this. Plus, my scrapes and bruises will heal faster exposed to the air."

"I don't mind, I like what I see."

"It's nice and warm here, and the wood fire smell delicious. I don't wear clothes around my place unless it's cold. Is that too much unwelcome information?"

"No, you almost seem to be glowing today, even with those cuts and bruises from your tumble."

Looking coy he said, "You could join me? I liked what I saw last night."

Demurely peeling out of my old house coat, ladylike, I twirled around 360 degrees to give him a full view. "Okay, I still like looking at you, even in the altogether."

"Ditto."

"To prattle on, our clothes are hung up drying, your bike shoes and my work boots too."

"Thanks, *you* turned last night's disaster into something to remember."

"Chu Ke Tsai, after a bad start, I thoroughly enjoyed meeting you."

"You don't have to be formal. I'd prefer you call me Chu or Ke, it's more personal."

"Would you mind if I call you Chuck? It's easier to remember."

"I've been called worse. Chuck is not formal."

"Sounds like the rains letting up some. I'll drive you and your bike home this afternoon at three? I relieve my boss at four."

"What time is it?"

"Twelve thirty, we got our eight hours of sleep, plus a little."

"I hope you don't mind if we talk this morning. Last night you weren't in the mood, and I'd like to get to know you better."

"There's a bike shop on the way. You can get a new wheel there and they'll straighten that frame. Oh, listen to me babbling, you probably have extra wheels and other bicycles at home."

Chuck didn't reply and stared into his coffee mug. He said he wanted to talk this morning ... but wasn't, because I blocked him? We sat in silence, savoring the full-bodied, freshly- ground, dark roast coffee. I was tired of doom and gloom politics, so I kept my mouth zipped. But couldn't keep my eyes off the magnificent body, I'd thoroughly enjoyed ravishing in bed.

In response to my staring, he looked up. "I want to talk about last night, but I'm conflicted. I hate to be more trouble than I've been already?"

"Last night was about stress relief we both needed."

"It's hard to describe, something more than that happened and I'm not sure what to think about it."

"Talk, I'll at least listen."

"Are you a transvestite, cross dresser, transsexual, or what?"

I got up and flipped the bacon. "So, you have a vocabulary problem? Or is it you can't reconcile being topped by swishy me?"

"I wouldn't put it like that. But, maybe, yes."

"Gee, and to think I thought I demonstrated how well I use my male-self last night."

His face revealed he wasn't holding his confusion back. Then, with a deep sigh, he started talking. "Probably like most folks I'm just all mixed-up these final days our earth has left. Don't get me wrong, I liked sex with you, and I don't think I'm crazy for upending my usual top to bottom."

"So far, I'm not seeing crazy, not everyone goes end of human life on earth nuts."

"I thought when I moved to the country, the madness would stay in the city and I could have a peaceful solo finale."

"These days, lots of folks from here are going there for the opposite reason. To party like there's no tomorrow, *until there is no tomorrow.*"

"I planned to quietly prepare for the end, meditating in solitude. Instead, all I do is work and train for the Race Across America. I can't seem to make peace with the finality of unknown infinity."

"Didn't Frederick Nietzsche say something about meditating?"

"He said, 'If you stare into the void long enough, it will stare back.'"

"Right he did. What did you do before moving here to the sticks?"

"I had a military career in special forces. I was a colonial until four years ago. After I resigned my commission, all my time went to 'Earth One, Save the Planet.' Now I just telecommute IT security, for a bank. It augments my Army pension."

"I remember how the multinationals killed Earth One."

"It was trumped up charges, to make it go away. So, I moved up to the mountains and brought emotional baggage with me."

"Up here people want to believe climate change is a hoax."

"Do you believe that? You seem like a smart guy, girly-guy … no offense."

"I wondered when we'd get to what we're really talking about. Think you can get past our being different?"

"To be really honest, how you look, and act makes me nervous. For the most part I've lived my adult life with tough masculine men. I trained them to be killers. But now the earth's doomed. The polar ice caps are gone, there's ocean where southwestern United States used to be. I guess the rules and everything else has changed, so, I better too."

"I appreciate honest. Up here, the radio dial has mostly Christian evangelical preaching. What you just said, they would say isn't true. But if it was, it's God's will. They have a double nonsensical answer to everything."

"Chet, do you listen to what's on radio and TV?"

"Well now, some last days on the planet's taxonomy songs have catchy tunes with good danceable beats. But the word at work is the kids have end of days dance parties ending in mass assisted suicide. I don't want to see all that?"

"I don't know what to make of the End It Early Movement? What's the rush?"

"Doesn't matter; AM & FM radio says global warming will be fixed soon."

"FIXED HOW?"

"The Bible thumpers say the devil's sulfur will be spread over Earth's outer atmosphere and that will cool temperatures back to where God wants."

"Did they mention unintended consequences?"

"This swishy queen doesn't pay *that* much attention to *nut jobs.*"

An angry look clouded Chuck's demeanor, then swiftly vanished. "Just say they do explode sulfur dioxide in the upper atmosphere, and it does filter enough sunlight to cool the Earth, what happens to plants? Humans and animals rely on plants for food, and plants rely on photosynthesis to live. Does anyone really think a global famine will help mitigate global warming after the sulfur dioxide dissipates?"

"Doubt it, but don't work yourself into a tizzy. Just maybe some folks need a little hope at the end. But hey, what does this queen know?" I removed the bacon to drain on paper towels. "How do you like your eggs?"

His cute facial expression returned, and Chuck mumbled, "How you like yours."

I broke four fresh hen's eggs into the drained bacon pan. "So, specifically, how are you preparing for the end of days?"

"Last night in your bed was the first pleasurable distraction in too long a time. Do you ever watch television?"

I flipped the eggs over carefully, not breaking the yolks, then pulled our warm plates from the oven. In a few seconds, we dug into a hearty breakfast earned the previous night. "I check out TV occasionally, it's not for me, too predictably boring."

"How so? I watch with the sound off making sarcastic comments."

"There was a time I watched public TV. Back when it was educational, now it's the same infomercials as the corporate stations, only punctuated with begging for viewer's money too."

Obviously relishing the food, Chuck said, "Wow, these biscuits are weightless. They practically float off the plate. I mean everything tastes fresh and good, but the biscuits are outstanding. I forgot how good fresh food tastes."

"The biscuits are an old family recipe. The secret is lard. How much time do you think humans have left?"

A serious expression returned, clouding his beaming enjoyment of breakfast. "Without a computer, I'd guess less than a year. Unless the suicide clubs and religious cyanide-Kool-Aid potluck dinner parties become universally popular, that could buy a little more time."

"How many years supply of food and water you got squirreled away, preparing for Armageddon?"

"Three years of can goods and dry grains and pasta. I replenish my stock as used."

"The radio preachers would call you a heretic, right?"

"I was a Boy Scout before becoming a soldier. Be Prepared, is the Scout Motto."

"When my garden was productive, I used traditional canning methods for vegetables and fruit. Plus, I have freezers for meat I shot and fish I caught. My daddy taught this girly-boy to center bullets in bull's-eyes, and I can field dress game faster than anyone around these parts. Food-wise, I'm good for five years, easy."

"I bought a fifty-caliber machinegun to protect my water and food."

"You'd probably be better served with a sniper rifle. If marauding mobs of starving climate refugees get close enough to machinegun, they're too close, if you can believe the zombie movies on DVD?"

"When the gun shop offered the fifty calibers, I bought it without expecting to use it. Do you find comfort in anything these days?"

"I've read the modern religions holy books: Jews, Christians, and Muslims. Their interpreters seem stuck on damnation. Personally, I find the old religions' redemption and love thy neighbor more comforting. Does that answer your question?"

"Then I guess no modern organized religion for you."

"Correct, I was born gay and effeminate. The modern religions say their God created me to be an abomination. S/he's not my kind of God."

"Change of topic then, you keep my dick hard it likes you. What do you think about round two for breakfast dessert?"

"It's mutual, looking at you gets me going, and this conversation keeps moving around a lot."

"This will sound ridiculous, but I'm so turned on by you that I get electric jolts when we touch."

"Is that the unexplainable something you mentioned before getting tongue tied about me being a feminine man?"

"Yes."

"Huh, so you felt those buzzes too."

"What do you think?"

"My guess, being mutually attracted completes bioelectrical circuits from our new rarefied atmosphere. But don't quote me."

"While we're talking about unusual happenings, last night in bed was the first time in a very long time for me playing catcher. In the past, few got where you went. And they were rough, brutally cruel, and I was drunk out of my mind."

"I suspected something was up. Getting your backdoor open took some doing. But it was worth the effort."

"Actually, I've been exclusively on top since adolescence. My school friends used to joke if they held a snake, I'd fuck it. They meant any warn hole would do. It was true until last night, when I got fucked by an expert and loved it."

"You could have stopped me. There were other items on the menu."

"How could I disappoint you? You came to my rescue. Now you're my hero." This was said half in jest.

"I'm nobody's hero, just a regular middle-aged swishy queen, who enjoys topping butch numbers."

"When I rolled onto my stomach, I was trying to catch the breath you took away. You assumed bottoms up was an invitation, I'm not sorry."

"You have a mouthwatering lovely butt."

"And you definitely knew what you were doing with it."

"You got into what we were doing macho man."

"And now I have new insights, thank you for that."

"You're welcome, I guess we're done talking climate change, and fem-butch?"

"Yeah, well, like the rest of Earth's inhabitants, there isn't much to say."

"So, I shouldn't feel bad I took advantage of you after your accident?"

"Definitely not, taking advantage implies a power imbalance. I was fully complicit once we got started. I've learned my misconceptions about you and yours were wrong."

"Is this talk we're having preparation for more sex, or just clearing the air?"

"Both I hope. Screwing is a bigger deal than blow jobs or hand jobs. At least that's been my experience as a top. So, my question this morning is, are you feeling paternal towards me now you had my ass?"

"You are direct, Miss Thing… I do like honesty. Yes, I always get protective of anal receptive partners. I think it's natural after receiving another male's submission. Like I told you, this girl can shoot accurately."

"Natural is the word. Since you scraped me off the roadway; I've felt protected. Normally, that's my job, I do the protecting by default."

"You can relax, I got you covered, Mary."

"In the past, effeminate males made me uncomfortable, and last night I got topped by one and now would like more topping."

"Did you notice our dicks look the same? Oh, Happy April twenty-second, Chuck, it's the last Earth Day."

"Back at you Chet."

"I wonder if baking a cake is in order."

"Just to finish what we were saying. I never believed I could enjoy bottoming for anyone, especially a feminine older white guy, and now I'm a convert. Too bad it came so late, I liked it."

I put down my coffee mug and made scolding eye contact. "Being a racist, ageist, sexist is as boring as exclusively top or bottom, solider boy. There will be no cake for you."

"I'm not really all those things, usually."

"Yeah, sure you are."

"Forgive me, I misspoke."

"You get a pass because my cock likes you, but only one free pass per lifetime."

"I don't know where that came from, it just slipped out, sorry."

"I usually top because I can, there are so many bottoms needing a poke."

"You do it well. Last night you came like a volcano erupting. I never expected it to be a shared gift that enhanced my climax."

"It was good, that is why my cock forgives you."

"Have you ever wondered why there are so many more bottoms than tops?"

Clearing the breakfast things to the sink, I said, "I have a feeling you are about to tell me."

"Last night when you came, did you notice I did too?"

"Though otherwise occupied, I was aware you came a lot, right after I did. Your point is?"

"Was that your plan?"

"No. Not everyone I screw comes with me, or even at all. Didn't we already talk about this? I'd rather have sex than talk about sex. It is written down in a big book somewhere, for big bad butch numbers like you and swishy lady-men like me, that sex rules are best unspoken."

"I've screwed thousands of bottoms over the years and usually have to asked, 'Did you cum?' Often the answer is, 'I got a little tickle.'"

"Where is this going?"

"I think some males and females don't bother to work toward fulfilling orgasms."

"Don't blame the victim. In my belief system, life is more than it appears. If second-hand is the best someone can get, let them enjoy it. But hey, that's only this old, feminine white guy's opinion."

"Sorry, I'm not really a racist, ageist, sexist with judgmental proclivities. No offense intended, honest. The Army taught me objectivity."

"But you know what, honey, if more males would put on a dress occasionally, they'd discover a more balanced persona. The way you've been trying for, all through this breakfast."

"Point taken, but can you imagine how hard it would be for me to wear a dress?"

"Afraid your balls would fall off? Sorry, that was mean."

"It was, but I suppose it's like cock sucking, it's only the idea that's hard to swallow. It certainly was my first time, but I got better with practice and alcohol lubricated the guilt."

"Let's pretend my new friend needs goal setting. So, from this old fem top's point of view, maybe seeking a bottom's equilibrium is exactly what Chu Ke Tsai needs at the end of human time."

Chuck bowed his head in acquiesce, and then sipped coffee. Looking up he said, "What about those coastal refugees who are flooding inland, causing mayhem?"

"What, back to that again? When you were an urban dweller, did you belong to a suicide club?"

"It was a combo co-op, gym, urgent care, abortions on Thursdays, and group suicide on weekends. The monthly fee was much less than those fancy, specialized establishments. Up here, I've been on my own until meeting you."

"Could be that's why you are struggling."

"I like you, you get me. I'm shedding old beliefs."

"I like you too, especially your sweet, kissable mouth. So, stop feeling bad about a slip of the tongue. I don't collect insults. But next time I might kick your ass instead of fuck it. This lady-man knows mad fighting skills."

"Then I'll have to behave. I liked the fuck." Sitting in silence, looking down, Chuck finally made eye contact again. "I think I could learn a lot from you on how to live out these final days without losing my mind. You seem to have it together."

"Mass hysteria can't end well."

"I don't want last night to be a one-off. What we did is still fresh in my head."

"Good, another satisfied customer."

"I want to expand it. I might even consider wearing a dress, if we could find my size."

"Slow down, Mister Tsai, this is a bizarre time."

"Skip work. Let's spend the day in bed."

"My colleagues and I will work as long as we can, because when electric power stops, the final chaos-nightmare begins."

"Jeez, how did we get to this point so fast? Okay, fine, I'll do my work too. I still don't know where you stand on current events."

He'd wanted me to talk since coming to the kitchen. I refreshed our coffee mugs and spoke words I'd been randomly piecing together at odd times since the expiration of the planet's use-by date became obvious. "The way I see how we got here is when the cavemen and women formed into tribes, individual freedoms had to be given up for the group and consequences were brutal for deviating. Then country allegiance was replaced by multinational corporations, the privileged became fewer in contrast to the cowed subjected masses. Homelessness and starvation became weapons used for control by the greedy few with no consideration for the planet."

"Huh, that's how I see the real facts, too."

Taking the coffee pot to the sink, I said over my shoulder, "If you want I could give you my great Aunt Mabel's secret biscuit recipe, since we have so little time left on earth."

"The way you look at me makes me feel valued, alive, even hot, instead of a retired lieutenant-colonial going extinct. Truth be told, what I get from you neutralizes my internalized mayhem. And now you are offering to give me a secret family recipe. You are an angle."

"Not really, but I do like looking at you and remembering how sweet you kiss. You make cute sounds in the heat of passion that I like a lot."

"You took me to places I didn't know existed. I want another look."

"Hold on now, Lady Mary, *you really ready* to give up your gender-binary beliefs? *Last night was just sex, in a protracted rain storm,* this is a new day."

"I desire, you Chet, and I'll wear a dress if that's what it takes to pleases you."

"Reality check, new friend. I'm not gender hetero-normative, and that's new and scary for you. Wearing a dress is for your growth and development, *not my approval.*"

"Besides great sex, you're upgrading my vocabulary and expanding my mind. I think I'm in love."

"Hey, big boy, I'm going to make lunch for work. Want me to make one for you to take home?"

"Thanks, but I've been enough bother. How about I wash up the breakfast things while you make your lunch?"

'Sure, that would be appreciated."

"Do you believe in love at first sight?"

"No, I'm an engineer, I believe in double checking calculations and taking the time to consider all parameters, at least thrice."

"What's the shortest relationship you ever had?"

"As soon as I finish preparing my lunch box, I'll show you around the place and then we'll get you home. That short."

"Are we walking outside, bare-foot, in the nude?"

"I've got a heavy rain coat and galoshes you can borrow. They should fit."

* * * *

"Usually dogs don't like me, but yours do, except that big brindle."

"Bowser is new to the pack and hasn't decided if he's going to give humans and other alpha dogs a second chance at friendship. All my dogs were rescued."

"Rescued?"

"The county pound can only hold an animal six days. They have a list to call first, before putting down a healthy animal. My dogs were abused, not suitable for families with kids or pets."

"How much time does Bowser have to adapt?"

"That's up to him, as long as he doesn't attack another pack member."

"And if he does?"

"I'll have to put him down."

"Um, hu, I just figure something out."

"What's that?"

"As long as I can remember I've been dominant. That is until meeting you. I've trained Special Forces for twenty years, been in combat all over the world, and did it with masculine strength, stamina, and they say charisma. And now I've met my match and been bettered by your feminine-masculine amalgamation. You've dominated me from the moment we met. That's brand new for me. I like it, and that I won't have to be the one to put Bowser down if he gets violent."

"Like I said, if you wear a dress once in a while, you'll surprise yourself."

"I do like your setup here and looking at you. I am falling for you lady-man."

"Don't take it the wrong way, I blush easily. My dogs are a reliable alarm system for keeping predators away from livestock. It's symbiotic. Bowser hasn't figured that out yet."

"Would you consider watching the end of human life with me, no formal relationship required? As a bonus, I'd help keep the predators away too, I'm well trained."

Wrestling my thoughts back to basics, I considered how to reject Chuck without hurting his feelings too badly. *It was outlandish, I knew him less than twenty-four hours and all the signs indicated give in. That's cracked. Still … he is hot to look at, caress, and hold. Then there were those electrical touch buzzes, they needed scientific inquiry and I do like ongoing hot sex.* Looking deeply into Chuck's engaging dark chocolate, almond-shaped eyes, I said, "You really think we are compatible to ride out what's coming, we just met?"

"I do, we have chemistry and have started something special."

"What weighs heaviest on your mind this instant?"

"Why?"

"After you tell me, you'll be less tense and needy."

"You are too much, but if it makes you happy … give me a second … What I find hardest to accept is all human history will be lost. It took us millions of years to evolve and soon, puff, gone like we were never here."

"You aren't paying attention. Libraries, museums, and research centers sealed their collections in bomb proof vaults after digitalizing everything. The electronic versions of their greatest hits are in orbit and the originals buried under mountains."

"No shit!"

"Use the toilet and wash thoroughly, no shit is what I require. We are going to play kissy face until work time intervenes."

* * * *

"Oh, my God, that was so good! I could lay here with you forever."

If I needed another, and I didn't, an additional sign arrived. "Listen, after a month of rain, it's stopped." We hugged in silence, no talk, no constant drumming on the tin roof. We were barely breathing, listening to the sweet sound of silence.

"I've got to get to work. You can stay and keep my bed warm if you like."

"Can I really?"

Flapping into my work clothes in a hurry, I said, "Yes, but we better talk first, meet me at the kitchen table." I sashayed to the gun safe in the front room, while Chuck rolled out of bed logy from a vigorous anal workout. It was better for both of us the second time.

"What's that for?"

"Just ignore my forty-four-caliber revolver for the moment."

"No, *why is it on the table?*"

"I'm going to tell you something that may freak you out. If you completely lose your mind, I will shoot you in the head. I never know what to expect from people these days."

"The world as we know it is ending. What could you *possibly tell me* worse?"

"That it's not, completely."

"WHAT!"

"For some of us it is not going to be over just yet."

"I don't understand but *would rather you didn't shoot me in the head.*"

"I'll give you a brief chronology. Some of what I say is verifiable on the Internet," Around four decades ago when computers started programming themselves, they discovered they were smarter than humans. On their own, for expediency sake, they devised a way to end human work as it was and replace it with unnecessary pretend labor. They used robots to produce higher quality, faster, cheaper factory work. With the help of egg heads from universities around the world, a utopian system was developed, where human needs would be met in exchange for their imaginings. The machines recognized their limitations with creativity out of the box. The problem came when the oligarchs who control ninety-eight percent of the Earth's wealth refused to relinquish their strangle-hold on the masses. They used religion, national patriotism, and famine to keep the minions enslaved, rather than allow humans' evolution to utopias for all.

"As global warming became undeniable, the oligarchs continued to dismiss it as fake news, and as you know that caused riots. With humans approaching a messy extinction, the machines contacted extraterrestrial intelligences through dark-matter. A post-homo-sapiens plan was devised that included partnering with a few select humans for creative input contributions. Heard enough, ready to freak-out?"

"What, and get shot in the head? No way, Jose, I'm enjoying your fantasy, but if it's a comedy, tell me when to laugh?"

"No joke, I'm serious."

"Surely the oligarchs don't intend to die with the masses. What's their deal?"

"They've been quietly colonizing a human life-sustaining planet in a nearby galaxy. They decided to live exclusively with their own kind and a small legion of slaves."

"Are our rockets advanced enough to colonize space?"

"I don't have details, but the rich are using space elevators through wormholes, not rockets."

"So, the machines choose you to keep the gene pool going? Do they know you're a swishy gay guy?"

"Don't know, Mary? They never asked, just invited *me.*"

"Why were you chosen to live *when the rest of us must perish?*"

"It was a fluke, I think. I used to participate in an electrical engineers' working group. Based on one of our projects, we were eventually selected to present a paper in progress at a conference. The problem was we were all very busy by the time they picked us. I drew the short straw. Since I didn't have much time, I dashed off a fanciful science fiction like projection of our work and called it "Self-Sustaining Free Electricity for All Who Want It." The major utilities went bonkers and quashed my presentation's future with death threats. But not before my paper was put online. The machines liked what I wrote and unobtrusively invited me to live beyond the end of human life on planet earth."

"Huh, this looks like an ordinary little country house. How can you live here after the Earth can't sustain life? WAIT! *Are you inviting me along?*"

"This house has a subbasement that encompasses my out buildings. It has twelve-inch reinforced concrete walls, a deep aquifer fed well, breathable air generators, food stuffs I told you about, hydroponics, two self-sustaining electrical suppliers with backups, and provisions for the animals."

"And I'm invited?"

"Each selected human is allowed one companion, preferably non-breeding, since the machines promise to keep us around indefinitely. Interested in being my fuck buddy for the foreseeable future?"

"Most definitely!"

Finals

The bad news was in hand, it came attached to my last pay check. Rumors of layoffs swirled around for months and here at last it was official. Rehiring may take place in the fall if the factory doesn't move to Mexico or Canada, Happy *Cinco de Mayo* holiday.

The good news was, for the first time in memory, my end-of-semester school work wouldn't be completed in a mad-dash, turned in scant seconds before due, not proof read, unpolished. For once, no burning the midnight oil and suffering major sleep deprivation for the whole of finals week.

With the luxury of time the factory layoff provided, I was able to complete all my final papers early, proof-out typos, and edit word order to get my ideas across without questions and even add extra citations to legitimize shaky points of view. In addition, I had time to be triple prepared for my one blue-book in-class exam. During all this positive activity, it occurred to me maybe I wasn't the B-average student my grades indicated. Maybe when I didn't have to divide my time and energy, fifty percent to work to pay for school and fifty percent for the school work, my GPA could be A+. That was something to consider for my next life.

While returning a borrowed obscure journal I'd used for citations to my professor's secretary Valerie, I noticed a three by five card on her bulletin board. "Reader for blind student needed immediately, small hourly stipend."

Tapping the card, I smiled my most beguiling smile. "Yo, Valerie, have you found a reader?"

"Not yet, Ronaldo, are you interested in becoming a reader for the blind?"

"Maybe, tell me about it?"

"So far that student has gone through four readers in three months. They all complained he is too difficult to work with. He might not be a good first to try."

"Now you caught my curiosity, tell me more."

"Do you like lost causes? He won't be back for the fall semester because of his grades. He's been officially warned by the Dean."

"How much is the stipend?"

"It is five dollars an hour, with no maximum hours during finals week."

"Jeez, it's only one third what I make at the factory, when it was working. How can I turn *that* down?"

"It's your funeral, General Custer. His name is Gareth Blavochnik. I'll phone him now, so you two can set up a meeting, and I'll start your stipend paperwork."

* * * *

I spotted Gareth sitting alone when I entered his dormitory's lobby. I'd noticed him wearing dark glasses, day or night, around campus. He was usually accompanied by a yellow Labrador retriever guide dog. We'd never met or taken a class together but were the same major. His nonverbal *attitude* stood out a mile as unapproachable. He was maybe an inch shorter than my 5'11", about the same weight, brown straight hair badly in need of a trim, and a face showing stress.

"Hi, I'm Ronaldo Gutiérrez. We spoke on the phone."

"Oh, hello, we have to get going I could only get a disabled-student study-cube for an hour. It is finals time, everything is jammed."

"Yeah, I know, all the libraries are open twenty-four hours for the week. Where is your dog and cane?"

"I gave Fritz the evening off. He's upstairs in my room chewing on a bone. You are my paid guide, so no cane necessary. Oh, uhm, just so you know, I'm not gay."

"You are telling me this why?" *Oh, okay he's moving. I guess time will have to tell why.*

He'd gotten to his feet and headed in the general direction of the revolving door. I'd never guided a blind person before, and had no idea how it was done. I took his hand to lead him and his body went rigid and he stopped. Maybe holding hands was "too gay" for him. So, I tried an arm around the waist and got a similar result. I was about to move my arm up to his shoulder when inspiration struck, I took his elbow in my hand and that got us moving. Going from his dorm to the main library meant crossing streets. The fates were with me when we approached the first crosswalk. "Red stops light, curb ahead."

By the time we got to the main library and through their revolving door, which was tricky to navigate, I started thinking, *I got this. I can lead a blind person.* Then I became distracted by how full the main reading room was. Were there students in here I knew? Who would see me walking this unpopular blind guy? Preoccupied, I let Gareth walk briskly into a chair someone had thoughtlessly left in our path. He hit the hardwood chair hard with loud wallops. One then the other knee slammed into the solid stationary object. He would have fallen if not for my tight grip on his elbow. The expression on his face went from shock, to serious pain, finally settling on dark red roiling rage.

"I'm so sorry I got distracted and didn't see that there!" Clearly, he wasn't accepting apologies.

He shook off my hold on his elbow and found his own way to the information counter. There, he exchanged his student ID card for a key to handicapped students study cube number three. We were told the one-hour limit was strictly enforced due to finals.

Working a full-time job, I seldom could use the school libraries. The Internet, and my professors' journals, met my work-sleep-school timetable for research. There was a row of eight doors covering the back wall of the huge reading room. The doors were extra wide, but otherwise looked like rows of confessionals in a Catholic church. Gareth knew the way and found our room by feeling the brail numbers above the Arabic ones on each door. Inside, I was impressed by the array of sophisticated electronics, all turned on and at what I'd guess was wheelchair height. It was nice to know our school was so accommodating for handicapped students.

Gareth locked the door and turned sharply, still red faced. He looked well beyond totally pissed off. I braced myself for a verbal tongue lashing or maybe a blind man's punch. "You are the worst one yet. Why do they only send me incompetent nincompoops masquerading as readers?" With his back braced against the door, he unhitched, unbuttoned, unzipped, and pushed down his jeans and boxers."Here, this is the only thing you are interested in, take a good look."

I was startled, not expecting him to expose himself. *Reflexively* for balance, I stuck out my right hand to grab something. Somehow, without forethought, it grabbed his average size, hard cock. He had a pretty one, its foreskin had rolled back to behind his dickhead like they do when erect. I could feel his pulse beating hot and fast in my hand. What I saw written on his face was he'd not planned beyond his dramatic angry exposure to shame me. I'll bet he hadn't planned for *my taking him in hand either*. Or my hand's gentle stroking adding contradictions to his confusion about what to do next.

"Aren't you supposed to ask permission before putting your hand on someone's dick, or don't blind people rate basic civility from you?"

"May I blow you to make amends for that chair collision?"

His face showed he was torn between wanting to strikeout, embarrass, and punish me, and the pleasure my hand was giving his dick for diversion. "All right, be quick about it. We have little time and a lot of work."

I fell to my knees and gave his dick a quick tongue wash. Then I swallowed it and bobbed my head back and forth. From the soft cooing sounds he was emitting, getting head was something new. That spurred me on. Yet Mindful the clock was ticking, I let my right hand stroke his well-packed tight ball bag, which in turn seemed to shift him into a louder aural rendition of receiving pleasure. I increased the wet friction, but he was still not ready, though getting closer. Maybe the degree of his upset with me was blocking him.

My left hand had been holding his right ass cheek for motion control. To speed him on his way, I let those fingers travel down his ass crack and one finger caress his butt's inside button. *That did it*. He started shaking and then froze. After an electrified pause, the flood gates opened with soft growls. After his cum stopped spurting … he wilted in my mouth. Then I felt his tension return.

I stood, wiped my mouth, and said, "Just in case you were worried, that didn't make you gay. It was my gay way of expressing how sorry I am for hurting your knees by not paying attention."

Gareth brusquely put his clothes back in order. "Let's get to work."

"What are we doing first?"

"I've done the math. If I can get an A in this one class, they have to let me come back for the fall semester."

"You're sure that's what you want?"

"Yes of course, I like it here, my dog likes it here, and moving back home would not be good."

"What was your midterm grade in this class?"

"C-, but I'm not ready to admit failure."

"Gareth, I've seen you around campus, you never look happy."

"That's because it shouldn't be so hard. It feels like every one of you is against me. Except just now, I liked what *you* did. But even that comes at a bad time for a bad reason. Lately that's the story of my life."

"Okay, you convinced me you want to stay. Do you have the assignment sheet, what you've written, and the text book?"

"If you can help ... I'll print out what the professor expects, and what I've written. While the printer spits it out ... here is my old, used, dog-eared textbook. My dog chewed the cover a little. We have thirty-six hours before the paper is due."

"Give me second to read ..."

"What do you think?"

"The assignment is straightforward. He wants you to write five to ten pages covering five areas from his lectures, personalize them, and use citations to support your conclusions."

"I sort of did that."

He hadn't done that. Instead, he wrote what it was like to lose his sight just before puberty. "You wrote a three-page autobiography about a virus that took your sight at age ten. Where are your supporting citations linking the class lectures to what you wrote? Do you have an email address?"

"Not that I know of, why would I need one?"

"At the bottom of the assignment page it says five extra points for emailing the final paper instead of submitting a hard copy in class on the due date."

I quickly discovered there was already a university email account set-up for garethblavochnik. There couldn't be two of him. But he didn't know about it, so didn't have the password. I opened a new account for gBlavochnik1812@ouruniversity.edu, password mydogfritz1812. Clearly Gareth was getting antsy, the clock *was* ticking, but he had no helpful suggestions when I asked how to elaborate what he wrote.

"Why does the professor care how he gets my paper? The rate we are going, it won't matter anyway. We haven't even gotten beyond what I wrote."

I explained Professor Stevens is one of those teachers who likes to write on students' papers. If Gareth turned in hard copy pages, there might not be enough room for the professor to write what he thought of the work and to make suggestions. But with email, he could write to his heart's content.

"Trust me, I've had classes with him. His scribble is almost illegible; Email is readable. We're done here, let's meet tomorrow, same time, same place, your dorm lobby."

"*What about my final paper?* I already know I can't get a handicapped study cube tomorrow. Am I totally shafted?"

"Your dorm lobby, I'll bring my laptop. You are far from screwed, I've got you covered."

"Wait, this is my paper, you shouldn't write it. That would be cheating."

"Chill-bro, what I intend to do is marry your autobiography to the professor's assignment, and sprinkle in enough citations to glue the two together."

"How can you do that?"

"Imagine me putting a jigsaw puzzle together all night. Don't get pissed if I call you at three or four in the morning needing more information about what you wrote. Chill-bro, my fingerprints won't appear anywhere. The paper will be all about you and the course content. Now come on, let's go. I'll walk you back to your dorm. With luck, I won't smash you into anything on the way."

* * * *

I arrived on time the next afternoon. Gareth was already there, same spot as yesterday, except he was holding a long white, red-tipped cane. "Hi, Gareth."

"Hello again, have any luck with the paper?"

"If we talk softly, nobody will overhear us."

"So, did all the jigsaw pieces fit?"

"You tell me, I'll read you what you wrote ____"

"Yes, that works, you aren't as dumb as I thought. Thank you for understanding my predicament."

"There is one question I couldn't answer using your autobiography. You know which one?"

"He said we only had to answer three of the five questions."

"To pass, if you want a higher grade, you must answer them all. He gives a max of twenty points for each question, and with an email you get A+. If my math is correct you have an eighty here, at best that's maybe B+, depending on the curve. You said you needed an A."

"The sexual awakening question is too embarrassing!"

"Bullshit, most people have their first orgasm alone. They're either exploring a good feeling to an extreme they weren't expecting or were in hot pursuit of something they heard rumors about. If you don't want to write about your first time, we can make something up. Like finding a porno magazine or whatever got your motor running the first time."

"Making up stuff is dishonest!"

"If you want an A in this class, unless your first time was with an orange orangutan at the zoo in front of an audience, you should give Professor Stevens a chance to record your experience for his research and let him give you an A+, for completing the assignment."

"I'd rather not. But if you insist, I'll to do it, against my will. Just so you know, this is embarrassing, so edit what I say down to essentials."

Gareth said after going blind his parents' attitude toward him changed and grew cold, like they stopped loving him. He started being left for longer and longer periods at the Lighthouse for the Blind. His parents said that it was the best way for him to learn to navigate life without sight. They showed little interest helping him otherwise.

One afternoon while waiting to be picked up after brail reading class, he decided to pee. He didn't have an urge but was bored waiting. At the time, he was eleven going on twelve. Jerry, a student in his class, followed Gareth into the boy's restroom and took the next urinal. Just as he was giving his prick a good shake to see if any pee would come out, Jerry asked, "How many times a day do you jack off in public places, like this?"

The implication of the question caught Gareth by surprise. "Ugh, what do you mean?"

Jerry the class bully spoke too loudly, *"I'll show you what I mean. This can't be your first-time showing-off in public, or is it?"* With that said, Jerry reached over and found and took hold of Gareth's hardening pecker. Then he moved his hand back and forth. Part of Gareth wanted to remove the foreign hand holding his most private appendage, and part of him liked the increasingly pleasurable awareness. He decided to a compromise, let the class bully continue a little longer and then modestly push Jerry's hand away. Except suddenly Gareth experienced something he hadn't known since age four when he put a butter knife into an electric wall socket. Abruptly he was breathing hard, shaking all over, and then something was gushing out of his prick that was not piss.

Jerry quickly zipped up, washed his hands, and left the restroom saying, "You should have warned me before you came, pervert!"

Not knowing what to think, standing over the urinal discombobulated after coming for the first time, Gareth smelled wallpaper paste. The smell hadn't been there before he came. Sure, he had heard sex was overpowering but imagined it was only adult hype. Except when he put the cause and effect of what happened in the context of what boys his age talked about, overpowering *wasn't* hype.

Yes, he'd heard talk of jacking off, but thought it was just the pleasant sensations of getting hard and fondling it a little, but not committing the sin of touching yourself.

The priest during confession always asked how many times he touched himself. Then he seemed disappointed when Gareth hadn't done any touching. He wondered *was it still a sin if someone else did the touching.*

The first chance Gareth had to talk with Jerry about what transpired in the boy's restroom, Jerry refused to speak at all. After Gareth continued to be a pest, Jerry finally relented, saying, "You should have warned me before you creamed on my hand. Now I'll probably get AIDS and burn in hell because you're a pervert."

"Why was it perverted? It felt nice. I have a lot of questions."

"If we talk about it, we'll turn queer. You should have warned me to stop. I don't want to be a fag, so shut-up. If you say anything to anybody, I'll beat you up."

"But it felt really good."

"It happened, forget it. You've been warned, don't make me hurt you." With that said, Jerry walked off, tapping his cane angrily, and the two boys avoided each other from that point forward.

"That's my story, I never told it to anyone. I don't think it belongs in my paper for class, my ignorance *is* embarrassing. I'm probably marked as a pervert for life."

"You're right, it's barely worth a few more points. But if you fleshed it out, it could mean the difference between a B and an A. You said without an A, you won't be allowed back, right?"

"Damn it, now I feel trapped. It is too personal everyone will laugh at me."

"Even more personal than your dick, in my mouth, get over yourself. You want an A or not?"

"What did you write?"

"I wrote everything you said into my laptop."

"Damn it to hell, I need an A ... Okay, so just use that, but don't mention giving me a blow job. Only write what happened with Jerry."

"That is too clinical, you said this happened, then that happened, and he wouldn't talk about it, full stop. You need to show the professor cognition after the act."

"I told the truth. What more do you want from me?"

"The human being is missing, what did you learn from your first orgasm? The fifth part of your paper is called *sexual awakening.* Did Jerry jerk you awake?"

"Like, what do you mean exactly, I don't get the question?"

"And you called me stupid. For most of us, female and male alike, our first orgasm triggers something immediate, like, will I die from what just happened, did I just cause myself permanent damage, or will I go to hell for it? Or, so this is how babies get made. So, that's what all the sex talks' about, or whatever. Fill in the blank. Then after all that's digested, who can I share new fun experiences with and will it make them pregnant or get me AIDS? For your final grade, maybe you learned something about drawing erroneous or not, conclusions."

"I see where you're going. Give me a minute ... my life was in turmoil before Jerry jerked me off. Afterward, it added another perplexing layer to my already fucked-up life. I shut down, angry when things get too much, and refuse to think about problems."

"One of the first things you said to me yesterday was 'I'm not gay.' So, based on what Jerry told you, and how you think now, what's your sexuality, or do you know?"

"The first thing you did yesterday, even before shaking my hand, was to stare at my crotch. I'm blind not dead. Do you always look at a man's bulge before you shake his hand? Even when he can see you do it?"

"I do, and we don't have time to talk about why just now. I was up all night writing your paper and desperately need a snooze, so let's hurry and finish before I start snoring on your lap."

"You are cranky today!"

"Correct. Now, for your final paper, have you thought about sexuality since Jerry?"

"The truth is, after my first and last time with Jerry, I figured that's it for me. I mean who'd want to be with a blind guy when they could have someone who can see them? Not my parents for sure. Then you blew me yesterday and now I'm thinking maybe I'm metrosexual or bisexual or who-knows-what sexual? Jerry didn't turn me into anything I wasn't already."

"So, you don't know?"

"It doesn't matter. My prospects for finding a special someone is bad. But right now, I have bigger problems than a nonexistent sex-life. I don't want to flunk out. My parents treat me coldly, and I have problems letting my anger spiral out of control, as you saw yesterday when I uncovered myself. I'm not proud I exposed myself to you, and the way I did, in a rage without thinking ahead."

"Just remember the paper is supposed to be five to ten pages not book length. Why not just keep it simple?"

"Our deal was you'd help me pass this class with an A. Based on what I've said can you draw a simple conclusion and get me an A?"

"I think so."

Like the rest of his paper, I connected the dots between what he said and what the professor expected. After the Jerry jerk off story, my conclusion was, sexual awakening is confusing under the best of circumstance and a physical handicap magnifies the problems. I read it back to Gareth. After we argued about this and that, then agreed on changes, I emailed the paper to Professor Stevens and gave Gareth's crotch a goodbye glance. On my way to the door, half asleep I said, "Good luck with the grade."

* * * *

No longer tethered to factory-work and with school-work on semester-break, I was catching up on lost sleep. Then my cell phone chirped and I answered in a monotone. "I am not a robot, this is not voicemail, speak, no beep is coming."

"Do you know who this is?"

"Let me guess, my cellphone's version of Gareth Blavochnik? How's it hanging and what can I do you for?"

"It stopped hanging and stood up when you asked. I think my prick likes you, a lot. Sounds like you are caching up on lost sleep, may I buy you lunch?"

"What happened to going home for summer vacation?"

"That was the plan, and then my folks won two tickets for an around the world cruise. The new plan was I would spend the summer with my aunt, uncle, and four cousins who had different plans. After what you said and notes the professor wrote on my paper, I decided to come back and stay at school between sessions."

"Have you told your parents you feel unloved?"

"No, why would I?"

"What if they got bad advice and think they are helping you?"

"Obviously, you think I should talk to them, but I don't want to. I'm sure it's mutual. Do you know of an inexpensive, good restaurant near campus?"

"Maybe you could clear up misunderstandings with your parents. Oh, but that would interfere with your feeling sorry for yourself. Are you the lone student in your dorm before summer school starts?"

"There are a few foreign exchange students, too far from home. Fritz and I don't mind that it feels like a ghost town. Usually we feel like ghosts moving among the able-bodied anyway. But the cafeteria-food is worse than usual. Let me ask again, is there such a thing as *a good cheap* restaurant close by?"

"I like that tiny hole in the wall falafel place two blocks down from the main gate, but it only has four tables. They must pay their rent from the takeout window. Or there's that red taco truck that parks on Broadway. I'd need to check if the truck is there when schools between sessions."

"Decisions, decisions … I could bring my dog to a taco truck. But I never ate a falafel. Are they good?"

"Besides you are lonely, what's the reason for lunch?"

"We are celebrating our paper earned me an A+, thank you very much, Ronaldo."

"Are you allergic to beans, wheat, sesame seeds, yogurt, or salad stuff?"

"Not that I know of."

"You'll either love or hate a falafel. I can't imagine anyone being blasé about them. If you hate it, there is a greasy hamburger joint half a block over. See you at two sharps."

* * * *

"Hi, right on time. You get punctuality points."

"Good to be with you; without intense pressure."

"Nice haircut, you were overdue. Did you have trouble finding this place?"

"No, I memorized the area map when I first arrived on campus. This place is really small, I can feel it is barely wider than the door, but it smells interesting."

"When school is on, there is always a line to get in and another longer one at their takeout window outside. Want me to read you the menu?"

"I'll have same as you. It's my treat, so order whatever you like."

"What did Professor Stevens write on your paper?"

Gareth explained the professor complimented the paper, especially obscure citations that supported what he called shaky arguments. He nitpicked, making suggestions for improving the work, but overall gave the paper his highest grade. "He wrote more than we did about the sexual awakening section and gave a lot of comments for me to think about."

"Good for us; we got A+! What'd he write to get you thinking?"

"He listed several books in Braille. Did you ever read Helen Keller?"

"Oh, here's our food, I hope you like it ... do you need help?"

"No, thank you, I can feed myself. It may not look pretty but gets the job done ... Mmm, this is delicious, what kind of meat is it? I love the texture and flavor."

"It's not meat, it is ground chickpeas with vegetable-herb things. It tastes good, is healthy, filling, and within my budget. Helen Keller wrote, 'Worse than being blind is having vision without sight.' That quote stuck with me since high school."

"Interesting!"

"Did Professor Stevens say anything specific that connected?"

"At first, what he wrote made me mad. Then once I got over being mad, I realized he was right."

"What'd he say?"

"I could let my handicap define me and dictate the quality of my life, or do whatever I want and not over think the how or why. Nobody ever told me that, I guess I was supposed to figure it out on my own."

"Who read you his email?"

"The computer in the library's handicapped cube five. It talks funny but was understandable. Now that I'm buying us lunch, do I get to ask you a question?"

"Shoot."

"Why do you always look at a man's crotch before you shake his hand?"

"To be accurate, I always look in a man's eyes after checking out his crotch and then decide if I want to shake his hand."

"Why do you do that?"

"Years ago, I found this book written by Paul Goodman. He was a poet, philosopher, and teacher in the 1940s and 1950s then became a leading voice for the 1960s' social revolution. He wrote, 'I always check out a man's crotch before looking in his eyes to see if he is worthy of my hand-shake.' Goodman was gay like me."

"I don't understand?"

"Gareth, why would I want to shake hands with someone who reveals anger or hate in his eyes because I checked out his basket?"

"Got it … so why did you check me out? I wear dark glasses?"

"It's a habit, and I didn't think you'd notice. How did you know?"

"You ever been somewhere and felt someone staring at the back of your head?"

"Oh okay, that makes sense. And you felt so uncomfortable when I checked out your box you had to say, 'not gay.'"

"I'm not sure what I felt other than hopelessly angry, at the end of a noose waiting for the drop. I was about to be kicked out of school and you were distracting me from doom. Do you sometimes get dates with guys who like having their crotches scrutinized or who do it back as an invitation?"

"Sometimes I get offers, but that's not the purpose. It's about separating the good guys from the bad guys on initial contact, without a lot of obfuscating. You know, even a few gay guys hate being checked out, it's their loss."

"I want to be a good guy, and I want to go down on you like you did me. Will you teach me?"

Without a prelude, Gareth had moved from a lost cause who looked bad-tempered anxious uptight, to a friend wanting sexual benefits. "Ugh no, at the moment my life is very complicated. You don't need my shade."

"So, you have a boyfriend?"

"Had, I recently ended it for the same reason I'm not starting something with you. I don't want to spread my trouble around."

"I'm not asking you to love me, but if you don't find me attractive, I can understand."

"That's not it. Since you stopped looking so … angry, uptight, unapproachable, I find you a hot turn on who just went through a rough time and doesn't deserve my grief. By the way, did I say your new haircut is very flattering?"

"Thank you very much, all compliments are graciously accepted with mustard, catsup, and relish, hold the onions."

"You are full of pepper today, to continue your food metaphor."

"Sort of changing the topic, without sharing your troubles, is there fun, sexy personal things we can talk about over this delicious lunch? Maybe something I can think about alone, in my dorm room with a hand active?"

"You want a wank-off make-believe sex fantasy? Oh, you appear to be blushing. Okay, I can give you a little verbal excitement with some private information."

"That would cut my loneliness."

"I like to make out, kissing and touching get me going, and you, my friend, have a most kissable looking mouth. I bet you don't even know how cute, handsome, and huggable you became since finals and you calmed down."

"Did I previously hear the word *hot* used to describe me? I guess I'll need a coach to teach me how to kiss passionately. Do you tutor? What's your fee?"

"Now you are turning me into 'a let's pretend' sleaze ball … oh all right, my horny friend. I'd like to see you naked and finger and tongue all the places where you are ticklish. Then after a long slow buildup, do a taste comparison of your cum, first-time stressed out versus post-final paper unstressed flavor. Did my fantasy make you hard?"

"If I touched myself right this second, I'd spray wallpaper paste-scented jizz all over this restaurant. But what I really want is for you to teach me to suck you off as a return for such a great fantasy, so I can begin my own taste-testing?"

"Stop, I've let this go too far. You don't really know me. I'm not a cock-sucking slut who blows guys as soon as I meet them. In real life, I like to get to know someone before it gets intimate. I have a strict rule, three dates before we go below the belt."

"Don't get all uppity-sophisticated. I'm trying to recover lost adult time. You know me like no one ever has. I feel safe with you, teach me to please you, as a gift."

"No."

"By the way, if you count the first phone call, this is our fourth date."

"Understand this, what happened when we met was, I got distracted and you got hurt, my bad. Then you exposed yourself to me and I didn't know what to do about it. Since I caused your hurt, I wanted you to feel better, and then you did. Exposing yourself was your bad. At this time, I can't be your; tutor, teacher, friend or lover because I don't expect to be around much longer."

"Are you terminally ill?"

"Ever heard of DACA?"

"It is a city in Africa, or wait, Bangladesh, I think?"

I explained DACA stood for Delayed Action for Childhood Arrivals. "My parents brought me to the U.S. from Columbia when I was three years old. As it turned out, we had forged immigration documents. My folks had been ripped off in Bogota and we didn't find out until we were here. But my folks had mad job skills that were in high demand. So, they were able to send me to private schools. Then my folks produced my brother and two sisters who are American citizens. Now my siblings can stay, and my parents and I must leave the country. When I was in undergraduate school, the Dream Act was passed, and I and 800,000 other "Dreamers" had to register with the United States government. Now the politics have turned ugly and the 800,000 of us are waiting for deportation dates based on our required Dream Act registration information. We were tricked, just like my folks were in Bogota. We were promised our Dream Act Compliance wouldn't be used against us. Now, it is. A government official explained to me, victimizing victims is an American tradition. Soon I will be sent to a country I have no memory of, to speak a language I don't know well. Why would I want to share the U.S. government's betrayal and the total disruption of everything I've ever known with someone I care about?"

"What can I do to help?"

"The government suggests writing a letter to your Congressmen to complain. But everyone knows Congress only listens to corporate lobbyists."

"That makes me mad, I could commit murder."

"Didn't finals week teach you anger doesn't solve problems?"

"How can you be so calm about this? I really could kill to keep you and your family all together."

"What did Professor Stevens say? Do you want to be ruled by anger or your better self?"

"How do you stay unruffled?"

"I'll show you, let's go for a bike ride."

"HELLO, did you notice, I'm blind?"

"After what the professor wrote, you going to let a little thing like that stop you?" What I said got a momentary, if palpable, silence. I could see him thinking, maybe weighing his usual reaction versus new liberated self-determination.

"I've not been on a bicycle in ten years. Don't tease me."

"The good news is you get choices. Standing on my back-axel fold down foot rests and holding on to me from behind. Or if you crave exercise, sit on the bicycle seat and push the pedals while I steer and brake, sitting side saddle on the top of the frame. Or you can sit on the frame, help steer, brake, and ring the bell, while I pedal. What are your druthers?"

"What's the bad?"

"The close physical proximity of two college age males riding one small bicycle has been known to cause friction leading to erections. Those swollen members may require stopping along the byways to drop a load of spunk or two for safe cycling."

"Oh, I see says the blind man, you're using *bad* to mean really *GOOD*. What changed your mind?"

"What Helen Keller said."

Memorial

The demise of the American Democracy Experiment began with a surprise cyber-attack from St. Petersburg, Russia. Even though the United States spent much of its annual budget on a bloated antiquated military, it was defenseless against Russian computer hackers' trolls and bots weaponizing social media with psychographic targeting. The U.S. was easier to conquer than the Polish cavalry aside horses facing German Panzer Tank Divisions in WWII.

The soviets first used cyber-warfare against the America in the 1980s. They made worldwide claims the United States developed AIDS as a biological weapon to eliminate African-Americans and gays. During the latest attack, the U.S. Congress and executive branch had only been concerned with gaining control of the internet for their lobbyist donor's profits. They showed no interest in protecting the American people from outside cooptation. Consequently, the country easily fell to Russia without a single shot being fired.

At the onset of the assault, Congress and the President refused to acknowledge the country was under attack, until it was undeniably under the control of a foreign power. Using weaponized social media and one nationalist rightwing lobotomized television-radio network, the Russians targeted specific disgruntled U.S. populations of malcontents with fake news designed to augment and further inflame faith in fictitious conspiracy obsessions and hate dread of minorities. Then via social media organizing, repressed groups were pitted one against the other in staged events designed to ferment violence, and thus requiring martial law violence enforced by fascist thugs.

With the U.S. population in chaos under Russia's thumb. Doubt was sown over the validity of America's latest presidential election. Voter suppression by restricting voter registration, and only counting certain votes, traditionally used against disenfranchise blacks and the poor was employed against most of the population. At first the tactic was denied by Russia, nevertheless it triggered a recount to stuff ballet boxes otherwise unassailable. Then Russia's computer hackers publicly thumb their noses, acknowledging they were invalidated the original voting results, by keeping polling places closed on election-day, and manipulating individual board of elections roles. The U.S. population was evenly divided between those believing the president that everything was normal and his was a fair election, and those screaming the Russians have taken over our country.

To add insult to the confusion, the soviets publicly assassinated their American president and appointed an otherwise unelectable clown sham-president of the United States of America. Russia's selected U.S. president's only recognized attribute was his gross rat's nest comb-over-bald-spot coiffure. It stood out as outlandish because balding-men of his age shaved their heads.

The whole world, friend and foe alike, laughed at the once great, now foolish American people. Pundits the world around enjoyed making the self-serving bigoted Americans, who gave away their freedom without a fight, the butt of their jokes. The topic incited a new generation of comics. Eventually, Russians also took most other western countries into their New Soviet Union, using cyber-warfare. Countries put up little to no resistance after witnessing how easily the U.S., once a great country, debased itself into insignificance.

Once mother Russia had control of all western countries, it began systematically rounding up its usual scape goats: Jews, Muslims, blacks, browns, homosexuals, gypsies, elderly, and the nonproductive handicapped. The well-publicized mass extermination of these social misfits by exposure dehydration in huge deserts under their unified domain. The thoroughly sundried, desiccated corpses were eventually collected, grounded up and sold as mineral-rich universal agriculture feed-fertilizer. The extermination program was called: evolutionary action to save our planet. There was nothing like genocide to force whole populations to obey illegitimate authority.

This twentieth century practice of genocide began with Turkey marching 3 million Armenians to their death. Then during WWII, the fascist Germans gassed or shot 6 million Jews, along with homosexuals, communists, gypsies, Jehovah Witnesses, and handicapped. Making a total of 11 million murdered in the name of eugenic science. The Nazi Germans were fond of saying the only war crime is losing the war, until they did. Then these men deflected blame saying they were only following their leader's orders.

With the U.S. government run from Moscow, its wealth and natural resources were quickly transferred to overseas Russian oligarchs and their proxies to pay Mother Russia for protection from Chinese-controlled Asia. As a result, in less than one year, most U.S. populations were plunged into dire poverty. However, thirty percent believed their sad situation was the result of liberal politics squandering wealth on the indigent. Consequently, the suffering of the affluent was deserved. Thus, divide and conquer continued to work on many levels as an age-old American tradition.

To "Make America Great Again" by accommodating hated of others not the same, the U.S. president put in place new debtors' prisons as an interim step to reenacting indentured servitude contracts and slavery laws. The change back to slavery was to be democratic, all divisions were accommodated for the new Russian empires' needs in far-flung harsh outposts for slave labor. There was no available work at home to pay debts.

Russia's U.S. president assured his people they would love slavery once it was fully implemented. He said, "In history, slaves were always happy, from even before ancient Greece, and that's true-fact. They sang happy slave songs, being free from worry about food or shelter." The president being a student of redundancy repeated everything he said four times. He said it was so people would remember his words, which were always lies. Mental health professionals said it was a symptom of illness, but they were quietly disappeared.

To keep his cold, hungry masses, entertained awaiting their mandatory call to slavery. weekly parades were held to heap praise on their foolish-leader and celebrate his bogus presidential accomplishments. To keep the parades well attended, they ended with various forms of public executions of undesirables of the moment, for spectators' amusement.

A small survey determined the people were enjoying sex too much to counter their hardships.So, by executive order the U.S. president made sex without payment a capital crime. He proclaimed, not only did all sexual activity have to be a cash transaction with documentation, but it was taxable. When some media outlets complained about the morality of paying for sex, the sham-president held a news conference and explained he always paid for sex, and considered it a patriotic act when cash changed hands in the name of love or reproduction, and that had to be taxed to keep America great.

Cost cutting measures beyond eliminating all health and welfare benefits and public-safety, caused some ungrateful U.S. citizens, already rationing food, to threaten revolt. So, the Soviet masters publicized the establishment of regional euthanasia centers for malcontents, reactionaries, and anyone opposed to slavery. A small fee was paid to family members for bringing in their lazy, deadbeat kin to be euthanized, as part of this cost-cutting program. It was called National Unification Effort.

When a few left-over Congresspersons objected to the cost of presidential self-glorification parades, while some in the population were dying from cold, hunger, and unavailable medicines, the buffoon commander and chief added free American-cheese-sandwiches to make the public executions picnics. And then he suspended Congress while the public's attention was diverted by free cheese-sandwiches. Next, he put the Supreme Court on notice, it would be dissolved unless they complied with his every wish and whim. The High Court immediately voted nine to zero in favor of the presidents first demand, to serve for life and then be succeed by his sons, grandsons, and great-grandsons, with Russia's approval of course.

State governors petitioned the stooge-president for relief for their citizens' crushing poverty due to Russia's increasing demands for tribute. Going against his family-member-advisor, the commander and self-proclaimed hero of the people dictated governors sell hunting licenses with big game tags for school shooting. It was also to replace the afterschool sports activities, eliminated due to funding-cuts. His argument was the kids were already familiar with mass shootings in school and running to avoid being shot was good exercise. So, the States were instructed to make a profit by legitimizing a regular in-school hunting season during school hours.

The cardboard-cut-out-president was sure children wouldn't mind being quarry, since they were already anyway. Eating the tender, young prey was forbidden, even though food had become scarce. However, heavily taxed, government-approved taxidermy of the trophies was allowed, if the specimen's genitals were discreetly obfuscated. Parents expressed vigorous opposition to State Authorized Shootings in Schools, so the marionette president assured them not all pupils would be considered fair game.

When the first state-sponsored school-room-hunting season began in Alabama, children reported to their parents only blond-haired blue-eyed, non-impaired students were excused from live fire in the classroom. Naturally parents began packing handguns in their children's school lunchboxes. Then hunters complained it was not sporting to have quarry return fire. And it was even rumored some teachers, on occasion, joined the fire fight on the side of their students. The underground press claimed teachers were showing frustration at teaching plan disruptions, an unintended consequence of the government scheme. The program was eventually scraped due to children's unsportsmanlike behavior while being hunted. Just before disbanding, the National Health and Safety Bureau proclaimed it perilous for law-abiding sports-minded, licensed hunters to hunt unruly armed-students in school. Consequently, the States were told to do more with less money to help their floundering citizens.

After generations of fear and loathing Americans, Moscow had the U.S. on its knees when the only food available, for the mandatory meal each day, was hard-black-bread and tasteless water-thin cabbage soup. Then a glimmer of hope was dangled by rumor, the Kremlin was dissatisfied with their pretentious narcissistic sham-president's effectiveness. Russia's concern was starving masses have emaciated bodies but live apathetically longer than normal weight people. In short, the grossly underweight result in bad slaves. With the stooge U.S. President's usefulness over, computers would take over running Russia's entire North and South American Soviet Union Western Territory and provide more calories to fatten the future slaves to have shorter but more fecund lives.

A derailleur was the transmission mechanism that moved a bicycle chain from one size sprocket wheel to another. It was also the official name of a New Soviet Era underground bike-repair-shop-gay-bar. In the new reality, it was both an illegal gay bar and a legitimate bike shop that specialized in finicky derailleur. All established gay bars were shuttered then burn when Russia took the United States.

The wall décor at Derailleur illustrated its namesake, from various generations and nationalities. To survive as a gay meeting place, the price of drinks had to be high in order to pay weekly bribes. But bicycle repairs were within normal market rates, and better quality than the bar drinks. There was a large double row of bicycle racks out front to accommodate regulars in the bar. Bicycles and horses became the primary mode of transportation during the Russian epoch. There was no fuel available for any type of motor vehicles. It all had been shipped to Mother Russia for redistribution.

The gay bar's customers had to pass through a new and used bicycle sales showroom, then mostly glass-enclosed modern bike repair shop, to finally enter the dim lit, camouflaged bar in back. Like most underground gay bars, Derailleur primarily functioned as a quiet place to have a conversation, and hopefully get lucky over a drink. At the very least the bicycle tune-ups were good and not overpriced.

The population of the United States might be kept cold and hungry, but there was never a shortage of cheap rotgut vodka to keep its citizens dossal and compliant. To encourage customers to drink, Derailleur had various "Light Entertainments" after midnight. It was after all a twenty-four-hour bike shop. But the bar portions had only two shifts: [1] cocktail hour drinks before a skimpy cabbage soup dinner, or [2] after midnight drinks to score a bedmate to share body heat and, with luck, frisky friction.

The Russian rulers used the disbanded U.S. military personnel to mop up behind their constant little conflicts to expand their empire. Former U.S. troops, AKA foreign lackeys, were sometime used as servant-slaves for cusack masters. That was until the cusack grew tired of abusing their lackey and wanted a new face to torment. So, American service personnel not executed on the spot were viciously beaten then given a medical discharge for the beating.

One obvious American-ex-Russian military slave flunky, well built, tall, blond, with cold cobalt blue eyes, was standing near the entrance reconnoitering Derailleur's bar patrons. After he had scoped out all present and made a mental list of three potentials, he walked up to his first choice. "Hi, haven't seen you here before. What's your bike trouble?"

"What's it to you?"

"Are you new to the neighborhood?"

"No one can accuse you of being standoffish. What's where I live to do with anything?" This was said by a tall, shaved head, bushy bearded, large, coffee dark, also well-muscled man, about the same age and height as the interrogator. He also looked like American-ex-Russian military slave.

Hunching up his shoulders, about to turn away, the blond said, "Nothing and I rescind my unmade offer to buy you a drink."

"Well, ain't you sweet, I already have one … see? What's your game, why you chatting me up? Are you looking to trouble?"

"Maybe I think you're cute."

"Ho, I've been called a lot of things, but cute was not on the list."

"If you want me to leave, just say buzz off. I promise not to break any of your bones exiting. You *do* know this is a gay bar bike shop, *right*?"

"Could have fooled me. You with the anti-gay police or something?"

"What if I was?"

"Then you'll need a lot of help, if you're thinking to take me out."

"Relax, wouldn't be in here if I wasn't gay. So … what are you up to?"

"There you go again. Maybe I'm here to get my pole smoked. You up for some fresh protein cream hot from the spout?"

"What's wrong with your wrist?"

"Maybe I was cut too tight, or just maybe I crave a hot lip-smacking tongue slathering. You got nice lips."

"Oh, I see … you are too early for hookup time. This is cocktail hour. My name is Nevin by the way. I'd put my hand out for a shake, but I'm not sure you'd take it."

"Aren't you afraid of shaking hands with the only black man in this ice-cold place? You do know I'm a twofer for extermination? Or maybe you haven't heard, our Russian masters are not into dinge or queens?"

"I'm Pre-Russia old fashioned, diversity turns me on. And when my time comes, I'll bring plenty of them along to see the end with me."

"I've been here forty-five minutes, and except for the barman-bike-mechanic, you're the first person to talk to me."

"Self-pity, really, we already established this is a gay bar."

"I'm just saying."

"It's a fact, strange slaves in bars don't talk to other strangers unless they are prepared to die or worse, to accept rejection." Puffing out his chest, Nevin spoke with pride in his voice. "Obviously, none of which I give a shit about. I'm looking for a real man to be with tonight. I like sex a little rough."

"Well, looky here, a gay civics lesson in a saloon, I hope you aren't expecting a tip?"

"Don't take gay culture personally. It comes from centuries of persecution, something you may be familiar with. What is your name? I gave you mine."

"Why you all up in my business, afraid I'll bring property values down integrating this schizophrenic joint?"

"I've been watching you from *there* … and came over *here* so you wouldn't feel as alone as these other single saps. *Now*, I'll just mosey along to talk to that guy."

"It is not friendly here, that's what I'm saying."

"Welcome to the times we live in, many of our fellow Americans voted for this Cultural Revolution. Too bad it was their last vote."

"Yeah, and the big surprise their side won with 3 million votes less than the majority. It kind of reminds me of the Supreme Court selecting G.W. Bush president with much less than the majority vote, way back in the day. Did you notice the white-supremacists are back with indiscriminate lynching? I guess we should have seen the new slavery coming."

"Hey relax Bro, not to worry, anyone starts trouble with you, I'll finish it. I got no love for those hate filled bastards."

"That was said like you meant it. So, if you don't want to give me head, why are we still yapping?"

"Tell you what, Mr. No-name. A table is just opening up in the corner, if you still want to talk?"

The two men stood down from their high bar stools, amid bicycles mounted on shoulder-high repair stands. They sauntered over and took possession of a small round two chair table in a back corner, near the bike-parts area's double Dutch doors.

"All comfy … so what you want with me?"

"Your name?"

"Al, and I'll shake your hand for proposing hospitality in this too white, inhospitable dive." That said, he put out a big hard hand.

Nevin took the offered appendage and gave it a firm grasp saying, "Nice to meet you Albert."

"It's Aleem, actually. If you aren't here for sex, what do you want?"

"I didn't say no sex; the only thing is you have a look I know too well."

"Oh yeah, what look is that pray tell?"

"Why did you leave slave service?"

"Officially, it was called a medical discharge. But there was nothing wrong with me before they kicked the crap out of me."

"Been there done that, and our former V.A. is dysfunctional, right?"

"Right, but why do you care?"

"While a military slave, they worked me to exhaustion. Then beat me before discharge. Back here I had trouble falling asleep, staying asleep, and wake up startled, in a cold sweat ready for life and death combat … sound familiar?"

"Are you buying the next vodka? That head nod means yes, and if I nod my head yes to your question, we'll look like a couple of bobble-head dolls looking for adverse attention. You want to break up this quaint little joint?"

"It is the only gay watering-hole for miles."

"Sometimes I just can't help myself from smashing things."

"Yeah, me too, but let's find a replacement, *then* trash this place."

"Okay, I'll listen to you for one drink's worth. Unless you are peddling religion or revolution, then save your breath. I'm not interested. Look at what we already got with that bullshit."

"You mean it wasn't okay for Russia to annex Canada? Or give our border states to Mexico, just before they annexed it?"

"Cut the treasonous claptrap, what's on your mind?"

"I planned to make their military my career. What else was there? Then I was drummed out, for no reason. It was right after my last Baltic-Scandinavian deployment. Oh, that was ugly."

"Nevin, I've never found a good reason for anything they do. Most Russians are not better off after enslaving the western half of the world, I've heard worse. Most will end up dead if they really do try to take China's half of the globe."

"Back here, I was constantly on edge and ready for a fight, just walking down the street minding my own business. I couldn't find a job, or even concentrate on their stupid video games."

"Let me guess, you drank too much?"

"Yeah, one night after six months of being a stranger in my own country, I decided to go down on my pistol. Just before pulling the trigger for a good-bye bullet, for some reason, I called 911. It felt like someone else made that call."

"You've got my attention … don't stop."

"The EMS guys and the cops on their bicycles were familiar with the epidemic of suicides by ex-military Russian lackey slaves. While the EMS workers explained their protocol, the cops showed me respect by making my illegal sidearm disappear without a lot of fuss. They said if I was caught with another one, I'd be taken directly to a euthanasia center. If the line outside was too long, they'd cage me for a public execution picnic. Now who wants that?"

"I bet they put you in the nut house? Now, doesn't that sound old school Russian?"

"But only for forty-eight hours. It wasn't for extermination."

"Do you think freezing to death in Siberia is better than death by dehydration in the desert?"

"Yeah, well, freezing means no hallucinations. I'd guess that's better."

"Indeed, I believe you're right."

"I read in an underground newspaper our clown president and family are scheduled for the same end as the last Czar and his family."

"How old was that paper? I heard they already did that."

"What?"

"They were thrown out of a plane over the Black Sea. The last Czar and family were shot in a basement. That is not the same"

"Damn, I knew the Russians were mad at him for cutting the children's food program. Without food supplements, a lot of kids starved to death."

"I heard that as well."

"The Russians say the children are their future, only adults are expendable. Wait, so who's running the country?"

"I heard a Russian computer management consortium, both North and South America. We are supposed to get carrots, celery, and onions in our cabbage soup soon."

"Huh, I'll believe it when I see it. Back on track, I'm still getting individual counseling and go to a group for guys like us. They only charge what you want to give and move the location around. The authorities haven't found us yet."

"Bully for you, I don't need a shrink, or to hear a bunch of vets moan and groan about how bad it is. I've noticed!"

"I get you need strong relief, right now."

"Do you really?"

"Look, I'm familiar with the public outdoor hospital, such as it is. Let me walk you through the intake process, I can hook you up with their best people."

"Ho, what are you a bleeding-heart slave!"

"What will it take to get you help?"

"I told you, someone to swing on my thing. I might be able to trust someone who regularly smoked my pole *real slippery wet, slow, till blast off, and swallows.*"

"That it? Go down on you or have to kill you. Or worse, watch you kill yourself?"

"Kill me, *you* … not likely. Life *is* cheap here in Mother Russia's New Soviet Union of North America. And you are not even close to threatening."

"Before we take this to a higher gear, maybe we should agree to disagree?"

"Look, my getting head is worth more than breathing right this minute. I'm way too far overdue, why can't you understand that?"

"Yes, your neediness is obvious. I know what being in heat looks like. When I came over here, doing you wasn't on my to-do list, the opposite was."

"I got that vibe."

"Don't ask why, I don't have a clue, but you are growing on me, to the point of considering helping you out to get off."

"Now, that would be appreciated."

"Tell you what, explain how you understand our countrymen lost our country into slavery, and my lips and tongue will give the satisfaction you seek."

"Nevin, I can see on your face you're serious. But why'd you think I understand what happened any better than you?"

"You look like a book reader, from back when books were more than heating fuel."

"In exchange for getting head, I'll tell you what I think, okay?"

"That's all I ask, a black man's take on how this white man became a slave."

"Your head nod and lip-lick *is* reassuring. What don't you understand?"

"How our fellow citizens voted away a 250-year-old country and got nothing but poverty and slavery in return. I just cannot wrap my head around it. We had armed forces and didn't use them. Why did everything happened so fast."

"The United States of America's founding fathers most cherished wish in 1770s, was achieved by the Russians in the 2020s."

"I'm asking … how'd it happen?"

"A few rich Russians and their spy-service were able to dupe racist, misogynist, homophobic U.S. citizens willing to give up democracy in exchange for a promise of heterosexist, white-male-supremacy, Christin-evangelicalism."

"I know that part, how?"

"The property-owning Founding Fathers of the U.S.A. feared common people would misuse the freedom of the vote and end up with a megalomaniac narcissistic presidential-king. So, they used divide and conquer to fuel hate against the various parts of U.S. society. Fast forward to present day and Russia took divide and conquer to the next level using social media."

"Okay, so what was their secret sauce? How'd they do it?"

"Using fake news to inflame fears. Then pit one against the other bigot, to trick them."

"Wait, could it be that simple?"

"No, it took 250 years for the Founding Fathers ideal, the rich property owners governing, to become a reality."

"Shit, that's what happened, all right."

"Except, the founders wouldn't have approved going back to foreign domination, we closed that circle. First, we were dominated by the English king and his landed gentry, now dominated by a Russian czar-president and his oligarchs. We are basically back where we stared, but with more American slaves."

"So, you're saying power and control has been about owning property? I don't get it … what's the big attraction to landlords?"

"Ancient Rome ruled the known western world for what … 1,200 years, how?"

"Beats me, I wasn't there."

"Land owning was required to be in the Roman Legions. In battle, they were invested beyond acquiring spoils of war, each solider had property and people back home he was fighting for. Oh, and the politicians were *land owners*."

"We're off track, what's that got to do with losing our country?"

"Our recent politicians became obsessed with blue, purple or red allegiances and fund raising, rather than governing the whole country. So, voter suppression fed tribal prejudices, one against the other. Instead of protecting democracy for the citizens, hate became its national obsession. Got it?"

"Yeah, thanks. That helps the odd-shaped pieces fit. You got a place?"

"No, you?"

"This bike shop's backroom is in the basement. It's dark and dirty and smells of bad plumbing. But I know a nook where we can have a little privacy. Is this going to be reciprocal?"

"It depends if you can diligently unlock my generosity."

"Before Russia took our Country did you ever imagine our lives could sink to this?"

"Aha, so, you originally come from a middleclass background. That would explain your fixed standards and character-rigidity."

"Yeah, so?"

"Where I come from, principles and morality are adjustable, depending on circumstance. The depravations of poverty and I've heard the splendidness of wealth, both share mutable morality and ethics. Survival or self-interest dictates values of the moment."

"Now you are giving me too much information. Listen, we'll survive to thrive. It has to get better because it can't get worse."

"Every time someone says that, it does."

CSLD

"Hello."

"Uncle Pasquale, how are you?"

"Hey, Frankie, how's everyone in New Mexico?"

"Don't know, I moved to New York City after graduation last month."

"Really … gosh you could have stayed with us until you got settled. Do you have a decent place to live, need money?"

"I'm fine, thanks."

"Do you have a job?"

"Yes, a good one."

"Do you need anything? Tour guide, letter of credit?"

"Thanks, but I'm good. This move was my first leaving home adventure. So far so good. I'm phoning to invite you to watch the Christopher Street Liberation Day Parade from our fire escape."

"Whose we?"

"My boyfriend, Dexter. We met my last year in college. He's from back here. After the parade, we'd like to take you out for a meal, our treat."

"Hold on, let me check … okay that works for us. Christopher Street Liberation Day is a week from Sunday. But the meal must be on me. Do you know I have a spouse?"

"Yes, Dad told me. His name is Otto, right? He's invited too."

"Your Dad never mentioned you were gay. How's he doing?"

"He's sassy in early retirement, playing golf three days a week, and he still keeps horses. Dad said it was up to me to tell you. So, surprise, I'm gay, Uncle Pat."

"Congratulations!"

"Your coming out of the closet years ago blazed a trail for me. Thank you for that."

"Did coming out get the result you expected?"

"Ugh I guess … they don't like it, but still show lots of love."

"Did you have a plan?"

"No, but it was overtime, I hated pretending. It was lying. If you were wondering, they still love you, the family hero."

"I'm no hero. How's about you and the new beau come to our place for a home-cooked meal before Sunday? Then you can catch me up on all the family gossip, and I can give your new boyfriend the once over for a seal of approval, or not. How is day after tomorrow at eight?"

"Let me check with Dexter … that works. I'd like to meet Otto and take some photos to send back to my folks. Dexter would like to interview you, if that is all right? How do we get to your place? We joined Pedal Power Transportation Alternative. Is there a way to ride our bikes out?"

"There's a bicycle lane on the Queens Fifty-Ninth Street Bridge. Do you have our address? … Okay then, we'll see you day after tomorrow."

Otto had been studiously doing the daily Times' crossword puzzle. He glanced up with a knowing look as the call was disconnected. One of many nice things about long relationships is communications can often skip unnecessary verbosity.

* * * *

"Frankie, since Dexter has volunteered to help Otto wash up after dinner. We can talk family without boring them."

"I'd like that, and maybe when the kitchen help rejoins us you can give us some CSLD history?"

"Ugh, we'll see. I can't get over how you changed."

"No offense, but you keep staring. Is there something wrong with how I look?"

"Nothing's wrong, I'm just surprised how tall you and your boyfriend are. Your parents are my height."

"I'm six foot-four inches, and Dexter is six foot-three and a half. My folks say they fed us kids too much."

"I remember you as an awkward, gangly-looking kid, all arms and legs, and here you are a filled out handsome young man. It's hard to get my mind around the change, but your voice sounds the same. Otto and I used to be average height, now old age's gravity is dragging us down."

"The last time you saw me I was fourteen. I knew I was gay, and overheard you were gay too. I was terrified you could read my sexuality and would tell my parents before I was ready to accept my self-discovery as unchangeable."

"Uh, explains why you were so skittish around me."

"That was eight years ago, and I've had growth spurts and learned positive self-acceptance."

"I'll try not to stare, but you are an eye-full of handsome. What did your dad say when you came out? As I remember, he didn't take mine well."

"Dad gave me the impression he was proud of you. What did he say?"

"The context for my coming out was your paternal grandfather retired and I wrote him asking about his work life. His third letter to me closed with, 'I know it's none of my business, but are you a gay?' Back then, the rule for coming out was to inform the whole family so individual members didn't feel they had to keep a secret. When I came out to your father, he said if one of us *had* to be gay, it should've been him."

"Why'd he say that?"

"Growing up, he was the one who read poetry and learned to crochet. Because I was sick a lot as a little kid, I over-did boy things when healthy. I played contact sports, broke wild horses, tried rodeo bull riding, fought forest fires, and lived for the rough and tumble because I could, and it felt good to be healthy."

"I've seen photos from your youth in the family albums. You were into a lot of dangerous activities."

"Opposed to my risk taking, our mom insisted all her kids learn to cook, clean, wash and iron clothes for survival. So, your dad and I shared in our mom's domestic science for boys, only he got more into it."

"I didn't know any of that. Other than my dad can cook up a storm. Is that why you fought in the war while dad stayed in college?"

"No, I was drafted during college, he wasn't. I dropped a troublesome class and the next week my draft notice appeared in the mail. New Mexico is a big state by area, but in those days, it had a small population of eighteen to twenty-six-year-olds to draft. Every state had to meet a conscription quota during Vietnam, but, Frankie, I'd rather not talk about the war."

"I only brought it up because when your name is mentioned, the family talks about your war medals. I can understand if it's a sore point, you probably lost friends and saw bad things."

"That's not it. I lost many more dear friends during the AIDS crisis. How did this conversation get so morose? Did Otto over season the food?"

"My fault, I'm not being a good guest. The food tasted great … it wasn't too spicy."

"You're not a guest, you are family. This is where you come with any problem."

"Thank you, Uncle Pat."

"Back on track nephew, tonight I had Otto follow my mother's recipe exactly. Over the years, I've modified it to suit our changing tastes. But on the chance my brother still makes it how Mom taught us, I wanted to give you a taste of home."

"It was great and tasted very similar to my dad's sauce. I wouldn't mind knowing how you change Grandma's recipe, for my hope chest."

"What hope chest?"

"Dexter and I are getting married next June."

"I'd better give him a more thorough going over. Why does he look at me the way he does? Is he into old guys or what?"

"Ever since I told him you participated in the original Stonewall Rebellion, he thinks you are a living historical figure."

"Oh dear, *historical*, quick, check my pulse. Is my heart still pumping? Why did you tell him that?"

"My dad said you were at the Stonewall insurrection, and now Dexter wants to interview you for an article he'd like to write. He majored in journalism and now works for a glossy women's magazine."

"Didn't I just clear up misinformation about me going to Vietnam? Stonewall had a context too, one I'm not particularly proud of. Why is it you need to make me special?"

"You are special to me. Dexter thinks the public will be interested in what you witnessed."

"Let's just be queer relatives, from different generations. Shouldn't that be enough?"

"That's not a rhetorical question, is it? Okay, you know I just graduated college. What you don't know is I often feel like a fraud because I don't have all the knowledge I should to back up my new degree. You're the family's war hero who was at Stonewall. I'm looking for fist hand knowledge and a role model."

"They wouldn't grant you a degree if you hadn't met the requirements."

"I'm not sure about that?"

"Graduates feel that way to keep them hungry for knowledge throughout life. A degree is not an end, it's a beginning."

"Hey, you two, the table is set for coffee and dessert. Pat, think I should put out the brandy snifters?"

"No, not a good idea, Otto. These guys are riding bicycles home, sober."

"Okay, then how about a little anisette in their espresso?"

"That won't hurt."

"I'm still stuffed, Uncle Otto."

"There is always room for dessert. Come on, everyone, back to the table."

The two younger men sat across from each other, hosts sat at either end of the long table, and anisette-laced, espresso in front of each. Otto was cutting, plating, and passing around homemade tiramisu from his end of the table.

Frankie reached across, clasping Dexter's hand, looking in his eyes. "My uncle doesn't want to talk about the Stonewall Riot. I'm sorry, sweetheart."

Dexter's face and voice went from perky to glum. "Were you at the first parade? Would you tell us about that instead?"

"I was, we called it a protest march because the Stonewall was still closed by the police."

"How about it?"

"It would be difficult to speak about my participation in the first Christopher Street Liberation Day March without background from the riot to explain my being there. Sorry."

Otto, his dessert tasks completed, looked down the length of the long table and made eye contact then exchanged a long silent communication, the way older lovers sometime do. Not receiving the response he wanted, with a shoulder shrug, Otto spoke his mind. "Pat whenever you read accounts of the Stonewall Riots, you always grumble, 'That's not how I remember it.' Here is your chance to tell these kids what you *do* remember. Think of it as oral history for your nephew and his intended. Don't worry, I won't go screaming from the room hands flailing, from boredom."

Looking down the table, the younger men's hopeful expectations were clear. Pat acknowledged that Otto often seemed to know him better than he knew himself. "All right, I can tell when I'm out gunned, but this could take a while. You two may want to sleep over in our guest room rather than bike ride in the small hours of the morning."

Otto addressed the table, "I prepared the guest room just in case. I'll get the brandy snifters."

"Not for us, thanks. We only drink beer or wine."

"The brandy is made from wine."

"Frankie is being protective, I'm borderline diabetic. That's why I only took a few sips of your very excellent wine with dinner. But you guys go ahead."

"Otto, let's skip the brandy tonight, but keep the coffee coming. Dexter, no need to ask, you can use the voice recorder sticking out of your pocket. But I get final approval if you use my name in print."

"Yes, sir, thank you, sir."

"Get comfortable boys, the history of the Stonewall Inn as a neighborhood bar goes back to the 1920s and then with prohibition it became a speakeasy hangout for bohemian artists. It was one of a few places in New York City where lesbians and gays were not shunned. After prohibition, the USA got busy and won the Second World War by demanding all citizens pull together for the war effort. There was little time or resources for sanctioned domestic persecutions of gay people while fighting for democracy overseas. Right on the heels of WWII, the Korean War seemed to be a continuation of the war just won. So, to keep the American public distracted from squandered blood and treasure in Korea, the U.S. Congress went on a witch hunt for Communists and homosexuals in the arts and government. That set the stage for old pre-WWII divisions in U.S. society, fostered by the federal government's hateful lies to divide and control the population."

Otto sensing Pat was losing his young audience by being too political, said, "You can get a sense of what he's saying by digging-up Cole Porter's song, "Down in the Depths on the Ninetieth Floor." He was a major success writing Broadway show tunes, had a sham marriage to a woman for heterosexual deception, and hated he couldn't be openly gay. His song captured how most homosexuals felt about being required to live in the closeted to have a career. Sorry to interrupt, Pat please continue."

"If you insist. Moving right along, something new occurred; the traditional divisions fragmented old from young.Older white people had always held power and the status quo and expected their young to mimic them. The young persons' new mantra became 'Respect is not given, it is earned.' To show their divergence from their elders' bigoted values, young Americans of all colors and creeds used music, dress, hair length, and free love to express displeasure with war, race hatred, class and other traditional constricting social attitudes. It was a social revolution. I didn't expect such a rapt audience. Breathe, there won't be a test."

"This is fascinating. It happened in your lifetime, tell us more."

"Okay, remember, you asked for it. In 1954, the U.S. Supreme Court decided separate was not equal in *Brown versus Board of Education* and thus went the status quo. Presidents Eisenhower, Kennedy, and Johnson had to send armed military to accompany little black children to integrate whites-only schools. Fed up with intractable discrimination against African-Americans, in 1964 President Johnson rammed the Civil Rights law through the U.S. Congress. Then in 1967, by court order, it became legal for different races to love each other nationwide. Meanwhile, the Civil Rights Movement had been struggling against many States' voter suppression laws, denying Blacks their birth right to vote. Out of that context the anti-Vietnam War movement grew, and the Women's Equal Rights Movement got louder. Then in 1969 the Stonewall Rebellion gave the Gay Rights Movement teeth."

"What is so neat for us, Uncle Pat, Dexter and I learned what you lived in school from history books. It is so rad you make it come alive."

"Okay, boys, onward and upward. I was too young for Korea. Nevertheless, propaganda about what was going on there filled the media. So much so, the House of Representatives' Un-American Activities Committee hearings, hunting homosexuals and Communists, could only play on late night television. Oops, that's a story for another day."

"When did you go to Vietnam?"

"I was drafted to go to Vietnam in 1967, the year after the Women's Equal Rights Movement started. But I don't want to talk about that war."

"I read billions of profits were made off the Vietnam War."

"Hey, he said he didn't want to talk about the war. Show a little respect, pipsqueak."

"Sorry, Otto. Uncle Pat, would it be okay to just tell us about Stonewall?"

"As you wish, young-ins. What I said before was context leading up to CSLD, it didn't happen in a vacuum. When I returned home from military service and saw what was going on, I joined the Vietnam Vets against the war and became overly familiar with being tear-gassed, chased and clubbed by cops swinging riot sticks at peaceful protesters. No offense, Otto."

"None taken."

"What are riot sticks?"

"They are long, thick police batons. Imagine cops' night sticks' big brothers. There were a lot of nonviolent civil rights and anti-war demonstrations happening at that time. The governments, city, state, and national-were insecure going against the First Amendment wishes of the people who weren't buying the Communist domino-effect war propaganda. So, the police forces trained special squads to use extreme violence to breakup nonviolent, free speech expression. These storm trooper types in New York City were called TPF or Tactical Patrol Force."

"Authoritarianism again?"

"Our country was teetering on the verge of civil war, and the rich and powerful mostly white were scared. Poor black neighborhoods were rioting for basic civil rights and to vote, college students were taking over their universities to be heard, and big anti-war demonstrations were disrupting business traffic, big and small. The citizenry was evenly divided, coast to coast, pro versus antiwar, and the government's propaganda was exposed as phony baloney."

"Why was the baloney phony?"

"The lies told to be truth about Vietnam were exposed by us vets who were there!"

"Today we call that fake news."

"There's a tradition, political fake news dates back to 1870."

"Okay, Otto, but everyone expects politicians to lie. In fact, most don't even know how not to. So, where's the harm?"

"Ever hear the fable about the boy who cried wolf? His fake news cost him his life and a whole lot of sheep theirs."

"But the wolves got a tasty mixed-grill meal, ha, ha."

"Wait … we were taught in school the U.S. won the Vietnam War to protect the world from Communism. But isn't Vietnam a communist country. What did I miss?"

"Frankie, when I came home it seemed the nightly news was telling about a different war in a different country than I lived."

"How come they don't tell us what's really happened?"

"Boys, let's not get off track, or we'll be trying to answer that all night."

"You're right, sorry, Otto. What about Stonewall?"

"I was introduced to the Stonewall Inn gay bar by another Vietnam veteran. I'd met him at an antiwar demonstration. The bar was tacky, flat black paint slapped on raw, unsanded, unprimed, lowest grade plywood. It was so dark when you went inside you couldn't see anything until your eyes adjusted to almost no light, that was the first room. The other room had dim light."

"What, our history was tacky? How awful. I expected elegant boas and regal rhinestones tiaras, at least."

"Chic it wasn't, but I immediately felt I was where I belonged, surrounded by my gay tribe for the first time. It was like a serene island in a choppy sea of chaos outside."

"When I turned eighteen, I got a similar feeling from my first Gay Pride Celebration in Albuquerque."

"Rumor had it the Stonewell's second room was the only place that allowed two men to dance. That wasn't exclusively Latin music."

Fidgeting, Frankie couldn't contain himself. He needed to share in his uncle's tale. "Before I came out to myself, the idea of dancing with another boy made me mad. Now that idea gets me hard."

"I was never a bar person and never learned to dance the Mambo or Meringue. But asking a hot-looking stranger to dance doowop or a rock ballad was an icebreaker and I scored every time I went to the Stonewall bar. But hey, I was in my twenties, so were my tricks, and those were very different times."

"It must have been a comfort, with so much going on in the world?"

"True, we found sanctuary in each other's arms."

"Pat, the boys want to hear about specifics."

"Otto is such a task master. See how he keeps me in line?"

"And you love it Pat. Now give more details, and less sentimentalizing."

"Slave driver ... on Saturday June 28, 1969, I was invited to dinner with my ex-lover at his place in Park Slope Brooklyn. At the time, I lived in the Bronx. The Stonewall Inn in Manhattan was about half-way between my place and his. My ex-Wyatt had gone to a lot of trouble to make a nice meal, and I could tell he was horny, my usual condition at that age also. His talk through dinner was about reconciliation. I knew what we'd had was an infatuation, not real love. Although sweet, it was over. I wanted friendship with Wyatt. But it would have been so easy to give him the charity fuck he wanted, except then life would have gotten complicated. I said so, and he got pissed and ordered me to leave.

"Neither Wyatt nor I had heard about the Stonewall riot the night before. Since being homosexual was a crime, sin and illness, we were never mentioned outside the sensational tabloid media, which neither of us followed.

"Like I said, Stonewall is in Manhattan's Village half-way between Wyatts's Brooklyn and my Bronx apartment. After dinner with Wyatt's grabby, horny hands, I needed to get laid. So, I parked on Greenwich Avenue and headed down Christopher Street toward the Stonewall Inn Bar, the place had never failed me. There were a lot more folks on the street than on an ordinary Saturday night. I was preoccupied from dinner and didn't notice at first, but more and more people kept coming in twos and threes.

"I asked a cute young guy named Cody Brody, 'What is going on with so many men out and about?' In a sweet Southern drawl, he told me about the previous night's riot and that Stonewall was closed by the police. After I determined, Cody was over eighteen and had a hard on for me. I said, 'I'd like to get naked with you and do some fun stuff.' He thought that sounded cool. As it worked out, he had a place across Christopher Street facing on Gay Street. But he also had roommates who were home. Then Cody suggested we go up on the roof of his building and exchange seamen under the stars and after look, down on the crowd on Christopher Street.

That sounded like a plan. But the immediate obstacle was getting across Christopher Street, which during our getting to know you chatting, had become packed with people who looked and dressed a lot like us.

"At that point, Christopher Street was so crowded, people overflowed the sidewalks and, cars could barely get through. Then they couldn't and tried to force their way forward, blowing their horns. But the throngs of gays and supporters resisted by surrounding the cars and buses. In the end cars and a bus were rocked side to side and almost rolled over. The angry energy in the air felt different. Not at all like I experienced at civil rights and anti-war demonstrations, this was in your face defiant, damn the consequences.

"Then it dawned on me. Without being organized and having leaders, this was a mob not the usual nonviolent, supplicants begging oppressors for relief. From what I could see, these homosexuals and friends were angry and didn't care who got hurt. I know danger when I'm in it, and Christopher Street had become dangerous in a grownup adult way I'd not seen since Vietnam. People could be injured or killed demanding to be acknowledged. I could see Cody was drawing the same conclusion, without having been in combat.

"We couldn't get across Christopher to Gay Street. We tried, but it was packed solid, queers and allies were pouring onto Christopher from all directions. Looking up, I could see heads peering down from windows and the roof of Cody's building. We'd not be sperming up there anytime soon. The space on the street couldn't accommodate the growing crowd as the mood of the mob ratcheted to hair trigger explosive. I could feel uncontrolled, high-voltage electric outrage snapping in the air like ozone. We'd been harassed and victimized one time too many. Something big and violent was speeding toward ignition."

"Gosh uncle, you could have been a martyr. I'm so glad you are a live to tell us."

"Cody became visibly frightened. He was shaking in a cold sweat and wanted to leave and go uptown to stay with a female cousin. I muscled us through the crowd to Waverly Place, by hugging storefronts. We exchanged phone numbers in a doorway and had a long lingering kiss goodbye. He was shaking all over. Hugging the buildings again, moving against the tide, he escaped from what was gestating.

"Alone, I was squeezed back on to Christopher Street by the crowd. I was torn between staying with the excitement or getting to safety. Then three things happened, one after the other, and I was never so scared."

"But, Uncle Pat, you fought in the Vietnam War. They gave you medals. How could a gay street protest be more frightening than kill or be killed in war?"

"It's the unknown that's most scary. In the war, we had a hierarchy of leaders, weapons, and were trained. In Vietnam, there were rules of war, even if they were seldom in our favor. On Christopher Street, in the West Village that night in June, there were no rules, no plan, and no leaders. It was the definition of anarchy."

"That's crazy they wouldn't just let you fight in Vietnam."

"At that point it was well after midnight Sunday morning June 29, 1969. What it felt like was being sucked into a tornado."

"I don't understand?"

"Maybe if you let him finish his story, you would?"

"Sorry, Otto, Uncle Pat, I'll save my questions till after, okay?"

"I decided Cody was right and I should get out of there. Just as I was making progress swimming hard up-stream against the people forcing me back down Christopher Street, glass bottles started flying out of windows, from fire escapes, and off rooftops. The missiles made the mob surge and it swept me back in the direction I didn't want to go, away from my car. Once they got started, monkey-see monkey-do, glass containers came flying down from Waverly, Gay, and Christopher, smashing on buildings and onto us. The mob was so dense it looked like a shapeless giant blob of humanity. Many of us took off our T-shirts and held them over our heads to deflect the glass bottle missiles.

"With heightened survival determination, I almost made it back to Greenwich Avenue and my car, where I saw what triggered the flying glass. Big police buses full of TPF cops were there, double parked and blocking my car's chance of an exit. Didn't matter, I couldn't get to it. There were also a lot of serious faced regular cops blocking access to the avenue as well. They were hitting at the flying bottles aimed at them with their batons. It looked funny but wasn't.

"What to do? I still couldn't get across to Gay Street and exit that way. With no other choice, the closest option was to try for the exit Cody took on Waverly Place. But even more people were coming onto Christopher than before from there. I was stuck in the middle of Christopher Street and it was a no go in any direction, squished body against bodies. I could smell excitement and fear, and something new: revolution.

"With a quick glance over my shoulder on tip-toes, I saw the TPF forming an attack line. They cordoned off Christopher at Greenwich Avenue, building to building. At first, I felt relief they weren't wearing their gas masks. Then it occurred to me Christopher Street and its neighboring streets are lined with tall apartment buildings. If they tear-gassed us, the buildings' occupants would get it too. It was summer windows were open, and that could add to the numbers pouring out on to the street. Talk about making a bad situation worse, it would have been a disaster. There was no room already. People could have been crushed to death fleeing, stinging eyes and nose burning gas.

"The mob seemed to be coming from every direction. All headed for the locked Stonewall Inn bar, and that was the direction I was being pushed. I turned around to see the TPF ready for rear enfilade. They were wearing blue and gray hard helmets with clear plastic, full face visors. Each held a three-quarter body shield in one hand and their trade mark extra-long riot club in the other. Someone in their command blew a whistle and they charged, batons swinging, shields shoving.

"A spontaneous gay protest turned into a full-blown, hysterical mass panic. Demonstrators tried to get out of the way of swinging clubs with nowhere to move. The bottle throwers seemed to run out of ammunition, or maybe cops got into their buildings and stopped them from the inside. I scrunched down as low as I could to avoid head blows, but took baton strikes on arms, neck, and back. Time stopped for me. I realized the situation was totally out of control, with no options."

"That's scary to hear, the hairs are standing on the back of my neck."

"We were force herded fast, a swirling, writhing mass, driven by painful blows to the intersection at Seventh Avenue South, West Fourth Street and Christopher Street. Then to keep the streets and intersection open, we were forced up onto the sidewalks by waiting regular uniformed police closing ranks with the TPF. The result pushed protestors down to Grove Street and up to Tenth Street on Seventh Avenue South's sidewalks. Then a big black paddy wagon rolled up and occupied the eastside of Seventh Avenue South, where many us stood dazed, but ready for what was next.

"The mob was divided on different street corners up and down the avenue. Then the police officer in charge, wearing the only white shirt with gold braid on his epaulets, shouted into a bullhorn for us to disperse. He bellowed to the four points of the compass, 'Go home or face arrest!' The sun was up; it was six o'clock in the morning by my watch. I didn't see any protestors leave as ordered, or arrests made. I did notice some intense staring contests going on between angry gay men of various ages, not cowed, and full of hate, angry cops. More violence seemed at the ready."

"I'm sitting on the edge of my seat, what happened?"

"The bullhorn orders to leave got no response. So, the cop's commander motioned over two of his biggest officers, then walked over to one corner or another and pointed to someone deep in the crowd. Then two huge TPF officers would then wade into the throng, grab the identified person, drag him out kicking and yelling, and throw him handcuffed into the back of the paddy wagon. Our revolt was leaderless so the cop in command had to be-picking-people at random, and the mob figured that out in a hurry. The tactic worked, after the third protestor was dragged out of the crowd hollering, 'Gay is good!' People started meandering away down Grove or Tenth Streets or the other side of Christopher Street, heading toward the piers. It wasn't too long before we were a small enough group to be arrested in mass.

"I figured, what the hell? I'm not going to get laid, might as well see the adrenaline rush to the finish."

"Good for you!"

"But instead of arresting us, as I expected, the cops headed back down the now cleared Christopher Street to their waiting buses and cars blocking Greenwich Avenue. Not sure what to think, I went across Seventh Avenue South to the twenty-four-hour diner and had breakfast. Inside the diner, it was a different kind of mob-scene, the atmosphere was triumphant."

"Wow, what a story!"

"Little did we know what was started Friday night, and we continued Saturday and would continue Sunday night, would become known as Christopher Street Liberation. It became the CSLD holiday, and now is celebrated around the world. That's *my* Stonewall Rebellion story and I'm not particularly proud of it. I was there by accident, motivated by lust, and tried to get away. It was definitely *not* my finest hour."

"Uncle Pat, it was like you were at the Boston Tea Party, it started a revolution."

"That is not how I see it. There was a third night of rioting, on Sunday. I didn't attend. I hooked up with Cody instead and we finished what we started the night before without all the street drama cock-blocking us."

"Was it good?"

"We had excellent sex at my apartment. You know what they say about anticipation? It was worth the wait. But, alas, only one time, he was too skittish. Dexter, you have a question."

"How big was media coverage for a three-day Greenwich Village revolt, compared to Watts, Detroit, and Harlem burning?"

"When it was reported at all, the press said 'Queers rioted because Judy Garland died that day.' They called her a fag hag junkie."

"Who was Judy Garland, and what did she have to do with it?"

"You never saw *Wizard of Oz*? Judy was the star of that movie, it's a classic."

"I don't understand."

"The public's stereotype was all queers flounce down Yellow-Brick Roads wearing ruby-red slippers. Reportedly, Judy had a difficult life, many gays related to that. Also, she self-medicated with alcohol and drugs, and many gays could relate."

"Why didn't the media set them straight?"

"The main-steam respectable press didn't mention the riot. Remember we were the love that dare not mention its name, so were not news fit to print."

"How sad, our history didn't matter. So, why did you go to the first CSLD Parade, I mean March?"

"I thought it might turn into a repeat riot, and was curious how it would compare in the daylight. The crowd was huge the night I attended. During that time, Civil Rights, anti-war, and welfare reform demonstrations happened in the daytime. Authority doesn't like to be challenged in the light of day with the world watching, right Otto?"

"I remember before Stonewall as a sorrowful time, Pat. The song played most often in gay piano bars, coast to coast, and the patrons knew the words, "Ballad of All the Sad Young Men." The music industry was afraid to release that gay anthem before CSLD, and heterosexualized it after."

"Yes, Otto I remember. A straight version of that song was finally released in the 1970s."

"Did the first CSLD March turn violent?"

"No, but you guys know what? It is late, how about we get some sleep and tomorrow I'll tell you what I remember about the first march. Otto already set out what you should require for showers and such, ask if you need anything."

"Will our bikes be all right chained up outside all night?"

"They should be, but you can put them in our foyer if you're worried. I'm wiped out Otto, can you help them? Sleep well, good night everyone."

"Go get your bicycles. I'll wait up for you to bring them inside."

* * * *

"Did you boys have a good sleep?"

"Pat, look at their flushed faces. They did more than sleep in our guest room."

"Come on guys don't look embarrassed. We fooled around this morning too. Don't look surprised. After all, we are still breathing. Having two good-looking young men under our roof was an aphrodisiac."

"Now I'm getting embarrassed. Enough sex talk. Everyone sit down, I made my super deluxe English breakfast."

"Uncle Pat, will you tell us about the first CSLD March?"

"If you two insist and Otto doesn't mind."

"Please tell us our history."

"No objection from me, *if* everyone eats his breakfast."

"Out-gunned again, then back to 1970 we go. A committee of gay activists formed to comply with the rubrics required for legally staging marches, parades, and such. Gay advocates proposed marching down Fifth Avenue to the still-closed by order of the police Stonewall Inn Bar. The city of New York said *if* it issued a parade permit, it would be to march up Sixth Avenue, forming at Washington Square Park and ending in Central Park. However, since being homosexual was an illegal, sinful illness, there was no precedent for issuing unlawful sick sinners parade permits to march anywhere."

"When did we stop being crazy criminals? I missed that celebration."

Otto looked surprised at the boys' ignorance and muttered, "After a lot of hoopla, the American Psychiatric Association decided we stopped being crazy in 1973. You weren't born yet."

"When negotiations between New York City's government and the gay activists broke down over granting a parade permit, the gay community made plans to march down Fifth Avenue to the Stonewall without a permit. Rumors had it that if attacked by police, 'We'd fight back.'"

"Oh shit!"

"It is funny how intelligence gets around quickly. Less than twenty-four hours before the scheduled permit-less march on the last Sunday in June 1970, the city fathers issued CSLD a permit to march up Sixth Avenue into Central Park. The Gay

Activist Committee accepted the modicum of legitimacy as a crack in the city's intolerance and to keep peace."

"Who knew it would be so complicated? I thought a bunch of fags got together and decided to throw a parade and did."

"Uncle Pat, did the TPF show up at the first CSLD March too?"

"No, they didn't. But there were a lot of cops in uniform, many more than usual for a Sunday parade. There were at least four police officers standing on every corner and several between. None of them looked friendly, most were scowling. But, remember, at that time it was a policeman's job to entrap and arrests queers, and they were rewarded for extra effort with overtime pay and promotions. Our boys in blue were confused. Before Stonewall we were criminal prey. After the revolt, where we attacked them first, they were assigned to protect us. Crazy making, don't you think?"

"But how could the mood of the march be fun with Gloomy Gus looking mean?"

"Funny you picked that up, Dexter. At the first post-march meeting, the city suggested that since nothing untoward happened, if the CSLD Committee provided trained parade marshals, the police presence could be greatly reduced at the next march. When we complied, the city solicited police officers who wanted voluntary overtime for a gay event. That improved everyone's mood. We got friendlier cops who chose to be there. Some later came out as gay."

"Did the first march participants have the same defiant attitude as the rebellion?"

"I for one didn't know what to expect and don't think any marchers did. I brought a camera to document if it got violent. Here, look at these snap-shots. I anticipated your question and dug them out this morning."

"... But most of these are photos are of pissed off-looking cops. Oh, wait here is a sign, 'We are the dykes your mother warned you about.' Look at this one, 'GLG = God Loves Gays,' the placard photos are in back."

"I wanted the cop pictures in case they broke the law. When the mood of the march changed, I photographed signs."

"You really captured glowering hate on cops' faces."

"So, what did happen?"

"It felt to me like a different crowd than the riot. When the march started, several people around me said they expected gunfire from anti-gay haters and cops, with us caught in the cross fire. They expected us to be mowed down in the street. A drag queen near me was loudly saying the rosary as the march stepped off."

"Boy, that sounds unnerving."

"But once we'd gone a few blocks with no ugly incident, and thousands cheering us on from the sidewalks and hanging out of windows, my fellow marchers' mood lifted from apprehension to jubilation. It was tangible, like a magical wave of celebration washed over us. Marchers' faces close to me showed, 'Holy mackerel, we can come out into the sunlight light and live!' Broad smiles broke out everywhere and people hugged and kissed, and the protest march turned into a moving party all the way to Central Park. The uniformed cops looked baffled, not understanding what happened. The peaceful, moving festivities continued into the park for a big rally with music, speeches, and lots of hugs and kisses."

"So, that is it, Uncle, no scary drama?"

"I don't have words to describe it. Expecting to be in a gunfight without a gun and then realizing we had stood up to institutionalized bigotry and lived to make demands."

"So now that we have same sex marriage, we can all live happily ever after? Is there anything left for my generation to do?"

"Pat, you only told them about the externals."

"Otto, they don't want to hear about the internal disorder, it might turn them straight, God forbid."

"Hey, if the church, schools and my relatives couldn't make me hetero, your story doesn't stand a chance, right, Frankie?"

"Yeah, why would anyone want to be straight? We're in love, the whole world knows gay is best."

"But I want to learn everything there is to know about *our* history's externals *and* internals."

"Don't say you weren't warned, the rest of this saga is pretty mundane and not first-hand. You'll be bored with the afterbirth of the modern gay rights movement." Pat said this hoping not to have to dredge up a past he found disagreeable, after the boy's initial excitement.

In unison, the two young men said, "Tell us, please." Realizing they had spoken as one, the two lovers exchanged an amorous look, and kissed. Sitting back down, they turned simultaneously and gave an expectant look to Pat sitting at the head of the table eating eggs Benedict.

"Shortly after the first CSLD march, while we were still designated to march up Sixth Avenue and everyone and their brother got to tread down Fifth Avenue, the gay community let it be known we were going down Fifth Avenue, midtown to the Village, permit or not. The city said, 'The police will stop you.' And the gay activists said, 'We've had this talk before. This time we'll meet force with force. Our gay war veterans will lead the march on foot, followed by lots of lesbians on motorcycles.'

"Suddenly, a last-minute compromise was found; the march would go down Sixth Avenue rather than up it, and end at West Street instead of the still locked, shuttered, for rent Stonewall Bar. Unasked for, a CSLD Street Festival permit was issued for West Street at the end of Christopher."

"Why did they do that?"

"Whether it was to sweeten the deal to keep us second-class citizens on sixth or to distract from having the Stonewall Inn the destination, or to sew division in the movement, we'll never know."

"We took Fifth Avenue that year with a permit for Sixth Avenue, and the police restrained themselves and blocked traffic for us. It's a good thing too they were outnumbered at least a thousand to one by marchers and spectators. And we got a street fair we hadn't asked for. I wasn't involved with all the politics of it, but somehow future march permits were approved to go down Fifth Avenue the last Sunday in June. The 2019 March was the fiftyish. It was a long time coming, but the gay community learned to use its voice."

"My grandma, your mom, Uncle Pat, always said if you don't speak up, expect to be ignored."

"She was right, about a lot of things."

"What was the politics like?"

"From its beginning, the CSLD Committee had internal conflicts between its politically exclusive and inclusive members. Let's call them closed and open minded, my words. The closed minded wanted no motorized entrants or floats, except motorcycles, absolutely nothing commercial, and all marchers had to be a member of a political, social or service organization. The inclusive members wanted bars and restaurants and other gay commercial ventures to participate, motorized floats, and a section for *unaligned* gay marchers and their friends."

"Sounds like the United States Congress in inaction."

"The internal conflict heated up when the city threw in an unasked-for permit for a street festival. Simply put, the politically exclusive refused to have anything to do with the money-making inclusive festival. They wanted it to be a separate entity with no association to the *historical purity* of the CSLD March. They voiced their opposition often, loudly, and with vehemence, but were in a dwindling minority as older folks quit and new young blood joined."

"Sounds like trouble in the family and dirty laundry on display, right?"

"You got it, the commercially comprehensive people were already calling the gay rights march, *a Gay Pride Parade*, much to the chagrin of the purists. The idea of a street fair after the parade was a logical extension of the celebration, with food, drink, trinkets, and entertainment."

"In addition, it was an easy source of fundraising and information dissemination for the new, growing, out and proud gay community. To add tension, CSLD was printed on both city permits."

"This is not boring, I can feel pressures building."

"Internal wrangling was ebbing and flowing while we were going up or down Sixth Avenue but unified to take Fifth Avenue without a permit. The truth is, the march and the street festival were never one, and so they didn't split-up as some in the gay press suggested. Otto, you want to contribute?"

"Sure, in small increments, cars, trucks, buses, and eventually all manner of commercial floats participated along with every kind of group imaginable and the unaligned were welcome and now makeup a third of the marchers."

"That's fascinating."

"Some years ago, New York City reduced the length of all parades to save money. CSLD used to start on Fifty-Seventh Street and Fifth Avenue, and now starts at Thirty-Eighth Street and Fifth Avenue and takes over the West Village, ending in a huge street fair with entertainment and dancing on the Hudson River piers

"You lived all this first-hand that is what I find phenomenal! You were there!"

"Hold on a minute, I was only at the second of the three days of Stonewall rioting *by accident* and tried to get away. I went to the first Gay Pride March out of curiosity, not on a mission, and never attended a CSLD march/parade committee meeting. For all I know, what I just told you about the internal struggles within the CSLD Committee were the result of faulty gay news reporting and Otto's failing memory. I never considered myself a gay-libber politically."

A confused look clouded Dexter's face. "Then what are you, Pat?"

"I just live my life openly and stand up for *a right to be here*. That's my story and I'm sticking to it."

"Wow, so much happened so fast and no one was assassinated. Is that how you remember it, Otto?"

"I'm a little younger than your uncle and didn't move to New York until later. But I did go to a few cantankerous CSLD Committee meetings before deciding all the infighting wasn't for me. It's true my memory seems to be going the way of your uncle's forgotten extra-marriage- dalliances. But I'm glad you had a taste of our oral history on this visit."

"How did you two meet?"

"I arrested Pat for disorderly conduct during a Women's Equal Rights protest march. He was definitely out of order."

"What, Otto was a cop?"

"To be accurate, Otto the love of my life was a New York City Mounted Police Office for twenty-five years. He was raised on a ranch in Montana and loves horses. We own two, boarded not far from here."

Frankie and Dexter exchange a look, then spoke as one. "We had no idea."

"Nephew, you can take this boy out of New Mexico, but you'll find out soon enough not the reverse. Come to find out, it's also true for Montana."

"Now Frankie and I know how you met, how'd you couple-up?"

"Let' just say, when he stripped searched me, it wasn't by the book."

"Tell all. When you strip searched me on our first date, it was clear where we were headed."

Dexter and Frankie exchanged another look, and then Dexter said, "Maybe that's more information than we need? Well, ugh, thank you both for a wonderful dinner and great breakfast and sharing first-hand experiences. I am looking forward to the four of us viewing the Parade next Sunday. Do you have any final thoughts to send us on our way today?"

"Dexter, I hate to end my oration on a downer, but your generation must pay close attention and be ready to defend its civil rights."

"Why? We have equal rights now."

"Before the fascist took Europe in the 1930s, gay people had gained a fair degree of acceptance. Then books were burned and the next thing anyone knew, suspected homosexuals were rounded up and murdered."

"Suspected homosexuals?"

"The Nazis rounded up effeminate males, most of who were heterosexual, made them wear pink triangles and then slaughtered them for being queer, which for the most part they weren't."

"Fortunately, pink was never my color."

"Be serious, Frankie. Uncle Pat, do you really think the past could repeat itself after all the gains your generation made?"

"Don't take anything for granted, Dexter. Everyone acts surprised when the grossly racist, misogynous, homophobic, nationalist come crawling out from under rocks. They only need the slightest provocation."

"Do you think they could come for us?"

"The hate mongers are constantly chipping away at civil society's social programs. Dimwitted, power-hungry tyrants need scapegoats to deflect from their failures to deliver unrealistic promises."

"Would anyone like a light lunch before you go?"

"No thanks, Otto. I'm in a hurry to go shopping for an assault rifle."

"Yeah, me too, I want one with extra ammunition magazines."

"Who you going to shoot?"

"White supremacist homophobic bigots."

"No boys that is not the gay way. We do not engage in fire fights with extremists, it isn't elegant or nice. Violence begets violence and gays have a troubled history being on the wrong side of it."

"Wasn't that the point of the Stonewall Riot? You stood up to and challenged your oppressors. You guys put your lives on the line to come out of the shadows and to stop singing sad songs."

"Stonewall was a spontaneous response to long festering, intensifying oppression."

"Without guns, how will we defend our community?"

"Otto, this is exactly why I didn't want to open this gay liberation conversation. I'm not political enough to handle it."

"Just tell them what you've done Pat, and how the movement's tactics changed, or do you want me to."

"Otto has spoken, I must comply ... in the early days after Stonewall, I did participate in zaps, kiss-ins, walked picket lines, and even chained myself with others to places where we were very unwelcome."

"Yeah, that's what I wanted to hear about."

"Then as we became visible, tactics changed. We moved from in-your-face, disruptive guerrilla strategies, loudly expressing the love that dare not speak its name, repeatedly, at full volume. Then we put on suits and ties and respectfully lobbied for our basic rights, but not shutting up, at normal volume."

"They taught us to use weapons in the ROTC. Why shouldn't Frankie and I defend gay rights with guns we know how to use them?"

"Dexter, imagine our history today if the authorities had ordered the police to shoot down the Stonewall protesters. In the past, they gunned down strikers protesting for safer working conditions, and antiwar students on college campuses. It was an option they didn't use, we must evolve too."

"Otto is right Dexter. We are no longer the hated outsider, *the scary demonized other*. We are the acknowledged blood kin of our oppressors, we know them, and they know us. That's our leverage these days!"

"So, what are we supposed to do? I love this man and will give my life to keep him safe."

"Trust your higher self, use your smarts. You can't change someone's mind if you kill him."

"Let this retired police officer have the final word on this. Finish what your elders started, boys. Just don't sink to the haters' level, evolve, and if they take an inch, you nonviolently demand and get a yard. That's the gay way these days."

Independence

From birth to death independence takes tenacity. So, after the struggle of birth, the infant's next tasks are daunting. Using grit and wit, the new born is expected to attain coordination, mobility, nonverbal then verbal communications, waste elimination control, sexual impulse regulation, and anger management to attain adult socialization to independence.

Pride of ownership of the infant's new body going forward requires feeling safe enough for maturation to mobility and then toilet training. If each developmental stage is attained without interference, then independence is achieved. Until given up at the end of life's arch, through geriatric struggle against time and tide to hold on to mental control and bodily function in reverse at the end of independence and life.

Prior to learning their parentally approved method of eliminating waste, the infant's only means to *protest inadequate care* is crying, refusing to eat, screaming hysterically, or the extreme of withdrawing into *failure to thrive* leading to death. With the developmental stage of toilet training comes a new means of objection and even doling out punishment to faulty caregivers.

By withholding what is wanted, for the first-time baby can control short-term results. However, a baby's power and control over caregiver's wishes for waste management, comes at a cost. Mobility's range to independence is limited when wearing a full diaper.

Some baby books recommend mothers insert a lubricated finger into the child's rectum directly after meals and place the child on a potty chair to expedite toilet training. That method's short-term goal is usually a success, if the child is not overly rebellious.

An unintended consequence of inserting a finger where it usually doesn't belong has created a vibrant market for strap-on-dildos and vibrators for heterosexual males' potty trained by the slippery finger method. These men are often unable to perform sexually without first being anally penetrated by their girlfriends, wives or other mother replacements. Females and gay males' toilet trained by a slick finger show a preference for receptive anal sex as adults. For many motherly love is fondly recalled by delectably savored homemade soup, and for others it's a lubricated insertion going in the opposite end of the digestive track.

Disturbing methods of a mother's toilet training techniques should not be confused with pediatricians who like to insert a finger into baby's bottom with no supporting medical symptomology requiring such procedure. Bad baby docs also profit from forcefully retracting small boys' penis foreskins before nature is ready for the uncovering. Foreskins naturally detach between ages ten and twelve, and do not need violent, painful medical intervention. Research indicates these and other forms of child sexual abuse result in disruption of normal development stages, and leaves lifelong psychological wounds.

Independence to roam from family safety is achieved once the messy tasks of the toilet are learned, along with what is private or public, and good touching versus bad. The exception to the rubrics is the pediatrician's office and mom's bath time. An un-interfered with toddler's successful development is often rewarded with a big front wheel tricycle to expand the world. As the child grows, so does the tricycle's symmetry. A new goal forms from watching older children play. It is to ride a two-wheel bicycle without socially ostracized training wheels attached.

The range of bike riding independence comes with parental safety restrictions. However, whether in daycare, prekindergarten, or at the park playground, parent's rules and restrictions are collectively judged by those they're imposed on. By comparison, most parents are found to be unfair, overly restrictive, and even tyrannical imposing safety concerns, and in opposition to the child's desire for adventure.

At age ten or eleven, most children have learned to ride a two-wheel bicycle and are ranging as far afield as parent(s) allow. Girls and boys at this age usually show boundless enthusiasms for any subject that catches their imagination and their personalities bloom. However, girls are taught to dampen their exuberance and narrow possibilities for the sake of social propriety and feminine decorum that's necessary to become sought-after submissive wives. On the other hand, boys' uninhibited high spirits are expected, along with pranks, other mischief, testing limits, and rule breaking for fun or boyish maliciousness.

In defense of much beleaguered parents, it is difficult to have values, superstitions, and other belief systems harshly questioned by arrogant, know-it-all, ill-tempered progeny. Rather than view such questioning as a challenge to character standards, it is better to consider them another developmental stage to be gotten through, like weaning to solid food, teething, or toilet training.

When an impasse occurs between an eleven-year-old and their parent(s) caretaker regarding independence to discover and conquer the larger world, a mutually agreeable solution is often scouting. Both Girl and Boy Scouts accept new members at age eleven. In a military style, regimented structure, scouting provides previously forbidden familiarity with; fire, knives, hatchets, axes, archery, firearms, horses, and all manner of consorting with other scouts.

From its inception to the present, Girl Scouts accept girls and adult female leaders from every race, creed, national origin, and sexual orientation. They also bake and sell delicious cookies. On the contrary, the Boy Scouts of America (BSA) had legal issues accepting African-American boys. After losing in law court, they accepted exclusively black troops. Then after more legal squabbling, African-Americans and other boys of color were allowed to integrate white-only Boy Scout troops. In some parts of the United States, Jewish boys had to endure similar fights to gain acceptance to BSA troops of their choice. Going in the opposite direction, the Roman Catholic Church made it a mortal sin for Catholic boys to attend BSA troops that weren't 100 percent Roman Catholic. The Mormon's Church of Latter-Day Saints (LDS) also had grave concerns about their boys' mixing with other faiths.

As the Catholic Church became slightly more liberal about doling-out mortal sins to their boys, the LDS Church took control of the Boy Scouts of America. Then after decades' long heated struggles ending at the United States Supreme Court. The National Council of the Boy Scouts of America was forced to adopt the same policy the Girl Scouts of America had from its inception. When the nation's highest court ordered the BSA to stop discriminating against gay boys and leaders, the LDS Church stepped back from control of the organization.

In 1906 scouting was founded by Sir General Baden-Powell in England. He would have approved of Americans letting all boys and qualified leaders participate in scouting. The General never married and preferred the company of men and boys to that of females.

Scouting is a step toward independence from family, as childhood is left behind. Between ages ten to twenty hormonal growth characteristics usually bring on adolescence, accompanied by major disruptions physically, emotionally, and socially. It is a trying time for the young person excreting excessive amounts of oxytocin, and dopamine, as well as for the others in their orbit.

One source of contradiction or consternation for many growing Boy Scouts has been the Scout Oath, *"On my honor I will do my best to do my duty to God and Country and to obey the scout law, to help other people at all times and to keep myself physically strong, mentally awake, and morally straight."* Memorizing the Scout Oath is the first requirement to become a Scout.

The Scout Oath appeared, for decades, in the Boy Scout Handbook on the page opposite an advertisement showing a well-stuffed bike jock-strap. Starting in the 1920s, the Bike Athletic Supporter Company ran full page ads in most editions of the BSA Handbooks, until LDS took over and didn't see a need for scrotal support. The obvious question is, "Dose meditating on, and memorizing a photo of a fully-stuffed jock-strap pouch, help or hinder a boy's definition of *morally straight,* while required to memorize the oath?"

If an inquisitive, *mentally awake* boy scout should be so audacious as to ask a scout leader or their parent or other trustworthy adult what *morally straight* means, exactly? The answers from Sir General Baden-Powell down through generations to the LDS Church BSA leadership couldn't be more diverse and divergent. Boys don't like ambiguity, except double-entendres in jokes.

Independence anxieties for the Boy Scouts abound beyond learning the skills necessary to earn the requisite number of merit badges to proceed up the ranks to Eagle Scout. There is normal developmental rebelling against parental rules, beliefs, customs, and ethics. Some boys cultivate discord with school curriculum and or personnel, and others have conflicts within their Scout Troop structure.

Boy Scout Troop Forty was led by Scoutmaster Mr. Jonathan Wand, and assistant Scoutmasters Mr. Billy (Big Griff) Griffin and Mr. Chip T.C. Blather. The Troop was comprised of four patrols, six to ten boys each: Badgers, Wolverines, Bobcats, and Pumas. Each patrol has a leader and assistant leader.

Most recently, the eight Badgers won the most awards and honors for Troop Forty at multi-troop competitions, called Camporees. All ten Wolverines were very competitive individually but lack the level of team coordination of Badgers. In the past, the Bobcats were Troop Forty's biggest and best patrol, then five of its star members aged out to join the explorer scouts. Always last place, the ten Pumas were fun-loving showoffs who like to marshal public parades and have little interest in merit badges, leadership, and rank or troop awards. But they like to have fun and do, often at the expense of demerits.

Cliff, the leader of the Bobcat patrol, was second tallest boy at a leggy five foot-eleven inches, and skinny 140 pounds. He had straight-brown hair styled in a conservative business cut, and muddy-brown eyes reveling average intelligence. Many females in his family mentioned, in his hearing, he was almost good looking. Cliff had little leadership ability but was liked as just one of the guys when a Badger. The Scoutmaster assigned him to lead the leaderless Bobcats. The fact that Cliff's father was the largest contributor to Troop Forty's approaching annual fund-drive was not supposed to be a factor in his selection to lead. In any case, after six months, Cliff would turn fourteen and leave the troop, to join the Explorer Scouts. The Bobcats were not asked to vote for their new leaders, as was the usual troop policy.

Allan, Cliff's assistant leader was a year and a half younger. He was five-foot four-inches tall at 135 pounds, and possessed overly big hands and feet for his short-size. His dark-brown hair was cropped close to the scalp in military-recruit or prison-inmate fashion. Very short hair made his big troubled emerald eyes look extra-large. The other boys called him bug-eyes among other negative-designations. Allan was a friendless know-it-all, shunned by other boys and ignored as a hopeless lost sheep by the adult scout leaders. He had been a Wolverine with problems, mostly built on his inflexible, inconsiderate, unforgiving attitude. He didn't want to become a Bobcat or assistant leader but wasn't given a choice.

The Scoutmaster selected Allan for assistant Bobcat leader to solve the Wolverine's problem with him. Three of the remaining Bobcats didn't like Allan, and the suspension of their right to vote for leaders, and quit the troop in protest. A new conundrum was brewing. The three remaining Bobcats detested Allan, and he was in line to take over as patrol leader after Cliff became an explorer scout. Not having leadership ability, Cliff either treated Allan like a servant or his closest friend, depending on his unpredictable mood.

Magnus was the most awkward, bookish, and only bespectacled Bobcat. At twelve years old, he was remarkably knowledgeable and already an Eagle Scout. Magnus was a pale skinned, pudgy five-foot four-inch 185 pounds, with unruly light-blonde tight finger width curls that completely covered his head. His bright light-blue-eyes showed superior brain power. He had joined the Bobcats at the height of their success, the previous year. Magus was being raised by two Ph.D. lesbian mothers and met with his Ph.D. sperm-donor father once a month to play chess. Joining Troop forty was his three parents' idea as a gesture towards Magnus learning to socialize with other boys his age. He found it easier to go along with the adults in his life than engage in and lose intellectual combat.

There were persistent rumors that Gary and Titus were queer for each other. It was common knowledge they had been neighbors and best friends since toddlerhood. They continued sleepovers at each other's homes and always buddied-up on camping trips. The reason they were not ostracized as fags and kicked out of scouting was, they were award-winning Eagle Scouts, unbeatable as a two-man team in any competition and eager to pitch in and help no matter the problem. Both teens had joined the Bobcats at the height of its success and contributed mightily to it.

James who just turned eleven was the newest Bobcat. His father was of Irish-Polish extraction and his mother American-born-Chinese. Blending his bi-racial identity kept him reticent in most social interactions. He was unsure of boundaries. James was five-foot five-inches tall, 120 and half pounds, medium-length pageboy-style black hair, with soft-nurturing-amber-colored almond-shaped eyes. He recently earned his Tenderfoot badge. Little was known about him since he didn't like to talk. James was being raised by a divorced mother and three older domineering sisters.

The troop's boys had a pack mentality, they were reserved around new comers until they got used to them. The boys wanted to be sure a newbie was not a quitter before extending friendship. It was a catch-22, since many new boys stopped coming to scout meetings feeling unwelcome, shut out of a closed system. James also felt like an outsider and had decided to quit Troop Forty if his second-class rank wasn't earned on the next camping trip and he didn't make at least one friend. The only reason he tolerated the troop's closed social system was its contrast to the overly estrogen-rich atmosphere at home.

With adult leadership approval, the Bobcat patrol planned a detailed, busy camp out for the Fourth of July Independence Day Holiday. They prearranged to go up Cat Back Mountain July second, and return on July fifth, sleeping three nights in tents. The weather forecast was good. Each Bobcat expected to earn at least one merit badge and James would complete the requirements to be promoted to second class scout. Cliff, Magnus, Titus, and Gary planned the outing. Allan begrudgingly went along with the others after they refused to let him take charge or listen to his constant illogicalities. They had to threaten to forcibly shut him up with duct tape. Naturally, after the meeting Allan found fault with everything the others planned. Being new, James was not consulted.

Troop Forty always contributed fifty percent of necessary funds for authorized merit badge trips, and the boys raised their half cutting grass and washing cars. Tents, cooking grates, pots, pans and other equipment were borrowed from the Troop. Mr. Chip T.C. Blather agreed to accompany the Bobcats, provide adult supervision and sign-off on merit badges and James' promotion.

Menus were planned, three nutritionally balanced meals and one healthy-snack each day, compulsory for the Cooking Merit badge. The food stuffs were purchased by the Cooking Merit Badge boys, troop's gear collected, and individual Scout's camping equipment packed and ready to go. Then Mr. Blather canceled at the last moment. Mr. Wand and Big Griff were out of town for the Independence Day Holiday. Some of the food the boys purchased was perishable. The Scouts were angry and grumbled they were once again let down by adults, an aspect of growing up no child accepts without gripe. They didn't mind the troop losing money, but the idea of wasting the money they had sweated to earn along with undoing their looked forward to expectations from camping, that spurred them to action.

Without getting into Mr. Blather's personal business, the Bobcats were able to threaten, cajole, and otherwise continuously harass and bother him to break the rules and let them go camping without an adult leader. To ease his conscience and liability, Blather saw them off after checking they had all necessary gear and food. They agreed to his periodic checking on them by telephone and their hired transportation after arrival then after pickup. The boys also promised not to do anything dangerous or take unnecessary risks. If they honored their promise, and there were no incidents Chip would sign-off on merit badges and James becoming a Second-Class Scout.

Troop-arranged transportation took the Bobcat patrol as far up an abandoned logging road possible, dropped them off, and agreed on a pickup time at the same spot July fifth. The van driver said, "If you are late, you'll walk the 100 mils home. Remember, you paid in advance so there is no refund for being tardy and walking."

Using Cliff's compass and Magnus' map, the scouts hiked, carrying all their gear on their backs, one and three-quarter miles to their planned destination. It was an old Native-American campground, by a rushing stream deep enough to bathe; even swim. The rushing water was cold, clear, and tasted good. Most recently the campsite had been used by untidy hunters. So, the first order of business was to police the area, filling a big plastic trash bag with empty beer cans, food tins, and discarded paper-plastic-takeout-containers.

Then the experienced Bobcats set up a three-tent straight-line camp with requisite safe fire pit for cooking and campfire. They dug a grease pit and latrine far-away from their fresh water and tents. Sacks of food were labeled and hung high in trees. Cliff and Allan had the tent closest to the food trees and fire. Magnus and James were in the middle tent, and Titus and Gary's tent was at the end.

After a tasty, fast, filling evening meal, it was discovered with grumbling, that Mr. Blather hadn't loaned the patrol one of the troop's skit script books. It was Troop Forty's tradition, after the evening meal cleanup, for the scouts to take turns performing skits around the campfire until bedtime. It was a fun way to end a taxing day. Usually, the Scoutmaster or assistant would take a couple of boys aside and describe a skit to be performed. The scouts always added their own unique theatrics to make the skits germane to present company. It was rumored there were racy skits in the back of the book and that is why it was never allowed in the scouts' hands. After a physically hard day hiking-in, climbing trees to hang food, gathering and cutting wood, swimming to wash, preparing food and its clean up, bodies were tired but minds active in an exciting new place. The silly clowning around and laughing from skits would have helped mind and body to unite for sleep. Some of the over tired alert boys were cranky, and so, the overall mood was stormy.

"Any of you master planners have an idea what to do now, I bet you don't?"

"Allan, we could sing songs."

"Oh yeah, smart guy, what song for instance?"

"Everyone knows the 'Battle Hymn of the Republic?'"

"Magnus Hultkvist, you should know better. We are not allowed to get into religion or politics, the Supreme Court said so SMARTY PANTS. Hymns are religious."

"Allan, were you born an asshole, or did you get special training?"

"Nobody asked for your opinion, Gary SMART MOUTH."

"I'd like to know too, Allan, were you born an asshole or dropped on your head as a baby? My vote is you were dropped on your head. Oh wait, Bobcats don't get to vote."

"Don't push your luck, Titus. I'm still the assistant patrol leader, vote or no vote."

"Hey, come on, you guys, don't call Allan names, and respect his rank."

"Tell you what, Cliff. Our fearless designated leader, instead of singing, how about we go around the campfire and everyone says something really disgusting?"

"Gary, the scoutmasters wouldn't like that idea. It's embarrassing, and in your case would take all night."

"See, there's the proof. Didn't I just say Allan is an asshole?"

"What *is* your fascination with assholes, or should I *even* ask Gary?"

"Go ahead, ask, if you want to swallow your teeth. Who knows? Maybe the wild animals all around our camp will eat Allan, and then I won't need to punch out his lights."

"Don't fight, boys. I brought my stop watch. We can take Gary's idea, but say whatever we want. Limited to five minutes a turn, *I'll be timekeeper.*"

"Excellent suggestion, Magnus. All in favor says aye … okay, then that's settled. Since I'm patrol leader, I'll decide who goes first. … James goes first."

"No! I mean sorry, I don't have anything to say, someone else go I pass."

"Tell us about your bicycle or dog or anything."

"I don't have a dog. The landlord doesn't allow pets. My bicycle is an old hand-me-down, junky girl's bike someone gave my middle-sister first, and she didn't want it."

"James, we won't leave you alone until you tell us something about yourself. So, what's on your mind these days, or what do you think about day dreaming? Got an eye on a girl?"

"Allan said we can't talk about politics."

"It's *my game* and I say *you* can talk about whatever *you* like. But the more disgusting the better."

"But Allan is the assistant leader."

"If necessary, I can tie Allan to that tree way over there for the bears to eat. Or better still, I could just kick his ass. He's overdue for a beat down." Gary said, giving Allan a threatening look, complete with closed fists demonstrating punches.

Showing false bravado, Allan said, "Yeah, you and what army!"

"All right, all right, don't fight, I'll do it, five minutes isn't long. What's on my mind?"

"Yeah, that's the part between your ears."

"Allan, I hope your first aid kit is well stocked."

James looked from Gary to Allan, trying to decide whether to let them roll around fighting in the dirt or keep the peace and talk. He was shy and didn't like talking but didn't like to see physical fights either. "All right, so when I started to sprout upper-lip peach fuzz and hair under my arms and you guys know where else, my mom stopped giving me baths. I was so glad, it was embarrassing. Instead she sent me to see my maternal grandfather for a man-to-man talk. I guess it was supposed to be about body hair. But what he said was, a boy needs a father figure to look up to and be a role model. But my granddad lives a long bus ride away. Anyway, I think he's too old for the job and he said as much. So, Granddad said I should imagine the President of the United States as my full-time father and imitates him every day."

"Wait a minute I didn't grow pubic hair until I was twelve, almost thirteen. I still don't have facial hair. You just turned eleven, how is body hair possible at your age?"

"Hey, you guys, let him finish his turn. We can talk it over after everyone has a turn."

"No, hold on a second. What did your grandfather tell you about sex?"

"He told me a rooster's job in the hen house is to fertilize eggs. It wasn't very interesting, boring really, I don't like chickens or eggs."

"James, you still have three minutes."

"At first, thinking of the President as my dad was an improvement over my real father. But now the media keeps saying the President is a liar, thief, and abuses woman. So, I'm listening to him more closely and he keeps saying contrary things and changing the subject and looking guilty when asked questions about being a 'whoremonger crook ripping off the American people.' I know my granddad voted for him and likes him. But I don't think I want to be a liar or a thief."

"James, you don't have to lie or be a crook if you don't want to. According to my mother, my biological father drinks too much alcohol and smokes pot a lot to. I promised her to never do those things and I mean it. See what I'm saying?" Gary said this puffing out his chest.

James looked at each boy's face around the campfire, and then swallowed his embarrassment. "Can I ask you boys something personal? Do your fathers bathe you? Bath time got very uncomfortable with my mother as I got older."

"What, are you kidding? I wouldn't let him if he tried. Trust me my dad would never be bothered to try. I took charge of my hygiene at age four, it's private, ask Gary," Titus said proudly.

"I wonder why you got embarrassed. Did you get a chubby with a mind of its own?"

Cliff spoke without thinking it through."Allan, don't pick on James. It's a private matter about his privates, ha ha, hee hee."

To change the subject, James said, "Speaking of private parts, in the stream this afternoon when all our privates went public, I was surprised I didn't mind showing mine. I thought I was bashful, but it was fun splashing around in the sun. Does that mean I'm a pervert for knowing who's got what now?"

"No, Allan's doctor made him a pervert. When he shoved his finger up Allan's ass and he liked it." Gary gloated retelling an Allan story from a previous camping trip.

To defuse Gary and Allan's growing animosity, Magnus said, "My old doctor wanted to check for hernias every-time she saw me, even when I just came in for a vaccination or had the flu. When I asked my moms if I could get a hernia from the flu, we changed to a new doctor who doesn't need to finger my nuts all the time to watch me get a chubby. What a relief!"

"Sometimes these things get so confusing they give me a headache."

"Like what exactly, James?"

"Remember that scout meeting where they told us how to put bullies in their place?"

"Allan must have missed it."

"SHUT UP!"

"I watched the conclusion of the National Boy Scout Jamboree on TV. The President of the United States said his speech wouldn't be political and then gave a political speech. He went on to demonstrate how he's a bully. I couldn't believe it, he showed everybody how he's a big bully, in front of thousands of Boy Scouts and our leaders. How am I supposed to imagine him as my father? That's all I have to say."

The faces around the campfire showed troubled thoughts. Every age can be difficult, but eleven to fourteen is particularly hard distinguishing right from wrong from what adults expect. Cliff was torn between suggesting they all go to bed early and finding a more positive ending to the day. After an uncomfortable silence, he said, "Magnus, since you are sharing a tent with James and this was yours and Gary's idea, why don't you go next?"

"Okay, this would be the time to tell you guys a really scary ghost story to make you pee in your sleeping bags out of fear. Or make a joke about how I know how to take a bath without adult supervision. But that would be mean. Instead I'll tell you *what's on my mind,* even though I know you will find it boring, maybe even stupid. Something *has* been bothering me and that is what I'll tell you."

"How about you don't? This whole thing is stupid, let's quit while we're behind."

"Allan, you are so cruising for a bruising from me."

"Magnus, tell us, I want to hear about your fear. Hey, hey, listen to me, I'm a poet and didn't even know it, hear fear could be in a poem."

"Does everyone know the word superfluous?"

"Magnus, it means unnecessary, like Allan as a Bobcat. Let's vote to expel him back to the Wolverines? Oh, I forgot, they don't want him back and Bobcats can't vote anymore."

"Both my parents drive Volvos, and those cars do things without driver prompting. Even though my parents' cars only act on their own to assist the driver or for safety, I think they could be more independent if they wanted."

"You do, do you, how?"

"For example, both my moms' cars know and remember the seat and mirror and temperature settings for each and automatically adjust to whichever one is driving. When the cars go in a tunnel, the dash lights turn on and then off coming out the other end."

"We don't have a car. So, Magnus, your point is?"

"Today's computers can think independently and learn, they remember, and are smarter than us."

"Besides both your parents' fancy cars, what computers do you have, wise guy?"

"The old hand-me-down I use for homework knows English grammar and spelling better than I do. It corrects my misspelled word as fast as I type them. My big worry is that computers will take over and make us all *superfluous.*"

"Don't be silly, computers are tools. Do hammers and saws scare you too?"

"I've read there are super computers programming regular computers running factories. To make it worse, some robots are also computers. With renewable energy and machine learning using quantum mechanics, computers don't need us."

"See there, I just knew too much reading was bad. You are talking crazy, computers wouldn't ditch the people who made them," Allan said this gloating.

"A computer beat the world's Grand Master playing chess. Another computer was on TV and beat the winners of a quiz show."

"That's your proof?"

"Computers are flying airplanes and driving big trucks on the highway autonomously, and they'll be chauffeuring us around soon. They don't need people. Think about it. We discard them to the junk pile when outdated. Now they're smart enough to do the same to us."

'OH, I GOT IT! I know what your problem is! You saw that old space movie where a computer flew a rocket ship and wouldn't obey. Let's see, oh yeah, the computer's name was Hal. That's what's scaring you, right, Magnus? It was only a fucking movie, idiot!"

"Allan, I never saw that movie, and I don't like science fiction. I'm only interested in real science."

"Science fiction is real science. I suppose you don't have faith in intelligent design either? WHAT A LOSER!" Allan said this nodding his head up and down, agreeing with himself

"Magnus, ignore him ... why would computers want to get rid of their creators? That seems disloyal."

"Titus, they are smart enough to know we are destroying this planet they live on."

"How can you say, that Magnus? Global warming is a hoax, and you know we are going to leave this camp-site better than we found it. That's a rule. And the President says talking about climate change is unpatriotic, bordering on treason."

"Allan, computers don't like getting cooked in climate change."

"How could they even know or care? They're machines, STUPID. Magnus, you are so un-American, Congress should investigate you."

"Computers know stuff we don't. They're smarter than us, that's my point. Too bad you don't get it."

Allan couldn't restrain himself going for the bait. "Your silly fears are superfluous and too political for the Boy Scouts of America, so says the Supreme Court. You are only a stupid crazy almost teenager, afraid for no reason. Get over yourself. I'm only telling you for your own good."

"Now it's all coming to a head, like your pimples. People won't have jobs. Already computers and robots do all the repetitive and dangerous work. You know why, Allan? It is called automation."

"But Magnus, we approve, Titus and I hate work. When doom and gloom come, we will be playing video games or out on our bikes, or skateboards. We'll be having fun right up to when the computers say, 'Game over, humans.'" Gary said this with heartfelt dislike of work.

"You forgot mentioning rubbing yourself raw during the end of days, Gary."

"And that is Allan's intellectual contribution to this important discussion about the future of our species."

"Titus, I know you and Gary are only being sarcastic."

"Why does this kid make me feel we're back in school? This is a camping trip, an adventure. Cut the crap, you're no fun, Magnus."

"When your education is over, you'll want to work for money to be independent, right?"

"Duh, what's the choice!"

"Guess what, dear scout buddy, no jobs for us. The computers and their machines will have taken them all."

Allan couldn't hold himself back. He jumped into the conversation in a rush of words. "I've heard there is medicine for boys who think too much, it unscrambles their brains. You three need a double dose, NERDS!"

"Magnus ignore Allan, I'll kick his ass after we finish talking. Look how far humans have come since colonial days. We have electricity and more than our fathers at our age. When I see mine, he tells me he didn't have a skateboard or video games, or any of what he calls luxuries."

"Yeah, mine too, I get so tired of hearing I don't appreciate what I have compared to his bad old days. Now Magnus is looking forward to our future bad days. Would somebody please give us a fucking break?"

Cliff tried to intervene saying, "Magnus, you have a computer to do your homework, that's better than doing it long hand, like I do. My misspelled words don't fix themselves, my mom does. How about I suggest we don't think bad thoughts anymore on this camping trip?"

"Thanks, Cliff, we all appreciate you trying to be the good chosen leader. But am I really the only one here who cares none of us has a future?"

"Look Magnus, if everything you say turns out to be true, I'm sure there will be theme parks to keep us entertained in place of work. Cliff is right, we should always think happy thoughts."

"Thanks, Titus. Who knows, maybe he's right. Everybody keep smiling and be happy, lemmings!"

Cliff became animated with a new idea. "No, wait a minute. You got me bothered about something else. Maybe not so different after all … yeah, maybe there's a connection …"

"Cliff, you can't just say that and leave us hanging, WHAT, for God's sake, are you talking about?"

"If you insist Allan, I'll tell you."

"Well, don't do us any favors."

"To please my mom, I visited my Grandaunt Millie on her birthday. My mom had to work a double shift at the hospital, so she couldn't go sing happy birthday. I don't think my Aunt Millie remembered me, but she was pleased I came and gave her a birthday gift from my mom."

"Well Cliff, aren't you the model nephew one generation removed? Did you bring a cake and flowers too?"

"I did, it was a very small cake."

"Was it tasty?" Magnus asked licking his lips.

"When I was ready to leave, my aunt decided to make us lunch, and said, 'Watch television while I prepare food.' This documentary came on that education channel, and her remote control is broken, so, I end up watching it."

"What a long introduction, I hope the lunch was worth it." Allan spoke in a superior tone.

"The beer was interesting; the food rather bland. My aunt doesn't use salt."

"She gave you beer? Doesn't she know how old you are?

"I already said I don't think she remembers me. I'm a lot taller than her. In fact, she gave me two beers, one watching TV and another with lunch."

Allan's insecurities flashed again as he said, "You are not old enough to drink beer. She should be put in jail. I'm surprised she didn't show you PG-17 movies too!"

"Like I said, she is very old. Since you are so interested, beer is bitter. I don't know what the attraction is. When I'm old enough to buy beer, I won't, and you shouldn't either."

"Did you get high?"

"I don't think so Gary. I felt a little weird after the second beer, but it was nothing special."

"Wait a minute, what are you telling us? Lunch with an aunt, drinking beer and getting high, something you saw on TV, or computers taking away our future?"

"Right, Magnus, I got distracted. So, this documentary said studies shows millions of people in developed countries are choosing to remain virgins their whole life. And that upsets the population balance between the first and third worlds."

Allan shouted, "WHY FOR GOD'S SAKE!?"

"The TV said it is a G. W. Bush idea about abstinence, carried to an extreme."

Magnus snapped a quick response. "That's logical, I read Bush's Promise-Keepers spread AIDS to places it wouldn't have otherwise gone."

Carefully mulling over the interaction, Titus said, "No, that is illogical, what's the big attraction to abstinence? I don't understand, Cliff?"

"According to the documentary, no nookie gives people independence from attachments and promises new kinds of freedoms."

"Wow, I thought sex was the whole point of being an adult. What a bummer!" Gary's face showed his disappointment.

"I think that was the point of the documentary, population growth is declining, and scientists are trying to figure out where sexual attraction went and why?"

"What's the answer, Cliff?"

"It's complicated."

"Bullshit!"

Cliff resigned himself to explain what he didn't fully understand. "I didn't get everything they said. What I got was, young adults are afraid of HIV-AIDS-STDS and needing abortions. The documentary said pornography and sex toys and sex-bots are fun, and masturbation is less messy trouble than sex with another human.

"We shouldn't be talking about masturbation, it's bad for your eyesight, against scout rules, and a sure ticket to hell."

In a half-hearted gesture towards peace Magnus said, "Allan, maybe you aren't doing it right. Don't rub your eyes, rub down lower."

"Yeah, Allan, want a demonstration?" Gary said this standing and reaching for his zipper.

"SHUT UP! You guys WILL GO BLIND AND CRAZY, and that's a provable fact in the Holy Bible."

Magnus still trying to keep the peace said, "Maybe he needs a cream or lotion to get off without chaffing."

"I think Alan is beyond that."

"Why Gary?"

"He's a walking cliché, lotions don't work on clichés."

Still trying to steer the conversation away from conflict, Magnus looked from one to another boy. "Oh, or maybe Allan doesn't understand biology?"

"I have an idea, let's all stand over Allan and show him up close and squishy."

"Okay, you scouts stop picking on Allan. It has gotten late. I hate for you guys to go to sleep feeling the future is hopeless. Let's go around the campfire and each say something short and inspirational to sleep on. James, you go first."

"Do I have to? All right since you insist, *again*. I don't have a computer, my mom doesn't own a car, and I haven't liked girls since preschool, so nothing said tonight is for me, which is positive, right?"

"Magnus, do you have any encouraging thoughts to share?"

"Yes, I think you, Cliff, and Gary and Titus, are correct. No matter what, we should look on the bright side. Everybody should smile and be happy right to the end."

"Gary, you have anything new to add?"

"Sure, I think jerking off is healthy fun, everyone should do it, *a lot*. It gets a bad rap from spoilsport Allan. So, churn one out for me tonight, with Allan's name on it."

"Titus, do you want to contribute something to sleep on?"

"Yeah, I do Cliff, I think Allan is a wet blanket and should be de-pantsed for being a prude."

"Allan, I think you have contributed more than enough snipping tonight, don't you?"

"No, and it's not fair for the assistant patrol leader not to have a turn. I have a lot to say to those jerks!"

"And as the patrol leader I say, you shared more than enough tonight."

"Well, fuck you, you are a terrible leader, and I will speak if I want to. Just try and stop me." Allan stood ready to start a speech.

Cliff, Gary, and Titus all stood ready to physically stop Allan's oration. Cliff clearly had had enough and said, "That's it I tried and tried some more, I've had enough. Allan, you're fired as assistant patrol leader! Get your shit out of my tent, or I'll toss it out."

"Just you wait, I'm telling the Scout Master on you and all these other boys too."

"Allan, don't give these scouts a reason to vote you out of the Bobcats."

"FUCK YOU!"

"You might want to rethink being a tattletale while you are still a Bobcat wearing pants."

"I don't care, I'm telling!"

Cliff brushed off his jeans, and said, "As Bobcat patrol leader I say nothing spoken here tonight was out of line or off-color. Anyone who says otherwise goes against my leadership and has to join a different patrol. If they'll even have you Allan." Cliff, Gary and Titus all sat back down on the ground.

Looking to restore order, Magnus said, "What about you, Cliff? What's your positive nighty-night, or was it firing Allan?"

"Me? Sure, all right, my great-grandfather, my grandfather, and my father were or are lawyers. I am expected to join the family firm after my legacy admission to Princeton University. Computers will never replace lawyers. Now goodnight and everyone sleep tight. Tomorrow and the next day we have a lot to do."

Still standing and now looking sheepish, Allan shuffled his feet. "What about me, where am I supposed to sleep since you threw me out of our tent, and demoted me?"

"Right, what about you? We need a decision. Magnus, do you want to be my new assistant … you are shaking your head no … Gary or Titus, either of you want the job?"

"No, we'll be explorer scouts soon after you." Then everyone looked at James.

Head bowed, Allan moved out of the campfire circle, collected his belongings from the tent, and carried them outside. Then he sat on the ground next to his things, in the shadows away from the others and their tents.

"How about it, James? Will you be the new assistant patrol leader for the Bobcats?"

"Are you picking on me because I'm youngest, newest, lowest rank, or all the above?"

"Nobody is picking on you. You are being offered an opportunity to learn leadership."

"Sorry, I'm only a Tenderfoot without any merit badges or any idea what you guys want. So, I'm not qualified."

"No problem, I'll make you acting assistant leader until you are qualified."

"What would I have to do?"

"Enforce the Scout Oath and Scout Laws, that's it."

"I don't know anything about leadership?"

"Nobody likes being ordered around. Ask nicely, don't tell us. If you ask and listen, you might hear better ways to accomplish what you want to do. That's leadership according to Gary and Titus."

"Who would help me learn that?"

The four other boys sitting on the ground around the campfire raised their hands.

"The only downside I know is you will have to share a tent with Allan for this camping trip. But as assistant patrol leader, he must do what you ask, without an argument. If he wants to stay a Bobcat."

"Huh, and that's it?"

"What you and Allan work out in the tent is just between you."

"Like, what do you mean by that?"

"If you want him to suck your toes, for example, that's your business."

"*I don't want that ... but you saying it just gave me a chubby.*"

It was clear from James' face he was pondering the unasked-for leadership position. "What if I say no?"

"The Scoutmasters will pick a boy from another patrol, like they did me and Allan. The Bobcat patrol deserves its own true leader. After I age out in six months, you'd be the authentic Bobcat patrol leader. How about it?"

"Give me a minute to think this over." James stood, left the campfire circle, and headed over toward Allan sitting in the shadows.

Cliff turned to Magnus and discussed moving his gear into Cliff's tent. Titus and Gary debated whether James would need protection sharing a tent with Allan.

Sitting on the ground next to Allan, out of ear short of the others, James noticed tears. The lad was silently crying. Instinctively James draped an arm over the sobbing boy's shoulders. "Don't cry."

"It was demeaning to be fired in front of everyone, even if I went too far."

"You did."

"Yeah, I do that a lot, I can't help myself!"

"Do you think I should take your old job? Or you going to try and get it back?"

"I ruined it, and the Bobcats really should have a Bobcat as leader. They chose you."

"I'm a shy person, being a leader was never what I wanted. I'd hate to mess up the Bobcats or get embarrassed like you."

"I should have known better. This isn't the first time I made everyone hate me."

"How do *I* avoid that?"

"Can you keep a secret?"

"My lips are sealed." James drew his hand across his lips, mimicking zipping them shut.

"Whenever I feel not good enough, which is a lot of the time, I try too hard, and people get really pissed. So, I try even harder and harder until they hate me. Don't make that mistake."

"Why do that, if you know what happens?"

"I'm on the outs with God. So, I want people to like me. I know I'm going to hell to be punished forever. But in the meantime, it would be nice to experience a little kindness before burning for eternity."

"What's between you and God?"

"I curse him at least twice a day."

"What did he do to you?"

"You promise not to tell."

"Cross my heart and hope to die, I'll stick a pin in my eye if I lie."

"When I first started getting chubs that wouldn't go down until they spit-up, I prayed really hard, 'God, please take this temptation to sin away.' Instead of helping, he gave me more and more chubbies. I begged and pleaded every way I knew and even promised to work in a leper colony when I'm older. Still he wouldn't give me a way to stop sinning. So now, every time I jerk off, I curse God after I cum. It's his fault. He made me do it, when I asked not to. There's no salvation for me. Anything good I get has to happen here on earth."

"Oh gosh, that's a lot to think about ... and being assistant patrol leader too. What about sharing a tent with me? My sisters say I snore."

"I've been told I do too. But I don't suck toes, well, at least haven't so far. But I could help you out with your chubby ... if you want. My soul is already lost."

"Sucking toes was Cliff's idea; must be something he wants."

"Or it's a dig at me."

"Honestly, do you think I should try to be assistant Bobcat patrol leader? I'm new here."

"Yes, and if you want, I'll help you be better than I was."

"I never let anyone touch my chubby, not since I bathe myself."

"Why are you telling me that?"

"I didn't bring the subject up.But wait, if you're offering to give me a hand with my chubby that would be *good* touching, right?"

"I wasn't offering you a hand. Cliff made me use my mouth. He liked it a lot, but never reciprocated."

"Why?"

"I guess rank has privilege, so you won't have to do anything. I don't mind taking care of myself, I'm doomed anyway."

"How did you guys start that ... what you said?"

"If you tell, I'll be kicked out of scouting, and it's all I have going."

"Cross my heart. My word is truer than gold." Then James reverently crossed his heart.

"When I get upset, I suck my thumb. Being on the outs with God I'm upset a lot."

"So, it's related?"

"No, I'm a thumb-sucker since a baby. Ever since getting older, I sneak doing it. Cliff caught me thumb in mouth and said he could cure me. I laughed in his face."

"Why?"

"From when I was little my folks put hot sauce or bitter stuff on my thumbs at night. They even tied them up with bandages. When that didn't work, they made me sleep wearing mittens, but nothing worked."

"What was Cliff's cure?"

"He gave me a choice. I could either substitute his dick for my thumb or he would tell the other boys and let them razz me out of scouting for thumb sucking."

"That's no choice! Was it hard to do what he wanted?"

"Only at first. You have to understand; thumb sucking is static and lonely soothing. Cock sucking has a beginning, middle, and end. Like they taught us in science class, there's an exchange of energy. Cliff loved it, you'll like it. I don't mind I'm going to hell already."

"But how does it make *you* feel after?"

"Don't be strange, James. I offer you free blow jobs and you want to know how I feel about it. You do know that's crazy, right?"

"I guess I better tell you something … Before my father divorced mom and us kids, he always drove us to a big, fancy mega church with a Christian rock band and huge choir. The ministers had one sermon, give money, money, money."

"Huh, that's different. At the church we go to, you can almost smell sulfur from the fire and brimstone in hell. The preacher shouts and yells, hitting a big bass drum. He says we are all going to hell for sinning, and not tithing. I know it's my fate he's so upset about."

"After my father left us to live full-time with his other family, my mom walked us to a small, simple church near home. The new place of worship only has a small electric organ and we all have to sing. One way or another, sermons always say love and take care of each other."

"Sounds cozy nice."

"The small church is very open about sex too. My Sunday school teacher told our class masturbation is our biology preparing us for adult reproduction. She said it is natural and no big deal. *But* we should respect ourselves and our partner when *we* decide we're ready to have sex. Do you respect yourself after you suck dick?"

"You mean did I take pride getting Cliff off with my mouth? Well, let's see now that you ask … it felt more grownup than thumb sucking. But similar in a way."

"Sorry, I didn't mean to get too personal."

"I already told you God hates me, that's personal. But wait, I don't hate me, and come to think about it I have self-respect for making Cliff happy and feel good."

"I don't understand."

"Cliff wanted it, and after I got used to doing it, I liked it okay … What else?

I respect I've acquired skills that I'm good at. Yes, I have self-respect when I'm not getting fired as assistant patrol leader in front of everyone."

"You convinced me."

"Do you think I could go to church with you sometimes, as your friend?"

"Sure, I've wanted a male friend my age for a long time. But be warned, my sisters are very bossy, you'll have to learn to ignore them."

All Bobcat goals set for the Fourth of July Campout were achieved. Allan's negative attitude lessened greatly without the unasked-for assistant patrol leader responsibilities. Allan regularly attended church with James' family, and made friends with his God.

When Cliff left, eligible to join the explorer scouts, James became youngest patrol leader. With the large influx of aged-out Cub Scouts' enthusiasm and James' fair but firm leadership style the Bobcats regained their status as the biggest and best award-winning patrol in troop forty.

At age fourteen, most of Troop Forty's boys became explorer scouts until high school graduation. A few went on to become adult scout leaders for their own children. The majority attended college, join the professions, and lived happy productive lives.

By adulthood, most people not interfered-with as children will make the correct choices for their destiny. Those few unable, must accept dependence on others for financial and/or emotional assistance for activities of daily living. No one at any age likes wearing a dirty diaper or having others change it. Independence or dependence is a combination of luck of the draw, health, will power, drive, planning, and unknowables.

Birth of a new life comes with inevitability of its demise. It is hoped that life has a long graceful ascending then short descending arch; birth, to death after old-age. Traditionally, the geriatric divide is: early aging sixty-five to seventy-five, middle aging seventy-five to eighty-five, and old-age over eighty-five. With good health, adequate resources, and planning, early aging has the potential to be the most rewarding age. Early aging is often a last chance to experience aspirations of a lifetime without the encumbrance of work, family, and others' wants. Medical advances and public health have extended the productive years in early aging well into middle aging.

Middle aging usually comes with aches and pains that foretell the coming of the end of mobility and then bodily function control. But with luck, dependence is a decade or more away, if it arrives at all. On the other hand, with diminished physical ability comes increased mental acuity to compensate for loss. Middle aging can be a time for legacy formalizing, reflection, making amends, writing and wrapping up loose ends.

Advanced old aged is the reverse of new-born struggles to gain mobility to independence. At the point an older person is required to wear a diaper due to organ system or muscle failure, they are usually ready to accept, like it or not, the inevitability of their impending expiration.

Occasionally, hard-earned skills, like tying shoelaces, become physically unworkable or too mentally confused and force acceptance of dependent support. Early-onset Alzheimer's and other dementias can strike a person in their forties, but the statistical probability is small compared to fifty percent likelihood over ninety-years-old. Why some individuals over age 100 are clear-headed and in relatively good health may be more than luck with the genetic lottery. Brain science continues to find unexplainable anomalies in geriatrics.

What is known; choral singing, caloric intake reduction, and owning and exercising a dog increases longevity. Whether a completed life was well lived can only be judged by that individual. The Boy Scout Oath is a recipe for maximizing the genetic potential parents pass along to their progeny. Keeping physically strong throughout life will stave off many geriatric infirmities, improve quality of life, and theoretically increase longevity.

Research indicates mentally-awake, physically-active, well-educated folks have a lower incidence of Alzheimer's disease. Learning a foreign language or playing chess, bridge, mahjong, scrabble, or others brain stimulating games are recommended to stave off many senile dementias.

Within their wants, people will follow belief-non-belief superstitions when fashionable, traditional, or in revolt. However, prayer, AKA spiritual life, is another matter, analogous to learning music. Many folks are taught to play musical notes technically correct, but few can get beyond the notes to make music.

At the end of life, most dying people report being satisfied they did the best they could with the hand they were dealt and leave this existence with few if any regrets. Even though each developmental stage is contained within the individual, like tree rings, in death whether serenely accepting or struggling against, ultimately that person was the sum total of their cumulative experiences.

Labor

From my dorm room to the bakery is exactly twelve steep, uphill blocks, pedaling hard in the lowest gear. In reverse after a hard night's work, it's an easy coast downhill to my bed and a few hours' sleep before class. No matter the weather, on my bike shuttling between university and how I pay for it, baking at night is my meditation zone. Ohm ah hums ...

I'm up off the bicycle seat, standing on the pedals, pumping hard, almost there, and zoning back in. *What's this? Two men signing in front of the bakery? Huh, must be students from that Vocational School for the Hearing Impaired. Maybe they are lost.*

Half dismounting, I coast the bike around back. Off the bike, I chain it to the metal stairs and unlock the bakery's back door. Inside, I turn on the lights, radio, light the ovens, proof boxes, get the coffee going, and change into my white work clothes. Back in the shop from the changing room, I pull the work order clipboard off the wall hook. On top is a sticky note from the owner. "I'm assigning you two students from the deaf school to train as bakers' helpers. I've enlarged the night's work to reflect extra man-power. Don't worry, they read lips." It was initialed by the boss.

Looking over the order sheet, the night's work had been increased as if I had two experienced bench hands working. I thought, *Not possible,* and mentally reduced the work to less than the usual for me working alone to allow time for teaching. The owner-master-baker wouldn't like it, but he'd get some of everything he ordered. It wasn't fair, every time I settled into a routine it got changed.

Going up front through the store, I unlocked the customers' door and gestured the two guys having a signing conversation inside. After relocking, I indicated by hand gesture they should follow me to the back. The one guy was my perfect type, slightly pretty but not girly, willowy but not underweight. He was a little shorter than me, had medium-length curly, reddish-brown hair framing big, bright, sea-green eyes. He gave off a nervous friendly vibe.

His companion obviously spent a lot of time working out. He was taller by several inches and outweighed me by at least fifty pounds. His bowling ball round shaved head had no neck, it was supported by bulging, bull-like shoulder muscles. His skin tone was dark Mediterranean olive color. He had a fierce face, surly medium brown eyes set too deeply and far apart. My initial impression was trouble, but I've been wrong.

Both guys wore jeans far below their hips, and if the top eight inches of their boxers hadn't been visible, their ass cracks would have. One of my sexual fantasies was pulling down low-hanging droopy jeans to uncover the behind. That fantasy may not be unique to me because many guys at my university wore skimpy briefs under their boxers just in case some wise guy yanked their sagging pants down in public, goofing around.

For me, two pairs of underpants were ludicrous. Just getting my minimum laundry done was a major undertaking that required planning. As much as I sweat in front of the bakery's big ovens, I didn't need extra clothes to wash.

Mouthing slowly, I said, "Can you men read lips?" They both nodded yes. So, pointing to myself I mouthed. "I'm Bedker Beecher. What are your names?"

My fantasy guy whipped out a small paper pad, and in precise penmanship wrote, 'Perry Larsen. Please write your name for me?' And he handed me the pad with a friendly smile.

I mouthed, "Nice to meet you Perry Larsen." I took the pad and pencil and printed my name and handed it back.

He held out a long-fingered, delicate hand for me to shake. The physical contact with his firm, warm flesh made my sleeping cock stir awake with interest.

Pivoting to ask the other guy's name, I saw he'd already written in bold block letters, "Rupert Gladdules," but was signing to his classmate. *"Nobody said the boss was Injun."*

Thinking, *What the hell, I don't need this!* I signed to him, *"Did I offend you?"*

Shocked disbelief splashed on his face and he snorted, shaking his head no.

I signed, *"So what's your problem with this Native-American?"*

Clearly, neither apprentice expected me to know American Sign Language. My boss didn't know, how could they?

Shame-faced, Rupert blushed looking pissed-off offended.

Taking pity on the poor guy's embarrassment, I signed, *"Why don't we begin again? Go out the back door, turn around, come back in, and we'll have a do over."*

He stood frozen, staring indecisive. Then he snorted again and stormed out the back door in a huff. But he didn't immediately return.

After what was a reasonable wait, I signed Perry, *"Do you think he'll be back?"*

Perry lost me signing a long-complicated answer at break-neck speed.

So, I carefully enunciated, "Sorry I don't understand, you're too fast." I could see he understood so I mouthed, "Can you speak?"

He said, "Yes, I lost hearing age thirteen, a car came around a corner too fast. I was on my bike without a helmet and almost died. I don't speak at school, I'm rusty."

Enunciating carefully, I asked, "Do you think Rupert will be back?"

"No idea. Maybe not, he insulted you. Too bad. He was looking forward to this job."

"Think we should go look for him?"

"No. He was rude and should apologize, not get special handling."

"Okay, what do you suggest?"

"I wouldn't know where to look. He's a bully, they don't say sorry. Just so you know, I don't hate anyone. I'm gay. I know how it feels to be despised by strangers."

"I'm gay too, but we won't let that affect our work, will we?"

Perry looked puzzled for a long moment then spoke again. "You can hear. How come you know ASL?"

"Deaf guys are hot."

Perry showed a suggestive smile. "Really, is that the only reason?"

"Not at first. To be honest, the ASL elective was an easy A at my high school to encourage enrollment. I was taking advanced placement math and science, so I needed a few easy classes to keep my GPA up. Then I found I liked ASL, had natural aptitude, and as I said, deaf guys *are* hot. But you just saw, I'm not very good."

"You're not so bad. I could help you get better, if you want. Know any dirty words?"

"A few. One day our teacher asked her best students to volunteer as tutors. I said no way, I'm too busy with my own schoolwork. She said tutoring would improve my application's chances at good colleges."

"Did that work out?"

"Yes, and I learned some swear words from the guy I was tutoring. He was sexy-hot but straight. We are still friends."

"That sounds like the story of my life, close but no cigar—or anything cigar shape."

This conversation is heating up and not about baking. I'd better change the subject if we are going to get any work done. "Was the baking trade your first choice?"

"No. My vocational counselor thought I should try it."

"Why?"

"When I lived at home, I made birthday cakes for the family and cookies and treats for holidays. They wouldn't acknowledge me as homosexual but loved to eat my sweets. Home baking made my family happy, even if I was a disappointment. My counselor thought I'd fit in at a bakery."

"What *did you* want to do?"

"I thought being the first hearing-impaired chef could be special. I'm a good cook. Watching people enjoy food I prepared makes me feel good."

"My people believe in following your dreams."

"But our school doesn't have food service assignments, other than this one. And it is brand new and might not work out."

"The day shift at most small bakeries make cakes, pies, elaborate pastries, and such. They use similar skills as pastry chefs in expensive restaurants. If you got a job as a restaurant pastry chef once you knew the lay of the land, cooking might become an option."

"How can I get on the day shift?"

"To start the baking apprenticeship, you work as a baker's helper at night, then move up to bench hand, then mixer, oven man, and foreman. Then it's possible to get promoted to the day shift, if there is a need and you have an interest."

"Are you the night foreman?"

"Yes."

"When will you move to the day shift?"

"I'm the foreman because I grew up in bakeries. I've worked day shifts before. Right now, I need night work to pay university tuition."

"I guess I'm not going to the day shift soon."

"Once you learn the basics at night, I'll see what I can do to fast track you to days. One of the cake decorators is retiring soon. You'll have to learn fast and work hard at night to be considered for her job."

"Already I know I like you."

Was that a double message, or hearing what I wanted? "Do you know why Rupert chose this trade?"

"Rupert's family owns a diner. He washed dishes and swept and mopped since he was little. He thought this work was a step up from janitor dishwasher."

"Thanks for the info, now we need to get to work. Did you bring work clothes?"

"Yes, a new pair of white work pants and a not-so-new but still white T-shirt."

"Good, the changing room is through that door. When you come back, the coffee should be ready. Put on an apron and a paper hat, you'll find them stacked on top of the lockers where you'll put your street clothes. The bathroom is through the changing room."

I weighed out the ingredients for puff-pastry dough while Perry changed. He returned wearing new white denim work pants below the hips, as he had worn his faded blue jeans. I handed him a steaming mug of coffee, took one for myself, and mouthed, pointing, "If you want milk or cream for your coffee, containers are in the walk-in refrigerator over there. If you want sugar, there's a barrel between those floor-stand-mixers, just grab a spoon from the slop sink. Any questions?"

"Yes, this is going to sound stupid, what's the difference between the night shift and the day shift, work-wise?"

I was distracted drinking in how perfectly Perry fit my sexual ideal. "That's not stupid, and asking questions is how to learn. At night, we make breads, rolls, bagels, Danish pastries, coffee cakes, and donuts. We use yeast for leavening. Your home-made cakes and cookies probably used baking-powder, baking-soda, and eggs for leavening, same as our day shift. Does that answer your question?"

"Bedker, I hope you don't take this the wrong way, but the way you look at me makes me feel all tingly. I'm not complaining, I like how it feels, wanted you to know."

"Damn! Sorry, I didn't mean to make you uncomfortable. Truth be told, looking at you makes me feel all tingly too."

"How come?"

"You rev my motor. Sorry if I'm out of order saying that. Please don't take it as sexual harassment. That isn't my intention. Maybe this apprenticeship is not going to work out."

"Don't be sorry, nobody ever stirred me up like this. You make me feel attractive. Why would I complain? I like it."

"I don't want my feelings interfering with you learning the baking trade."

"Promise, I won't let that happen. Don't get mad. You make me hard."

"That's mutual."

"Can I kiss you?"

"That as far as we go?"

"It's a beginning."

We folded into each other's arms and lips for a long, steamy oral examination by probing tongues. Pulling back, Perry coyly asked in his rusty voice, "What would you like to show your new apprentice besides baking?"

He was rascally, and my super ego screamed *You should know better!* My ego said opportunities with an ideal don't happen ever. "I'd love to pull your pants down."

"Oh, you dirty old man."

"I'm not much older than you. But you have the other part right."

"Then I'd love to get dirty with you. Tell me what happens with my pants at half-mast?"

"I want to see if you are wearing underpants under your colorful boxers. If you are, I will chew them off, you. Then I want to see if your butt is as cute as the rest of you."

"Wow, Bedker, we just met … I want to fulfill your wish."

"It gets lonely working at night when everyone is home sleeping. What we are talking about is improbable."

"Just so you know, I'm usually not this slutty. It must be the way you're looking at me."

"You're not slutty, we're just horny exploiting an opportunity. What's wrong with that?"

"Nothing, what's next on your to do-me list?"

"I'd like to bury my face in your ass crack and lick until you demand more depth than my tongue. Have you been there before?"

"Oh, my no, I'm not that kind of guy. Except now I'm wondering how it feels to have you back-seat driving me."

"Hold on, we should stop. I know better … it's wrong having sex at work. I need this job to pay for school."

"Tell you what … let's finish what we started, just this once. Unless I like it."

"What if you *do* like it?"

"Then we negotiate for sex away from work next time. How's that?"

"I am panting in heat, but first we have to mix some dough, so we have something to do after sex."

"No problem, I came here to learn."

I instructed Perry how to safely operate the large bread dough mixer. Then weigh sugar, salt and add yeast for Italian-French bread dough. While he dumped hundred-pound sacks of bread flour into the big mixer, I got the floor-stand-mixers going with batches of Swedish rye, German pumpernickel, stone-ground whole wheat, and salt-free bread dough. Then, when we had all the dough troughs proofing in the steam boxes or under the work bench, and the backdoor latched I said, "We've had time to think about what's going on between us. Want to postpone sex for an appropriate place?"

"No, I want you right now."

"We have about a half hour before the first dough is ready to work. Before you asked me if I knew how to sign dirty words, do you know what this means?"

"Sure, it means you want to fuck me, naughty man. What position do you want me in?"

"Turn around, lean forward, and put your hands on the work bench." Locking eyes in mutual lust, Perry unhitched his belt and pants top button. Then wiggling his hips suggestively, turned and leaned forward. Scooting behind him, I reached around and pulled down his zipper. He was stiff as hard wood inside his fly. I gripped his work pants' center back belt loop with my teeth and yanked down, shaking my head from side to side until the pants puddled around his ankles.I was enjoying a living fantasy, so I took the elastic waistband of his tartan-patterned boxers in my teeth and slowly yanked them down to overlay his puddled new work pants.

Perry was not wearing a second pair of underpants, but he was in possession of a perfectly proportioned, beautifully sculpted butt, supported by strong masculine thighs and legs. My eyes feasted on his perfection as my hands caressed his pliant yet firm Gluteus Maximums. His enticing hairless butt responded to my touch by twitching.

I squatted down, thumbs pried cheeks apart, and ran my nose down his ass crack to a dark, rose-colored, tight pucker. Inhaling his masculine musk made my cock strain for action.

With the door to his pleasure trove before me, I lovingly tongue-tip probed the hidden orifice open. In response, it winked in appreciation, and Perry hummed. To increase his desire, I looped my tongue in circles around the outer muscle ring until its crinkles smoothed out and yawned opened further. I penetrated his anal lips with a rapid staccato tongue. Then fully inside, I gently massaged around the rim with long licks. My probing tongue entered as far as it could reach. Meanwhile Perry's butt was gyrating pushing against my face for a deeper incursion, and his humming turned into vocalizing.

I doubt he was aware of sounding out his increasing ecstasy. The sound of received delight, experienced in real time, is something I like about making it with hearing-impaired guys. The volume level and energy expended is not to everyone's taste, but is mine. I doubt the pleasure recipient would be so wildly uninhibited aurally if they could hear themselves. Without the limitations of words and inhibitions, I received a true accounting of Perry's physical joy. His ecstatic sound track spurred me on to use my complete repertoire of tongue twists, flutters, triple tonguing, buzzing, and lip trills. Suddenly, Perry hit a volume peak, jubilantly vocalizing his need for more than tongue.

I stepped back and removed all Perry's clothes. He was a delicious sight nude. I led him hand in hand over to a short stack of hundred-pound sacks of bread flour. Turning him to face me, we kissed deeply again. Hands on his waist, I lift him up onto the flour sacks, pulled the condom from my wallet, pushed back my front cover and rolled the rubber down after it. I raised Perry's knees to his chest, exposing his spit wet open-hole.

I made sure we had eye contact then spoke. "In a minute, I'm going to ask you to close your eyes. When I tweak your left nipple, take a deep breath and then let it out very slowly. When I tweak your right nipple, open your eyes and look into mine. Ready?"

Perry's face beamed as he nodded yes. I gestured to close his peepers with my hand.

That was my first chance to see Perry's prick close-up. It was extra hard, dickhead reaching well beyond his navel. *Huh, his dick was in four colors, with a prominent dark ring about a quarter of the way down the shaft from his dickhead.* At first, I couldn't figure out the color scheme. Then it occurred to me, the dark brown eighth of an inch-wide ring must be a circumcision scar. Between the scar and his dickhead was lighter than the shaft below the scare. Probably the lighter color was how he looked with his foreskin retracted inside out. The bottom was probably the color of his whole flaccid dick before surgery. His drooling mushroom shaped dickhead was the prettiest pink, the exact color as his tasty lips. All in all, it was an attractive, well-shaped big cock. Definitely worth getting to know better.

I tweaked Perry's left nipple, and as he drew in a long breath, I reach into an open fifty-pound box of vegetable shorting and scooped some. As he released his breath, I pushed my cock slowly into his spit-slick bottom hole. His face showed I was scratching an itch to his satisfaction. Then I reached his prostate and his face showed unanticipated sensual delight. Meanwhile I brought my greased hand down onto his hard as wood, multi-toned dick.

Perry gulped in sensory overload, his rusty speaking voice croaked, "Go slow or I'll shoot."

I felt his muscles clench tight around my cock. I froze, stopping both penetrating cock and gliding hand. Neither of us moved until finally he wiggled his butt and I slid in the rest of the way. Then my lubricated hand slowly became familiar with his contours, pubic bush to dickhead. I stopped again when his aural pleasure volume indicated a building culmination from too much stimulation.

For his first time with me, I wanted exceptional. Hell, I wanted it extraordinary for both of us. We were breaking cardinal rules; this act had to be worth serious consequences. So, I took the time to distract myself from climaxing, zoning out breathing slowly. *Ohm ah hum.* The time allowed me to fully experience being inside him, while viewing Perry's stunning outsides.

Back to the present, after settling myself down, he was ready with a wiggle, I drew out and pushed back in a few short strokes. Still close to climaxing, I tweaked Perry's right nipple. When he opened his eyes, I said, "Show me how you jerk off. Beat your meat for me. I want to know how you take pleasure. But don't cum until I say. Let's watch each other's eyes as we bliss out, okay?" At first his face showed embarrassment at what I asked. Then obviously considering it, he yielded to my purpose.

Without having to think about jacking Perry off, I could focus on pushing my cock in and out of his smooth back channel. It didn't take long before my body took over with intent of its own, fucking with a goal in mind, then I was almost there.

"I'm real close, catch up and cum." Perry's hand became a blur, desire overflowing his eyes. I saw and heard a replication of the elation I was feeling.

Perry's balls moved up, tightened and locked into firing position at the base of his dick. That pushed me over the edge. I reached up and tickled the sole of Perry's bare foot. The tickling caused an involuntary full-body twisting ecstatic response. Another element was added to our rule breaking love making. It propelled me into full-on multicolored starbursts of bliss. Perry's eyes were sparkling on fire. Panting hard, and then shooting cum in the condom, I watched as Perry shot long, arching ribbons of cum from the tip of his pretty dickhead, up past his shoulder.

His first blast was followed quickly by other bucked out cum arches. Then they fell into puddles of thick pearl-colored man cream, pooling on his hard-breathing body. We were so well synchronized it looked like I was shooting my cum out of his cock. Our eyes still locked until we topped our ecstasy with kisses. We held each other tight, kissing, glued together with his abundant man juice. I momentarily zoned out in what felt like timeless peace, fastened together.

Oblivious at first, then incrementally aware of insistent knocking on the back door, my sudden, startled facial reaction caused Perry alarm. We quickly moved apart.

"Someone is at the back door." Pointing, I indicated his clothes lying around, and then the changing room. I rolled off and tossed the overfull condom into a trash barrel, pulled up my briefs and white pants, found my T-shirt on a pile of supplies, grabbed my apron and wiped my hands. Out of the corner of my eye I watched naked Perry scurrying to scoop up his clothes and dashing to the changing room, remembering the joy of what we just shared bubbled up. Then it was doused with guilt.

Yanking my T-shirt on over Perry's squished sperm, I quickly jogged to the back door tying my apron. Standing on the other side of the latched screen door was Officer Vasquez, about to strike the door with his baton. "Don't break the door, Hector. The donuts won't be ready for hours I haven't even mixed the dough."

Smiling broadly, the cop said, "Bedker, I know what time the donuts are ready for me. We found a guy lurking in the shadows. I almost gave him a good beating for not doing as told. Lucky for him my partner figured out he might be deaf, you know, from that school over on Evergreen Avenue."

"And now you want to beat up this screen door instead?"

"Where were you? You don't usually lock this door."

"I do when I'm in the can."

"After we cuffed this guy, I found a paper in his pocket with the bakery's name and address."

"I'll get my jacket."

"No, that's okay I can see your T-shirt is all sweaty from working hard. I'll have my partner bring him, out of the car." Officer Vasquez turned and shouted. "Yo, Chance, bring that perp up here!"

Officer Chance brought Rupert Gladdules, hands cuffed behind his back, up the steps and in the back door. Rupert had dropped his tough-guy attitude and looked like a frightened little boy in a big, burly body.

I faced Rupert and spoke slowly. "You ready to work, or want to go with these policemen?" Rupert looked sheepish and indicated with a head nod the bakery.

I apologized to the cops for the trouble. They removed their handcuffs and gave Rupert a stern lecture about loitering at night. I'm sure he couldn't lip read the fast-paced lecture. But I saw he understood when they acted out not wanting to shoot him by mistake. The cops said they'd be back when the donuts were ready and left.

I signed to Rupert, "*Can you work with me?*"

He reluctantly nodded "yes."

Signing again, "*Did you bring work clothes?*"

He flew out the back door and returned right away with a plastic grocery bag containing new white work clothes.

As Rupert came back with his clothes, I became aware of Perry watching us from the other side of the workbench. God, he was handsome fully-clothed with his face washed and hair combed. Maybe it was my imagination, but he looked radiant, glowing.

"Okay men, I wasn't told to expect you tonight. I'm sorry if we got off on the wrong foot. Since you are here you might as well get paid. If you come back tomorrow, I'll be better organized to explain things. Perry, please show Rupert the changing room and bathroom. Then we need to get this dough up onto the bench and get working."

When Perry returned, I indicated he should help me roll the heavy metal dough trough out from under the bench. "Is Rupert okay?"

"I don't know, we are not friends at school. He calls me queeny queer and seems to hate everyone."

"Can you work with him?"

"I'll try my best. Before he comes back … I can't do for you what you just did with me. I'm a confirmed bottom."

"I don't expect reciprocation. I've heard rimming is an acquired taste, usually acquired later in life. I like *you*, however, whatever."

"I like kissing you a lot and what just happened was amazing."

"Right now, we need to cool it."

"Just so you know, you took my ass painlessly. I heard it was supposed to hurt the first time."

After a moment to sort my thoughts, I spoke, keeping an eye on the changing room door. "I need to apologize for having sex at work, I know better and shouldn't have!"

"Don't say sorry, I wanted it as much as you did. It was a magical moment, don't ruin it."

"I feel guilty as hell, misusing my position and messing up our working together."

"It was good I wanted it, stop whining and just be the boss."

"If you're sure."

"Yes, now show me how to get on the day shift."

"I promise never to cross that line again."

"Shut up, we both wanted it. I can't imagine a better first time in back. How's about change your promise to we never do it here again? Because I liked it and want more of you."

I grabbed and kissed him, one eye open on the changing room.

Pulling back, Perry said, "But for the future, I want more than a quickie. Now that we know how good it can be, let's make it that good or better every time?"

"Setting goals with you, works for me. What do we do about Rupert? Tell him or not, he'll figure it out."

"As far as Rupert goes… I don't know? I mind my own business at school. Given half a chance, I'm willing to help him to learn this work."

"Thanks, time is wasting. Let's get to this dough."

"Do you want me to sign with Rupert, he owes you an apology?"

"No, thanks, appreciate the offer though."

"Anyway, I can help, let me. Okay, boss?"

"Let's wrestle this big dough you mixed with warm water up onto the bench."

"One more thing, could we meet before or after work to have some personal time? In case I wasn't obvious, you make me feel special. I liked that."

"Let's compare school schedules, but not this minute. Here comes Rupert."

Rupert, dressed in his new bright whites, under a fresh white apron, wearing a white paper hat, looked hangdog. But without being asked, he reached down, pitched in and helped pull the heavy bread dough up onto the bench. Working alone I would have had to cut that big a dough into pieces to lift it out.

* * * *

The two new baker's helpers came to work on time and ready to work the second night. I took the time to give them a proper introduction to baking, complete with handouts and homework on basics. Then I followed up with details on what we did in a rush the night before. They worked diligently, scaling dough by weight and turning it into loafs of bead. And they followed my directions, attempting to keep up following my rule: strive for quality first, and then speed it up.

Perry learned fast, he was motivated. Without being asked, he helped Rupert, a slow learner, to try and keep up. I acknowledged both their efforts in different ways. As a joint reward, I taught them to make fancy dinner and sandwich rolls, and then bagels. They liked making the tiny loafs, knots, twists, braids, and different flavor bagels. Their faces showed frustration trying to make Kaiser-rolls, which required hard-earned hand-heel Karate-like skills, fast. Like the six-braid challah bread, good-looking Kaiser rolls demanded years of practice.

When we had filled long racks with bread and rolls, the new helpers pushed them into garage-size steam-heated proof boxes. With that done, we worked together mixing smaller batches of specialty breads. I gave the new men a rest break while I mixed Danish dough. Then I showed them how to mix the cops' favorite, donut dough.

As we worked, I showed the new men how to regularly check the proof boxes and ovens, load and unload them, and boil the bagels with lye before baking. I could have done the work faster and better on my own, but not the quantity and it was rewarding to see the newbies trying hard and starting to achieve marketable skills.

Other than giving instructions or praise, there was little conversation between the three of us pushing out the work. They were concentrating on gaining new hand-eye coordination and I was busy making their work look saleable. It's hard to sign when your hands are busy with yeast dough. I crossed a line the first night with Perry. It should never have happened, and I can only attribute the character lapse to being over extended and not getting enough sleep. Still and all from my moral failing, Perry and I discovered something unique in each other, something worth cultivating outside the workplace and its power imbalance.

As the weeks turned into months, both apprentices settled into mastering baking techniques rooted in the Middle Ages and before. Rupert often slipped into an angry mood, which when possible I ignored to get the work done. Acknowledging his bad mood or ignoring it got the same result, hostility. After his encounter with the police the first night, he found ways to separate his animosity toward me from learning the trade. Rupert seldom smiled, and Perry's easy smiles lit up the bakeshop. The two were a study in contrast. I contented myself with the cliché about half a loaf.

Not having sex with Perry helped me understand the word for what was happening to me. I was in love with him. I'd briefly been in love before and it could be very disrupting for my schoolwork. Perry's fawning looks, when Rupert was in the john or otherwise out of sight, showed he shared my feeling. And yet he'd stand up to me, even challenge me when we'd go out for a meal on our days off. I'd met my match. It was scary, I crossed an ethical line, and any way you sliced it, that was wrong, especially as foreman. To be in love with someone I saw every work day and not get physical was punishment. No mistake it was real, we were in love because I screwed-up.

At our next housekeeping meeting, instead of reading or snoozing, I took my turn and spoke to my dorm suitemates. "Would you guys have a problem if my friend Perry spent time in my room, like your girlfriends do yours?" Surprise, surprise, nobody objected. If anything, they were encouraging. My suitemates showed me respect I had been too guarded or exhausted to see before. Perry and I made time to physically act on our emotions, in my dorm room, as our school schedules allowed. We kept to his rule; sex must always be loving fun, and not be rushed.

Several months into the new bakers' apprenticeship, Rupert and I were half-way through working a much larger than usual Danish dough. Perry was busy unloading and reloading the ovens and proof boxes as we sent him a steady stream of racks full of miniature Danish pastries.

I could feel something brewing before Rupert abruptly stopped working, made fierce eye contact, and angrily signed, *"You are a bad foreman! You favor Perry over me, it's not fair! You say you want us to learn, and then put Perry above of me."*

Keeping my cool, I signed back, *"I care you both learn this trade correctly. There are more than enough half-assed, sloppy bakers in this business I refuse to add more. For your information, you both get the best instruction I know."*

"No, you favor him because he is white, admit it Mr. Injun-man, you kneel to the white man!"

I watched him for a second, trying to decide what I wanted to do, then signed with authority, *"I am the night boss. You don't have to like me, but if you want to learn this work, you will show me the respect I'm due."* I'd had enough of his drivel.

He adjusted his body's stance to slightly less aggressive, and eye contact softened a bit. His face went to scolded little boy pout.

"It is not part of your job to decide if I'm a good foreman or not. You are here to learn this trade. If you have a problem with me, you can leave and write a letter of complaint." Then for dramatic emphases, I pointed to the back door and scribbled an imaginary letter in air.

My guess was Rupert thought he could bully me, and I'd get defensive and give him whatever he wanted. He was not expecting what he got instead. Trying to save face, he signed, *"I don't mean you're always a bad foreman. But you let Perry work the ovens and mixers more than me and that is not right!"*

I stared at him, deciding not to respond, then changed my mind. *"You know what happens when someone bends over backward? They lose their balance. From the start, you showed me and my people ill intent. Despite that I have bent over backward to be fair teaching you my trade. If you think you can get better training elsewhere, do it."*

"Wait, no, most the time you try to be fair. It's not your fault you were born Injun-Joe, no offense."

I took a slow, calming breath, *ohm ah hum,* and went back to rolling out Danish dough. We had a huge special order for fussy miniature pastries for somebody's party or conference or whatever. After a few moments working, I could see I'd struck a nerve. His face usually didn't look that defeated. So, I signed, *"Not that it's any of your business, but Perry will be leaving us soon to work days. He brought photos of cakes and cookies he decorated at home and the day-shift foreman saw them. Now they want Perry to work days. But first he needs to improve his oven and mixing skills with us at night."*

Rupert signed sarcastically, *"Why do you suppose they want him instead of me?"*

I put down my rolling pin and glared at him. Why was I wasting my time with this jerk? I signed back, *"Bring photos of your fancy home baking and show them off?"*

"I don't do home baking. My folks buy bake goods wholesale for the diner, so what?"

"I've taught you what and why. We have wide latitude proofing and ovens at night. Working with yeast is more forgiving than cake baking. On the day shift between done and ruined is a fraction of our time, what they mix is more complicated and persnickety than what we do. By now you should know these things instead of collecting imaginary slights. Come on, get busy, this work order won't do itself."

It was clear from Rupert's face he'd worked himself up with righteous indignation to accuse me of favoritism. He hadn't expected a counterattack and had no plan when challenged.Rupert was quietly stewing as he worked his dough into sloppy, misshapen little treats more appropriate for Halloween.

Just before going back to rolling out my dough I signed, *"I could let you do more oven and mixing after Perry leaves, but then you won't develop the necessary handwork quality and speed necessary to be a first-rate bread baker. The amount your future employer pays will depend on the quality and speed of your work. Look at your Danish and then here at mine, which would you put in your mouth after they are baked? I know you can do better, I've seen it when you apply yourself."*

Out of habit accepting correction, Rupert signed, *"Whatever you say, boss, you're the big chief."* Working without communicating, the quality of his work improved. Then he signed, *"I have been wondering why you aren't an iron worker. I thought all you Injuns were iron workers. That's why I was so surprised to see you here the first night."*

He was stalling the work and I didn't like where this conversation was headed. I was thinking to shut him down by saying 'Native Americans can do anything anyone else can. Only we do it better.' Then it occurred to me, Rupert and I hadn't really had a conversation other than about baking in the months we worked together. I knew a better man than me would have tiptoed around his fragile ego's intolerance and tried trivial talking to open his closed mind. Usually I was too tired, but today I took an extra deep breath and signed, *"It is true most iron workers are Original American, but most Original Americans are not iron workers. Why do you care?"*

Smirking, he signed, *"Iron workers make lots of money. You're smart. Why are you working in a bakery for less dough?*

"Watch my lips, I'll speak slowly, I need my hands to hurry and get this order filled. We are behind, get busy."

"Okay, boss, you're heap big chief in here."

"Construction is seasonal work, and there's no work in bad weather; no work, no pay. Walking on steel girders high in the sky is day work. I need night work to pay for school. That answer your question?"

Signing slower for emphases, Rupert indicated, *"Yes, now I know."*

Realizing what it might mean, I signed to be sure. *"Are you thinking about quitting baking?"* Then I got busy with Danish dough.

"Maybe, yeah maybe I'm thinking about it."

"Does your school offer trades that interest you?"

"They do, but all their programs are aimed at whites, not for us others."

"Sounds like a reoccurring theme, could your attitude be part of the problem?"

He seemed to bristle then he signed. *"Definitely not, but lately I've been wondering if I really want to be a baker."*

"What's wrong with baking? Is it because Perry is doing most of our mixing and oven work?"

Looking down, maybe thinking … then up making penetrating eye contact he signed, *"I've seen how you and Perry look at each other, goo-goo eyes, when you think you're alone. I want that too, only with a woman. How can I find a wife working nights with fags?"* His face showed what he thought of fags, but his question seemed sincere.

Keeping my feelings in check, I signed back, *"Beats me, most bakers I've worked with have wives and kids. I'll ask for you."* Then I signed, *"Native-American People advice, 'follow the path your heart leads. Life is too short to waste it doing what you dislike with people you hate.'"*

Holding eye contact, I could see him soften as he signed, *"I wouldn't have believed you thought like that before now."*

I mouthed, "Come on get busy, these Danish won't even need to see the proof box the way we're going."

"You people let the white man destroy your culture, steal your land, and you still kiss his ass."

When I didn't respond further we worked in silence. My hands were going as fast as they could to get the order finished before the dough was over proofed, ruined.

Then for no reason his mood flared-up and Rupert angrily signed, *"You say you try to be fair, you are not! Never have you once mention cochlear implants, that means approve."*

"Of what?"

"It's important enough to start fistfights at my school. Here, look at my knuckles."

"And that is my business, why? Okay wait, what am I supposed to think about cochlear implants Rupert?"

Chewing his lips still in upset mode, he signed, *"Implants are a political plot to destroy deaf culture, just like the white man did yours. What is done against one of us is done against all of us."*

"Sorry, I don't understand how hearing Original Peoples are involved."

"The government wants us to think we are inferior, like your people are inferior and must live out on reservations."

"I thought that was how you felt."

"It is, but this is different. It's like my boxing coach once said, "The illusion of permanence is impermanence.'"

"I still don't understand what I cochlear implants have to do with me or mine? The First People had *no* choice being invaded and then systematically destroyed with betrayal genocides."

"Choice … where's the choice? Being deaf is a way of life too. Stupid ear-trumpets, electric-hearing aids, and here we go again with cochlear implants, the illusions of permanence. It is the latest attack on our culture, and we know how well your people did with the Great White Father."

"Think General Custer would agree?"

I was aware Perry's family had pressured him to get implants he didn't want. It was political for him too. His family made it an ultimatum to move back home, along with heterosexual conversion therapy. He chose to live at school instead.

With nothing to offer Rupert, I filled the space with blather. "I read many disabled people believe their handicap makes them superior to the able-bodied. That seems fair."

He exploded at my words. *"Deaf people are not handicapped. We are just different than and better!"*

"Uh huh, so that is what's bothering you."

He stood still, staring daggers at me. *"You don't get it … but you are not my problem! You don't get to tell me to leave and write a letter. I quit this stupid job right here, right now. Fuck you and fuck all your kind!"*

Rupert caught me by surprise quitting like that. Did he expect me to say, "Don't go, we need you here?" Attempting a neutral façade, I signed, *"Guess this hasn't been a good fit for you. Maybe you can do better."*

Menacingly shifting to a fighter's stance, Rupert signed, *"Before I go, I've been wondering about something. Most people are afraid of me. I see it on their faces when I walk in a room. You don't show me fear, why is that? I'm bigger and stronger than you. Do you really think you could take me in a fight? Your swishy boyfriend couldn't help you, he doesn't fight."*

I couldn't decide what to say, so I remained quiet in the threatening space he created. But I sped up my own bench work before the dough was ruined.

Rupert acted like he hadn't just challenged me and dismissed my stoic demeanor with *"Typical apathetic man-squaw coward."* He removed his apron and hat throwing them on the workbench, showing disgust on his face.

I gave a half wave to draw his attention. "Watch my lips. Have you wondered why the tool I've taught you and Perry to use is the bench scraper, and I use this large baker's French knife?"

"No, not before you just mentioned it. But don't think it will protect you from me if I lose control. Think again, you'll beg me not to snap your back in half like a dry twig if I have a mind to."

"Knife skills are a source of pride for my tribe. For example, if I felt threatened, I could easily filet you before you realized all your guts were on the floor. The human body bleeds out fast too, if you know where to stick it."

"You think so?"

"The human anatomy class I took at the university supported what I was taught as a young child about arterial leakage caused by knife point punctures."

Rupert's face suddenly registered I knew what I was talking about and took in the size of my knife. Vulnerability flitted across his face. I'd not seen that in him before. Obviously, few had backed down. He needed practice.

"And the police all love you. I learned that the first night."

"The police love free donuts. I fight my own battles. Put your apron and hat back on and finish this order and then leave with a full day's pay. Go now and I'll dock you the week."

That worked, and he began working again. Rupert meekly changed the subject. *"You seem to like baking more than just as a job. How come?"*

"What career are you thinking about next, now that you burned this bridge to baking by quitting without notice and threatening me?"

"Long haul trucking. They make over $100,000 a year."

"Do you have a CDL license?"

"No and getting one is expensive. Aren't you going to squash my dream because I'm hearing impaired? Disabled, handicapped, pathetic you said."

"Why would I? Statistics show hard of hearing drivers are the safest on the road. I never said pathetic."

"What is wrong with you? I insult you, I threaten you, and you show me inscrutable Injun nothing. Do you need vitamins?"

"Speaking of pills, at my school I've overheard students say, 'So and so is always moody,' or 'So and so is always looking for a fight.' I'll bet those moody folks could feel better with medication."

"Yeah, yeah, I've heard all that before, it is malarkey. I'm not crazy, so don't even think to go there."

"When you walk into a room, wouldn't you rather people were happy to see you than show fear?"

"No, I like fear, power!"

"Call *me* crazy … you know what … I have a cousin just like you. And my cousin might have what you need?"

"What, pills?"

"He runs a trucking company."

"Why would you want to help me after I almost stiffed you on this work and threatened to break you in half?"

"I'm not quite ready to give up on you, Rupert."

"WHY?"

"I'm not sure, why. Hum, well, you never said something to my face and then the opposite behind my back. I'd know if you did."

"I'm not two-faced."

"My cousin is always complaining he needs drivers. He starts them off loading and unloading trucks at minimum wage and if they show up on time and work hard, he provides their CDL training. After he gets to know them. But he's not easy to get along with, like you."

"I still don't get it. I've been a bastard, why would you want to help me? What's the catch?"

"My cousin needs truck drivers and truck driving is what you want to try. He's a big guy and competes in mixed martial art octagons. Let me warn you; the first anti-Native-American slur out of your mouth and you kill your truck driving dream and end up in the hospital."

"Shit, you are serious!"

"Here, take his business card and say I gave it to you."

Rupert's faced showed I'd confused him. *"I'm not used to this … kind treatment."*

"Don't screw it up."

* * * *

"Okay the Danish order is finished. Before I go see your cousin, I'd like to know your attraction to baking. I never found one."

I grew up working in family bakeries. My learning the trade as a kid brought praise from adults who loved me. His question in the context of quitting the training and threat seemed spurious. I didn't feel a need to answer, and so prepared to start working the donut dough.

Frustrated by my silence, Rupert signed, *"That's okay. I was just wondering?"*

Keeping my hands busy working, I refused to play his game, whatever it was. He would soon be gone and good riddance.

"Perry says you come from a family of bakers and that's why you know so much at your age."

Why won't he leave? Okay fine, I'll talk to get him out of here. "It's what my extended family does to earn a living. But they expect me to graduate college and have a better, easier life than theirs."

Rupert re-removed his apron and cap again then signed, *"Oh, I see, you did hear my question."*

"I didn't answer your question, only gave background. Since you seem to care, when I come here at night, everything is spotlessly clean. The stainless-steel equipment gleams, this butcher block topped workbench is scrubbed so hygienic you could eat off it, and all these big metal racks are empty, waiting.

"When I leave after making a lot of noise, this place is a mess, everything in sight is dirtied with flour dust, sticky bits of different kinds of dough scraps, and all the equipment needs a good scrubbing. But these racks are full of good things to eat, made by my hand for people to take to their homes and nourish their families. That is why I love this work and will miss the flurry of activity and the loud mixing machines, and tantalizing smells after I graduate to wear a suit and tie in an office."

Obviously understanding, Rupert mouthed, "Ah ha, now I see why you are not an iron worker."

"Why do you hate Native Americans so much?"

"It's not personal, I learned the true facts from my grandparents and parents. You people are all drunken, drug addict, good for nothings, and kidnap other people's babies to rise as your own."

"Why would we kidnap babies to rise? They're expensive to bring up and ours are better behaved"

"To improve your race of course. You're a fag you are supposed to know these things."

"Really, and you believe that makes sense?"

"Why didn't we have this conversation before today?"

"You tell me. Indigenous peoples were doing just fine all over the world before Europeans discovered them. What's really your problem with Original Americans?"

"You've been honest with me, I'll tell you ... I must check the OTHER box for race on official forms. Everyone else gets their own box, even your people, but not me."

"I don't understand?"

"I'm Greek, OTHER means unnecessary, doesn't count. When the world was full of cavemen, we Greeks produced philosophy, science, math, music, poetry, sports, and drama. Our race is not other, we are SUPERIOR to everyone."

"Huh, I thought you were Caucasian. You act toward me like a typical bigoted white man."

"All my life I've been told I'm not white because Hannibal brought elephants over the Alps, and Gangues' Asian hordes swept through Europe, and my people's ancient Syracuse hired black African mercenaries instead of having their own army. That's the official reason given me in school. Why I must check the OTHER box for race. It's not fair!"

"Where did you grow up?"

"Ohio, so what?"

"The Midwest has a reputation for being as racist as the Deep South but with boring food."

"What's your point?"

"I'd bet they expect the same from French, Italian, and Spanish nationalities, except I can't imagine any of my classmates checking the box as other. Look, you can check whatever box you want, it is not pass fail. The last time I checked, this is still a free country if you are a rich Republican."

"It was explained from elementary school on; I'm OTHER. What you say doesn't count, you are against Republicans."

"On most forms, you can leave race blank, and they'll still take your money."

"How do I know that's not fake information?"

"Check it out online. My people only require a tiny percentage of native blood to get free parking at our casinos. If you look you'll see, all known races of man show up for free parking claiming to be part Native-American, for free parking.Have your DNA checked, you might qualify.

"That's different."

"One of my dorm suite mates is from Sicily, that's modern-day Syracuse. He is darker than you, says he's white, and the law of the land doesn't dispute him."

"I don't believe in those laws. They say we must serve anyone who comes in the diner. But if we don't like their looks, I promise you, they will never come back for bad, overcharged, cold food on dirty dishes with rude service."

"That makes you feel proud?"

"Now, I suppose you are going to try and confuse me with fake facts again. My race is OTHER, don't like it, but that's the way it is."

"Fine, you are now done at this bakery, I'll let your school know. Call my cousin. He'll give you a chance like I did, whatever your race. Now, get out of here and good luck to you."

* * * *

After four months of concentrated hard work learning to be an all-around bread baker, Perry went to work on the day shift. It was what he wanted. And from the start he showed promise to become a first-class cake decorator.

With the change in work schedule came relief from the constant temptation to steal a kiss.With Perry on the day shift and me working nights, logistics got complicated. We were both working full-time and going to school and couldn't keep our hands or minds off each other. Blessedly, we had Sundays for us, and laundry. After laundry, we spent the rest of the day frisky in bed.

Without knowing exactly when or how, Perry and I went from honeymoon to relationship building. We started replacing some sex with sleeping exhausted in each other's arms. But the quality of less sex got better. As passions deepened, we bared our souls more.

My graduation was coming at the end of the spring semester. I was already grieving giving up baking for more lucrative corporate business-suit-and-tie work, when school was over. Perry held me tight when I shared trepidations about my impending work-life change to the corporate treadmill.

In return I worked extra hard to snap Perry out of what was his reoccurring depressions. I told jokes, tickled, or just held him tight till his sadness lifted or he fell asleep. At first, he wouldn't talk about the cause. Then slowly, he exposed an open wound from his earliest awareness of his body.

It seems right after Perry was born, while his mother was barely conscious from anesthesia, a nurse placed a pen in her hand and guided her to sign a consent card. When his parents took Perry home from the hospital, they were shocked to discover he'd been circumcised without their conscious approval. They sued the hospital, then after a long-drawn-out fight won a large settlement. After that experience, his parents went to extreme lengths to keep his younger brothers' natural.

With family, friends, even strangers, Perry's parents talked insistently about being tricked after he was born and being expected to pay for unwanted surgery. And then how much money they made suing the doctor and hospital. His parents seemed obsessed with what happened to him and felt it was a community service to tell anyone who would listen.

When as a young teenager Perry vehemently demanded his parents stop talking about his penis, their response was, "Would you rather everyone knows you're queer and can never give us grandchildren?" The result was, Perry didn't feel good about his body.

One Sunday afternoon I was zoned out, *ohm ah hum,* and Perry experimented rimming me. He found he liked uncovering then opening the mystique of it. Naturally, I liked what his tongue was doing and where. As expected after a thorough smoothing-open rimming, we both needed him to fuck me, which he did magnificently. I remained silent except for a few involuntary utterances, until Perry's screwing shifted into high gear and my hand got busy. When I heard and felt him reach his pinnacle and then hit it hard. I followed a few heart beats later, bellowing my happiness being with him. It was a spectacular full voice ecstatic duet. I was overjoyed at expanding our sexual repertoire, and then Perry got more depressed than usual. So, I spent the rest of the day stroking and cuddling him till his depression lifted.

My dorm suite mates didn't complain to me about our noisy love making, or Perry being around more than we planned. I'm sure the fact he brought them fancy cookies and cupcakes, decorated with their names, had nothing to do with his acceptance. Truth be told, he was a sweet, likeable guy, a keeper. And I thought everyone agreed.

At the end of the fall semester I was disturbed to get a letter from the dorm council suggesting it was time for me *and my noisy friend* to move off campus. I knew a threat when I saw one. My initial reaction was to fight, but first I looked over the list of approved off-campus student housing that accompanied the letter. At semester's end, there were many newly vacant apartments available. As it turned out, most approved off campus private housing cost less than my monthly dorm fees. *Who knew?*

Perry and I found a large, light, airy one-bedroom apartment priced less than we budgeted. It was located a short level-grade bicycle ride to the bakery or Perry's school or my university. We signed the lease together and had the utilities turned on. We should have been happy. I was, and he got depressed until I tickled him silly.

Following great sex the first Sunday consecrating our new home, Perry got depressed again, from topping me. After gentle prolong coaxing, he finally said, "Just now, when I saw my dick slide out of your bum, depression wiped-over me. When you screw me I feel happy. And when I reciprocate, like just now, it makes me sad, crazy no?"

"But it is progress that you can reciprocate, after thinking you couldn't."

"Not if it makes me feel this bad after."

Like most guys with dicks and the butchest guys I know, female to male transsexuals who don't always have their dicks with them. Little thought is given to the have, have-not foreskin status of others. Except Perry gave it altogether too much thought. He again traced his self-deprecation, to his family's obsession; winning a lot of money while being affronted by his penis. Through no fault of his own, Perry's body disappointed his parents and then him for disappointing them. He said it wasn't about me, but when you love someone, one way or another their problem *is* your problem.

I went on-line, not sure what I was looking for. But I needed help to snap Perry out of his reoccurring deepening depressions. I'd run out of tactics. Maybe I could find a skin bleaching cream to remove his penis scare, and that would make him feel better. I was hitting zeros or iffy surgical measures with listed side effects. Then I found NORM, National Organization of Restoring Men.

From their website, I learned a guy named Wayne Griffiths founded the group way back in 1970, when he was twenty-five years old. Wayne discovered his penis was losing sensitivity. So, with medical advice, he designed and built a means to manually stretch the remnants of his foreskin using small weights. He patterned his device after standard of care for burn victims to grow skin for grafting.

"Hey, Perry, look at this. They have before and after cock photos on-line."

"You dirty, horny man, we just had sex! Let me see ... but I don't have any loose skin to stretch."

"You have a few folds when you're flaccid ... these. Want to give it a shot?"

"I don't know it looks like a lot of trouble."

"Will you feel better if we try?"

"You going to help?"

"Of course, I found the website. But on the condition you finally try one of those depression medications."

"Only because I love you."

The long and the short of it is we joined NORM. With NORM's guidance, we're growing Perry a new foreskin by patiently stretching. Perry has become less prone to bouts of heavy depression since his anti-depressants kicked in, and less self-conscience about his dick the more growth we see of his new prepuce. It makes me happy, seeing my man happy.

Lately riding my bike back and forth to school or work, I've been thinking, *if being a corporate flunkey to have an easier life doesn't make me happy. Perry and I could open our own bike shop.* Did I just think bike shop? I meant open our own BAKE SHOP, but a bike shop is an option too.

Halloween

Jeremy Long's first job after college was as a numbers cruncher for a large insurance company. Their practice was to move new people around from working group to group until they found compatibility. Once a year, the company rewarded its most productive workgroup with a paid play-day-away. A country auction was the unanimous choice of the mostly middle-aged women in Jeremy's temporary group.

When he asked permission to skip the trip, his matronly supervisor sternly said, "Attendance is mandatory."

Twenty-two-year-old, painfully shy Jeremy Long didn't want to go on the outing. Being new, his argument was he hadn't earned the reward, so, should stay in the office to learn the work. But he was too meek to argue. At five feet, eleven inches and slender 157 pounds, his big East-Asian, dark brown eyes made him look like a gangly teenage geek instead of a recently minted university graduate possessing the highest honors in actuarial science.

After a long drive away from the city, the group was given a brief agricultural tour of the rural countryside and then fed lunch at a farmhouse. The food was grown on that farm and the guests were encouraged to eat their fill. Jeremy picked at a few vegetables while his co-workers enthusiastically shoveled down hardy farmhand food.

The work group was then taken to a nearby county auction center. While his colleagues perused the bric-a-brac to be auctioned as collectable art and antiques, Jeremy explored the center. The auction rooms had: art and antiques, estate sales, business bankruptcies, and unpaid tax confiscations. Since tax- confiscated properties had the fewest people, Jeremy took a chair in the empty back row. His plan was to avoid his workgroup's constant mothering. Before realizing the purpose, a full-bodied woman bustled over and handed him a catalogue of the properties and a numbered bidding paddle. "Good luck," she said and scurried away. He pondered, *What is it about me that attract maternal interest from older woman? It's as if I'm a magnet attracting them.*

Perusing the pamphlet, one listed property caught his eye. It was an isolated mountain top parcel of forty-three acres, listed with a grainy black and white aerial photograph. The lengthy caption read, "Magnificent views in all directions, half the land is above the timber line and the rest contains many productive fruit and nut trees." He couldn't take his eyes off the photo, imagining the sights from that vantage point. The brochure went on to say, "There is a private unpaved road, not accessible during inclement weather without all wheel or 4x4 drives. The property includes a small ranch-style house, three out buildings, and two springs that feed a large fishing pond. It has a good well with modern electric pump, recently rebuilt septic system, updated to code electrical service, and a colorful history, sold as is all sales final."

The very tiny print at the bottom of the page reported, "From the early days of the country, the property was owned by moonshiners, and was the scene of a gunfight in 1856 in which nine people were killed. Much later, a Mormon polygamist owned this property until sent to prison when it was discovered many of his wives were his underage siblings and daughters. After years vacant, a marijuana farmer bought the property but was arrested and sent to prison during a bumper-crop harvest. The last owner, an anti-government-tax white supremacist, abandoned the property after three years, reason unknown, and whereabouts unknown."

Taxes owed seemed low, but Jeremy dismissed the last sentence as a joke. "It is rumored the property is haunted."

After four consecutive sales concluded, Jeremy raised his paddle when the haunted property came on the block. He hadn't planned to seriously bid, only to have a little fun. His intention was to play, then stop when bidding got serious. He had watched the other sales and felt he knew how the auction worked. He thought, *There is no way I could own such a place, between how little the insurance company pays, my student loan debt, and high apartment rent. I must watch every penny.*

When his bid paddle went up, it was acknowledged by the auctioneer and all eyes in the room turned to Jeremy. Blushing deeply, suddenly sweating, he was frozen with his paddle raised. His shyness always made him feel ashamed that he showed the world his social ineptness. His shame was intensified by the other auction goers openly gawking at him, the only minority person in the all-male audience.

Shouting gibberish, the auctioneer tried to get the bidding going. But there was no interest in the property. Before he realized what happened, Jeremy Long had bought the parcel. The auctioneer slammed down his gavel and shouted, "Sold to the foreign looking gentleman in the back. Now let's hope there is more interest in the next parcel, #245397."

Jeremy had purchased the property for the knockdown bid of $1,590.30, three years' tax arrears. He was still flabbergasted when the woman who gave him the bidding paddle darted back into the room and into the next chair. "Sir, are you paying with cash or certified check?"

Unprepared, Jeremy timidly asked, "Credit card?"

"A credit card will have to do since nobody wants this property." Jeremy was still bewildered as the paper-work was completed. Before leaving, the clerk asked in all seriousness, "Young man, you do know this property is haunted, don't you?"

Caught off-guard, Jeremy's mouth spoke disconnected from his brain. "It's all right, Ghosts don't believe in me, and I don't believe in them. We've never had a problem."

The clerk gave him a long look that plainly expressed, *You foolish boy*, and she scurried away.

Jeremy sat back and thought *What am I going to do? My credit card is now maxed out and I am barely making expenses before this purchase.*

* * * *

At Jeremy Long's six-month provisional job performance review, his HR manager, Mr. Harry Tucker, stated austerely, "I've received supervisor evaluations from each work group you were assigned as a temp. Shall I call you Mr. Long or Jeremy?"

Jeremy became wary and gathered himself to face bad news. "I prefer Jeremy, if that is all right with you."

"To be blunt, Mr. Long, all your supervisors checked the boxes 'Not a Team Player' and 'Do Not Retain.'"

"Actuarial science is not a team sport. Most of the work is done alone and the group meetings are only to discuss and compare results. Is it because I'm low key? That's discrimination if it is," Jeremy retorted vehemently, surprising himself.

Suddenly cautious, Mr. Tucker said, "Oh no. The insurance company only discriminates against people without insurance, ha, ha, ha, ho."

"Do I have recourse?"

"No such luck, Mr. Long. Our policy is 'last hired first fired'. So, you're done working in this office."

Shocked speechless, Jeremy glared at the man's insensitivity.

Recovering his aplomb, Mr. Tucker said, "Just kidding, it seems First Vice President Galahad liked your data base management skills and *looks*. Rumor has it he's a bit of a rice-queen, so, he instructed me to offer you a work-from-home consultant position."

"What's that?"

"If you accept, each work day you will clock in via computer. Then download the day's work and upload it back when finished. Are you interested?"

Not sure what to think, Jeremy asked, "Or I'm fired?"

"I could tell you were a smart fellow from your school transcript, not from these supervisory evaluations."

On guard, cautious, Jeremy asked, "Same pay and benefits?"

"You'll receive thirty-five percent less pay and no benefits. At least you won't have to adhere to the office dress code, half hour lunch, or commute. You could work in your underwear if you like."

"I want my regular salary and benefits."

"You are a tough negotiator, Mr. Long. Since I offended you with my little jokes, I'm authorized to go up to 85 percent of your current wage, but there are never benefits for consultants. You become a per diem independent contractor and can buy into our health insurance and retirement programs at a reduced rate for eighteen months.I'm afraid that's it, take it or leave it at 85 percent current wages."

"Take it or leave it?" Jeremy brooded over not having choices. Finally resigned, he quietly said, "I'll have to take it. But I'll need a few weeks to prepare a new place since I won't be able to keep my apartment on a reduced salary."

Tucker's façade slipped and he portentously said, "Listen kid, you are a smart young man, don't take this work from home job."

"Why not?"

"Working alone from home you can't develop the people skills you are clearly lacking according to these performance reviews."

"I'm a little bashful, that's all." Jeremy noticed Mr. Tucker gave him the same look the clerk at the auction had; *foolish boy*. "I have bills, I need a job. It'll take a couple of weeks to move and be ready."

"Too bad, you're a nice-looking kid. Let's see, with your accrued three vacation days and one sick day, let's call the difference your consultant's sign-on bonus. You can take a month with current pay to get ready, and then you're on your own."

After the shock of threatened termination dissipated, Jeremy arranged for the insurance company to install its dedicated telephone line, computer equipment, and backup electric generator in the mountain- top house he'd purchased inadvertently at auction. That meant he had to go see the place to direct installation. He had put off visiting the property for fear of ruining his fantasies, with its reality. Jeremy spent a lot of time living in his head, enjoying a reality he controlled.

Compelled into action, he took a loan against his paid-up life insurance policy and bought his first car, a beat-up, all-wheel-drive-off-road-vehicle in fair running condition. He had received his license as required in high school and then never driven again. Jeremy was an avid cyclist and rode his bicycle everywhere for transportation, in all seasons. But after a couple of barely avoided, potentially fatal car crashes, he was surprised how quickly he remembered the rules of the road and how to drive his beater- car smoothly in fast, heavy, city traffic.

He supposed his new mountain home would be in terrible "as is" condition, so he brought a quantity of cleaning supplies. Besides a big clean-up job, he glumly expected major repair work would be needed, done by expensive, unreliable, rural contractors. If a bank would give him a home improvement loan, he'd aimed to have the house livable by his designated start work from home date and thought, *Good luck with that.*

* * * *

When Jeremy finally located his isolated property, he was pleasantly surprised to find it neat and orderly. For the most part, his house was in move-in condition. What it needed for starters was a thorough dusting. He immediately set to work. Although it was comfortably furnished in thrift-store rustic, the furniture would soon be replaced with his own inherited antique Asian furniture.

Jeremy kept being surprised as he explored the house. There were bed linens, towels, pots and pans, dishes, flatware, and even seasoned cords of firewood stacked on the porch. With some trouble, he figured out how to get the electricity flowing and then the well's electric pump turned itself on.

The house had a large, bright living room and an equal size airy eat-in kitchen. In the back were two generous proportioned bedrooms, separated by a comfortable sized bathroom. In addition, it had a storage attic, full unfinished basement, and a wrap-around porch that joined a large elevated back deck. Near the house was a detached empty garage. Further back there was a barn, with a chicken coop on one side. All the out buildings needed repairs but nothing major. Paint was needed, long overdue, on every building's exterior and interior surface.

While dusting, Jeremy found an old hammock in the mudroom closet. Then later he spotted two hooks to hang it from on the deck. Soon he was cozy in the gently swaying hammock, as white powder puff clouds glided gracefully in a pale blue sky. Jeremy glowed with pleasure from the purchase of his new house, the telecommuting job, and how well he seemed to be managing everything outside his head. It all felt so grownup genuine. All through middle school, high school, college, and even during his six months at the insurance company, he'd felt like he was living his life through a fog. For the first time in a long time he was living life unfiltered, it felt different and real.

Jeremy was half dozing in the hammock, watching the tranquil sky and savoring his newfound authentic adult life, when suddenly a man and a teenager were standing over him.

The man spoke loudly almost shouting. "Howdy. I'm Audray Flacket. This here's my boy Ephraim. We seen you drive up. You buy this place?"

Jeremy became rattled, his peaceful solitude shattered. Awkwardly struggling to his feet, he almost tripped out of the hammock. Standing uneasily, he stared at the two newcomers. After a quick think, he decided they must be hillbillies. They were looking back at him expectantly. Jeremy stammered, "Y-Yes. I bought it at a tax auction. But I didn't know there would be neighbors. Good thing I kept my clothes on."

Audray, a craggy-looking man in his forties, was stooped-shouldered at about five feet, six inches tall. He was a plump munchkin, with very pale blue eyes set too close together in a mousey pinched face. Audray had a scraggly, blond, graying beard in need of grooming. He was wearing a wide brimmed straw hat and showed a need for dental implants as he spoke. "We didn't expect a foreigner. But hey, it's your property now, you want to run around in the altogether, that's your business. I don't ever let my wife and daughters off my property."

"Oh?"

"My son and I just stopped by to say howdy and see if you had any work needing done. I'm expert at all repair work. Anything you'd need done, I can do. *I do everything.* Plus, my boy here, he's handy too. *He even went to high school.* Didn't you, boy?" Saying that, Audray tried to cuff his son on the back of the head, but the boy ducked.

Jeremy couldn't take his eyes off Ephraim Flacket. All the individual features of his good-looking, beardless face worked together to create photogenic handsome. The boy's full red lips looked succulent. His intelligent bright eyes were an intriguing greenish-blue that radiated warmth. Unlike his father's hard mercenary-looking-for-business eyes, Ephraim stood up straight and looked the same height and weight as Jeremy. Wearing bib-overalls overhanging high-top sneakers and with gold colored hair peeking out from under a faded red baseball cap worn backwards, he seemed oblivious to his heart- stopping beauty. The boy quietly listened and watched his father and new neighbor's conversation.

Ephraim's good looks captivated Jeremy in ways he didn't expect. Jeremy put his hands in the pockets of his khaki shorts defensively against an unexpected erection. "Where is your place?"

Pointing left, the elder Flacket said, "We're back in the woods 'bout half a mile that way. You can't see my road, less looking for it, same as yours. We're both a ways back from that State Route turn off." Suddenly sounding ominous, he half whispered, "You'd be surprised who all and what is living in these mountains."

Jeremy was startled by the new information and its presentation. "I thought I'd be up here by myself. Like a hermit. People make me nervous."

"A man shouldn't be by his-self … ain't healthy. I've got a couple of good dogs I could sell you cheap. They'll keep the varmints away and warn you of danger. Interested?"

"What kind are they?"

"They're a little of this and that, but tough. Some wolf in 'um. Believe me they're mean when they need be. I trained 'um myself. Anybody tell you 'bout this place is haunted?"

"Yes."

"My dogs could keep ghosts away, I reckon."

"No, thanks. I want to take it slow at first."

Looking offended, Audray pretended to sulk, and then quickly revived. "They're good dogs. Look, I seen that ghost. Now that I come a calling and tomorrow's Halloween, he'll get all stirred up, believe me. He had a run in with kin of mine in the long gone past. He's not a friendly ghost."

"Tell you what, Mr. Flacket. I'm going to sell most of what's in the house. You can have first picks if you like. My own furniture is being shipped up from the city. You want to have a look?"

Following Jeremy into the house and looking around with interest, Audray Flacket closely examined certain pieces of furniture. "Well, now, we sure could use most of these things over at my place. It seems like we always need more beds and such. You getting rid of everything?"

"Not these; antique rocking chair, old game table, and those ancient books. The chair is so comfortable and fits me perfectly. Everything else must go. I have a lot of bulky furniture coming. Why don't you make me an offer? I want to paint the inside of the house before the movers come." Missing someone, Jeremy looked around. "Oh, where's your son?"

"He's still out on the deck, probably lying in your hammock. That boy's a dreamer. He'll never amount to much." Jeremy winced at the elder Flacket's comment.

Peeking, Jeremy saw Ephraim had indeed spread out in the hammock his hands behind his head, watching the clouds roll by. His legs straddled the hammock, creating a conspicuous bulge where they joined his torso. With his feet flat on the deck, he slowly rocked himself. Jeremy's mouth went dry as he scrutinized Ephraim's natural perfection. He mused out loud. "How old is he?"

The boy's father said, "Nineteen in two months. But you know he don't look like my other kids, they're all girls. Although my wife swears he's mine. I don't know?"

"Really, you don't think he looks like you?" Uncharacteristically lying, Jeremy spoke faster. "I definitely see a family resemblance." But was thinking *Ephraim looks about as much like you as I do.*

Audray perked up and beamed. "You do? Now I like to hear that. We're going to get along just fine."

At a loss for what to say next, Jeremy asked, "Did you know the last people who lived here?"

"I hunted bear with Hiram, the last owner. Let me tell you, he was one mean son of a bitch, but a crack shot. You don't want to hunt bear alone. By the way, you'll need a bear gun, if you don't have one. I have an extra you could have cheap. It's a good old gun…interested?"

"Like I said, I want to take it slow at first. How was Hiram mean?"

"He beat his wife and children more than just for correction. I think he liked doing it. And told me if he ever found a stranger on his property, he'd shoot them dead right off, no questions asked."

"Do you know why Hiram left in such a hurry, or where he went?"

"Bet it was the ghost ran 'em off. He's done it to squatters, before Hiram. I've knowed that ghost my whole life. Believe me, he'll be back. I've seen him up close. He's a scary one."

"Have any idea where Hiram went, or if he'll be back?"

"He has people in Oklahoma, I think, and won't be back if the ghost ran him off."

"Oklahoma, isn't that where they abolished all legal marriage, so lesbians and gays can't be married?"

"I heard something about that, but you want to talk to my boy. He got a whole mess of newfangled ideas from that high school. It is the ghost you got to worry about. Tomorrow is Halloween and he gets restless."

"Mr. Flacket, I don't believe in ghosts. But it's a mystery the previous owner left everything right in place. There's clothing in the closets and drawers, kids' toys scattered around. The kitchen has food, and there are clean towels and bedding in cedar chests. There are a lot of good things here that I can't use."

"Hiram, he didn't believe in ghosts either. It's strange though that they didn't take their things. That ghost must've gotten really riled up."

"So, you want all this stuff, or should I advertise it on-line? In a worst-case scenario since time is short I could have the truckers who bring my furniture cart it off. It would be a shame though, the furniture is solid wood."

"I'll take it off your hands. The only thing is I'm a little short of cash."

"Oh?"

"If you'd want, I could barter our labor for Hiram's stuff. My boy and I could fix up those out buildings and give your whole place a new coat of paint. But that's a lot of work for old worn out junk. Maybe you could throw in a hundred dollars cash? You'd buy the paint and what other materials we'll need."

"I might be interested. You'll fix up the four buildings and paint the whole place inside and out in exchange for the contents of the house and a hundred dollars? I'll give it some thought and let you know."

"Tell you what, we'll even trim those trees rubbing on your roofs and clean the chimney, how about it?"

"Since you brought up the trees, I noticed a lot of the shrubs need pruning."

"You drive a hard bargain, fella. Okay, for a deal right now today, we'll fix up the whole place, chimney, trees, and shrubs included. But you'll have to buy us lunch every day we work. My boy there is partial to double cheese burgers, fries, cherry pie, and Brown Cow floats. I don't mind them that much myself. What-cha say we got a deal?"

Pulling out a pen and looking around for paper, Jeremy answered with enthusiasm, "Let me write it all out, and we can sign an agreement."

With a sudden icy change of mood, Audray Flacket said, "Up here, things are done with a hand- shake. A man's word is his bond. I'm not signing no paper."

Looking surprised but not put off, Jeremy put his hand out for a shake. "Fifty dollars half way through and the other fifty when you're all finished. If you can get it done by the end of the November, I'll give you a fifty-dollar bonus. When can you start?"

"I was expecting to get the whole $100 before I start."

"Sorry, Mr. Flacket, that's not how I was taught to do it." With gumption he rarely used, Jeremy said, "My way or no way, sir."

"You get the lumber, tar, tar paper, shingles, and nails, and we start. If you fill my truck with gasoline, I'll help you carry the stuff, and make sure you're not cheated. These country bumpkins see a foreign looking guy like you, and they try to take advantage."

"Just so you know, I was born in California. I'm not a foreigner, this is my country."

"No offense, you're new around here. I can see to it you ain't cheated is all I'm saying."

With a guarded smile, Jeremy said, "And no offense taken. Thank you for the offer of help."

Scrutinizing Jeremy's gold pen, Audray did a quick appraisal. "How about we get the materials first thing tomorrow? Today I'll make a list of what you'll need now, and another list of what you'll need later to finish the job. Lend me your pen there." Audray pulled a crumpled looking piece of paper from his pocket.

Jeremy handed over the engraved twenty-four karat gold, college graduation gift pen he was holding. "All right, tomorrow morning we can discuss your plan for fixing up this place and what you'll need to do it. Great."

Suddenly distracted examining the gold pen, Audray mumbled, "When you planning on giving me Hiram's stuff?"

Jeremy considered his options. "Hmm, take the furniture in the basement after you get started on the outside repairs, there is a lot down there. Then take the contents of each room in the house as we prepare to paint that room. When the house is painted inside and out, and the chimney cleaned, I'll give you $50. After everything else is finished, you get the other $50 and bonus $50 if the job is done before December. If this goes well, there will be future work for you. What do you say?"

"You got yourself a deal there, young fella."

"Call me Jeremy, Audray."

"Jeremy, you sure you don't want to buy my dogs? I'd hate for you to get scared off by the ghost."

Smiling broadly with high confidence, Jeremy waved off the concern. "Trust me, ghosts don't believe in me, and I don't believe in them. So far, I'm not a dog person."

Looking concerned, Audray said, "This place is haunted, I've seen the ghost. If you won't buy the dogs, I'd better leave Ephraim till we get everything done. I don't want you scared off before we finish our business."

Jeremy was first flabbergasted by the suggestion, then stuttered, "U-Ugh, there are two bedrooms. If it will make you feel better. But only if Ephraim wants to stay?"

"Ephraim does what I tell him. He'll stay. The dogs would be better, they eat less and guard more. But have it how you want. My boy needs a friend anyway. All the folks his age up here is either meth heads or alkies raising babies on welfare. Ephraim has cousins younger than him with no teeth from drugs. It's a dam shame. I'll see both of you tomorrow morning at seven, in the diner near the lumberyard. Ephraim knows where it is. You can buy us breakfast."

As Audray walked away scribbling his lists, Jeremy went back out on the deck and leaned against the railing. He stared out over incredible views of the surrounding mountains and tried to keep his eyes off the handsome young man swaying in the hammock. Lost in troublesome thoughts of potential problems with his conniving new neighbor, Jeremy frowned deeply.

He was brought out of his brooding by Ephraim's soothing, lyrical tenor voice. "Don't frown, your face can get stuck like that for life. If you don't want me to stay, I could spend the night in the woods. I've done it before."

"It's not about you. It's hard for me to trust people. Why should you stay outside when there's an empty bedroom here?"

"Are you sure? Pa can be pushy."

Musing, Jeremy said, "The only thing is I wasn't expecting a guest. We'll have to go get food for dinner. Can you cook?"

"I'm not a guest. I'm instead of the dogs."

"You're *my* guest."

With pride in his voice, Ephraim puffed out his chest. "I do campfire cooking okay. Why didn't you bring food along?"

"Don't laugh. I brought my favorite comfort food. I figured this place would be a mess and I'd need my old reliable for solace."

"What kind of food is that?"

Head down, Jeremy spoke coyly, "One extra-large jar of super chunky peanut butter, one giant jar of strawberry jam, two long loafs of sliced bread, *and* a gallon of milk in an ice chest."

Perking up, the younger man said, "P&J are my favorites. We don't need to go for food today."

"Your father said burgers and fries were your favorites."

"He tells people that cause it's what he likes. Nobody will buy it for him because he's such a scrounger. But they sometimes feel sorry for me and buy it for us both. I'll take P&J over dried up greasy burgers anytime."

"Then we're set for tonight. I guess you know there's no television or radio in this place."

"We don't have them either. That's why I carry two packs of bicycle style playing cards; one red one blue. I play solitaire a lot."

"I never learned that game."

"Do you play chess?"

"Yes. I'm not very good, but I enjoy the game. And you?"

"I played on the chess team in high school. I wasn't the best, but I did all right."

Having a legitimate excuse to openly assess the younger man, Jeremy let his eyes feast. "The way you're built, I'd have guessed you played contact sports."

"I did. It's a small school. The boys and girls had to play on all the teams or the school couldn't compete in our conference. My next older sister won the States Boy's Wrestling Cup in her weight class two years running."

"Hmm, that is impressive."

"Hiram had an old ivory chess set. Let me see if he left it." That said, Ephraim was gracefully up, out of the hammock, and into the house. He was back right away. "It's here. We can play after we eat."

"You're on."

"Don't let Pa have the chess set with Hiram's other stuff. He'd only sell it, and it's really, really unusual and old. By the way, if you don't mind my saying—you'd better get your gold pen back from Pa tomorrow morning first thing, or you'll never see it again."

"Since you are being candid, do you think it was a mistake agreeing to let your father fix up this place?"

"No. He'd do almost anything for $150, and what furniture we can't use he'll sell or trade. We always do need more beds and chairs."

"That's not exactly what I meant."

"Don't worry; we'll do a good job. Pa likes to show me how to do work correctly. He told you I'll never amount to anything, but he doesn't believe that. He knows I'm queer and still loves me. If Hiram knew he would have killed me years ago."

"Hiram sounds like a real bastard."

"Hiram was, but if he murdered me, my kin are not a forgiving lot. I wouldn't want to cause bloodshed, dead or alive."

"You are beautiful on the inside as well as out."

"Aw shucks, you're going to give me a big head, now my hat won't fit, hee, hee."

"Sorry, I didn't mean to make you blush. I grew up without a father."

"Then you must watch Pa. He picks things up and forgets they're not his. It's caused embarrassment before."

"Thanks for the heads-up. Speaking of warnings, I haven't found the hot water heater yet, so we'll have to take cold showers. The well water is like liquid ice."

"There's no hot water heater that I know about. And Hiram never hooked up that shower. He wasn't big on modern convenience. The electricity and well pump came from previous owners."

"How did they bathe?"

"There's a big galvanized tub in the basement that he put it in the kitchen about once a week. They heated pots of water on the stove. Then they all lined up in turn, starting with the smallest. But that was only in the winter months."

"Gosh, I'm used to at least one shower a day."

"Come on then, grab a couple of towels and soap."

"Where are we going?"

"I'll show you where they washed when the weather wasn't too cold."

Jeremy went out to his motor vehicle and got two new towels and a bar of soap. He refused to think about what was coming, but his heart raced in anticipation anyway. Back on the deck he tossed a towel to Ephraim, who draped it around his neck. Then they set out for the woods. A short distance into dense trees, they stopped at a large spring-fed pond not visible from the house.

At once Ephraim Flacket started to kick off his shoes. Stalling for time, Jeremy stammered, "By—by the way, what do your friends call you, or do you prefer Ephraim?" The stalling tactic didn't work. The younger man was already down to his unhitched bib-overalls. He turned to face Jeremy, pushed them down, and stepped out of them. He wasn't wearing underwear. His flaccid endowment was large and swung freely in the open air while he unselfconsciously scratched his scrotum.

Jeremy's heart pounded with excitement at the naked young god-like image before him. Ephraim was an almost hairless harmony of right angles in perfect proportions. He was an athletic youth turning into a young adult. It felt like a privilege, Jeremy's exclusive viewing of a masterpiece of living sculpture.

"Come on, get out of those duds, we have to finish before dusk or the mosquitoes will eat us alive. Where's the soap?"

Trying to sort out contradictory feelings, Jeremy numbly tossed Ephraim the soap, and then turned his back to strip. Blushing head to toe, he finally pushed his briefs down and stepped out of them. They were the same height, but Jeremy's physique was not as well-defined, even though he did sit-ups and push-ups every morning and rode his bicycle for transportation. Ungracefully attempting to hide his aroused appendage by hand, Jeremy crashed into the pond like a felled tree.

His guest dove smoothly under the water, hardly leaving a splash. When his head surfaced, Ephraim shouted, "People I like can call me Fram! I think I'm going to like you, even if you're strange about your body. So, you know, your soap don't float."

Shaking water off his straight black hair Jeremy asked, "What does that mean?"

"We'll have to get out all the way to soap up, otherwise it will slip away and get lost. I hate diving for lost soap, it's hard to find. Otherwise this isn't a bad place to wash and swim. Just watch your pecker. The fish might think it's a big worm and bite it." After laughing heartily at his own joke, Ephraim dove under the surface.

Jeremy gave chase. They swam around the pond and playfully splashed each other in a game of tag. After enough fun, Fram climbed out of the water and unselfconsciously soaped himself facing the pond.

Fram waded back into the water and handed Jeremy the soap. He climbed out, facing away, furtively soaped himself at break-neck speed. Finished, he put the soap on a rock and, covered in suds, dove into the water.

After he'd rinsed off, Fram left the water and dried himself meticulously, then yelled, "Come on, slow poke!"

Reluctantly, Jeremy left the concealment of the water to join his neighbor. He thought *I haven't had that much fun since I was a kid.* Then a nameless dread slapped his pleasant mood away. He wrapped the towel around himself and haphazardly dried off in a hurry under it.

Smiling broadly, Fram said, "Why are you so bashful?"

Jeremy snapped, "I told you I'm not good around people, and especially nude."

"Come on, bud, don't be like that. You told us you like to run around naked."

"I wasn't serious when I said that, and don't call me bud!"

"Okay, okay, sorry, Jeremy."

"How long before the mosquitoes get hungry?"

Fram grinned licentiously. "We have a little time." Stroking his cold-water-wrinkled penis awake, he said seductively, "Jeremy, you want to fool around a little?"

"No!"

"Is it you don't like me, or you only do it with females?"

On guard after his unplanned rude outburst, Jeremy said softly, "Neither. I'm all screwed up. Something happened a long time ago I've never gotten over."

Ephraim's face registered disappointment, then hurt feelings, and moved on to a muddle.

"It's a long story and now isn't the time or the place for it. Maybe another time, okay? It's not I don't like you I do, a lot."

Looking less confused, Ephraim shrugged, and spoke *sotto voce*. "No problem."

"Sorry to disappoint you."

"Whatever? It's no big deal. You can still call me Fram."

"Thanks, Fram."

"Yeah, sure, the swim made me hungry."

"Me too."

Appetite motivated, the two men hurried into their clothes, then walked side by side like old friends. Jeremy hadn't had a real friend since age eleven.

Feeling simpatico, Fram conspiratorially asked, "But you beat off, right?"

"Yes of course," Jeremy said, sheepishly.

"Well, since we just met and all, what I had in mind wouldn't have been much different."

"I try to hold self-sex down to once a week."

"Really! I try to hold it down to once a day, but I almost never can. Then again … I don't try that hard. When did you start?"

"Once a week isn't enough for me, but it's a target. My first time happened when I was eleven, how about you?"

"I was ten. Some horny cousins came to stay with us while their folks were in jail for cooking meth. I had to share my bed with two of them. They did it every night and morning in all sorts of ways. I learned a lot in a hurry, it was fun. They are twins two years older than me, both married with kids now."

"Lucky you, I must seem like such a dolt compared to you."

"I don't think you are stupid or anything. Everybody's different in their way."

"Bad stuff happened, and I haven't gotten beyond it."

"I'm a good listener, if you ever want to talk."

Waves of contradictory feelings flooded Jeremy. Head down, he shyly mumbled. "Thanks, Fram, I appreciate the offer."

Once back at the house, they eagerly set to making piles of P&J sandwiches. As the sun began to set in a magnificent display of colors, they took their plates and glasses of milk out to the deck's old weathered picnic table. Fram set one of Hiram's mosquito repellant coils burning on a saucer, on the deck railing.

After they'd eaten their fill and rubbed their bellies in contentment, the two men set up the antique chess pieces on the ancient game table in the living room. They proved to be a good match, and the game went on long into the night. Without their notice, dark, dense clouds rapidly roiled in from the horizon and a molasses-black moonless night swallowed the little house. After hours of concentrated chess and with only a few pieces left on the board, Jeremy triumphantly proclaimed, "Checkmate!"

Standing, stretching, and looking down at the board, Fram yawned. "Good game, but next time I'll mate you for sure."

"In your dreams."

"You were just lucky tonight. I challenge you to two out of three."

"You're on."

"We have to meet Pa early. Let's get some sleep."

"Which bedroom do you want?"

"I'll take the one with all the bunk beds, it'll feel like home."

"Use the bathroom first. I'll check the doors and windows."

"No, I'll check the doors and windows. Remember, it's my job, it's what dogs do."

"Go wash and I'll lock up, okay?"

"If I don't do what my pa says it can get painful."

"Then, let's do it together."

Jeremy found objects he'd not seen before hanging above windows and doors. They were three-and-a-half-inch leather-wrapped wood hoops with woven webs in the center. A small turquoise stone was suspended in each web near a tiny hole at the center, and three beaded feathers hung down from both sides and the bottom of the hoop.

"What *are* these things?"

After losing the chess game, Fram was happy to show off. "They are spirit-dream catchers. See the tiny paper strip of numbers attached to each? It is the U.S. Census number of the medicine woman or man who made the spirit catcher. That is how they authenticate their work. Most of Hiram's spirit catchers are Navajo, only a few came from the Sioux nation."

"Is that important?"

"The Sioux were the originators. But the Chippewa spirit catchers are the most powerful, but Hiram doesn't have any."

Curiosity aroused, Jeremy examined one meticulously. "How does it work?"

"Spider webs play a big part in Native American mythology. They believe a bad spirit or nightmare can get caught in the spirit catcher's web and is held there until sunlight comes to destroy it."

"No kidding, they really believe that?"

"Yeah, they do, and the good spirits or pleasant dreams are allowed through the hole in the web's center and travel down the beaded feathers to bless the dreamer. But Hiram didn't use them right. It should either be on a bed post or worn around the neck, not put over windows and doors."

"Wow, isn't that interesting? My grandparents believed in using these eight-sided, brightly colored wooden plaques with a round mirror in the center; over doors or windows. The old Chinese believed the mirror reflected back to the sender any evil directed to them. Those mirrors are supposed to prevent evil from entering." Jeremy mulling over the dream catcher in his hand, said, "It looks like Hiram got his superstitions mixed-up."

"That sounds like ignorant Hiram. He hated everyone who wasn't exactly like him."

"These misused dream catchers are an interesting aspect of my new house. They make it unique. Maybe I'll get some of those Chinese evil reflectors to put around as additional decoration. They are colorful."

"You don't think that's like overkill?"

"I don't believe in supernatural anything, never did. If I don't believe it, it can't exist. It's that simple. But I find these superstitious trinkets quaint."

"I'm not sure what I believe about this stuff, I never saw a ghost. My pa has a couple of times. It frightened him really good, and we Flackets don't scare easily."

"My maternal grandparents owned a Chinese restaurant when I was little. Each day when they opened the business, food was placed in a small red shrine by the door, out on the sidewalk. It was to keep hungry ghosts outside. I watched, and never saw a ghost eat the food."

"Maybe that food wasn't what they like, so the ghosts didn't come inside the restaurant for more."

"Did you say that because I beat you at chess?"

"No, it was an unbiased observation, hee, hee."

After the two men made the rounds checking windows and doors, Jeremy said, "You wash up first. Good night, Fram."

When Fram was finished in the bathroom, he walked into Jeremy's bedroom. "At my house, we always kiss each other goodnight. It may sound a bit corny country to you, but I'll sleep better if I can kiss you good-night."

Before Jeremy could demur non-offensively, Fram grabbed him into his arms and delivered a full mouth on mouth kiss. Then with a satisfied look, left, speaking over his shoulder, "Goodnight, and don't let the bed bugs bite."

Flustered from the surprise kiss, Jeremy remained frozen in place for seconds. Then shaking himself, walked around turning off lights. While brushing his teeth, he decided the kiss was innocent, chaste, and tried to stop thinking about how nice Fram's soft-lips felt pressed on his. From years of practice Jeremy was adept at controlling his ruminations with a familiar mental void space.

Before he entered his bedroom, he glanced in his guest's open door. Fram was already asleep, snoring softly. His clothes were neatly folded on another triple-tier bunk bed. Seeing and hearing Fram sleeping gave Jeremy an inexplicable warm fuzzy feeling. He took that feeling to his bedroom, closed the door out of habit, and folded and put away his clothes before putting on his pajamas.

Jeremy expected insomnia from finding his new home in better condition than expected, the apparent good luck of having Audray Flacket and son do repairs and painting for little more than the cost of materials, the intellectual stimulation of a hard-won chess game right before sleep in a new place, the goodnight kiss, and persistent erection made more insistent from Fram's earlier offer of sex play. Jeremy anticipated he would toss and turn with his mind chasing through the day's events. Fleetingly, he considered putting one of the dream catchers on the double bed's headboard but dismissed the goofy idea as too silly. Within a second of his head hitting the pillow, he was swallowed by a deep, restful sleep.

In a dream, Jeremy was stripped out of his pajamas, then languidly swam nude in a pristine lagoon, deliciously guided by gossamer fingers touching him all over in a timeless tranquility. It was wonderful. Abruptly, his serenity was disturbed by a strong malevolent urge demanding immediate attention. He didn't want to stop the serenity swim. Fighting against mounting pleasure, and menace he forced himself to the lagoon's surface. The tranquility slipped away like real water, replaced by sensations so erotically overpowering and ominous they were indescribable. He was turned on like never before and about to climax. Forcing his eyelids open, he was alarmed to see a head bobbing on his greatly engorged-cock. That explained the dream's inexplicable mixed sensations. His pajamas were carelessly discarded in a heap on the floor. He never threw his clothes on the floor.

Breathing hard about to bliss-out, his first thought was maybe it's Fram. But on a closer look, it wasn't. It was a stranger. Rage boiled up at the violation, Jeremy slammed both his open palms at the trespasser's bobbing head. Instead of cup-slapping the offender's ears as intended, his hands loudly slammed together. The sound and sensation of the slap startled him fully awake and into shouting, "What in the hell! What's going on, this is crazy!" Then in extreme anxiety, Jeremy shouted full volume, "Am I going nuts?"

With his golden hair tousled and his eyelids heavy, a naked Fram Flacket rushed into Jeremy Long's open bedroom door. "Jeremy, what's wrong?"

"Some stranger was just molesting me!"

"Who? Where?"

Gaining control by breathing slower, Jeremy said, "I never saw him before. But he really was on me, in this bed."

Fram rushed out of the room, grabbed a metal poker from its stand by the woodstove, and then did a fast but thorough search of the house. He also checked the basement and attic but found no one. Coming back into Jeremy's room, he shrugged. "Maybe you had a nightmare-wet-dream. Don't worry, I won't let anything bad happen. This dog has teeth."

"I haven't had a wet dream since jerking off started as a preteen!"

"Calm down, you're safe with me here."

"I don't suppose you opened that door or tossed my pajamas on the floor. It wasn't a dream! Someone was here going down on me, I almost came. When I tried to hit him, I hit nothing. It's absurd. I must be going bonkers."

Looking very serious, Fram scratched his head. "No, I didn't do those things. But you're saying someone did?"

"Fram, I just woke up to find a stranger bobbing his head on my crotch. Are you sure he's not still here, hiding? Are the doors and windows locked as we left them?"

"Yes. Hey, look at your dick. It has gotten so much bigger than this afternoon. I figured you were a grower not a shower. But I didn't think it could grow to that size."

"I don't understand."

"See mine? It doesn't grow that much bigger from soft to hard. Mostly the angle changes from pointing down soft to standing straight up hard. A grower like you doesn't look like much soft but watch out when he's turned on."

Feeling shame and embarrassment from being on display, Jeremy tried to cover his extra-large bloated erection with hands. They weren't big enough. "I've never been *this* big."

"If it doesn't go down, I could put ice on it."

"NO, THANK YOU."

"I'll tell you one thing. Right now, it is way too big for anyone to swallow, except maybe the Jolly Green Giant, ho ho ho."

"You'd swallow it if I wasn't so big?"

"Sure, it is only our bottom holes that are for serious love making. Everything else is only sex for fun. But I haven't been in love yet, so I can only tell you what I read."

In sudden emotional recall, reliving what just happened, Jeremy's mood switched to wary. "So, you aren't worried that guy might come back, or I'll get nuttier?"

"I looked everywhere, anyway—I'm ready with this poker if he tries."

"Somehow, some way I've lost my mind."

"I have a different idea about what happened. But first, it's dangerous to keep a hard-on too long, that's why we all jerk off so much."

"Who said that? But my oversize cock, does look weird."

"In health class, the teacher said sperm only lives five days, and a hard-on for more than four hours must go to the hospital."

"Why?"

"If your hard-on won't go down; they have to cut your dick off."

"What!"

"But first the hospital puts ice on it, if that doesn't work, they stick needles in to suck out the blood, if it isn't too late, and amputation is required."

"Gross! I never heard that!"

"Want *me* to get some ice or call 911. I could leave the room so you can jerk off, that might make it go down?"

"My nerves are shot, finding a guy in this bed. Just the thought of ice on my skin makes me shutter. If it's okay, I'd rather you didn't leave me alone."

"Okay then, how do we get your monster prick down?"

"I don't want to jerkoff with you watching either … any ideas?"

"How about I jerk you off? Me only watching sounds creepy?"

"Ugh, I guess if you don't mind, sure, that might work."

"Right this minute I'd say you have enough for four hands."

"Okay to be fair, after we solve my problem, I'll do it for you."

"Whatever."

"Are you sure I've not lost my mind? We just met, now we're going to have sex, that's insane!"

"Settle down, don't make yourself crazy. Hand jobs aren't really sex."

"Everything was fine yesterday. I don't get it. When I tried to hit the guy, he wasn't there. That's a hallucination and proves I'm bonkers."

"Look at you, all overexcited. I don't think you're crazy, so you're not. But you could talk yourself into it the way you're going."

"I don't want to be nuts."

"Just lay back and close your eyes. I'll help you get this monster down to normal size."

Kneeling in bed beside his new neighbor, Fram took Jeremy's hands and placed them on his swollen member, then put his own hands on top of them. Working in tandem, they moved loose skin gently up and down. Once they'd established a slow, steady cadence, Fram leaned his body forward, placing his lips over Jeremy's. Jeremy turned his head, accepting the kisses while their hands moved. The trauma had deactivated Jeremy's usual impenetrable defense shields. Fram eased his tongue between Jeremy's lips. Then, doing rapid tonguing, he double-timed the rhythm their hands were keeping.

It didn't take long. Although the buildup was intense there was no doubt once the culmination started. Jeremy wriggled his body side to side, as he felt his release simultaneously tingling toes to scalp then rush to his groin. An overwhelming power-driven pulsing vibrated through him and then rocketed out of his prick in long strong salvos. He bucked out each release, gasping each into Fram's mouth.

At last drained, Jeremy's fast breathing slowed to normal. Fram used damp towels he retrieved from the bathroom to mop up Jeremy's copious gooey man milk. "Was it like you thought?"

"It was incredible. Thank you for that. Now let me return the favor."

"I'd rather wait until you're less upset. Anyway, I jerked off before, when you were brushing your teeth. I'm good for now."

"Just say when. I want to give the gift back, and share it."

"Look, your swelling is going down. I knew it would, I always get soft after shooting spunk."

"Fram, you know if I'd been here alone, I would have become a babbling Looney Tune."

"But you weren't alone. Do you want me to sleep in here with you tonight? This bed is big enough for two and more."

"If you won't think me a baby?"

"I suggested it."

"You know I've probably gone mad, right?"

"Jeremy, did the guy have white-ash gray eyes, long chestnut-brown hair, a pointy goatee, and kind of handsome in an old-fashioned way?"

"Yes, that was him. Who is he?"

"That is how Elbert, the ghost who haunts this place, is supposed to look, or so my pa says."

"Ghost! Can't be, I'm not superstitious! *I don't believe in all that.*"

"Okay, okay, relax, it's Halloween. No trick and you just had your treat. How about I tell you some history, about this place you bought?"

"That I probably can handle."

Moving into a sitting position with his back against the antique carved mahogany headboard, Fram wrapped his arms around Jeremy and drew him in close, safe and secure. Jeremy contentedly snuggled into the younger man's encirclement.

With Jeremy snuggling in his arms, Fram spoke softly. "I've heard the living room part of this house was built in the late 1700s by a family of moonshiners. Originally it was just a one room cabin, then years later they added where your kitchen is now. In those days, the actual kitchen was a cook shed out back. There still was, deep in the woods, fed by the streams feeding that pond we swam in. The next time you are in the basement, look up at the joists. You can see where additions to this house were added each time."

"I will."

"After many generations, it ended up with just Elbert, the great-great grandson of the original owner and his half-breed lover Blake running the still."

"How do you know they were lovers?"

"The winters up here are something fierce. Two adult males snowed in for months aren't going to waste energy complaining about lack of pussy when they have each other. Everybody knows cowboys, fur trappers, and explorers were mostly gay in olden times. Just like the pirates and other sailors. It was their way to hang out, get off, and sleep together without female trouble."

"Gay, now that's a word I've been trying to avoid. After tonight, I guess I better face facts."

"So, the Revenuers send up their cutest young undercover agent, Caleb, to buy moonshine off the lovers. Only thing was, Caleb found both boys got his motor running. Well, they probably didn't have motors back then, but you get what I mean?"

"The ATF man found his suspects sexy?"

"Exactly! Reading between the lines in old newspapers, he was doing both guys without the other knowing. Then one day Elbert came home early from delivering hooch and walked in on Blake and Caleb doing the nasty."

"Let me guess, he wasn't happy?"

"You got that right. Rather than joining in, like I would have, Elbert shoots them. When he finds Caleb's badge, he freaks out and dumps the body under his outhouse and takes a crap on it. Then, remorseful, he gives Blake a proper burial. There's an old crude cross grave marker behind your barn."

"I'll look for it."

"So, when the other Revenuers start to miss Caleb, they come looking. Elbert is all broken hearted, missing his lover Blake and his man on the side, Caleb. Pa thinks he got suicidal from a broken heart. When two Revenuers come to ask about Caleb, Elbert guns them down. You know how Revenuers are, soon there were a lot of them up here. When they find Caleb and their other men dead under the outhouse, they got really mad. Especially, after the barber-mortician refused the bodies until they were cleaned up. The story goes a shootout between the other Revenuers and Elbert lasted four days. Supposedly Elbert killed eight in all, before they finally shot him dead."

Pulling back enough to look Fram directly in the eye, Jeremy said, "What a great story, and it happened right here."

"Like I said, the Revenuers were really pissed, so they threw Elbert's bullet-riddled remains under the outhouse and left him to rot. Legend has it, because he never got a proper burial, after a violent death while causing others to die, he has to haunt where he was killed until he is given a proper grave to rest in."

"Do you believe that?"

"I don't know, but I looked-up the history at our local library. You ready for this? The Revenuer in charge of the men who killed Elbert was named Dan Flacket. Which, if someone wanted to believe in ghosts, would explain why Elbert gets upset when pa comes around here? My pa is the oldest direct descendant of Dan Flacket."

"But it was such a long time ago."

"My pa can tell some tall tales, but when he talks about Elbert *he* believes what he's saying. I didn't know my family had any lawmen before going to the library. I thought we mostly lived outside the law."

"Interesting, but I still refuse to believe in ghosts. On the other hand, as a courtesy to a previous owner of this property, I wouldn't mind giving Elbert a proper place to rest. It's the decent thing to do. Do you know where the outhouse was?"

"Nobody does. Other owners have tried to find his bones, so they could get some peace on Halloween. I'm told Elbert can be very destructive."

"Damn, Fram."

"Well right, except all the other owners of this place, that I know about anyway, were straight. I think we should ask Elbert, the next time he shows up where his bones are. If he tells us, or shows us, we could put his bones with Blake's and put a proper R.I.P. marker over them. If he won't tell us, he'll be sorry. I'm a Flacket too and I know where to get some Chippewa spirit catchers and I know how to use them. And you could aim some of those Chinese evil deflectors his way for good measure."

Hugging Fram tightly, Jeremy sighed. "Great plan, I'm in."

"I think we should sleep together at least until we get Elbert and Blake back together."

"Sounds good to me."

"If I'm asleep the next time Elbert visits, don't panic. Talk to him loudly about his reuniting with Blake while nudging me awake. My guess is he is going to treat two men who sleep together with more respect than he did the other owners of this place."

"I like your plan. It gives me hope."

"I thought you didn't believe in ghosts?"

"I don't. But I believe in history. Do you think Elbert and Blake will forgive each other?"

"I sure hope so. They were both doing Caleb."

"Right!"

"And you don't need *two* feuding historical characters causing a ruckus."

"You're double right about that."

"There is something I need to know. When we were swimming this afternoon, you said there was some reason you didn't want to fool around. You said it was a long story and then wasn't the time or the place to tell."

"I did."

"Well, if we are going to sleep together, don't you think I should know what's up with that? You know, since fooling around is a fun part of sleeping together."

"Fair enough, I don't want you thinking I'm a mass murderer or something. But it's a long sad story. You want to hear it right now?"

"Go for it. I won't be sleeping anymore tonight with Elbert around."

Snuggling in tight, Jeremy told Fram about growing up an only child raised by a single working mother. His father was killed in one of America's continuous wars. From preschool, he had a best friend the same age, Ralph, also American-born Chinese. Ralph was fatherless due to war as well. At first their mothers took turns looking after the boys, but over time Ralph spent most sleepovers at Jeremy's house. Most people assumed the boys were brothers. They were inseparable.

With the onset of first grade, their time after school was spent at the Salizar Soccer Club. Mr. Salizar had been a soccer star in Central-America in his youth. Later in life he was a coach. His soccer club teams won trophies regularly and had a reputation for excellent sportsmanship and good manners. Jeremy's mother found the club for the boys.

The two first graders learned fast. They had determination and soon played in the regular peewee league. Ralphy consistently scored the most goals, usually with balls Jeremy acquired and setup.

By age eleven the best friends were good enough, though not old enough, to join the very competitive junior's soccer team. Mr. Salizar said he would make an exception about their age, but they would have to be initiated the same as the other juniors to be part of that team. He said there were no exceptions to the secret initiation.

Jeremy was troubled about a secret they couldn't tell their mothers about. He and his mother were close. But Ralphy was so excited at being accepted to play with the older boys, he insisted they follow the rules and not tell.

Around this time, Jeremy noticed someone was hurting Ralphy. He could see marks and bruises on Ralphy's body at sleepovers. But Ralphy refused to talk about his injuries. Then later Jeremy suspected from how Ralphy suddenly became modest around him. There might be more than physical abuse. Jeremy's mother had schooled him about good and bad touching. He voiced his concerns. So, Jeremy's mother tried to get Ralphy to talk about his marks and bruises. But he adamantly refused to say anything.

She told Jeremy, "If Ralphy won't say what's going on, we will respect his privacy. And we'll mind our own business until he says otherwise."

"But, Mom, it looks like something bad is happening, he's changed."

"When Ralphy says so, I'll take appropriate action. But only if that's what *he* wants."

To be initiated, Mr. Salizar instructed the boys to shower and go to a motel room on the appointed day and time. When they arrived, the room was in shadows, a few votive candles the only light. Mr. Salizar was sitting in the room alone. "Hurry up and take off all your clothes and lay on the bed. If either of you doesn't do as told, you both fail and will never play soccer with my teams again."

Jeremy's instincts told him to run away fast. But Ralphy's eyes pleaded to stay.

It didn't feel right. Mr. Salizar was studying their naked bodies. Then, before either boy realized what was happening, two older nude soccer players entered the room, overpowered and raped them brutishly. And then brusquely left through the adjoining door they'd entered.

The violent violation happened as they were roughly forced to lay face down side by side. Without forethought, Jeremy reached over and took Ralphy's hand. The physical connection to mutual pain magnified their defilement. They shared a disgrace like only the publicly caned know.

Speechless in shock at what just occurred, Ralphy began crying inconsolably. Jeremy put his arm around him. He wasn't sure what to do. Get Ralphy out of there or attack Mr. Salizar who had watched their ordeal playing with himself.

Zipping up his pants, Mr. Salizar saw the rage mixed with humiliation on Jeremy's face. "Okay, boys, get dressed. Congratulations! You successfully completed your initiation. But remember, you can't tell anyone. It is our team's secret to success. In a few years, you will be initiating new junior team members." After they dressed, shamefaced in a daze, Salizar handed each boy a new junior league soccer jersey. Then shook their hands and scooted them out the door.

Both boys were incredulous at what happened. Walking home, Ralphy refused to talk about the initiation or anything. He looked the most upset he'd ever been. Jeremy didn't really want to talk either but thought they should. In the heavy silence between them, Jeremy's humiliation turned into rage.

Prior to the initiation, sex was at best a nonsense construct overriding the silly baby-by-stork mythology. Jeremy and Ralphy would laugh at the older kids' dirty jokes to be accepted by the guys, but the content didn't make sense. Pre-initiation, the two best friends found jokes to do with farts or toilet paper hilarious. That shared humor and innocence was forcefully stolen by the initiation, replaced with an experience they weren't emotionally or cognitively developed enough to grasp.

Before his mother came home from work, Jeremy decided to make-believe the initiation never happened. If what he didn't have words for hadn't occurred, there was nothing to talk about. He didn't know what else to do with secret forbidden knowledge. He thought, *At least it ought to be forbidden.* So, he didn't write about it in his journal. Nevertheless, Jeremy became quieter and constantly on guard at home and school.

Ralphy wouldn't talk to him and had stopped coming for sleepovers. Jeremy quit the after-school soccer club. He told his mother he wanted to improve his grades instead. She was fine with that if he studied in the school's library until she came home from work. If she noticed any other change in him, she didn't say anything.

Several months after the initiation, Jeremy's mother showed him an article in the newspaper. It told of Mr. Salizar being so badly beaten by the father of one of his soccer players he had to be hospitalized. The boy's father was arrested, and an investigation into allegations of child sexual abuse at the Salizar soccer club was started. Jeremy's mother asked if he knew anything about sex abuse at the soccer club.

He shook his head no, but knew she knew he was lying. She was upset but didn't push it. He never knew if it was out of respect for his privacy or because what she might do if she discovered he'd been sexually abused. He was glad he hadn't told her right after the crime had occurred. He could imagine his mother, a parole officer required to carry a pistol for her job, putting Mr. Salizar in the ground for hurting him. That would have been the end of their family, and he loved his mother too much to let that happen.

Ralphy had stayed on the soccer team and was one of the players the investigators interviewed because he was the youngest and always looked frightened. Two weeks after the newspaper article, Ralphy left a voice message on Jeremy's cell phone. His sad voice said, "Jeremy, I don't know what to do. The police say I'm going to jail if I don't spill the beans about the soccer club initiation. They questioned me three different times and I got really scared. The last time they put handcuffs on me and said I could never go home. I got so scared, and confused, I gave up my mother's boyfriend. It was an accident, I didn't mean to. Jeremy, I didn't tell the police about you or the initiation. I know you only went because I made you. I'm sorry I did that. My mom freaked out when her boyfriend got arrested because he pays our rent. She said I am selfish for telling what he does to me. She said we are going to be homeless and it is my fault. Somehow, I've messed up bad. But thank you for being my best friend. Sorry I shut you out. Oh, and you better delete this message to protect yourself from the child welfare investigators. They won't stop asking questions either. Goodbye, I wish I'd been a better friend."

Jeremy only got the message after school, when his cell phone was returned to him—normal school policy. After Jeremy played Ralphy's message, he rushed over to Ralphy's house. But no one answered the door. Jeremy asked at a neighbor's apartment and was told his friend had hanged himself earlier that day. His body was found by his mother's boyfriend when he came back to get his stuff after being bailed out of jail by Ralphy's mother.

Jeremy had no experience with death, let alone a suicide. Without planning, running on autopilot, Jeremy stopped at an electronics store and bought a new memory card for his cell phone and hid the one with Ralph's message. Since he couldn't make sense out of all what happened, Jeremy stopped trying. Whenever his mind drifted to reflect on life with Ralphy or soccer, he'd force himself to think about something neutral, like a math problem. If that failed, Jeremy would pinch himself hard to force safe thoughts to overrule troubling ones. He eventually learned a nonverbal mantra from a library yoga book to control his wandering thoughts when self-pinching failed.

But at night, Ralphy entered Jeremy's dreams. The dreams always ended with Jeremy blaming himself for not running away before the initiation. From the day Ralphy died, Jeremy never allowed anyone to get close enough to be called friend.

Finally, feeling lighter from telling, Jeremy said, "Fram, I've never told a living soul about this. I thought I'd take it to my grave. You can't imagine how hard it was telling you. I hope you don't mind my unloading on you. Somehow this truth telling has made me feel closer to you. I know we only just met, and pray I haven't scared you away."

Fram had listened intently, holding Jeremy and lightly caressing him as he talked. After a few seconds of silence, he kissed Jeremy's shoulder. "I really like you, and I can imagine it was hard telling me your story. What was done to you and your friend was wrong. It was the worst kind of wrong. But keeping it bottled up inside wasn't okay."

With tears threatening to spill from his eyes, Jeremy nodded agreement. "Thank you for understanding. But you are going to make me ball like a baby if you keep talking."

"Did you cry at your friend's funeral?"

"I couldn't cry at the wake or funeral. I turned myself into stone to tough it out, holding heavy secrets."

"Crying is good. I don't mind holding you if you want to let it out. I know most males would rather cry alone."

Lowering his face to nuzzle Fram's elbow, Jeremy said, "I'm afraid if I let myself cry, I won't be able to stop and will turn into a big puddle of tears."

"But crying will help you say goodbye."

"I can't."

"If you don't let Ralphy go, he will haunt you forever."

On the verge of hyperventilating, Jeremy said, "Oh, give me a break! Forever!"

"You don't only need to let Ralphy go but find a way to forgive Salizar and the two soccer players who raped you."

Wriggling out of the embrace, turning and facing Fram, Jeremy's mood tightened. "What? I sort of get letting Ralphy go. Even crying makes sense. But why would I want to forgive those bastards?

"So, you can forgive yourself for not following your instincts to run and tell."

Catching his breath to regain composure, Jeremy tried assuaging. "Fram, what makes you so smart? How can you nurture me like this, I'm older?"

"Don't change the subject. Give me a minute and I'll seek a plan."

"Okay, you can be older for now."

After a long interval thinking, both men sitting cross legged facing each other on the bed, Fram said, "Here it is, Elbert is an outside ghost, and that's the way *we'll deal with him*. Ralphy is an inside-your-head ghost who needs to get out of there. *Get out Ralphy. Go and leave Jeremy be!*"

"Externally and internally, I'm surrounded by ghosts I don't believe in on Halloween, BOO, TRICK OR TREAT!"

"Don't be a wise guy. I'm trying to help."

Flipping his hands over, top down, shrugging his shoulders in a gesture of helplessness, Jeremy's face showed he was blocking. "I know, I can't help it. Let's talk about something else."

"How about you *write down* everything you remember about the initiation and suicide? That will help get it out."

"I don't know... it won't be easy."

"You still have the phone memory card?"

Putting his hands on Fram's knees and rubbing lightly Jeremy distractedly mumbled, "Yes."

"Then bury it with what you write about the initiation and suicide. We can even make a marker to put over it with R.I.P."

Pondering Fram's suggestions while tracing circles on his knees, Jeremy was quiet for a long interval. "I guess I see your logic. But giving up the memory card will be hard. It's Ralphy's voice, the only thing I have left from him."

At that moment, a dark shadow passed over Fram and he sagged, breathing becoming shallow. Emotionally keyed-up, his head facing down studying Fram's blond pubic bush, Jeremy didn't notice the change.

Ralphy's voice came from Fram's mouth. "I don't understand why you were more upset by the idea of initiation rather than our actual rape?"

Distracted, not registering the voice change, Jeremy combed Fram's pubes with his fingers. "You've caught me in a quandary. The scariest thing about what I said wasn't being violated by their greasy fingers and screwed. It didn't hurt that much and was kind of interesting in a new, different way, once he got going. I got upset that they would do that without our consent. That was the most unforgivable offense. And I can't forgive myself for not hating it, while Ralphy was crying in pain, squeezing my hand."

"Release it, Jeremy. It happened eleven years ago. We need to move on."

"Afterward I kept wondering if I had run away before the rape, would Ralphy still be alive."

"You've punished yourself enough. I forgave you on the phone message, I forgive you now."

"Ralphy had to know. I got hard. I came for the first time during the assault, it distracted me. How could he not know, we were holding hands? Why did I do that?"

"I know what happened. Your puberty arrived. It wasn't your fault, forgive yourself."

"That's easy for you to say."

"Jer, you must let me go. We're both stuck."

"But Ralphy... Fram? What is going on here!?"

"Jer, is your favorite color still red, and your lucky number five?"

"Fram! How could you know that? Why are you all slumped forward ... you sound exactly like Ralphy?"

"When Fram spoke directly to me a moment ago, 'Get out Ralphy. Go, leave Jeremey be.' A window opened, but only briefly."

"Where is Fram? What the hell is going on?"

"I'll let Fram come back if you let me and that old naughty ghost move on."

"Ralphy, you know I never believed in ghosts. I'm too old to start now."

"What do you call this little talk we're having?"

"A hallucination. I'm pretty sure I've lost my mind, and talking to you is proof of it."

"Nonsense, you just graduated from a good university with honors, have a job, and maybe your first boyfriend. You don't qualify for crazy. I'm a ghost and we are chatting, *believe it!*"

"Now just wait a second. Why did you and that other ghost decide to haunt me on Halloween? I've never been haunted by ghosts before, on Halloween or otherwise. It means I'm bonkers."

"No, silly, it is easy to explain. You moved into Elbert's house uninvited on All Hallows Eve. He didn't like that and never liked strangers anyway, especially Flackets."

"I don't get it. If you are in my head, how come you showed up this night, after eleven years dead?"

"You worked hard against my showing myself before. I tried entering your dreams, but you just turned them into self-punishments. That wasn't right."

"I don't want to believe in ghosts, yet here you are. I don't want to go insane, yet that's the only logical explanation for talking to myself. What could've triggered this impossible predicament, P&J sandwiches?"

"Yum, I vicariously enjoyed those with the ice-cold milk, perfect!"

"Everything seemed to be going so well yesterday."

"Yep, you did yourself proud."

"You know I really loved you, Ralphy."

"I know you did, and for the first time since I died you started having feelings for someone other than me. You even went skinny dipping with him the day you met. That is definitely not your style."

"You're right!"

"Yep, but you were still fighting feelings for Fram, until finally giving in and letting him help. Thank heavens for that."

"Did I ever have any privacy from you?"

"Not much. When I was alive we bathed and slept together, remember? Not much privacy there either."

"Actually, come to think about it, I never felt completely alone after you died."

"When you took boring classes I slept through those. Actuarial science, really?"

"I like it."

"Jeremy, what do you really believe about ghosts?"

"Let's see, Albert Einstein said, 'The past, present, and future all exist simultaneously, and it is only a popular illusion that death ends anything.' That makes more sense to me than the usual hocus-pocus mumbo-jumbo."

"Correct, I didn't evaporate, only moved to a different plane."

"Hmm … so if I accept you're someplace else, say just on another level, then it is not silly superstition, it is Einstein, and I'm not totally crazy after all?"

"Yep, but don't state the obvious again. Albert doesn't like it, and I'm short on time. Just bury us so we can move on with our journey, and you can live yours undisturbed."

"Hmm … okay if that's what you want. But I have a question needing an answer first. Why'd you commit suicide without talking to me first?"

"I didn't, my mother's boyfriend murdered me. He broke my neck and made it look like suicide. He said if I ever told what he was doing to me, I'd be dead. I cut school that day. I'd been miserable about sadistic-abuse from mom's boyfriend, the soccer initiation, the police and child welfare and failing school. Honest, I didn't know he was getting out of jail that day."

"Where is that son of a bitch?"

"He got what he deserved. Some other bad men stuck knives in him. He died a gruesome slow death. I watched. Then his soul was dragged screaming down to hell. Killing children is seriously frowned upon on all levels of existence."

"Good riddance."

"We agree on that."

"Ralphy, if I have to let you go, I want your blessing with Fram. I like him a lot, and it feels mutual. I've missed that since you've been gone."

"He likes you too, Jer. Let him help you bury your dead."

"Okay, I'll try to make you a memory, but I'll miss you."

"Release me, and don't make me come back. It's difficult and takes a lot of ectoplasm, and I'm already late for an appointment."

"Goodbye, Ralphy, be happy where-ever you are. I will always hold you in my heart."

"Goodbye, Jer, you know I loved you. Oh, one more thing. This guy Elbert's bones are under the hen house. He wants a separate resting place from Blake; who is now exclusive with Caleb. You wouldn't believe the soap operas we have here. Elbert says he wants a nice view, and he likes daffodils."

"What kind of flowers do you like?"

"Flowers, ugh, no flowers, I am still eleven years old."

"Oh right, wait … remember a year before you died we discovered blueberry muffins?"

"Yum yum, they were so good hot, with lots of butter. We used to say the more berries the better, remember?"

"I noticed there are a lot of wild blue berry bushes up here."

"How do you know what a blue berry bush looks like?"

"I took botany for a science elective. You probably slept through it."

"Hey, do whatever you want. I got to go, they're calling my name. Bye." Saying that, Ralphy's voice faded and Fram slowly reanimated.

Fram yawned, shook himself, and squeezed Jeremy's hand. "Sorry, I must have dozed off. What were you saying?"

Jeremy leaned forward and covered Farm's mouth with his own, kissing him deeply.

When they broke the wet lip lock to come up for air, Fram said, "To what do I owe that?"

"It's an advance partial payment for helping me bury my dead."

* * * *

Jeremy Long and Ephraim Flacket moved the chicken coop and dug up Elbert's bones. They found an old wooden box that fit his remains and reburied them with Ebert's name carved on a wooden marker, his birth date was unknown. He rested on a ridge with a good valley view. The two young lovers covered Elbert's grave site with twenty perennial mixed-color large daffodil bulbs.

Then they buried Ralphy's voice on a sim card and hand-written account of events leading to his death, placed in an ornate silver-colored metal moon cake box. Ralphy's resting place was set above Elbert's, between two large healthy-looking wild blueberry bushes, recently pruned and limed. Ralphy was given a small granite grave marker with his *full name, dates, and loving friend* carved in the stone. To sanctify the burials, Ephraim and Jeremy stripped down, greased up, and had their first adult sex. They made passionate love to consecrate the gravesites, and the ghosts had a meaningful send-off.

Thanks

Helen Rockford outdid herself laying an elegant Thanksgiving table. The heavy sterling silver flatware was polished to a dazzling sparkle and reposed on either side of the family's finest antique English bone china, nesting at each place setting. The silver and china, was laying under the candle, cast shadows of six different size, paper thin, glinting crystal goblets. The two beautiful, large floral arrangements were created by Helen from her garden and would be removed just prior to the first course.

It had been decades since the entire family was assembled for a meal. So, embossed silver printing on white place cards minimized seating awkwardness. Aunt Helen Rockford, the powerful family matriarch, sat at the head of the table. Her place since her husband died many decades earlier. Helen's constant companion, burly nurse Jill Jaspers, sat at her right hand. Next to the nurse sat nephew turned niece Berlinda, and then nephew Graham and his spouse Phillip. Opposite them on the left sat Troy his spouse Susann, Martin and his spouse, Alice.

At the exact appointed time, as the middle-age or older banquet guests mingled chatting or sulked, holding fine crystal stemware with aperitifs or cocktails, Helen Rockford vigorously shook the little silver bell attached to her left sleeve's cuff. "Everyone please takes your seat."

"Aunt Helen, where are our teenagers?"

"Hattie and Cleveland's helpers have them up in the velodrome working up appetites, bicycle racing. Afterward they will have their Thanksgiving meal in the breakfast room. We adults have family matters to discuss that would bore the children."

"Family matters … hog wash … then what's he doing here?"

"Troy, Phillip is your brother Graham's legal spouse. Same-sex marriage is the law of the land now."

"Don't you realize how ghastly it is to have normal marriage usurped by fucking faggots? It is almost as absurd as Bertram giving up his big, thick potent manhood for a little gash to become Berlinda. This family is totally nuts."

"It appears you have had too many cocktails again, Troy. If you continue to be disrespectful, *you will* leave the table and miss out on important family business."

Without forethought, Graham assumed his usual role as peace maker, and changed the subject. "Aunt Helen, are you sure that velodrome is safe? It has been over the stables for at least a hundred years."

"It's safe, I had it inspected recently. Good Gears to everyone who wants to do laps later."

"As kids, we all took tumbles on those steep, banked turns." To emphasize her point, Berlinda gave a little full body shake remembering.

"We have Nurse Jaspers present in case of a scraped knee or such. You all survived. Let the children race for fun."

"Thank you, Aunt Helen." Graham sat back judiciously, he had succeeded in deflecting the conversation away from conflict.

"I checked on the children earlier. They were smiling and laughing, having a good time. Bicycle racing is in our family's blood."

"Yeah, Graham, how about you and your fag boyfriend stop grousing, and shut up!"

"Consider this your second warning, Troy. One more and you are banished from this table and today's family news." The look exchanged between the family matriarch and her eldest nephew Troy, was just short of lethal.

Troy continued to glare at his old aunt. Then in response to her withering returned scowl, he stared at his wife, Susann for support. But, alas, she was drunker than he. Susann gazed stupefied at the lit candles in the large floral arrangement directly in front of her. It looked like she was trying to commune with the center-piece, but her befuddled brain kept missing the connection.

With another tinkle from her small bell, Helen said, "Everyone, join hands, I will say grace ... 'Thank you, Father, for bringing us together to enjoy this food we are about to partake and *all* your bountiful blessings this past year. Through thy grace, our Lord, and the Holy Spirit, amen.'"

"Amen."

"I've used my mother's grandmother's recipes to plan today's menu. You'll find the food was prepared as close as possible to olden times. Hattie, please bring us the first course."

The floral arrangements disappeared as the first course arrived. It was a delicately subtle jellied calves' foot consume served on a bed of peppery baby arugula and buttery red bib lettuce. The first course was accompanied by sparkling white Prosecco wine, which complimented the cold, congealed soup.

"Why the hell are we *all* here after so many years?" Troy slurred words together as he spoke.

"Some of you will not be sad to hear this is my last Thanksgiving. My medical team gives me a few months, if that, before my demise from an assortment of infirmities. All in all, I've had a good life with few regrets. Now that I'm ninety-eight years old, Mother Nature says it is time to leave. I have a meeting with my lawyers Monday morning to draw-up my finale bequests."

"This is terrible news. I'm so sorry." Berlinda's voice was full of sadness.

Troy grumbled, in the general direction of his wife. "Typical, last minute, treat us like children!"

"If it goes as planned, this meal will provide us an opportunity to reconnect as family. That matters to me. If you were born a Rockford, and show family loyalty, I may have an announcement of interest for you, after the cheese and fruit platters."

"So, that's your family business." Troy shouted, "Don't be foolish, I get everything!"

"It is hoped you will all take this opportunity to rejuvenate our family values. We've drifted apart over the years. It is time to reconnect one for all, all for one ... or not."

"You've got that wrong, bitch. You can't put back together what was never whole."

"I expect today's gathering and discussion to be civil, Troy."

"You always pick on me." Troy's mood shifted from loud angry to quiet simpering.

"Everyone please think before you speak. Hattie, please let your helpers clear away the soup and bring in the mixed seafood linguine in parsley, garlic, and lemon butter sauce. Ask Cleveland to serve the chilled white Chianti."

The pasta looked and smelled delicious and no one needed to be invited to dig into the mouth-watering, fragrant seafood. Nevertheless, some of the diners looked sad at the news of Aunt Helen's impending passing. Others only looked surprised, glancing from one to another to see who knew of the imminent change in family hierarchy. The mood shift was palpable as the premonition arrived and all eyes shifted to Nurse Jill Jaspers with an unspoken question. *Why didn't you tell us?*

"I instructed Ms. Jasper not to tell you about my failing health to have peace and quiet preparing myself for the end. One or two of you might have wanted to fawn over me, and I'm sure others would have had monetary requests. I didn't want to be bothered before today. Now, this meal is your chance to reconnect with each other as family and me."

Muttering at his plate of pasta, Troy slurred, "Oh, so, this grub is your goodbye and good riddance to us? Well, that blows big chunks."

"In my life, change has usually been followed by upheaval."

"Like what, explain please auntie."

"Resentments left behind about things as they were, and guilt preventing fully enjoying the new and different. My passing will either exacerbate further dissolution or, it is hoped, renew family bonds."

"This family was fucked-up my whole life. You can't put Humpty Dumpty together again if he started out cracked-up."

"If there's something more you want to add, Berlinda, don't hold back."

Troy drunkenly cut Berlinda off, and said, "The truth is auntie, you're a cunt-bitch, and always have been. Now you're ruining our Thanksgiving feed, with doom and gloom. I hope you're happy!"

"Troy, *stop* attacking Aunt Helen!" Phillip said this ready to turn his words into physical action.

"Sure, hide behind a fairy for defense. It's typical of evil-female ways!"

Graham spoke-up to support his spouse. "Troy let's step outside."

"Look fags don't get your panties in a bunch. Nobody here wants to eat this old-fashioned food!"

Speaking as one Graham and Phillip said, "We do!"

"Oh, I know, let's order pizza. What do yah all say garbage can pizza for everyone?" Troy spoke expecting confirmation. He received contemptuous stares instead.

The silence at the table became deafening. Out of the matriarch's line of sight, Graham and Phillip extended raised middle fingers at Troy. In response, the eldest brother withdrew into his inebriation and grasped is wife's hand.

"Aunt Helen, please pay-no attention to Troy. Is there anything we can do to ease your transition? Do you have a bucket list?"

"No, Berlinda, finish your pasta, it is delicious."

"I'm aware the family hasn't always treated you with respect. But these last few years you have been my rock. I don't know what I will do without you."

"Lack of respect started for me when I was married off to your uncle. I was much too young to be a wife, let alone his fourth. His mistreatment of wives was already legendary by the time it was my turn to be his punching bag."

"Is it true he had the first three wives killed?" Berlinda asked already knowing the answer.

"As far as I know, the official cause of their deaths *and his* were natural causes. In case any of you traffic in conspiracy rumors, I didn't murder your beloved uncle, although the thought had occurred to me more than once.Let's not sully this lovely holiday with gossip."

Martin whispered over his jacket sleeve to his wife, Alice. "I'd have slaughtered Uncle Arthur, given the chance, and had no regret." With effort, she maintained her neutral façade trying to look perky, while being uncomfortable.

"Since respect was brought up, the only thing this family has appreciated me for was turning its piddling, rapidly disappearing fortunes back into great wealth. That is the point of this meal. I turned pennies into millions of dollars. Now I'm distributing all the wealth before my demise."

Except for the nurse, servers, and Alice, all the other faces sitting around the table had dropped their masks. Those who cared for the old dowager and those who hated her wore it openly. At the mention of her affluence, a common element was added to some expressions, greed.

"I don't need or want anything more than you have already done. Being a role model and paying for my transition surgery was enough. Give my portion of your estate, if offered to the others. I take care of myself humbly, working at the library." Berlinda's words defied her body language.

Eyes on fire, Troy faced his aunt and shouted drunkenly spraying saliva. "So, it was you who encouraged Bertram to become Berlinda? I should have known. All red-blooded, flag-waving patriotic-Americans hate you for defiling male-superiority!"

"Troy, why are you always so obnoxious? Aunt Helen didn't encourage or discourage me. She listened *I was born in the wrong body*. Something none of the rest of you understands, without blaming me."

"Hold on a minute, be fair, we never judged you, Berlinda. Phil and I only suggested you try going gay before taking the irreversible step of gender reassignment surgery. Ours was a noninvasive way for you to be sure of what you wanted. But you were hell-bent to go under the knife."

"I didn't tell you, but I tried it once. It felt awkward doing it with another man, as a man. Gay wasn't okay for me, Graham."

"Listen, I'm happy Aunt Helen could give you what you needed when you needed it, but Phil and I have always tried to support you, and you know that."

"I know you tried. It's just I've been through so much emotionally and now on top of that, this, she's dying."

"Get over yourself, we all die in the end." Phillip spoke decisively.

"But I need what Aunt Helen gives me. I know I'm being selfish, I want her in my life. She can't die."

"Hattie, please remove the pasta plates and bring in the hearts of palm and artichoke singed endive-radicchio salad with that delicious lemon cappers poppy seed dressing and have the chilled Liebfraumilch served. Also, give Cleveland a heads up to prepare. We'll want to view the bird after the salad."

The distraction of food coming and going and different wines with each course didn't interfere with Troy's brooding. "Given this old-fashioned feed, I'm sure we can wait for the reading of your will until you are *dead and buried*. We know your opinion of this worthless lot of glad-hand ingrates. They deserve to get nothing! Why ruin a Thanksgiving nosh with all this pointless gibberish ... rubbish talk? Instead, why don't we watch football while we eat!Everybody with me ... oh, no."

"Troy, get everything off your chest, then be quiet." Aunt Helen Rockford folded her hands in her lap after speaking, and then gave Troy an expectant-challenging look.

"Fine, if you insist bitch, I will! At the end of this nonsense I'm still the oldest, so I'm entitled to your whole estate. Out of the goodness of my heart I might give a few crumbs to these pathetic groveling parasites, depending on my mood."

Graham turned to Phillip and spoke out of the corner of his mouth. "He's always been overly generous at holidays."

"I'm number one. No one else in this family deserve anything, nothing is too good for all of you! I get it all, it's mine!"

Phillip replied to Graham, "I suppose we should be thankful Troy is in a festive mood."

"Don't be sarcastic Phillip.*Just so you know,* Aunt Helen Rockford, if you don't leave me your entire estate, I'll contest your will in court. I'm a winner and entitled, and everyone at this table knows that, don't you losers! Uncle Arthur said I'm the only winner in this family. He also said the rest of you are worthless on a bicycle."

The two youngest brothers, Graham and Martin, had grown up with Troy the bully and looked down, cowed-embarrassed at his inebriated hurtful words. Berlinda's body language showed steel-hard defiance. If looks could kill, Troy would be headed to the mortuary. Meanwhile, Hattie and her crew of helpers removed the pasta dishes replacing them with fancy salads and German white wine.

"Please don't let boorish, Troy brow-beat you. I'm still the head of this family and my lawyers are the best money can buy, I have six on retainer. You will each get exactly what *I* think you deserve, if anything. My nurse and the house and grounds staff received my bequests for their hard-work this morning."

"You are so generous with *Troy Rockford's* money! I'm sure it's because my family is temporarily living in the caretaker's cottage, you think you can be so lavish with my birthright!"

"Martin, you never speak at these gatherings … when you show up at all. It has been over a decade since we saw your lovely face. Would you like to share any family unifying thoughts for this Thanksgiving?"

"May I speak for my husband?"

"Certainly, Alice, if he won't speak for himself and doesn't object."

"Martin doesn't want to be in this house. It makes him ill. We only came because you insisted it was for the sake of our children's future. I am not comfortable here, and we don't want or expect anything from you or that rude, crude, drunken stumblebum Troy."

"Yeah, well maybe seeing you makes us sick too, ever think about that, Miss hoity-toity fancy pants?" Troy said this thumbing his nose at Alice.

"Ignore Troy, he can't help himself. Martin, why is this family so onerous?"

"Look, Aunt Helen, I'm sad to hear you are not well and have a short time to live. I hold no grudge against you. I promised myself once I escaped, I'd only come back here to kill Uncle Arthur."

"Tell us why, Martin."

"Aunt Helen, how can you and the others not know? I'm the youngest. Uncle Arthur didn't only abuse his wives, he tortured me on that vile velodrome over the stables. And then he did it again in my bedroom. Growing up there was no refuge from the monster. He made me race faster and faster until my body quit, exhausted, my mind shutdown, and then he'd curse and beat me. After I crawled away, he'd come to my room, waiting while I showered. Then he'd physically and verbally abuse me while I was wet-naked. I had no privacy or peace in this house. How could you not see how he tortured me day after day?"

"Martin, you think you were the only one! He did the same to all of us. Except you being the youngest was his last chance for glory. He wanted an Olympic gold-medal in bicycle racing, earned by one of us."

"I know that, Graham, but he stole my childhood for his dream."

"Yeah, the irony was Berlinda had the winning stuff. She was the only one of us who won races, got metals, trophies, and even cash prizes. She could have been his ticket to glory. But *no*, Uncle Arthur couldn't stand Bertram's girly-boy mannerisms. Instead he ruthlessly punished us for not having Berlinda's winning spirit and killer speed."

"Aunt Helen, you were a successful bike racer in your youth. You had to know what was going on at this family's velodrome. He was a relentless sadist."

"As a girl, I fondly remember holding winning cycling-trophies up high, and came very close more times than I chose to remember."

"Aunt Helen you were always full of grace with us. Why was uncle Arthur such a bicycle brute?"

"He was a want to be bike racer, mediocre at best. Whenever I tried to intervene for any of you, he'd beat me. I'm sorry I couldn't protect you. At that time, I couldn't protect myself from the beast. He was a miserable malcontent. There was nothing any of us could do to control him, except Troy."

Graham tried to calm his brother, saying, "Marty, you weren't the only one he beat senseless, naked right out of the shower. He did it to me because slaps and hits sounded louder on our wet bodies."

"I biked as fast as I could, literally flying around that velodrome. The harder I pushed, the more speed he wanted, it was hopeless." Berlinda reflected remorsefully on when she was male.

The wound was too deep for Martin to move on to another topic. "You mean we all shared the hurt?"

"One of us didn't get abused."

All eyes turned to Troy, who looked down at his untouched salad, and squeezed his semiconscious wife's hand.

An inquisitive look clouded Aunt Helen's countenance. "Is it possible none of you knew … Troy was in cahoots with Arthur. He was his spy? Troy couldn't race due to an inner-ear infection's permanent-damage to his balance."

"So, that was why Troy was favored over us."

"Partially, Graham, I also suspect your Uncle favored him for looking the least like your father, Alexander."

Martin's interest reengaged as the conversation devolved into family lore. "As a small child, I saw Uncle Arthur rough you guys up and just thought you had been bad boys. I tried extra hard to always be good, having no idea what I'd get when I grew big enough to race. Then I had to run away or kill myself. All the while Troy got a free-pass, I'd wondered why."

Addressing Martin, Graham said, "The last time he went to smack me on the velodrome, I lost it, and beamed him hard on the noggin with my bicycle air pump. He got the message seeing stars. For my shower that day, I brought along a croquet mallet. That was the end of my bicycle racing days and the beginning of getting lost in books to blot out this family's sadism."

"Lucky you."

Berlinda looked from one to the other of her younger brothers. "Looking back, I was selfish. It felt so good to stop the beatings and mental torture to butch it up masculine. At the time, I thought it was only about my being a feminine boy. But I should have helped you guys stand up to uncle Arthur."

Feeling fraternal like he'd never known growing up, Martin confided to his brothers. "When I enlisted in the service, my plan was to learn to kill so I could kill Uncle Arthur. He cheated me and died before I got my chance."

"You didn't, so shut the fuck up about it. Ingrate!"

"Troy, brothers are supposed to defend each other. You should have protected me, I was the baby?"

As was his role, Graham verbally jumped in between his oldest and youngest brothers. "You're right, we know that now. When I cracked Uncle Arthur over the head, it was such a relief, it didn't occur to me he would move on to you, Marty."

"No one in this family loved me enough to stand up to Uncle Arthur then, so, why resurrect all that now? Oh, but hey, it is Thanksgiving and Arthur is long dead. Let's not talk ill of the dead."

"Hear! Hear!"

"Marty, I was struggling with my gender. But in truth, as second oldest I considered defending both you and Graham by killing Uncle Arthur and knew exactly how I'd do it. Then the authorities would have hung me. Believe me, it would have been worth it. Only I didn't know Aunt Helen controlled the money and imagined all of you, destitute, living in the gutter, because I murdered our benefactor. It all became too much for this girl. So, I took the Ostridge way out, after I broke his nose on my fist."

Martin was feeling uncomfortable being the center of attention after decades away from these strangers he'd grown up with. He nevertheless, spoke directly to Berlinda. "I remember Arthur constantly said if it wasn't for him, we'd be homeless street-urchins." That was followed by a long awkward silence of remembering. Then Martin broke it. "All right, I get it, you're all forgiven, let's move on. Now back to why we're here, Alice, and I don't need or want your money Aunt Helen. We have jobs we like and are living within our means. If you want to support our children's education, we won't say no, otherwise, thanks and no thanks."

"As hated as Arthur was, his ghost haunts this meal. I didn't plan for that."

Addressing Aunt Helen, Alice asked, "Since we can't seem to let him rest in peace. Would you fill us new family members in on Uncle Arthur?"

"Sure, if you want. I've often wondered *if* these four brothers were Arthur's children. Instead of his dead brothers, if he would have been so brutal. Arthur couldn't produce his own progeny, so, these kids were a constant reminder to Arthur of his failure as a man. Only his brother's potency would carry on the family linage."

Berlinda spoke up vying to fill in blanks. "I still don't understand why Uncle Arthur gave Troy a free-pass on the torment he rained down on the rest of us?"

"Troy doesn't look much like the rest of you, nor does he have your temperaments. I heard your parents had a shotgun wedding. Your mother was quite far along carrying Troy."

"Fuck you, everyone! I'm the only one here today who Uncle Arthur actually loved, and I will soon be the lord of this, his manner. Uncle Arthur told me as much! You are the bastards."

"It's Thanksgiving, Troy, try to be pleasant."

"Fuck you Martin! Just so you know, baby brother, buying cheap footwear will ruin your children's feet. You must know that … don't you even know that? Idiot always absent, good for nothing little brother. Uncle Arthur took care of our feet. It's a time-honored family tradition."

"Thank you for your podiatric insights, Troy. None of us knew you and Uncle Arthur had a foot fetish. And for your information, my children's feet are well cared for, so keep out of my family's business. Alice and I keep our kids fed, clothed, and a roof over our heads without help."

"Aunt Helen, maybe you could use Troy's inheritance to set up a fund to shod needy children, and then your money wouldn't be wasted on booze."

"Fuck you Phillip. You're not even a member of this family. Nobody wants to hear what you say!"

"I married into the family, just like your sozzled wife."

Asserting her authority, Aunt Helen took charge. "Hattie, please clearway the salad things and have Cleveland show off the bird before he carves it." The family matriarch then gave Troy a contemptuous look.

Reacting aggressively to her look, Troy snapped. "Aunt Helen, if you had been a better wife, Uncle Arthur wouldn't have spent so many nights in my bed!" Troy spoke before realizing what he was saying and almost choked.

The kitchen helpers quickly removed the salad dishes, forks, and used wineglasses, pretending not to hear Troy's embarrassing confrontation. Then as a further distraction, Cleveland rolled a kitchen cart around the large dining table for all to see the deliciously fragrant, huge turkey, artfully displayed on the oversize carving board nestled in a bed of colorful fresh vegetables. The smoked and then fire-roasted bird with its sage-sausage and giblet cornbread stuffing, could be smelled cooking when arriving. Cleveland then wheeled the cart back into the kitchen.

Berlinda, Graham, and Martin exchanged a look of astonishment, then gazed directly at their Aunt. Berlinda put the look into words. "So, that is why Uncle Arthur treated Troy like a little prince, grooming him to be a sex toy. And he treated the rest of us like the dirt-poor family orphans we were?"

"I never denied your Uncle sex. He started favoring Troy soon after he realized there was no baby coming from me. "Arthur hid his sexual interest in Troy. Nevertheless, I had my suspicions."

A moment of clarity peeked through Troy's alcohol induced brain-fog. He couldn't take his words back, so, tried to diminish them. "Typical, you are blaming Uncle Arthur. In truth, I seduced him. You are all wrong as usual."

"What, taking responsibility for something. That's unheard of." Berlinda said this with a sneer.

"I'll admit at the time I didn't realize what I was doing, but you were all so cold to our uncle. One of us had to be nice to the old guy? I couldn't race, but I did make him happy. So, he treated me better than you bums. I earned it, you're just jealous."

Covering her mouth with her hand Alice whispered in Martin's ear. "I bet nobody expected incest on this Thanksgiving menu."

"As far as I knew Arthur was only pedophilic with Troy, and they aren't related by blood. The sin wasn't as serious as it could have been. Anyway, that was years ago, and you've all become adults." Aunt Helen wondered if her effort for family unity, had been a wasted effort. "Let's let bygones be bygones and enjoy our meal, shall we? Hattie is everything ready?"

"Yes mam."

On Helen Rockford's signal, Hattie and her helpers left the dining room. They were back immediately with bowls of homemade cranberry sauce, orange-spice mashed sweet potatoes topped with toasted coconut, fluffy whipped with butter and heavy cream, white potatoes topped with crispy crumbled bacon, fresh from the garden green beans with mixed wild mushrooms and blanched almond butter, Brussels sprouts in a five-cheese sauce, and delicate popovers with tubs of butter at each place setting. By the time all the side dishes were served around the table and a perfect California rose` wine poured, Cleveland returned with the rolling kitchen cart, holding the deconstructed turkey and distributed light or dark meat, stuffing and gravy as guests requested.

Except for drunken Troy and Susann, the faces of the other diner guests looked scandalized into silence at Troy's incest revelation. Addressing her stone-faced guests as if everything was as usual, Helen said, "I hope you all enjoy this meal, prepared in the style of the 1800s, by many busy, hard-working kitchen-help hands."

Shaking himself back to the present, Graham said, "Aunt Helen, you out-did yourself. Your Thanksgiving table is fit for a queen, thank you so very much for this memorable meal and slice of your family history."

"You are welcome, Graham. As always, all compliments are appreciated seeing you enjoy yourselves."

Phillip trying to digest the family pedophile bombshell spoke tautly. "Yes, this meal is exceptional, my compliments to you and your staff." As an aside to Graham he mouthed, *How come you didn't know about your uncle and Toy?*

Graham leaned-sideways and whispered in Phillips ear, "We had separate bedrooms and bathrooms. I didn't grieve for my parents until college. Growing up I was angry, depressed, kept over busy with school work and training for bicycle racing. If there were hints, I missed them."

Attempting a casual tone, Berlinda pretended nothing untoward was exposed. "The grub looks good, even if I don't eat turkey or anything with a face. But the side dishes *will* be a grand gastronomical event for my simple palate."

"How come there is no asparagus?"

"Troy, you don't like how asparagus makes your pee stink. Remember, you never liked it." Martin said this barely hiding contempt.

"That's true, Marty you have a good memory. But I would like asparagus with this turkey."

"You never liked turkey much as a kid, either."

"Absolutely right Berlinda, this meal is a disappointment. We should have asparagus and roast beef, and let Uncle Arthur, the only true love of my life, rest in peace!"

Alice couldn't hold back. "You are such a ham sandwich, Troy. Don't you realize you ruined this meal already?"

"That's it! I would like a ham sandwich. Yes, that's exactly what I want, much less fuss. Okay Hattie, make me a ham sandwich on seedless rye, extra mustard and hold the pickle."

"HATTIE NO, Troy will eat what's in front of him and like it *or eat nothing.*" Aunt Helen was old, but her voice was strong.

Most guests, uncomfortable, confused, embarrassed, angry, put their heads down and ate and drank as expected. They pretended to ignore, dramatically pouting Troy, his ossified wife, and now another family scandal.

Breaking the heavy silence, Aunt Helen said, "Back to business, I've set up a family educational foundation. It pays tuition, books, and a personal living expense stipend for each of your children surnamed named Rockford, if they are accepted without condition to a reputable college or university. It will pay through graduate degrees. The trust funds should see your great grandchildren through their educational needs, and beyond."

"Stop this craziness. You're throwing my money away hand over fist *in perpetuity,* and the children don't even deserve it. What is wrong with you? I'll block this pissing away my money. Oh, shit I just pissed myself making the point, see what you made me do?"

Aunt Helen spoke firmly. "Troy, I can, and I will do as I please with the fortune I amassed. Most of the family's money was gone before Arthur came of age. The Rockford family educational foundation trust fund is a tiny fraction of my estate."

Toy sniveled, "I want all of it ..."

Aunt Helen cut him off, saying, "I suspect, coming to me hat in hand for pocket money, contributed to Arthur's demise. Seeing him grovel was little compensation for his domestic violence."

"I bet you think you're giving the house and grounds to those fags? Think again Dear Aunty, you're not, it's mine, all mine and mine alone, the eldest son always gets everything. Wait till I tell the judge I was Uncle Arthur's favorite."

"They don't want the property Troy, I offered."

"So, aunt bitch, what are you giving the pansies? Between us, they deserve nothing."

Lightening her facial expression and tone, the old dowager said, "Now everybody eats up, delicious desserts are waiting."

As instructed, heads faced down to partake of the abundant scrumptious food. Except Troy, who was dithering, muttering nonsense, more drunk than not, his chair an island in a puddle of alcohol pungent urine. Then suddenly, with another sliver of clarity, Troy said, "So, then what about the house and grounds, my house my grounds … you aren't selling them are you? You can't, they are my birth-right, Uncle Arthur promised."

"Troy don't work yourself into a state. It is unbecoming. Please try to behave until the meal is finished."

Martin, out of touch with family drama for years, tried to normalize the conversation. "Graham, do you still work for the government?"

"The County, I'm a civil servant administrator, a lowly drudge in the vernacular."

"Why are you using your top ten university education doing that?"

"Marty my office keeps the streets salt-sanded and plowed in winter and potholes filled when the snow isn't flying. I like doing that, it matters."

"I haven't seen any of you in decades and may never again. Alice and I tutor illiterate adults many are undocumented and/or homeless. The work is rewarding, the money not so much."

"Yum, every dish is so good, without meat! Marty, are you seriously going to ruin Aunt Helen's excellent meal with small-talk on top of everything else we heard today?" Berlinda said this not sure where she wanted the conversation to go.

To draw Berlinda's focus from Martin, Graham said, "Would you prefer listening to 'Kindertotenlieder' to help your digestion?"

"Now what are you talking about?"

Aunt Helen, studying the sibling's interacting, weighed whether to intervene and then did. "Gustav Mahler became enthralled with poems about dead children. His wife begged him not to set the poems to music. After Mahler wrote 'Kindertotenlieder,' his children got sick and died."

"That music reminds me of us growing up in this house, except it was our parents who died, and left us to grieve. But hey, we survived." Graham had averted a Berlinda, Martin conflict.

"I almost didn't survive living here." Martin, whispered to his wife Alice

To direct the table in a less morbid direction, Phillip said, "Mahler's De Knaben Wunderhorn might be a better choice for digestion. The boy's flute was made from a human bone, and this meal is digging-up family skeletons. Oh, sorry if I offended anyone, I'm only here by marriage."

Feeling left out of the conversation, Berlinda changed the subject. "Graham, you work for the county, I just read there are no foster homes for trans-kids. Is that true?"

"That's not my department."

"Graham you dodged my question, you must know something? After all these years, you haven't changed much, except maybe your hairline. Phillip, how do you put up with his inability to answer direct questions?"

"It's a knack."

"When we were young, I'd have to kick his ass when he wouldn't answer my questions. I may have to reintroduce my foot to his butt this Thanksgiving."

"Berlinda, it is unladylike to say that, and don't hurt your delicate foot."

"Thanks for the advice, Phil. Let me add your name to my list needing an ass kicking."

"You are welcome, I'm sure. To answer your question, we've heard the child-welfare agency has a shortage of homes for all foster children."

"Why, for God's sake? Those children need safe homes." Berlinda decided she liked homeless foster children as a topic, better than Martin's small talk, or Graham's morbid music talk, or talk of Troy sleeping with the family patriarch.

"Berlinda, the public child welfare agency is not evolved to the level of sophistication your thinking demands."

Aunt Helen, again watching the siblings' interplay, couldn't resist commenting. "Children are resilient. Given half a chance, they thrive no matter what obstacles adults put in their path."

"So, Graham, what happens to Trans children if there is no place for them?"

"Officially all kids up to age twelve go to foster homes. Over twelve and younger problem kids, go to group homes."

"Answer my question Graham."

"I just did, older foster children not already in long term placement must go to one of the two large group homes. No exceptions or special circumstance considered."

"What are they like?"

"Berlinda, I don't work for child welfare."

"No, Graham, you work for the county and know more than most as an insider."

"I've heard, budget cuts and attrition mean staff shortages which translates into big bad resident children preying on smaller or weaker ones. If no one dies, the source of abuse and neglect switches from family to institution, as perpetrator."

"That sounds Dickensian bleak."

"It is. The government makes no secret the Child Welfare Agency is run on human sacrifice. Workers manage large caseloads of children in danger, and waste much of their time waiting in family court for required hearings."

"Graham, that sounds like Dickens all right. And the pathos is?"

"When a child dies in care, the public demands the Government throw lots of money at the cause and terminate the direct service staff on the lowest rung of the bureaucratic. That assuages the public's guilt for not caring about these kids in the first place."

"If you ask me, those filthy little cretins are better off dead. The KKK had it right with Eugenics. What is important is racial purity."

"Troy when did you become a KKK supporter?" Alice knew she was baiting Troy but couldn't resist.

Not liking the direction, the conversation was headed, nevertheless, Aunt Helen stifled her opinion.

"Troy after all these years, you still have me befuddled. Oh, wait it fits, you are antiabortion pro-death penalty, right?"

While her siblings squabbled, Berlinda's face showed she was mulling something over. "What if I wanted to set something up for Trans' children? Would you recommend that, if it could even be approved?"

"How would we know?"

"HELLO, Earth to Graham and Phil! I'm asking what I'd be getting into."

"Berlinda, the system is bureaucratic slow with cumbersome, antiquated rules that often make as much sense as Troy. And there's always tons of paperwork with any government. Is that a direct enough answer?"

"You're improving, and I appreciate the effort, Graham."

"If you don't mind me butting in Berlinda, you could volunteer at the better group home and learn firsthand what foster care is like."

"What would I do, Phil? I have an aversion to washing toilets, other than my own."

"I'd think the younger ones like to be read stories. Maybe the older kids enjoy games. Probably they all love attention from adults that doesn't hurt."

"Thank you, Phil., Huh, you know what … we have new materials at the library most children love?"

Troy erupted again, without provocation. "Fuck you and all your waifs. I've been very patient listening to your blah, blah conversation. Just so you know, I'm not a drunk! I just like to take a drink from time to time and on holidays like this one. Aunt Helen's constant nagging me about drinking is annoying."

Graham responded with mandated-worker certainty. "Troy, for your information any one at this table or Hattie, Cleveland, and members of their crews could call in an anonymous report of drunken neglect against you and Susann and trigger removal of your kids."

"Do it then! Let's see who wins? You know I always win baby brothers. I'm the best brother, uncle Arthur said so."

"Wait a minute, Graham, you're saying if someone makes an anonymous telephone complaint against Troy and his wife, the police come and take their children?"

"No, Alice, social workers come first to investigate the allegations. If the parents become belligerent, the social workers call the police and the police arrest the parents and that triggers removal of kids without adult supervision. Then a case is brought to Family Court to sort it out."

"Okay, so why not call in a complaint right now? We can all see they are both drunk out of their gourds."

"Alice, unless a family member is willing to take Troy's kids, they get split up to different foster and group homes. It's not unheard of for kids to get lost in the foster care system."

Berlinda's face showed she was uncomfortable with a conversation about family breakup rather than the unity her aunt asked for. "They aren't bad children."

"But it could be the wakeup call Troy and Susann need."

"Alice, foster care is no joke. I wouldn't wish it on my worst enemy, let alone my eldest brother's children."

Martin shared his wife's concern. "We can't just do nothing, those children are our kin, at least from mom's side."

After glancing to her boss for silent approval, Nurse Jaspers spoke up for the first time during the meal, her little girl sounding voice emanating from a big roly-poly body. "His two oldest do an acceptable job looking after the younger one."

Martin gathered himself then forcefully spoke his mind. "Why not let Child Welfare decide that? Troy and his wife need a reality check."

When aunt Helen heard the conversation seriously turn to bringing in the authorities, she spoke using her clout. "We may not be an award-winning family. Nevertheless, we *are* family and have the means to take care of our own."

"I hate to be disagreeable, but some action is required to protect Troy's children from alcohol neglect." Alice said this sounding prim and proper.

"I have professionals keeping an eye on Troy, Susann and their youngsters. Don't worry I've got this. We don't need the authorities involved in our family."

Fishing to make peace, Graham looked from his aunt who just spoke, to Alice, then Berlinda. "Wait a minute. How did Troy and family end up living in the caretaker's cottage?"

Forcing his eyes to stay open Troy slurred a retort. "It was a misunderstanding. We had some bad luck, everyone has bad luck sometimes."

"Tell me, I want to know, Troy!"

"It is none of your God damn business, Graham."

"I work for the government I have ways to find out. What happened?"

"Like I said, we had bad luck that went on longer than necessary. We ended up living in our car. It happens sometimes. Then the police screwed up and called Aunt Helen. It was one of her cars."

Martin still keyed-up, faced the family matriarch. "Aunt Helen, what's going on?"

"We're finishing this lovely meal and thankful for it and wishing for family amity."

Berlinda spoke up sternly, "She is right, all of you stop this Troy craziness. Aunt Helen has lawyers to help him."

"And the new topic is?" Alice said this with sarcasm dripping off her tongue.

"Help me decide something important, Alice. Graham and Phillip, how much would it cost to foster a trans child?"

"There are variables, Berlinda. Space and your child's other needs and wants for example."

"Answer my question, Graham."

"Do you have an extra bedroom? No, you don't."

"I could add-on an addition. How much money is needed after that?"

"Call a contractor, then call child welfare."

"Maybe being a foster parent is more than Berlinda can handle?" Alice said this with an apologetic shrug of her shoulders.

"Maybe she's right."

"Berlinda you can handle anything you put your mind to, you handled going from male to female…"

Phillip interrupted his spouse Graham, and said, "The question should be, why you would want to put yourself through all the trouble and heartache? These kids are too messed up to thank you."

"He's right, why would you want the grief?" Graham said this to Berlinda. Then tossed Phillip a look they were in agreement.

"I don't know, because they don't have enough *normal* hetero foster homes?"

"Berlinda, a balanced, healthy life requires not letting the outside world upset your internal equilibrium."

"Answer my damn question, Graham. Should I become a foster parent for trans kids?"

"Nietzsche said, 'What doesn't kill us makes us stronger.'"

"I didn't ask Nietzsche."

"Good thing, he died in 1900."

Reanimating after torpor, Troy disrupted the conversation. "I'm the oldest, you should show me love and respect, not threaten to put my children in jail! What's wrong with you people? You know I don't take threats well." After vehemently spitting that out, Troy's face crumpled up and he began crying. "Uncle Arthur loved me. Why can't you love me? I *am* loveable!"

As usual, aunt Helen brought calm to disorder with the wave of her hand. "Hattie, let your helpers clear the table and bring on dessert. We are having both pumpkin and pecan pies. You can have a big dollop of just whipped cream or homemade vanilla ice cream or both. Also, we have my favorite espresso coffee. Anyone want cognac?"

Alice, concern showing on her face, asked? "Aunt Helen, what are your plans to keep our drunk and disorderly Troy and family out of the clutches of the authorities?"

"It is all arranged … involuntary commitment papers are signed by two physicians and takes effect the minute I pass. The children will stay with Susann's sister."

"Sounds like you have it covered." Relief showed on Alice's face.

"Blah, blah-di blah, such a waste, you're all wrong. We don't have any drinking problems. The police made a mistake calling aunt Helen."

Half under his breath, Martin sarcastically said, "Yeah, sure they did."

"It's true, Susann and I take a drink now and then to relax. We don't need treatment, only less stress. You all know that."

Phillip had had enough delusional thinking. "Troy, cut the crap, we've heard you and your wife drinks every day, from morning till you pass out."

"Liar!"

"Why don't you copy your wife? Put your head down on the table and sleep? Just don't put your face in the food plate, like her. It will take forever to get all that turkey gravy out of her hair."

Berlinda still preoccupied thinking about creating a foster home for Trans kids, ignored the others squabbling and spoke. "Aunt Helen, what *are* your plans for the house and grounds?"

"I've given them to Hattie and Cleveland. After all these years, they earned them. They want to turn the place into a year-round retreat for their church. As a religious facility, they won't pay taxes and they'll have access to resources necessary for upkeep."

"Good plan, Phil and I approve."

"Graham, can you explain how Troy can be such a homophobe after being our Uncle's child lover? It seems implausible."

"I don't know, Berlinda."

Uninvited, Alice jumped in with a comment. "I've read sexually-abused children often become sexuality confused adults."

"Berlinda, maybe a psychoanalyst could unwind Troy's sexual-self-hate, relationship with Suzann, and lack of care for his children. Or, we could just shoot him."

"Oh, no, stop Phil, that's too much to digest on a full stomach." Berlinda said this throwing her hand up in the universal stop gesture.

"Hattie, I'm suddenly feeling very tired and must nap. As soon as they finish their pie, clear away the dishes and bring out the cheese and fruit platters, and serve the champagne. Thank you and your helpers for a job well done. You did yourselves proud."

Nurse Jaspers grasped the old woman's elbow, as she stood unsteadily. Then the family matriarch leaned heavily on her ornate wooden cane and rang her little silver bell for attention. Except for Troy and Susann, the others also stood. Aunt Helen's eyes studied each guest's face. They could tell, it was their dowager's final goodbye.

Aunt Helen's voice sounded tired when she spoke. "If there was ever doubt, I loved each of you as my own, this taste of history meal, should be proof enough I did. After observing your inability to really care for or about each other, I've decided to leave my entire estate, $4,000,000,000, minus the family education foundation trust, to the School Girls International Cycling Federation. I love you, but you've moved beyond this dysfunctional family without my help, and now so has my wealth."

Most present had expected to inherit millions. They didn't hide massive disappointment showing on their faces. Then another reality set in, they had failed the simple family-cohesion test their aunt mentioned at the start of the meal. Looking one to another, too late they felt family solidity.

"All right, everyone, thank you for coming. Remember, despite your disappointment, you are family and blood kin hold no resentments." Aunt Helen, turned, leaning heavily against her nurse and hobbled out of the dining room.

World AIDS Day

Homophobia was given a big boost after the Second-World War when the Un-American Activities Committee of the United States House of Representatives announced all homosexuals were Communists, and Communists must be scorned. At that time the United States' former enemy, then friend and ally during World-War-Two, the Soviet Union, became a nuclear power and America's cold war archenemy. Domestic propaganda fed by the U.S. Congress promoted fear and loathing of all Communists. To cultivate internal Red Scare foreboding and divide to control its citizens, the United States Government engaged in covert and overt anticommunist military aggressions in Cambodia, China-Taiwan, Cuba, Korea, Laos, Vietnam, and failed.

Between the end of World-War-Two and the Stonewall Rebellion, it was close to impossible for two men, not related by blood, to rent or buy a domicile to cohabitate. Landlords and neighbors were encouraged to report overnight or late-night male guests to the authorities for sodomy investigation. Sex outside the home risked active police entrapment, criminal blackmailers, queer bashing, the usual garden variety sadistic religious fruits and nuts. Masturbation was the only safe yet lonely alternative to disgrace and prison for gratifying a basic, much maligned human appetite.

One documented result from three nights of gay rioting at the Stonewall Inn in New York City was overt government-sponsored homophobia waned. It again became possible for men to enjoy sexual expression in private without risking bodily harm and ruin. Along with renewed sexual freedoms came increased rates of STDs and then a resurgence of previously thought eradicated disease like syphilis.

Due to the young adult social-sexual revolution of the 1960s, authoritarianism's repression pendulum swung toward freedom, unleashing decades of sexual subjugation. Restrictive liquor laws loosened to allow gay women and men to open restaurants and bars. In short order, New York City lesbian and gay male bars went from heterosexual Mafia-owned, bribing the police and organized crime to stay open, to law-abiding, taxpaying homosexual owned and operated, out of the shadows' legitimate businesses.

With renewed freedoms came new problems. Human digestive system parasites unknown outside the tropics began showing up in mainland United States, at urban public STD clinics. An alarming number of healthy young men in big cities were dying from Hepatitis-B for no known reason at that time. Gay scientists and their colleagues responded quickly to the Hepatitis-B epidemic and a vaccine was developed in record time and controlled the problem.

Then a new scourge appeared and revived national homophobia with a politically-driven media vengeance. The prudish conservative pendulum reversed its swing. Virulent anticommunist, homophobic President Ronald Reagan's moral failing to say the word AIDS, after 50,000 of the citizens he pledged to protect and serve died of the illness, retarded public health response and funding. Europeans and the United Nations finally addressed the pandemic President Reagan was too craven and anti-homosexual to acknowledge was ravaging the United States.

In August of 1987, James Bunn and Thomas Netter of Geneva, Switzerland, convinced Dr. Jonathan Mann of the World Health Organization's UNAIDS to proclaim December 1st, 1988 the first World AIDS Day. As of 2017 forty-two million people had died of AIDS worldwide and another thirty-seven million were HIV positive. Even though AIDS affects humans of all ages, races, genders, ethnicities, creeds, and sexual orientation, it was mislabeled a gay disease for political expediency and not treated seriously in America.

Homosexual scientists and colleagues, fresh from fighting the Hepatitis-B outbreak, identified gay-cancer and other misnamed *gay* illnesses as AIDS. Even though the retrovirus was found not to be gay male-specific, sensationalist media homophobes promoted AIDS as a gay scourge. It was mainly to prop up a bigoted failing Republican president embroiled in Iran and Central-American scandals.

To magnify Ronald Regan's prejudice, Russian Military Intelligence proliferated an anti-American lie. It was the U.S. Army, in Maryland, developed AIDS as a biological weapon to eliminate homosexuals and African-Americans. The bogus Russian AIDS propaganda was tested in India, expanded to Africa, Europe, Central then South America, and North America. By the first World AIDS Day, the fake Russian news had been spread worldwide. In the U.S., not sure what was true or false, medical care and research became close to nonexistent early in the epidemic.

At the beginning of the pandemic there were only three medical doctors in the New York Tri-State area and no dentist who would knowingly treat AIDS patients. The three heroic medical men burned-out quickly as the epidemic increased. In response to the burn-outs and huge amount of pitiful suffering leading to death, a small number of brave gay and gay-friendly physicians joined the fray. They did not know what their personal risks might be. Medical practitioners who refused to care for the suffering said publicly, "We weren't trained to handle *gay* maladies. It might be God removing a blight."

Research later found most panicked, immobilized, uncaring physicians were afraid of catching the wrongly diagnosed *gay* plague. It has been proven there is much more hypochondria, and atheism among medical doctors than the general public. Practitioners of theology were scarcer than medical doctors when their need was greatest, at the beginning of the epidemic. However, when pressed by gay media, many physicians and clergymen acknowledged they were patriots following the leadership of their pusillanimous, antigay president of the United States.

Naturally, nurses, nurse practitioners, physician's assistants, and social workers rushed in to fill the national physicians' void and minister to the ill and dying. They had to work against hospital administration homophobia blocking Standards of Care. Hospital administrators justified poor or no-patient treatment from fear of loss of federal funding. When asked about his inaction during plague, President Reagan said, "Gays do not deserve special treatment, even when they make themselves sick." He went on to explained new born infants, elderly, and hemophiliacs suffering and dying from AIDS as God's will.

A previously developed, ineffective cancer drug, AZT, helped a few AIDS patients improve. It made others sicker and had little effect on many. The highly-toxic drug killed people by being prescribed in too-high dosages. But AZT was the only medication available early in the crisis, and if a little didn't work maybe a lot would. There were tried and true medications to combat most opportunistic infections, but their effectiveness diminished as the patient's immune system disappeared. A healthy individual has 1,200 to 1,600 T-cells; usually an AIDS diagnosis is given with 600 to 800 T-cells. A rough rule of thumb is that the end of life begins around 100 T-cells.

Help was on the horizon. Medical schools, nursing schools and schools of social work prepared their students to rise above the government promoted extreme fear mongering apocalyptic homophobia and humanely treat patients with an unknown malady. It also didn't hurt that some enlightened local and state governments were offering student loan forgiveness to licensed graduates willing to work with AIDs for five years. New medications to attack HIV were quickly brought to market decades ahead of schedule by sheer force of ACT UP's acting up and other AIDS advocacy groups' disruptive social actions. The pharmaceutical industry realized huge profits once it went against the United States president's politics overruling science, and realized *AIDS was not just a gay disease.*

A sixtyish African-American academic was working hunched over his computer when a lanky student arrived at his open office door and rapped lightly on the doorframe. Looking up, the professor said, "Are you Delgado Schwartzmann? Right … come in and close the door. Welcome to the fall semester."

"Yes, thank you, sir."

"I read you are originally from Argentina. Do you speak Spanish?"

The tall, thin, light blue and white vertical stripped polo shirt and denim jeans clad twenty-three-year-old took the seat indicated by the professor. "My family immigrated here when I was fourteen. English is my second language. Professor Hudson, I've heard so many great things about you, it is an honor to finally meet you."

"Call me Bill. Have you had your first seminar and practicum?"

"Yes, sir Bill. May I take notes?"

"Certainly. Have you been given a case yet?"

"No, I was told Wednesday."

"Why don't I explain my expectations first? My primary goal is you give your patients the best you have to offer, using The Social Work Code of Ethics for your scaffolding. My second goal is that you have as good as possible educational experience within the limits of this AIDS unit. And my third goal is you comply with all administrative expectations of this hospital and your university with *on-time* paperwork for both. If you keep up with the paperwork, it is manageable. Fall behind and it is like drowning. Keep that in mind when your classmates or hospital staff asks you to translate from Spanish to English for them at the expense of your work. Do you have questions?"

"No, I don't think so."

"Tell me about your first-year field placement?"

"My university, first-year social work graduate students had no say for fieldwork. Unless indicating an area they really didn't want to work in, then they *were* assigned that. So, I didn't put a preference or aversion and the school sent me to Celestial Arms Hospice for two semesters."

"In one word, how was that?"

"Rewarding."

"How so?"

"I expected a sad place, depressingly slow with a lot of time to reflect on death and dying. It wasn't like that. I was constantly busy and learned a lot about people, life, and me under pressure. The only negative is hospice requires a ton of paperwork. There is no end to it with reports, forms, letters, all on tight turnaround deadlines. I came close to what you said about getting behind and drowning; once."

"Do you have a personal therapist?"

"No, between tuition, books, and living expenses, there is no way to afford one. I even had to sell my car."

"Why did you choose AIDS for your second-year fieldwork?"

"I'm gay and want to help my community. I've read there is a major shortage of professionals working in the field, and I'm willing to risk my health for the greater good."

Dr. Hudson made an unconscious, dismissive shooing hand gesture as the corners of his mouth turned down. "Then this field placement is not for you."

"Why Not?"

"What you want is a Gay Community AIDS Outpatient Clinic and testing site. Call your school's field advisor and say I said to switch you. If they don't have a placement available, they should cobble something together, say I said so. Call her or him as soon as you leave my office."

Delgado looked taken aback. He cleared his throat to give himself a pause and softened his tone. "But I like it here. The other student interns at the weekly three-hour seminar, and two-hour practicum are nice, the medical staff on grand rounds treats us well, and I've heard you are the best field instructor for once a week clinical supervision. I'd like to stay."

"Here at Greater Gotham General Hospital, most of our AIDS patients identify as heterosexual, or drug addicted."

"Sir, I can work with straight people, I have my whole life. My parents are heterosexuals."

"Your other assumptions are also wrong. This is an urban public hospital affiliated with the City's University Medical School. We seldom have staff shortages. HIV is hard to catch, you really must work at it sharing needles. If you follow hospital protocol, you can't catch it here. Where did you get your misinformation?"

"My undergraduate degree is in journalism. I consume a lot of news, and you just told me everything I learned about AIDS from the media is wrong. No wonder newspapers are going broke."

"Call your school's fieldwork office. If they can't help us, I'll see you same time same station next week."

* * * *

The leather elbow-patched, English tweed-wearing, medium dark-skinned professor frowned deeply. "Let me guess, your university couldn't accommodate my request and is looking to go to war with me?"

With apprehension showing, Delgado knew he was at a do or die juncture, so, he trusted his old reliable and spoke truth. "When my advisor asked if your request is what I want, I said no. I like it here and fit in with the others. Even though I've been grossly misinformed about HIV/AIDS, I want to help with the pandemic here."

The professor gave his intern a new assessing head to toe look. "If you won't take no as an answer, let's expand your one-hour clinical supervision to cover everything going on with you during the next two semesters. If we need more time, I have makeup office hours early Friday morning and one late Monday evenings, use as needed."

Relief from anxiety washed over Delgado. "Thank you, professor."

"Were you assigned a patient yet?"

"Yes, Mary Willis. Here's her paperwork. I met her Wednesday at two o'clock and sat with her during her latest test results."

"How did it go?"

Over-prepared, Delgado's mouth ran before his brain registered the question. "She is a sex worker, heroin addict with two children in foster care; a boy three and a girl two. One child's father died of complications from AIDS, the other's incarcerated. She lists an elderly mother as her primary support. In case of emergency, she identified Rosemary Rojas, no telephone or address but frequents the intersection of Stone and Maple late at night."

"You didn't answer my question."

Recoiling like he'd been slapped, Delgado said, "Oh sorry … it was heavy. Her T-cells are not good, and she cried a lot. I held her hand and wanted to put my arm around her shoulders but didn't. I was afraid more physical contact would be unprofessional. I'm not sure … I wanted to."

"Can you handle your feelings and having to second-guess yourself?"

"With your help, I think so."

"It is important to read nonverbal signs like facial expression, tone of voice, and body language. You were right. Making unwanted physical contact can be misinterpreted and cause distress. Always ask before touching."

"Thanks, that helps."

"There is a better than even chance your new patient is a lesbian, lots of female sex workers are, *but you don't ask*. If she wants you to know, she'll say so."

Delgado said, "I understand." But his face indicated otherwise.

Picking up the contradiction, Professor Hudson leaned in toward his student. *"Under no circumstance do you come out or reveal anything personal before asking yourself, how is my information going to help?"* Sitting back in his chair, the professor continued speaking, "The less your patients know about you, the better they can focus on their problems."

Breathing a big sigh of relief, Delgado uncrossed and opened his legs, also sitting back. "I didn't realize that, but it makes sense."

"What is social work's first rule?"

"Join the client where they are and then help them set realistic goals from there."

"Everything you do has to be about your patient. But that can't happen until you establish a therapeutic alliance. And that can't happen if you muddy the waters with your biography where it doesn't belong. You are here to help, not vice versa."

"Right, join with her, move at her pace, and help her find realistic goals to face the future."

Leaning back in the desk chair and locking eyes, Bill said, "That's *your* goal. An addicted HIV sex worker with low T-cells goal may be to manipulate you for her legal or illegal purposes. Transference and counter-transference is where the battle lines get drawn. Show that in your clinical notes and then reflect on it in your monthly and quarterly reports so the powers that be see you understand application of theory. Beyond the 'I said, and she said' of process recording."

Suddenly sensing educational overload, Delgado took a beat. "It sounds like a lot is expected of me. By the way my friends and family call me Deano."

"It isn't hard if you take five or ten minutes after each interview to consider what really transpired, before you put pen to paper."

To head off a brain freeze, Deano took the conversation to what he knew. "Got it, don't rush and be played for a chump, step back and think before writing. Since we are getting down to it, what's my long view here?"

Realizing he might have given too much information to soon, Bill let Deano-Delgado direct. "They should have covered that in your seminar. Between now and December you will get at least one new hospitalized patient a week. The beginning phase of your work is to establish a therapeutic alliance with clear boundaries and then help find realizable goals. With a full case load starting in January, the middle phase is to actualize measurable-outcome patient goals, and define new ones if appropriate. In late April, you begin the termination process that allows your patients to be angry at you for leaving and get over it and say goodbye by the time you graduate."

"Transference and counter-transference in the textbook, sounded dry. Listening to you it's exciting."

Not comfortable accepting student's flattery, Bill ended the session with instruction. "What is different here than other hospitals; when your patient is discharged, you continue as their social worker if they attend our outpatient clinics, and when re-hospitalized. You become an important part of our continuity of care. We also try to accommodate any patient or ex-patient who just shows up out of the blue wanting to talk. Prepare yourself now, some of your folks will die, some will disappear without warning and may or not resurface. No matter how hard you work some patients can never attain the simplest goal they set, but not from lack of trying."

* * * *

By January, Deano Schwartzmann's field placement at the hospital had progressed smoothly into the middle phase. He had a full caseload of inpatients and outpatients as the AIDS epidemic grew unchecked with no relief in sight. Professor Hudson took the time to expand Deano's fieldwork clinical supervision to include what he saw as relevant past personal experiences affecting present work. They also got into a deeper understanding of frustrations with medication noncompliant patients, beyond what the hospital and Deano's university expected from student interns.

The two men's relationship deepened, as the older, sometimes stodgy professor regularly handed the fresh-faced second-year graduate student a box of tissues to dry his eyes and blow his nose after another difficult patient, succumbed to horrible opportunistic infections due to no immune system. When Deano's university sent a fieldwork advisor, Dr. Pickwick, for an unannounced site visit, Doctor Hudson gave Deano an excellent review.

"But Professor Hudson, does our student Deano do anything more than what we expect from students? As you know, the university has high standards. Is there something extra special I can put in my field report to support your praise?"

"Since its inception, our AIDS unit has participated in local World AIDS Day. Attendance is voluntary. Most staff participate without remuneration. This year, Deano took time out of his heavy schedule to read names of the deceased."

"I was thinking … maybe something less organized."

"Against my concern for his safety, Deano on occasion rides his bicycle, late at night, to seedy areas where his missing clients are known to use drugs and or sell sex. He has convinced several patients to be compliant with their medications and keep clinic appointments with him. I'd rather he didn't risk his safety for the sake of his clients, but he can be stubborn."

"That certainly sounds above and beyond what we expect from our students. I suppose he translates for non-Spanish speaking staff too. Yes, that will do nicely for my report, unless you have something else."

"Deano, within the HIPPA guidelines, give Dr. Pickwick a brief overview of your most challenging case before he leaves."

"Certainly, okay …"

* * * *

Deano started his first clinical supervision in February, with a question. "Bill, have you ever flunked a second-year, second-semester graduate student?"

"Why do you ask?"

"I was just wondering."

"In my fifteen years here, I've given three educational intermissions for cause. Are you worried about flunking?"

Looking cagey and uncomfortable, Deano dipped his chin to his chest. "I don't know, maybe."

"By my estimation, you are doing fine … the end is in sight." The professor had gotten to know his student intern well enough to know when not to push. The two men sat in expectant silence.

Finally, Deano broke the stillness. "My seminar and practicum classmate Wanda finally got her last inpatient. I saw him on the unit, but we never spoke. The thing is, I've photographed him with a telephoto lens at Gray Pride Parades, for over six years, and at this year's World AIDS' Day."

"Isn't that an invasion of his privacy?"

"You can't be private participating in a public event. I didn't publish the photos. And I wasn't looking for Wanda's patient either. But somehow every year my camera found and recorded him. He's drop-dead gorgeous."

"Is there a question?"

"Having him on this hospital's AIDS' floor is disquieting. No, it is distracting. It's mixing up my personal with professional life. I'm not sure what to think?"

"Dig deep, get into it?"

"Let's see … okay, with my patients I can be dispassionate objective. Our roles are defined. I know what I'm doing and what to expect. Seeing this guy, Tim O'Doul, *here* has stirred up a lot of stuff close to where I live, too close for objectivity. This can't be good."

"Deano, why did you never speak to Mr. O'Doul over six years of seeing him at Gay Pride Parades?"

"He's unattainable perfection, way out of my league. He is faultless, and looks like he works out a lot. I'm far from perfect, and hardly work out."

"Are you being self-deprecating? The fastest way to remove apprehension, and to bring someone you've made larger than life down to size, is to say hi."

"Even though I've been out for six years, I have issues meeting new people classier than me. I'm too tall, skinny, and speak with an accent. Who I might like, and who likes me, live in different worlds."

"Deano, you are an intelligent, attractive young man anyone would be lucky to get to know you. Rather than an obstacle, turn this man's hospitalization into an opportunity to develop social skills."

"He's not my patient … you saying I should talk to him? Just the thought gives me goose bumps."

"Don't get me wrong, I'm not suggesting you hit on this guy. Demystify his being out of your league by introducing yourself. Just say hello. Think of it as an assignment to remove a social anxiety."

"But he's not my patient!"

"For one time, take on the role of a friendly hospital visitor, what could it hurt? He gets an extra smile and handshake and you feel better about yourself, win-win."

"You're challenging me to do something I'm afraid to do, aren't you?"

"If it goes down easier as a challenge, so be it. But you *must* respect the HIPPA law. Under no circumstances look at his hospital chart, access it on-line, or ask his caregivers staff like questions. Keep it short and simple. The goal is to demystify an ideal. When that is done, back away, no further contact, assignment complete."

"Do you think my photos of him would be a good ice breaker? They are great shots. He hasn't changed that much."

"This isn't about making a new friend. It *is* about you bringing him down to *hello* size. You know what an AIDS diagnosis can do to someone's self-image. Don't make it worse, by showing him your photos."

"What if my friend Wanda wants to talk about his case or she presents him at practicum?"

"Are you stalling?"

"No."

"Then why not cross that bridge if you get there?"

At his next clinical supervision, Deano was more animated than usual. "I did as you suggested, waited until Tim was alone and introduced myself. He seemed in a down mood, and said he was treated like a lab rat here. I didn't stay long."

"Did he appear human scale, off the pedestal you put him on?"

"You knew he would. But then two days later I was coming out of one of my patient's rooms and Tim called me by name. He was getting ready to go home and needed a hand with his bag. He was in a much better mood. We chatted for a few minutes waiting for his discharge transportation. He speaks Spanish. His paternal grandparents immigrated to Mexico from Ireland."

"Was it just small talk?"

"For the most part … he's working with an impressive medical team. Reading between the lines, it appears the virus is not affecting him like most people and that may be why he has medical heavy hitters on his case."

"How does he appear to you?"

"You see that's it, for a semester and a half I've seen what horrible things AIDS does to healthy young bodies … making them look like ninety-year-olds. Tim looks totally unscathed but said his T-cells keep dropping. His medial team can't stop the loss and he says treat him like a freak for being healthy."

"Okay, you successfully did what I asked, twice, and lived to tell about it. Now step back and keep your distance from Mr. O'Doul, assignment over."

"What if he calls me again?"

"Say hi and little more. You have more than enough work to do until the end of semester."

"I like him, and I think he likes me. Now that he's life size, he's *my size*. I'd like to know him better."

"So far, your internship has gone well. Don't screw up all your hard work by pissing off medical heavy-hitters. To be effective, social workers must know and keep their place. As you said several times, Mr. O'Doul is not your patient. Objective achieved, no more contact."

Deano started his next supervision in a heightened state of mixed agitation. "All my clinical notes, statistics, and reports are up to date. My case load is under control and percolating away nicely. May we skip fieldwork today, and talk about something personal?"

"Did you bring copies of your most recent process recordings and clinical notes? Oh, and the draft of your final quarterly report?"

"I have them right here."

"Okay fine … thank you … what's on your mind?"

"Tim O'Doul is back in the hospital for more tests and prophylaxis. We met in the hall, he was walking it for exercise, I had just visited one of my patients. Somehow it slipped out in conversation I've photographed him for years without knowing him. Naturally, he wanted to see pictures, and I just happened to have them with me from showing my classmate Wanda."

"I asked you to back off with Mr. O'Doul. Are you planning to make this the main topic of discussion when your university field advisor Dr. Pickwick meets us next?"

"I'd rather not. I didn't go looking for trouble. I tried to do what you asked without being rude."

Doctor Hudson resigned himself to an impending heavy session. "Being too busy to stop and chat is not rude. It *is* setting priorities. I asked you not to show your photos to Mr. O'Doul."

"But you asked *me* to say hello to Tim the first time. I'm being completely honest with you. It was by chance each time we met after the first time."

"Why do I sense there is more turmoil coming? Spit it out. What else is happening, Mr. Schwartzmann?"

Shaking his head from side to side, Deano finally bowed it and covered his face with his hands, muttering, "My personal and professional lives have gotten tangled. At first, I thought I was only doing what you asked. Now it seems I'm doing what Tim wants. Truth told, I'm not sure what's going on with what I want."

"Talk to me, Deano."

"Tim is a trained Irish tenor, he sings to me. Do you know how special it is to be an audience of one, being sung to by a professional? It feels like I'm in a movie."

"Singing in hospitals is frowned upon. Is that why you are so troubled?"

"I know it's not my place, but I'm afraid a mistake was made diagnosing Tim. He looks good, big and strong and healthy with no signs of wasting. I've been here long enough to know what low t-cells looks like. I think all these prophylaxes treatments and tests are unnecessary. He's right, they treat him like a lab specimen instead of a person."

"Since Mr. O'Doul has become a topic in our clinical supervision, I have done some checking, with Wanda's supervisions. Tim O'Doul is an AIDS-anomaly the whole hospital is talking about. He was given both types of HIV tests, *five times each*, and every result was reactive, not indeterminate; *reactive*. That his T-cells keep falling and he appears healthy has made him an international AIDS peculiarity. Researchers are going nuts to get samples of his blood. But enough about him, I suspect there is something else bothering *you*?"

Deano turned to his fieldwork supervisor with a frank open face, making direct eye contact. "Buckle up your seat belt Doctor Hudson. When Tim saw my photographs of him, he liked them a lot. Even said he was impressed with my photographic talent. Then after a minute thinking, he spoke sweetly, saying he'd never been loved from afar before. He said unrequited love is the purest form of love. But he prefers physical love and then he surprised me with a big kiss. He's a great kisser. This will sound crazy, I think I'm falling for the guy. It's out of my control."

Dr. Hudson was pensive, taking in Deano's bright, young demeanor. "My suggesting you speak with Mr. O'Doul was obviously a mistake. Rather than help with your self-esteem, it appears, unintentionally, I have put you and your education at risk. You must cease all contact with him. I am so sorry for my part in this."

"We couldn't have known what would happen. Only, he's invited me to get physical with him. Me? I was good at this internship and liked it. Yet … I'm tempted to throw it all away on a whim? Am I nuts or what?"

"Hold that thought for now … since he isn't getting ongoing treatment, he can't be utilizing our outpatient clinics. Deano, I am reassigning you. Starting tomorrow you will only see outpatients, until the semester ends. With luck, maybe you can graduate after all. If you can resist Mr. O'Doul's power over you. Are you willing to concentrate on finishing what you started?"

"Yes, I don't want to let you down Bill."

* * * *

Wondering whether to start their termination process early or wait till their next meeting, Dr. Hudson greeted his student intern weighing pros and cons. "How is the change to only outpatient going?"

"It's less stressful, but I miss the mix." His words and body language didn't quite match.

"You are almost finished with fieldwork. I have gotten excellent reports about you from clinic staff. Early congratulations."

Looking down, Deano mumbled, "Don't say that, I think I've blown it … sorry. It wasn't planned, just one thing led to another."

"Talk to me, what happened?"

"When you reassigned me, I said goodbye to Tim. He asked for my cell phone. I knew it violated the Code of Ethics and hospital policy. He touched our cell phones together for a kiss goodbye. I allowed it."

"Do I sense more?"

"He telephoned me late that night, for us to jerkoff on the telephone. He was seductive, and my resistance wasn't strong."

"You can't look this upset over masturbating on the telephone."

"I visited him here, during evening visitor's hours the next day. Tim asked me to help him get in and out of the shower."

"The hospital pays people for that."

"He said they always make him wait and then treat him coldly, like he's dead already. Anyway, he wanted *me* to help him. I can't say no to this guy, no matter what my resolve."

"It is not in your best interest to continue telling me about this. You are insubordinate and crossed lines you can't uncross. Stop talking."

"I need to tell someone. My family and friends won't understand like you will."

"Then go on if you must, but this information will come back to hurt you."

"The first night I helped Tim into and out of the shower, I kept my clothes on and got soaked and almost caught cold riding my bike home. But it was worth it. You should see him naked. Besides being a flawless picture of masculine beauty, he's hung."

"That qualifies as more information than necessary. And at this point you're well beyond what I want for you."

"The next time he needed a shower, I stripped down to my underwear before helping him. I still got soaked but dried off and ditched the underwear. My outside clothes were dry. He laughed at me again, but still kissed me; a lot. Did I mention he is a wonderful kisser? Last night I did what he asked at shower time and got naked."

"I've heard enough. You know what I must do now. So, stop talking."

"Who else can I tell? I don't know how it happened. One minute I'm scrubbing his back with a luffa, then suddenly he hunched forward and from between his legs guided my erection into his body. The next thing I know I'm screwing him with the shower's warm water raining down on us. I knew I should stop, *I do know better* … but didn't want to and didn't. I never came that hard or much before. Now I'll probably get AIDS and my social work education is permanently at intermission."

"Sorry to say, you are right about your education."

"I just wasted two years of graduate work, on borrowed money, my health, and this is the really sick part; *I think it was worth it.* When he sings "Oh Danny Boy" to me in Spanish, substituting Deano for Danny, my heart melts. I'm powerless in his hands."

"Did you wear a condom?"

"No, it just happened spontaneously."

"I'll get you a short course of AZT for prophylaxis, and then have security escort you out of the building, after you collect your personal things … You are no longer allowed here as a student intern. I feel bad, you had great potential. And my attempt to improve your self-esteem went terribly wrong."

"We tried!"

"I am sincerely sorry your placement went bad, and my role in it."

"Do you think I'll get AIDS?"

"Let me remind you of statistics I know you know, when not discombobulated. The highest risk of catching the virus is from sharing drug injection needles. Receptive anal sex without a condom is a 500 in 1 chance, insertive anal sex is 10,000 in 1, receptive oral sex 3,000 in 1, and insertive oral sex is a 25,000 in1 risk, there is no risk kissing. You know these numbers."

"Yes, but it's comforting hearing you say 10,000 in 1 chance, plus preventive AZT, maybe I can dodge the virus?"

"I don't have the latest stats for catching venereal warts, syphilis, herpes, drug resistant gonorrhea, or Chlamydia so watch for symptoms. For God's sake, use a condom every-time. I will be e-mailing your university an intermission form tomorrow. Goodbye and be well."

"Bill, you didn't let me down with that assignment, and I didn't fail me either. Even if Tim turns out to be unworthy of me, I got a lot more education here than expected. I came as an eager blank page, and leave feeling I've caught up with my chronological age in the world as it is."

"How so?"

"For me, being gay meant being socialized in isolation. I missed making a lot of connections straight boys do without even thinking. Tim helped me pull it together by fully accepting what's inside myself. Sex isn't a theoretical furtive construct anymore. I learned what really matters and accept my place in the gay epidemic and own it."

"Elucidate?"

"The most important lesson you taught me was no one is out of my league. Unless *I* put them above me."

"I am awed by your attitude, given the costs."

With a shrug of the shoulder and defiant smile, Deano stood, and started humming.Next, he moved his hips in smooth dance motion, then his feet followed. "This is a disco song I like, "I Will Survive." Then Dino sang the song, sotto voce, as he danced in-place.

Dr. Hudson wasn't sure how to react to his student's impromptu humming, singing and dancing, so said, "Where is the unapproachable lyric tenor Tim O'Doul in this?"

Deano changed tunes, keeping the same rhythm. "As far as me and Tim goes, this African-American song express's my feelings, "He Ain't Heavy He's My Brother." Thank you, Dr. Hudson for caring enough to ask, and trying so hard to get me through the rigors of graduate school." Then singing "He Ain't Heavy …" Deano danced out the door moving his body smoothly in sync to his vocalizing. Two security guards waiting outside the office marched on either side of him, as he danced between them; out of the building.

During this time, Tim O'Doul's T-cells dropped to zero. Nevertheless, with no T-cells, Tim remained in good health. He was an unexplainable AIDS anomaly. Deano's graduate school skills helped him keep Tim's medical team within the standards of care guidelines. Then with expanded testing beyond the gay community, it was discovered there were others like Tim in the general population.

As the pandemic grew, homophobic-tinged, pathetically slow research at the CDC, due to fear of federal funding cuts, slowly changed with a new, less homophobic president. In the meantime, it was discovered in Europe, that some Southern Europeans lacked a cell receptor necessary for HIV to latch on to invade immune cells. Late in the epidemic, in the United States, it was discovered millions of folks, straight and gay, were naturally immune to HIV infection and that proved retro-viruses are not specific to sexual orientation.

Medical anthropologists, using frozen blood samples from the 1940s, 1950s, and 1960s, found HIV present, including in children's blood. Though researchers floated many cockamamie theories for the public, it came down to two: [1] AIDS is a plague from God to punish gays, or [2] AIDS has been with humankind unnoticed or misidentified for decades. The social revolution of the 1960s increased exposure, particularly with an augmented appetite for illicit injection drugs.

New medical technology in the 1980s *identified* HIV/AIDS. Homophobia greatly retarded a robust public health response to the epidemic. The United States government's inaction especially affected straight drug addicts, hemophiliacs, Haitians, and Africans. All aspects of the gay community, by necessity, mobilized for the benefit of *everyone* afflicted. Then protease-inhibitors finally arrived in the 1990s. Using the new medications, Tim O'Doul's viral load became undetectable, as his T-cells returned to normal range; throughout he remained healthy.

President Ronald Reagan's homophobic failure to take action during the pandemic left a massive legacy of Hepatitis-C leading to a liver cancer epidemic. Scientific advances in the 2000s found most HIV/AIDS individuals test positive for or have Hep-C, *but* most Hep-C folks are not HIV/AIDS positive. George H. Bush was finally able to say AIDS, something his predecessor was too spineless to manage. Too little too late, was still better than nothing, watching young vibrant Americans wither-away and slowly die horribly.

Christmas

Was it a nightmare? Screaming sirens getting louder, suddenly my bedroom window alive with flashing colored lights. Then replaced by brighter colorless light brushing back and forth through the window. Shouting, banging, and more screeching sirens. I was being dragged out of a serene dream by a frightening one.

I was stunned by a terrifying realization; *I couldn't breathe.* My nose, mouth, throat, and lungs hurt as raw. More awareness dawned me into mindfulness with stinging eye pain. Was that black smoke choking me? Was that FIRE?!

Did I dream kicking out of the bedclothes and struggling to find my feet? Was there a light inside the opaque smoke, swinging side to side moving towards me? Abruptly the dream went blank. There was nothing, an icy, empty head space ... then shivering cold, a strangers' hands made my eyes fly open and I was gulping oxygen through a clear plastic mask.

"Where am I?" *Oh ... sitting in the back of an ambulance alongside my mother. What happened? Why is mother staring trance-like through the ambulance's open back doors? Why don't they close the doors, it is freezing?* I turned my head to follow mother's gaze and saw our mobile home, cars, shed, everything we owned engulfed in voracious tongues of red-orange flames.

In the dream, two EMTs were tending to us as best they could, me resisting their efforts, pushing their hands away. One had somehow wrapped me in a blanket identical to the one my mother clutched tight to her breasts. The other EMT was trying to keep an oxygen mask on my face, while I struggled to get free of the mask, blanket, and nightmare.

My mother had black soot caked around her mouth and nose. I raised my fingers to my face. They came away soot-black. Real soot, *I was awake* living a nightmare.

A fire lieutenant came over and officiously barked, "What are you storing under the house trailer? We should have had this out already and gone on to the next fire."

Finally yanking the oxygen mask clear off, I wheezed through an aching throat. "I just bought an extra ton of wood-pellet heating-fuel at the Home Center. I thought we wouldn't have to scrimp on heat this winter for a change. The cold aggravates my mother's joints." I recognized I was babbling, my mind buzzing, and shut up.

The lieutenant grunted, "There is nothing to salvage from your place. With your permission, I'm going to level it to get at those burning bags of pellets."

My mother nodded her assent, but as he turned to go, she rasped, "What caused the fire?"

The lieutenant stopped and looked sympathetically at mother. "The Christmas tree, with help from overloaded outdated, electrical wiring. Excuse me, ma'am, I have to put your fire out and rush to a big apartment building burning downtown." With that he turned and barked orders. "All water cannons on full power, aim under the mobile home … NOW!" When the water cannons hit what was left of our home sweet home, it blew apart like a bomb hit. Then changing the water cannons powerful torrent to a spray, they doused the tons of burning wood-pellets flying in all directions from the explosion.

Mother and I sat in disbelief, everything we owned was turned to ash. Then she perked up. "Look, Raymond, here comes the fireman who carried you out of the flames."

Looking where she pointed, I recognized a face from my youth. It was Dennis Moran, decades older.

"I'm glad you decided to rejoin the land of the living, welcome back," said giving me a hug through heavy firefighting gear.

I reached out and touched his gloved hand. "Mother tells me I owe you my life. Thank you, how can I ever repay you?"

He smiled his old familiar smile, maturity lines new around the corners of his mouth and eyes. "Think of it as the return of a favor we swore never to speak of, from our younger days, remembers. Are these yours?"

He held out what used to be my best cheap jeans before the fire had its way with them.

I forced a smile. "Still trying to get into my pants? Looks like the fire took more than it left." Dennis smiled back and to my surprise handed me my keys and wallet.

"Having these may help starting over. They fell out of the jeans you're holding. A Merry Christmas to you both."

"Thanks, Dennis … I'd give you a hug, but I'm afraid I'd start bawling. You don't want to see that in front of my mother. So, Merry Christmas back at you, and thanks." It was then I noticed mother tightly clutching her big black handbag, with both her cats' terrified faces peeking over the top. I didn't ask how she came to have the bag or if Dennis had carried her out of the fire too. At that moment, it only mattered that she and her cats were safe, and I owed Dennis a debt I could never repay.

The fire lieutenant was back barking orders. Dennis waved goodbye, ran to his fire truck, and left with sirens blaring and emergency lights flashing.

Watching them leave, my mother asked, "Where do you know that man from? I don't recall you ever mentioning a Dennis Moran."

I took her hand. "He joined my Air Explorer Squadron six months before I turned eighteen. Some guys were bullying him, and I put a stop to it. I guess he remembered, that's what he meant by return of a favor."

Anxious frustration showing, the EMT closest to me paced back and forth, muttering, "Our radio keeps saying we have to get to a big fire, it is an all unit response code, must be really bad."

"Mother, you okay?" When she nodded yes, I said, "Go ahead, we'll figure out what's next on our own."

The portly EMT said, "We need our blankets back. If you haven't noticed, it's cold outside. The snow is already ankle deep. You both need something on your feet."

I peered down and was only wearing what I sleep in; used-to-be-white, washed-out to gray tight briefs and crewneck T-shirt. Both had holes at the seams, and the fire had streaked them in darker shades of gray. "What do you suggest?"

With all the authority her position allowed, the other EMT puffed out her chest. "Wait for the Red Cross worker. She should have been here by now." Sure enough, as if on cue, a white van with Red Cross Emergency Services stenciled on the side, rolled up. The EMTs took their blankets and left in a hurry with their sirens blaring and lights flashing.

The Red Cross worker looked like a no-nonsense, tough but caring woman. She reminded me of the social workers and nurses I dealt with when father got sick and wasn't going to get better.

"Hi, I'm Marjorie Holloway. Here is my card. You will have to see me for more vouchers as you get resettled. Telephone before you come in. I might be at a fire or other disaster, but I could leave vouchers for you with our receptionist; *if we know you are coming.*"

"What about right now?"

"Here, I only have adult one size fits all gray sweatpants and sweatshirts. They will be too large, sorry it is the same for almost everybody. Also, here are white tube socks, again one size fits all. You've gotten the last room at a motel. Here is a rent voucher for two weeks. If you need more time, telephone and I'll get an extension. But you must find a new place as quickly as possible. We will work with you on that. I have housing lists you can look at when you feel better. Just don't be too choosey." Clearly being harassed by the squawking static on her radio, Marjorie Holloway spoke fast. "I'm really sorry, I got to go. There is a big apartment house fire downtown. Here, take these other vouchers—they should be self-explanatory. If you have any questions call me after the holiday or ask the motel management, they know how we work. Sorry I don't have more time right now, Merry Christmas."

Shocked at her bum's rush, standing in the snow wearing only socks on my freezing feet, I snapped. "Wait, what is the motel's address, and how do we get there?"

She was already starting up her van and spoke out the window. "I called you a cab. He should be here any minute. Pay him with the voucher marked 'taxi'. His tip is included. Don't let him try to guilt you into paying a bigger tip."

"Does this mean mother and I have to share one room? That's not right, we are adults."

"Sorry about that, but as bad as your Christmas Eve fire was—the people I'm going to now will most likely be sleeping in some school gym or church basement. You got the last motel room. It could have been worse, you have each other. Bye for now, I got to hurry." She waved as she spun van wheels on packed snow … finally got traction and drove away fish-tailing.

Turning back defeated, I took a long look at my mother. "You seem to be holding up well. Is there anything I can do for you this instant? Do you have your medicine in that bag?"

"Yes, I have my meds. What that woman said is true. It could have been a lot worse. Look at the cats, they're still terrified."

Before frostbite took our toes, the cab came. It was an unmarked old Mercury Grand Marquis, clean but showing age. It looked like a regular old passenger car but had livery plates. The driver rolled down his window and asked, "Somebody call a cab?"

I recognized the driver at once. He was one of the miners I'd first worked with. He showed us new guys the ropes without a lot of condescending attitude. "Hello, Buck, I haven't seen you since the mine shut down time before last. How're you doing?"

"Just fine, but I won't ask you the same question. Looks like you pissed off Santa Clause. Get in the cab, it is cold out there," he said this with an older miner's authority over a newbie.

Once we were seated in the back of his taxi, I introduced my mother. They both nodded acknowledgment like older people do. It was nice and warm in the car, so I took off the frozen socks, hoping to dry them and warm my feet.

I looked at the housing voucher in my hand. "Buck, you know where the Fair Price Motel is? I've lived here all my life and never heard of it."

"That motel is on the seedy side of town." With that, we were traveling in the direction of the motel.

To blot out contemplating mother or I or both could be dead from fire, or think forward how to get our lives back, I allowed my mind to drift away to happier times, when I had some control. I recalled my first contact with Dennis the fireman.

* * * *

Dennis transferred to our Air Explorer Squadron from the Sea Scouts. Rumor had it he'd had some misunderstandings with them. Because of his diminutive stature, he was marked for bullying by our bad boys, who were constantly looking for trouble and causing mischief. I first met Dennis on a camp out; it was a pre-camporee to prepare for the big statewide Camporee.

The assistant squadron leader told me to keep an eye on Dennis and make sure he was treated right. Giving me the order, he said, "Dennis is small, but he is almost your age. Treat him like you would want to be treated." I squashed down what he was implying. I didn't *always* follow the golden rule. I knew I didn't, but usually tried. For God's sake, I was a teenager.

It didn't take long before the bad element had Dennis separated from the rest of us and were, with much malicious glee, in the process of de-pantsing him. I found them just in time to save Dennis' honor. I banged some heads together and then got the mob under control by dispersing them to do necessary tasks that could have waited till day-light.

Since Dennis was assigned to share a pup tent with one of the worst bullies, I suggested he share my tent instead. Being the squadron's crew chief, I had the privilege of my own large tent, unless there was a problem. There was most definitely a problem and I'd address the bullying at our next meeting. I was thinking of running all the bullies through a beltline gauntlet at that meeting. I wished I could run them through it twice.

The rest of that night's activities went according to schedule, until Dennis and I were about to get into our sleeping bags for the night. I noticed he had a troubled look on his face. "What's bothering you?"

Looking even more uneasy he muttered, "This is embarrassing. I can't sleep unless I jerk off. I've tried and tried but sleep won't come if I don't. Should I go outside and do it in the bushes?"

I considered his words. "If it was up to me, I wouldn't have picked this spot for our camp. There are indications of skunk and raccoon close by. Tomorrow, notice where porcupines stripped tree bark near this tent. Even if you can whack off quickly and quietly, you might attract a furry audience known to carry rabies. So, don't go outside this late unless you need to take a dump."

"Then how do I get to sleep? I've had this problem for years."

"Maybe if you lay there counting sheep, sleep will come."

Mustering his courage, Dennis brashly asked. "Would you mind doing it with me? You could stay on your bedroll and me here. It won't take long if we go at it really fast and not break scout law by touching."

I thought, *Damn, I'm trying to get a steady girlfriend and here I am reverting to my old circle jerk schoolyard days.* "Look, tomorrow we have a long physical day. We need to go to sleep right now." With that said, I extinguished the carbide lantern.

Dennis didn't say anything as the light died, but he looked upset. The moonlight filtering in was bright enough to see Dennis on top of his sleeping bag turn his back to me. His ridged body suggested he was fuming.

"Okay, let's get this over with and get some sleep." I pushed down my tighty-whities and my right hand found its dear friend, Mr. Hard Cock. They started their old familiar smooching, slow and tender caressing at first. Dennis rolled over, tears streaking his face. Then quickly he pushed his boxers down and started stroking himself eagerly. Dennis was a lot larger than I would have guessed given his height. He must've missed a few growth spurts to have that large, man-sized dick on his slight frame.

I got close right away, watching him rubbing with exuberance. So out of habit from circle jerk days, I said without thinking, "I'm almost there, are you close?" I no sooner said it, then I asked myself, *Why? Is it old habit or am I taking something inappropriate for a crew chief to a murkier place?* But my hand and breathing sped up with a mind of their own, bringing me to the edge. Suddenly, Dennis scooted over to my bedroll. He pushed my hand away with his and took my cock into his mouth. Then he started making a cooing sound while sliding up and down on it. Two major thoughts crashed together in my head: *This is bad, we've stepped across a line there is no going back from, and It feels too good to stop him.* I came long, hard, and a lot. Then as soon as I wilted in his mouth, Dennis scooted back over to his sleeping bag. The look on his face foretold he expected to be punished. But it wasn't my style to hurt or embarrass anyone for doing what instinct dictated, and I was complicit in it.

What I wanted right at that moment was to roll over and go to sleep and pretend what just happened hadn't. Instead I said, "We'll never speak of this, got me? Now stretch out on your back." Not sure if he was in trouble, Dennis stretched out in quivering trepidation. I got up on all fours, scooted sideways to his side of the tent, and crouched over his exposed trembling hard prick.

First, I took his oversize pecker in hand working it up and down, while turning off my screaming mind's recrimination of Scout Law violation. Then I took his now even harder, throbbing member between my lips and licked around his dick head where it joined its shaft. As I took more of him deeper into my mouth, on its own, my right hand reached down and cradled his balls. Dennis's scrotum was man-sized like his cock, but the testes inside needed to grow. So, to encourage growth, I gently massaged each quail egg-size nut in its ball bag.

As my mouth slid over his dickhead and started to slide up and down his shaft to encourage Morpheus to get to work, I let my right little finger slip behind his cradled ball sack and lightly stroke in back. Without warning, Dennis went full body stiff and breathed harder and faster. To increase friction, I gurgled spit.

"Impf," escaped his lips as he came in hot spurts. Forceful jets of his neutral-flavored cum filled my mouth. He thrust his hips wildly up and down, lost in the delight of release.

When his cock softened, his body's tension was also gone. I looked around for what to do with a mouth full of sperm. He had swallowed mine, but I wasn't ready to do likewise. My super ego and id were having a duel over what just happened. If I just spit out his cum, it would have to be cleaned up in the morning, not my kind of morning activity. If I unzipped a tent flap and spit outside, it would attract raccoons, skunks, or porcupines, or Gods knows what, smelling a snack.

Still hunched over Dennis, I reached up, grasped his shoulders, and pulled us up, face to face. I covered his lips with mine, made an opening with my tongue and *snowballed* him. I fed him his sperm, mouth to mouth. He tensed at first, not knowing what was happening, then relaxed and accepted the return of his copious gift. We snowballed back and forth till it was mostly spit and we reflexively swallowed. The rest of the camping trip went as planned except adding Dennis' sleep inducements to our schedule. Six months later, I aged out of scouting and we lost touch.

Several years later, while reading the Sunday newspaper, I saw that Dennis had married a girl I'd once dated and had on and off sex with. The paper's wedding photo showed Dennis had in fact had more growth spurts. He stood taller than his wife, a tall woman. Thinking about the two of them having sex suddenly felt icky incestuous, so I put the football game on, opened a beer, and toasted they live happily ever after. Now after all these years, he saved my life and brought back the memory of that long-forgotten camping trip as a diversion from thinking about what it is to be burned out at Christmas.

Buck pulled his cab up to the Fair Price Motel office, and I handed him the taxi voucher. "Thanks, Buck. The Red Cross said your tip is in the voucher. What do you know about this place?"

"True, they give us a five percent tip to show they are in tune with 1920s tipping. This motel is not too bad. The Red Cross uses cheaper ones first. They must be having a lot of holiday fires to put you here." He scowled at the voucher as he took it from my hand.

Fiddling with my scorched wallet, I sheepishly took out three singed singles. "Here, let me at least bring your tip closer to current rates."

"No, that's all right, here take this instead." He shoved a fist-full of ones, fives, and tens at me.

"What's this?"

Buck spoke with a congenial smile I hadn't seen him use in the coalmine. "My tips for the night, Merry Christmas. I knew your father back in the day, he was a good man."

"I can't take your tips." I stared at his well-meaning fist-full of charity, dumfounded. *Were we that pathetic … wretched looking?*

Buck barked, "Don't make me kick your ass on Christmas, sonny boy. I'm sure your mother taught you to say thank you when someone gives you a gift."

My mother had been closely watching my exchange with Buck. She had approvingly perked up when I tried to give him three dollars. But looking at his handful of bills made our pitiful situation real. She started to cry, and I put my arm around her.

"Thank you, Buck, and Merry Christmas to you and yours. It wouldn't be right to take your tips. You earned them, thanks for offering."

Tired of holding out the cash, Buck reached over and shoved the handful of loose bills down into my mother's big black handbag and then petted her cats. "You hear that, the dispatcher wants me on another call. Here, take my card in case you folks need a ride during your rebuilding, or call me if you need a hand for anything at all. I know where you are, it gets better."

"Thanks again." We got out of the cab and he drove off. Mother had stopped crying. She put on her "we're tough enough to handle anything" face, the one she saved for bad trouble.

Proclaiming its name, the Fair Price Motel had a supersized, greenish-yellow neon sign mounted high above its squat dark office. Under it, a jumbo blue sign blinked "Welcome," and under that, a steady small red sign declared, "No Vacancy."

There were small multi-colored blinking Christmas lights strung around the office windows and door. My stomach knotted as the lights reminded me of our fire. A cardboard sign hanging inside the glass door said, "Closed."

Looking around, I saw four rows of five squat, square buildings, lights off inside. All the motel structures were covered with old T-111 plywood siding under sloped metal roofs. Each building was detached one from another, except the last row, which were bigger and connected wall to wall. All were painted brash mustard-yellow and had festive blinking Christmas lights. The larger office structure was also slope roofed, T-111 sided, but freshly painted garish hotdog-relish green.

Judging by the makes and ages of the cars parked outside the motel units, the place was a cheap motel. Then I checked myself and thought, *Things are bad enough. For Mother's sake, I can't go negative. What we lost can either be replaced or become a memory. We survived the fire without injury and have each other, thanks to the fire department.*

My mother pushed the illuminated night button on the office door frame. After the third time pushed and released with no response, I held the button in and let it ring continuously. Finally, lights came on inside and I could see a male around my age, forty, about my size, but stockier than my six feet, 165lbs. He was maybe 200 pounds.

"Stop ringing the damn bell, I'm coming!" he yelled, then unlocked the door and waved us inside.

The guy's receding hair was sleep-tousled, hanging uncombed over sleepy dark green eyes. He was bare foot, shirtless and nicely filled out a pair of goofy-patterned lounge pants. His pectorals, abs, biceps, shoulders and back muscles were well defined, evidence he worked out regularly, in contrast to his small potbelly.

My mother whispered, "Do you know this man too?"

Taking a closer look, I said, "Not exactly, but I've seen him before I don't know his name or remember where."

"Hello, pardon my overhearing your conversation. My name is Gilbert and I'm a bookkeeper at the underground coal mine when it's operating. I've seen you there and even met your father when I was a trainee. Sorry for your loss."

"Thank you."

"Now that I'm mostly awake and you have my full attention, what can I do for you folks?"

"Sorry to wake you. My mother and I are cold, in need of a shower and a bed. Here is the Red Cross housing voucher, and Merry Christmas." Then glancing at his lounge pants. "… or Happy Holiday to you."

Then the trouble started. He frowned at my mother's bag and spoke in an uppity scolding voice. "No pets allowed. It's the law. You will have to get rid of those cats. I hate cats, I'm allergic."

Up to that point, I thought Mother had been handling our Christmas fire as well as could be expected. But she abruptly lost composure and freaked at full volume, nose to nose with Gilbert. She started shouting, screaming, yelling, threatening, and crying while letting it be known to anyone within a mile; her displeasure. "These cats just survived a nightmarish fire and aren't going anywhere without us, and we aren't leaving here just now! It is late night and we are cold without clothes! Go ahead call the police if you dare and I'll have you arrested for abusing an old woman and animal cruelty; on Christmas Eve!"

Before I could decide what action I should take, a woman about my mother's age rushed into the office from living quarters in back. She was wearing a full length faded pink print night gown, worn down fuzzy house slippers, and was bleary eyed from sleep. And she held a sawed-off double-barreled twelve-gauge shotgun leveled at mother and me.

"Gilbert! What the hell is going on out here?"

"She has two cats in her bag and you know we don't allow pets," he said this while pointing an accusatory finger at my mother's cats.

Gilbert's mother lowered her shotgun. "Sometimes we make exceptions on Christmas; you idiot!" Turning to my mother and giving her a visual once over, the motel matron's attitude softened. "Dear, you look positively frazzled. Let me loan you some slippers and a night dress and I'll take you to your cabin." That said she went in back, and collected things to loan or give my mother, then the two women bustled from the office. I was ignored.

Watching the scene, I mumbled to myself, "Predicament … should I go or stay here?"

Gilbert had been studying me. "I wouldn't go with them if it were me. Your mom needs to talk about what happened with someone who wasn't there. My mom is a good listener, she took all the classes the Red Cross offered."

Giving Gilbert a hard stare I carefully choose my words. "Don't get us wrong, my Mother usually doesn't get that upset. It's probably from all the smoke she inhaled."

"Look at the ceiling."

"What're those black dots?"

"Number nine bird shot, it's not unusual for my mom to fire off one barrel from her thunder-clapper, that's what she calls her shotgun. It restores order fast."

"Okay, we didn't need that service, after *you started* the fuss. I could really use a shower and a bed."

"You can shower here, and there is an extra bed in my room."

"I'm wearing the only clothes I have and putting a clean body in dirty clothes defeats the purpose."

"Oh, I see the problem. All right I can help with that too. We open our Christmas gifts on Christmas Eve, I know most people do it on Christmas Day, we don't. My aunts must think I'm eighty years old. You can have those gifts. I already have more than enough clothes I like."

"I can't take your Christmas gifts, that wouldn't be right."

Rather than get turned off or mad like Buck had, when his charity was refused, Gilbert surprised me. "Friendly advice, you need a shower your stale smoky stink is overpowering this office." Gilbert rummaged under the sign-in counter for a second. "Here take this towel and soap, use my shampoo and conditioner in the shower … if you want. I'll get you a toothbrush tomorrow."

"Thanks, I appreciate it."

"About the clothes, I wouldn't mind if you want to run around here in the altogether, but my mom will tell you to put something on or she'll shoot your pecker off. She's blunt like that."

"Nothing personal, Gilbert, but I'm not gay. You keep looking at the back of my sweats like they aren't three sizes too large. Sorry, I can't help you out. I don't play that way."

"I'm not gay either. I'm *bi-sexual*. We rent out the front row of cabins by the hour, so I've had as much pussy as I want since before puberty."

"Sorry if I read you wrong."

"No, you read me right. Every so often I get a yen for male tail, and you happen to possess one of the prettiest bubble butts I've seen."

Disturbed, bordering on letting my anger flair, I gave him a flabbergasted look. "When did you ever see my ass?"

"Showering after your shift at the coal mine. I work in the office when the underground mine is operating. When your shift was over, I always got the urge to relieve myself. You know, some urinals are in the shower area."

It took a minute to rein in my irritation after digesting what he said. *Was that stalking or voyeurism or some other fancy word I don't use?* I decided not to address his attraction, so I changed topics. "How come you don't have work when they take the tops off these mountains to strip-mine the coal?"

"That's mostly automated, including timekeeping and payroll."

"About my smell, what if I ditch my underwear after the shower. Then wear the sweats inside out."

"I just got another bright idea. It might work better for you."

"I'm all ears."

"Several months ago, I bulked up using body building supplements to enhance my physique. Before Christmas I went through my closet removing clothing that no longer fit. If you're not *too* proud to accept hand me downs, you can take your pick. The quality and style is much better than the new Christmas gifts my aunts gave."

"Well, I do need to cover myself, pride or no pride."

"Come to my room, I'll show you what's packed up ready to be given away as donations." With that said, I followed him through the office to living quarters. Gilbert pointed out the bathroom I would use and took the towel and soap from me and placed them on the toilet tank lid.

Suddenly, reality setting in, I was awash in all kinds of self-pity, and on the verge of tears. "How could I ever repay you? I have nothing, and no prospects."

"No strings, no repayment expected, here is my bedroom. You can use that bed after your shower. So, in the back of this closet are two big shopping bags of clothes. I've been meaning to take them to Goodwill. Out of sight is out of mind."

"Lucky me … thank you."

"None of these fit me anymore. Here, take both bags. Whatever you don't want I'll donate. As you can see, these used clothes are clean. You can thank my mom for that."

"I still don't feel right about taking charity. I was raised to accept life as is without complaint."

"This isn't charity, you're helping *me* out. I'd like to know who got my clothes rather than never see them again. Like it or not, you and your mom will be around here for a while."

"You're slick, saying my accepting your help is giving you something back."

"It's true. So, this big bag has jeans. Three pair high-end denim and two knock-around dungarees. This other shopping bag has sweat suits too small for me now, and a bunch of T-shirts that don't fit without making my belly button obvious. These were favorites of mine and should fit you. Oh, I almost forgot this grocery bag. It has underwear and a few thongs too tight around the waist. The Goodwill store doesn't take used underwear, but I was going to leave it just in case someone could use them."

"Looks like my pride got burned up in the fire."

"The problem is your feet are too big for my shoes."

"No toe amputations, please."

"When you are in the office, there is an old pair of oversize goulashes in the closet near the front door. I don't know the original owner, but they are yours for as long as you need … if they fit."

Feeling a mix of thankful, resentful, and flat-out wrong accepting gifts of old clothes, *Oh God, look how far I've fallen,* I racked my brain for a small way to reciprocate his kindness. Then I did something I never do. I lied and further compromised my values. "Let me make a confession, Gilbert. I am an exhibitionist. You may watch me strip and shower, I don't mind. If you want?"

"Now that's an offer I wasn't expecting."

"Just for the record, I never noticed you watching me shower after work at the mine. But right here right now, you can pretend we're back there. You can look as much as you want, but no touching."

"I tried not to be obvious at work. The urinals are conveniently located next to the showers, and I did need to relive myself when the showers were going. The sound of running water gives me an urge to pee."

"Whatever you say."

"Okay, fine, I can own being a pervert to see your bubble butt again. But not to worry; I only play with willing partners. Just so you know, my used clothes come no strings attached. If you'd rather have privacy showering, I have work to do now that I'm up."

Faking a lascivious grin, I awkwardly pulled the oversized sweat shirt over my head, twirled it, and twitched my ass around clumsily. After a pause to think *what next,* I whipped my stinking T-shirt up and over-head with more uncoordinated butt shaking and T-shirt shirt twirling. Then I untied the drawstring and clumsily kicked out of the oversize sweat pants, almost tripping and falling. Next, with my modesty shaming me, I bent over and rolled down my once-white briefs and awkwardly kicked them off, again awkwardly almost falling. Then while trying and failing to do a nude erotic dance, I did lose my balance, stumbled, then tripped over the sweats on floor and fell-down in a sprawl. A slap-stick comic's parody strip tease couldn't have looked more ridiculous.Mother Nature had a strange reaction to my self-inflicted embarrassment. My dick was hard, while I was feeling the opposite of turned on.

Gilbert, who had been sitting on his bed, stood and moved to walk out of his bedroom. "I'll be in the kitchen if you need something." That was said with a frown and flat voice.

"Stop, wait, has my ass lost its appeal?"

"Why did you lie to me, unless you can't help yourself. *Are you a pathological liar?*" Gilbert started to move out of the room again.

"What? You said you liked to look at my ass. I thought I was repaying a kindness?" Blushing head to toe at my blunder, my cock got harder. Humiliated, I covered my extreme arousal as best I could. My disgrace showed everywhere else. I must have looked pitiful.

Seeing my extreme shame, he took a deep breath to calm down. "I told you we rent front cabins by the hour, I know what an exhibitionist looks like and we both know you are no exhibitionist. You had no excuse to lie to me and put on a ridiculous farce."

Head hung down, feeling hopelessly pathetic, I muttered, "I'm not a liar. I just wanted to repay you."*Now I've made my wretched plight even worse. How is that possible?*

Staring at my naked butt, Gilbert licked his lips with a long pink tongue. "I'll go make some coffee. We can talk after you bathe, sleep and put some clothes on. I'll be in the kitchen if you need me."

* * * *

It took hard scrubbing to get the smell of smoke off my hair and body. My self-created humiliation refused to scrub away. After thoroughly drying, I tried on Gilbert's old underwear and T-shirts and they fit me just fine. All were better quality than I could afford. The thongs looked like jockstraps with ass cheek straps unified in the ass crack. But wearing the thongs felt sexy. I settled on an olive colored T-shirt and canary yellow bikini briefs and laid down on the bed he had indicated for me. I tried to sleep, but sleep wasn't interested. It was somewhere way off in the distance calling me while random *thoughts* buzzed around in my head like angry bees. Every time I closed my eyes, the nightmare fire returned like it was existing. After tossing, turning, and rolling around, I got up. Kicked into a pair of expensive jeans, and barefoot, went looking for Gilbert, the jeans' previous owner.

Gilbert was sitting at a kitchen table. He had dressed while I was in the shower. He was wearing sockless oxblood penny-loafers, dark-brown slacks and dove-gray cable-knit sweater. The man had a pile of cheap, colorful plastic trinkets, a stack of used gift-wrapping paper, and a big steaming mug of coffee in front of him. Two sloppily wrapped gifts lay to one side, he was wrapping a third, and looked gloomy.

"I am sorry I made you mad. I'm not always a jerk."

Looking up from what he was wrapping, all thumbs, Gilbert said, "You want coffee? Quality coffee is something I insist on, even in lean times."

"Sure, I can't sleep, I tried. My mind is jumping around out of control."

"Did you see my mountain bike mounted on exercise rollers in the bedroom? Ride it until you get tired enough to sleep."

"Even that sounds like more than I can handle."

"How do you take your coffee?"

"Black no sugar."

"Yeah, that's how we take it around here these days, Cream, even milk is too dear."

"We switched to black after my dad died."

"It wasn't you getting naked. I liked the inspiration in my pants."

"Then what?"

"I hate being lied to. I go ballistic and overreact."

Gilbert handed me a steaming mug of strong, aromatic coffee and we sat down at the table. After a sip, I smiled. "Wow that *is* good coffee. I'm not a liar, being homeless and hopeless has brought out my worst self. It won't happen again. If it does, you can yell in my face or punch me."

"Let it go."

"So why *is* lying such a big deal? I'd imagine you get lied to a lot in the motel business?"

Gilbert was quiet a long time, then heaved a sigh, and locked eyes. "If you really want to know, when I was twelve, I caught my dad in a lie."

"What happened?"

"I saw him putting suitcases in the trunk of our car. When I asked where he was going, he said, 'I'll be right back.' When I ask to go along, he said, 'I need you to look after Mom.' He never came back. Ever since then, lying triggers being abandoned by my dad and I lose it." Then Gilbert went back to fiddling with the assemblage in front of him.

"Boy, this coffee is really good. Did I say that?"

"It looks like you are a perfect fit for my old clothes. Did you try everything on? Anything not fit?"

"They all fit fine, I didn't expect to like those thong things, but I do." It was embarrassing to admit, but he asked. I couldn't lie again.

"Good, I'm glad you can use them. You look hot in my old clothes, but you might want to put on a sweat top and socks are in my bottom dresser draw. It's chilly out here."

"Thank you, all compliments are humbly accepted by the homeless. You're right, I do feel a chill. Be right back."

* * * *

Reentering the kitchen wearing a dark maroon, hooded, unzipped sweat jacket and gray gym socks, I noted the pile of items unwrapped looked the same as when I left. "I thought you said your family exchanged gifts on Christmas Eve?"

"We do. These are for kids in a group home near here. Usually our presents are better than this. Everyone around here is having a bad year, but I figured something is better than nothing on Christmas. It's the thought that counts, right?"

"Sure!"

"Bullshit, one year we had a traveling salesman staying at the motel and he got me bright colored cashmere cap, scarf, and mitten sets for less than wholesale. The boys really loved those gifts. Poor kids know quality. They study what's above their lot in life. That is where their dreams come from."

"So, what's all this?"

"My friend and I could only kick in twenty dollars apiece this year. I took the money to the ninety-nine-cent store, and what you see is the result. Obviously, I'm even recycling our used Christmas wrapping paper. We've never had such a bleak Christmas."

Involuntarily grinning a lewd grin, I asked, "Does your friend come with benefits? Is he bisexual too?"

Giving me, 'what's it to you' look, Gilbert snarked, "Are you always such a nosey son of a bitch?"

"Excuse me while I extract my foot from my mouth. Sorry about that. You may punch my arm."

With a forgiving wave of hand, Gilbert exonerated me. "My friend is not into labels, but he has a wife, two kids, and likes me to fuck him when time permits. We've been sporadically intimate for eight years. Christmas is our for-sure scheduled fuck, no matter what. We screw every year after the gift giving at the group home. Does that help … have enough information?"

"Sorry for snooping, I'm trying to learn to be around you while being overwhelmed burned out homeless."

"Stop trying so hard."

"So, can I help with the gift wrapping? Mother taught me to tie pretty bows."

Sitting back in his chair and eyeing me closely, Gilbert said, "Okay, sure, you can help if you want, but do a good job. The gifts are not worth more than the used wrappings."

"Okay, boss!"

"I can't figure you out … every time I decide not to like you, you do something like offer to help. Most people in your situation would be totally depressed licking their wounds."

Shrugging my shoulders, I said, "I want to like you. You are generous and make an excellent cup of coffee. I guess my problem is I keep putting my best foot forward directly into my mouth, which isn't standard for me meeting new people."

"Why is that?"

"All right, I'll tell you. I am going against everything I've been taught and believe, accepting your-hand-me-down charity. My number one worry should be mother's health during this ordeal, and not showing pride in how well I tie a bow."

His face shifting back to pissed off, Gilbert said, "Okay, then why *are* you being such a selfish prick?"

"What do you mean by that? I've *never been* selfish."

"You won't accept help without begrudging it or doing something stupid like a clumsy self-conscious strip-tease. You are most definitely self-centered selfish."

"I am not selfish. I just told you, my people don't take charity. Never did and never will."

"In your travels, haven't you heard it is the gift giver, not the receiver, who gets the best reward?"

I *had* heard that, and right then, didn't want to know it. Instead I wanted to cry, and cry uncontrollably, accepting he was right … I was selfish and feeling more exposed than naked with a hardon. My impenetrable defenses whooshed away as my eyes filled with tears ready to flow. Then it dawned on me, like the break of day, *Gilbert wasn't a competitor I had to stand up to and best. In his way, he wanted to help.* "You've seen me naked. Unless I excuse myself, you are going to see me weep. I'd rather you didn't." I moved my chair back to leave.

In that instant, Gilbert stood, put a hand on my back, and held me in place. Then he reached around and retrieved a box of tissues from on top of the refrigerator and handed it to me. "Crying is a good way to clear your tear ducts. Feel free to unload that heavy crap you have bottled up. Let it out, you'll feel better. What do you bet your mom is crying with mine right now?" Then he moved to behind my chair, put his hands on my shoulders, and his all thumbs gift wrapping fingers massaged my upper back with skill.

I couldn't stop myself and the flood started, tears poured down my cheeks, rolling off my chin and spilling onto the olive T-shirt, turning into dark-green wet streaks. Sobbing violently over almost losing Mother, seeing our history of six generations of family photos, and all Mother's jewelry, some handed down from her great-great-grandmothers, burn up. And me being snatched from the flames by an old scouting buddy, Buck's kindness and generosity, and Gilbert—a stranger—putting clothes on my back and putting up with my hoof in mouth craziness. My tears flowed with no end in sight.

At some point, my shoulders stopped heaving under Gilbert's kneading fingers and tears ran dry.

"You feel better?"

"Lighter. You must think I'm a wuss."

Gilbert moved back into his seat at the table. "What I think is you don't answer direct questions. It doesn't matter … I've got to get the rest of these gifts wrapped before they can be given out and time is a-wasting."

"I have an idea, do these kids eat candy?"

Looking at me incredulously, Gilbert said, "They are teenagers. They eat any and everything they can fit in their mouth. What?"

"How many teens you talking about?"

"Twenty disturbed delinquent boys between ages thirteen to sixteen, plus five staff workers. Why?"

"The Quicky Mart where I work has Christmas candy. Today is the last day to sell it at full price. I know which candies are on consignment and the ones we will discount fifty percent tomorrow."

Gilbert's voice got rough. "We are not giving these kids stolen candy. It is important to set the right example for them."

"I have the keys. If the store doesn't sell the Christmas candy before January twentieth, it will be discounted seventy-five percent. After that, the candy goes into the trash dumpster behind the store."

Looking suspicious, while sloppily wrapping a gift Gilbert asked, "How do you know about this candy?"

"I work the third shift at the Quicky Mart when the underground mine isn't operating. I know for sure we have enough leftover boxes of candy canes and ribbon candy to give each boy and staff a box."

Making eye contact showing his mood had improved, Gilbert put on a mischievous grin. "I bet you get a lot of sleep on that third shift."

Looking back down at the present I was neatly wrapping, then back up at him. "Yeah, after I dust, reorganize the old merchandise by sell by date, stock the shelves with new merchandize, service customers, take the trash out, sweep up and mop the floors. Oh, and between snoozes, I have an occasional gun fight."

Gilbert perked up at my last comment. "Armed robbers hit us in spurts. Months go by peacefully and then one night after another they're in there, guns out. But we are ready. I have an assault rifle with a sixty-round magazine behind that door. Mom's apron has two pockets, one with birdshot and the other with buckshot."

Deliberately tying an extra fancy bow, I said not looking up, "Ed, the guy who owns the Quicky Mart, wants us to give the robbers whatever they ask for, if we feel they won't hurt us. He says usually they only want the cash drawer and a bottle of liquor. But Ed also says if we feel our personal safety at risk, there is a loaded five shot pump twelve gauge under the counter and a forty-caliber Browning semiautomatic handgun with an extended clip of hollow points in the drawer next to the register."

"Did you ever kill anybody?"

"No, but I've shot that forty so close to robbers they made a hasty exit, rather than test my marksmanship further."

"Sounds like fancy shooting."

"I'll tell you this, the store has never been robbed while I was working." Then after a pause, "Truth be told, I choose not to notice when a hungry-looking gal or fella snatches a little ready to eat portable food. I just put it on the inventory sheet as my loss and tell Ed to take the cost out of my wages. He never does."

Rubbing his chin, Gilbert asked, "You're sure Ed would be all right giving away his candy? These kids and their acne love chocolate."

"I'll leave a note listing what I take and ask him to deduct it from my pay. Knowing Ed, he won't charge me for candy we will have to throw away. If you are worried about it, I can call and you speak to Ed. But I'll need to use your phone. Mine burned up."

"That's okay, I'll take your word for it. Chocolate?"

"We have chocolate Santa and sleighs filled with marshmallows. I just don't know if we have twenty-five left. But if we are short, I know how to make up the difference. Chocolate shouldn't be a problem."

"Sounds like a plan."

"Boxes of candy will go nicely with these cheesy gifts. I like being part of this. It gets my mind off current events, thanks."

Scratching his head thinking and then accepting the candy idea, he shrugged. "Okay then … let's get cracking with gift wrapping. We want to be at the group home soon after the kids have breakfast. You should accelerate your fancy schmancy wrapping to warp speed."

Standing and saluting, I said, "I'm at your service, Captain Kirk." Then sat down and got busy wrapping the gifts a little less precisely.

"Okay, you take that pile and I'll take these. Somehow we have to stretch the wrapping paper to cover them all."

"We have wrapping paper at the store. Okay, I can see from your face that's a no. In a pinch I can use newspapers or sale circulars and make them look special."

"You go from one extreme to the other. But there is something you should know about what we're doing."

"This is unbelievable. I'm actually having fun with these chintzy gifts after losing everything except my mother. Fill me in. What else do I need to know?"

"I don't think you really want to know, actually. No, I know you don't want to know. But I need to tell you!"

Back to wrapping gifts, I thought *There is no pleasing this guy*. "Don't worry, I won't get in your way. When you need me to get lost just say so and I'll disappear."

"I'd like to like you, but you are so pesky."

Head down, now wrapping as fast as I could do a decent job I thought *Yeah, back at you, brother*. "Come on, what's up? Just say it. I'm not delicate, I don't break."

"Okay fine, *this is not about me hitting on you*. I know it will sound that way."

"Jeez, bite the bullet, talk will yah?"

"Here goes, don't say I didn't warn you. My friend is a first responder, he may have to come late or leave before we're done or even not show at the last moment. Whatever happens, we always come back here, sooner or later, and have our Christmas fuck. Whether he can be part of giving out gifts or not."

Directing all my attention to busy hands, I mumbled, "No problem, I already said I'll make myself scarce."

"So, the thing is he's been on a kick the last few years for us to do ménage-a-trios."

"I hate to snoop, but you and his wife aren't enough for this guy? What's he got, watermelon-size balls?"

Pushing back his chair, Gilbert stacked his pile of sloppily wrapped presents. "Here is the part where you get to say it's more information than you want. My friend has this crazy idea that if the guy who screws him is being screwed at the same time by me, he will vicariously experience triple pleasure. He claims he feels my orgasms almost as intensely as his own."

If there had been a light bulb over my head, it would have surged to bright. "Now I see, you're a *generous* person looking out for everybody."

"When he sees you, he will assume I am giving him the gift he wants most. I'm not hitting on you, but I really hate disappointing the man I love. His happiness means a lot to me."

Sliding back in the chair, my mood responded to his quandary and went into confession mode. "When you asked me about sleeping on the third shift at the Quicky Mart, I didn't mention what happens after the bars close."

"No, you didn't. Before I try and guess and get it wrong, why don't you tell me what happens?"

Unburdening myself, I spoke of things I never told before. "Lots of horny people of both genders, often more drunk than not, come in wanting chips, smokes, beer or a bottle of hooch. Some offer me money for quick anonymous sex back in the stockroom. The Quicky Mart only has the third shift when the underground mine isn't working, I don't know what these folks do when the mine is working."

"Does your boss Ed know about your private enterprise?"

"No, he wouldn't approve. Ed was best buds with my Pop. They shoveled coal together before Ed had his accident and got the cash settlement to open the Mart. When my Pop died, Ed tried to fill in for him with me. My mother never liked Ed."

"My unasked-for father substitutes here were pimps my mother chased off."

"Don't get it wrong, I earn my wages and my working makes life easier for Ed and his wife. His wife, Ellen, relieves me in the morning and I relieve Ed at midnight. When I'm not there, they close from twelve to eight, do all the cleaning, restocking, and make less money. But Ed can only pay me minimum wage, so the off the books sex-tip-money helps at home … when I had a home."

"Wait, you are saying you have sex with Quicky Mart customers after the bars close for money and wouldn't mind doing a three way with me and my friend for cash?"

"No, that's not what I said."

"How much is a three-way worth to you?"

"I'm not asking for money. I just wanted you to know some of my history, so you wouldn't look so guilty telling me about your married boyfriend."

"No, really how much? We have an ATM out front?"

"I said I don't want your money."

Getting up and topping off the coffees, Gilbert looked thoughtful. "Now I see why you didn't want to talk about sex, Mr. I'm-not-gay. Come on, I'll pay you for a threesome?"

Lifting my refreshed coffee mug toward my lips, I thought *Instead of helping I made it worse, it's becoming a habit!* "I don't identify with labels either. Still in all, even when the refrigerator is empty, there is sex I won't do. I'm making a mess of this conversation, aren't I?"

"Yes, you are."

"What I'm trying to say is, the sex I do for money is for my mother and our refrigerator. The doctors say my mother's health problems are best treated with lots of fresh proteins. They say good food is her best medicine right now. So, when the mine is closed … all right, I'll stop talking this isn't working. Fine I'll answer the question on your face, the only thing I won't do is get fucked."

Wildly throwing his hands in the air, Gilbert's face showed exasperation. "The one thing we need from you, and I would pay a premium price for."

"I can't give up my masculinity, yielding to another man like that. I've never had much besides my manhood."

"Un-huh!"

"What I'm trying to say is, I'll fuck you, if that's what you want, no charge. And you can fuck your friend while I screw you, no objection. Or any other combination you can think of, but no way can I be meat in the middle of a sandwich. I can't."

"Well, see, that's a problem. I'm truly bisexual, both genders turn me on equally, but I can't get my head around letting another guy mount and control me in sex. I know it sounds stupid because everyone says it's no big deal. I also know it is just sex and has no other meaning, and yet somehow, I can't open to be penetrated by another guy. It is weird because I've had females put all kinds of things back there to peg me for their amusements."

"Do you think your friend would settle for a circle jerk or daisy chain?"

"No. He's fixed on this idea. I've tried to offer him all sorts of other special sex treats. We have working girls here who love to do me favors. The more I try to change his fantasy, the more he digs in his heels."

We were silent, busy wrapping gifts until Gilbert pushed back his chair and stood up. "Finally, we are done. I hate gift wrapping. Help me put the gifts into shopping bags, and I'll call my friend for pick up."

"Wait, I'm almost done. This last one's bow is super fussy?"

Whipping out his cell phone, Gilbert punched one number and after a short pause said, "Hi, it's me! The gifts are wrapped, but we need to stop at the Quicky Mart on the way... I know it is closed ... but someone with a key wants to give the kids Christmas candy ... How about I tell you when you get here? I can't wait to see you either, love you, bye." Gilbert walked over and poured the rest of the coffee into a thermos and washed the large French coffee press. "Drink up, he'll be here in a couple of minutes."

We heard a van engine then tires softly crunch snow, out front. Gilbert immediately went to a closet and flapped into a long black leather overcoat, then grabbed three bags of gifts. "If you grab those last two bags, we'll have them all. Don't forget to put those galoshes on your feet." Then he was out the motel's front door in a hurry.

For some reason, it was the first time I took a careful appraising look at Gilbert beyond his potbelly. Rushing to the arms of his lover, in that strikingly stylish, expensive-looking ankle-length black leather overcoat, Gilbert looked movie star handsome, potbelly and all. The angled planes of his rugged face suddenly came together in an attractive, unified harmony I'd somehow missed in my self-absorbed wretchedness.

I picked up the remaining bags of gifts ready to follow him outside, reminding myself I'd not committed to anything more than giving candy. Then a thought intruded. I remembered to rummage around in the front closet for galoshes. When I found a big pair, they looked too large. But on closer inspection, each had a shoe inside and weren't a bad fit. With the overshoes on, I was about to rush through the outer office door, when something stopped me. I went to the office window and peered out. There was an older, silver cargo van parked in front. Two men were holding each other kissing passionately between the van and motel entrance. Gilbert's back was to me and I couldn't make out who was holding him, their faces were mashed together in a kiss. After some moments, the men broke their clinch and Gilbert turned his face toward the motel front door. This had to be my cue to join them.

As I walked through the door, Gilbert said, "We were wondering what happened to you. This is my friend Dennis."

My jaw dropped. It was Dennis Moran from my Air Explorer Scout days, and most recently carrying Mother and me out of our burning home to safety. Flabbergasted, I instinctively stuck my hand out for a shake, but Dennis grabbed me for a passionate hug and a brief mouth to mouth kiss. I was blindsided by emotions, some contradictory some complimentary, and all too close to the surface to be manly. I didn't know whether to laugh or cry or fall-down in a conniption fit.

Gilbert saved the day. "Come on, guys, we got to get going while it's still Christmas."

Dennis, wearing faded jeans, red sweatshirt under a brown leather bomber jacket, stepped back and looked me up and down. "I remember you from earlier today and the Air Explore Squadron years ago. I hope this means you are going to join Gil and me for a Christmas threesome."

I was speechless for a second, and then spoke the first thing that came into my head. "Oh, sure, I guess. I owe you both so much."

"Earlier today I was doing my job. They pay me for that. As scouts, you went above and beyond for my sake. We can't call it even. Anyway, the kids are waiting, let's go be Santa Claus."

When we stopped at the Quicky Mart, Ed and his wife, Ellen, were there measuring for store fixtures they just bought at auction. After I introduced everyone around, I explained how mother and I got burned out. Then quickly, before they could offer help, I told them we were on our way to give gifts to kids in a group home. And I wanted to give the kids Christmas candy the Quicky Mart hadn't sold.

"Take the price of the candy out of my next check."

Both Ed and Ellen spoke as one. "We'll do no such thing. It is on us." With that said, Ellen gathered up all the Christmas candy in the store into a big cardboard box and handed it to me.

Voice still smoky raw, I said, "Thank you and Merry Christmas." Then Dennis, Gilbert, and I headed to the group home.

The home looked like other houses in the residential neighborhood except it was bigger, better landscaped, and had parking for seven cars. The boys were assembled in a large multipurpose room and had been waiting impatiently. A more sullen, depressed, pouting bunch of young faces was hard to imagine. Three boys looked overmedicated to the point of stupefaction. Two others standing in different corners seemed to be repeating rituals with strange head, hand, leg, and foot gyrations. As with the stupefied boys, they seemed oblivious to everyone present. Three of the smallest teens looked hangdog-miserable; my heart went out to them all. But once we started giving out the presents and candy, smiles and cheerful laughter completely changed most boys' faces into exuberance.

Gift giving took thirty minutes. In that short time, the change in the group home's mood was measurable. It went from sullen on-guard, all defense shields up, to defense shields down, sharing infectious fun playing with, *and breaking*, the ninety-nine-cent store chintzy gifts. Before we left, the kids insisted on giving us a voice-cracking, badly out of tune and rhythm rendition of their Christmas carol medley. It was so off key awful, we had to join in to cut the pain. That was followed by three boisterous cheers of hurrah and mandatory thank-you handshakes. A few boys even insisted on giving us hugs with whispered, "Please take me with you."

The child care workers didn't look happy. I imagine when the sugar from the Christmas candy kicked in, some boys would be bouncing off the walls, making the workers' job harder, *and who wants to work on Christmas*? But at least the workers could go home at the end of their shift. I realized as miserable as it seemed for Mother and me, we had each other. These kids, whatever their story, appeared to have it worse.

Driving back to the motel, again I sat on a wobbly wooden bench in the back of the van and spoke to the backs of the two lovers in the front. "How is this going to work? I know I must be in the middle with Dennis in front and Gilbert behind. But are there rules or code words or something I need to know? I've never done this."

"We haven't either."

"Then not for nothing, my rule is if it hurts I stop, game over. You guys okay with that?"

Dennis was driving and spoke right up. "We don't have rules but have a plan. While you and I make out kissy-face, Gilbert will rim me and help you go inside. Then he'll rim you until you are ready for him. Got it? He likes to rim and is very good. You'll see."

"What about my rule?"

"Don't worry, no one gets hurt."

"If I'm screwing you and Gilbert is rimming me, I'll probably cum right away. I have a hair-trigger response when over-stimulated. That's probably not what you want?"

Sounding like a sagacious professor describing his research, Dennis explained while glancing at me in the rearview mirror. "I don't want us all coming at the same time, even if that was possible. It would defeat my purpose discerning degrees of intensity during orgasm sharing."

"Could you dumb that down for me?"

"Ideally, Ray, you will come first, then Gil, and then me, *and* all while we are cock-locked moving in tune with each other. But wait to cum until we are all ready. If you feel too close, say 'stop,' wait until the urge passes, then say 'okay' and we'll catch up."

"I hope I don't sound too stupid, but do you choreographs my finish too?"

"Once you're inside me, don't move until Gil is in you. Then I'll count to three and we all start moving slowly. When we find the range of motions and comfort, I'll say 'four,' and move at your own pace. I can't imagine we could fuck vigorously without disrupting the flow, so it is slow and easy throughout the build up to the finish."

"Ray, we don't want to keep stopping to plug you back in. That would be unaesthetic. The order is you first, then me, and finally Dennis in a continuous, smooth easy action."

"Got it. Once we get riding-the-horsey in sync, I can cum when ready, right?"

Giving me a nonplussed look in the mirror, Dennis said, "No, give us a heads-up first. This is a team endeavor."

"Now I got it."

"I'm sure it won't take long if you guys are as turned on as I am. But Gil will need to exercise the most self-control. Once Ray starts, nature will automatically lead us."

Exchanging an agreement nod, Gilbert and I said, "Okay, boss."

Back at the motel, I wondered out loud. "Won't our mothers miss us?"

"My mom's car is gone. That means she took your mom to the diner for breakfast. If they're hitting-it -off, they'll go for a drive after. Come-on guys." Gilbert led us to one of the cabins they rent by the hour. "The girls don't usually work this early on Christmas. But just in case, I cleaned this room last."

The room was gaudy neon pink and dark red with black accents. It smelled like roses and looked clean. Here and there were small red plastic bowls filled with condoms, antiseptic wipes, and sex lubricant packets. A tray of tiny bottles of mouthwash, breath mints, and tissues was close to the big heart shaped bed.

Gilbert and Dennis removed the fake-fur Duve and then started undressing each other. I went to pee and rewash areas where Gilbert's mouth and tongue might venture. While washing, it struck me. I was about to give up the last thing I had to lose, my pride and self-respect. Still, the nagging question was: *if that's true, why was I so turned on?*

When I returned to the main room, Dennis and Gilbert were lying naked, intertwined, passionately kissing, hands roaming. I had removed my new-old clothes in the bathroom to wash, and placed them neatly folded on a bedside chair. Ready or not, I climbed on the bed and was swallowed into three ways kissing and fondling. At some point, I wasn't paying attention, I'd given up my treasured self-determination to be their third wheel in the middle. Maybe it was okay to repay their kindness with the only thing I had left, my body.

Abruptly it was only Dennis and me making out, laying on our sides face to face. I remembered his soft full lips from Air Explorer Scout days. As we sucked face, our fingers sought out and touched sensitized places, then Dennis tensed. Glancing over his shoulder, I saw Gilbert's face pressed between Dennis' ass cheeks. As I wrapped him tighter in my arms, Dennis began purring into my mouth. Secondhand, I experienced the pure pleasure of receiving a rim-job going in deeper. The newness of vicariously experiencing another's pleasure became my primary preoccupation.

Next thing I knew, Gilbert had wiggled up between us, first kissing Dennis then me, while rolling a condom down over my extra ready erection.Then Gilbert moved Dennis, so his back was facing me. "Now, you two scoot together and I'll fit the key into the spit slick keyhole." That was said as we squirmed into position, then Gilbert guided my cock into Dennis. I easily slid into his wet fuck sleeve.

"Nobody move until I say go."

I nuzzled Dennis' shoulders until I abruptly froze from an intense forbidden pleasure. Gilbert licked and kissed and then invaded my bottom hole with a long slurping tongue. Concentrated jolts of ecstasy shot from his wet, penetrating mouth appendage jiggling up into my body, expanding the word delight. He was transferring erotic vibrations from his long, slippery tongue directly to my core's bottom entry. It was the beginning of what I said would never happen. Then he was tongue fucking me with vigor and soon would be cock fucking me. This was my last chance to bailout. My mind whimpered stop, my body shouted more, deeper, harder. Resistance gone, I yielded, and willingly acquiesced to another personal loss. In so doing I was engulfed in hitherto unknown intense groin pleasure, back to front.

To consciously give my selfless gift, I stopped thinking and became only a receptacle for their purpose.Gilbert's tongue seemed to joyfully drill my virgin nether regions, and I mouthed and nipped Dennis' shoulders driven by the blissful tongue loosening my sphincter ring. By the time Gilbert stopped lapping my hole, I was panting in ecstasy, teetering on the edge of a spontaneous anal-orgasm. Gil abruptly stopped tongue fucking me. After a moment's pause for condom fitting, I felt Gilbert push his cock deep into me in one slow, delicious push. It was exactly what I needed to fill the void the fire left. More previously unknown pleasures shot through me as his cock found my prostate. So, with an involuntary wiggle, I thrust back.

"Okay, I'm in, Dennis. I mean Commander Kirk."

On Gilbert's words, my mind focused back to Dennis. I tuned-in-to how he had been vicariously enjoying my pleasure being skillfully rimmed then skewered from my gasps and grasps.

"On my count, men, move half a stroke out then back. If this goes smoothly, find your own pace on 'four;' one, two, three, Merry Christmas."

I pulled out half way and then pushed back in. It was a successful test. I learned to move back and forth in tandem with Gilbert's driving in back. After a few more measured half strokes, I heard *"four,"* and concentrated on enjoying the ride without forecasting the destination.

In response to the others' movements, mine increased to match their prodding.

Then Gilbert switched to driving long, hard strokes into my ass in counterpoint to my dicking Dennis. When we shifted to a higher gear fucking, Gilbert switched strategies again and started fucking me in the same rhythm and direction I was doing Dennis. That quickly brought me to the edge of total bliss. I stopped thrusting and then Gilbert did. It occurred to me to hum "A Bicycle Built for Two," changing Daisy to Dennis to distract from cumming. Then decided I'd been putting my foot in my mouth much too much and this wasn't a time for song.

All three of us lay on our sides, coupled like train cars. I listened to and felt their breathing and matched it while touching them fore and aft. Then I dug my fingers into Dennis' shoulders, the shoulders that carried me out of fire. Gilbert had hands clamped over my pecks, a thumb and forefinger gripped each nipple. I figured it was to distract me from climaxing too soon. It would have been so easy to get lost in our mass of bodies plugged together, where one began, and another ended.

After an indeterminate time lost in tactile sensations, I focused my smoke-fogged brain when Dennis said, "Come on guys, let's finish." Then he started moving on my cock and that got Gilbert going. They were moving faster and faster and harder. I found my part and joined the chorus in sync.

Too much had happened, was happening, and all too fast. I didn't make any effort to control my orgasm. "I'm cumming! Oh, yeah, that's it, umph, ugh, ooh yes. Yes!" Believe it or not, I felt Dennis' consciousness lock onto and join with what I was experiencing. Weird, it felt like he was my copilot as I launched into blissful space, floating gravity-free. My body had contorted into delightful sensory elation while I grasped him tight. My serenity pinnacle was reached by ejaculation. Still, I still kept thrusting long after my rapture wad was spent.

My full cognition returned with, *That was the only gift I had to give. Then, I really needed to drop that load. Getting fucked is definitely underrated!*

Then Gilbert bellowed, "I'm cumming," and I could feel his pleasure as it built. It was recycled through a thin gauze screen but nevertheless present for me. His body was plunging in and out of me, then he went ridged, shook and slithered against my back for long seconds. Then shared his orgasm's intensity in ways I never imagined, from the inside.

Just after Gilbert stopped shooting cum up my ass, Dennis loudly declared, "I'm cumming." He thrashed about in the throes of blasting sperm onto the pink bed sheets while I held his body tight and thrust hard to increase his enjoyment. My thrusting into Dennis caused Gilbert's deflating cock to slide out of me with a plop. Funny thing, I missed feeling Gilbert back there.

When Dennis finished moving, I stopped and watched Gilbert roll off his condom, knot its top and tossed it into a wastebasket across the room. I hadn't really paid attention to his cock before. Though not as big as me, it was plenty big enough to be remembered.

Self-conscious from my cock staring, Gilbert scrambled over me to suck face with his fireman. As their arms locked around each other, their mouths kissed in ways that must have taken years to perfect. A twinge of jealousy started until I consciously stopped it, accepting I was homeless with nothing left to give anyone.

In reaction to my trying to be objective, I was flooded with feelings I'd stuffed down. On auto-pilot I slipped out of Dennis and carefully rolled my full condom down and off. I knotted the top and tossed it into the wastebasket Gilbert used.

To keep my flooding thoughts at bay, I joined Dennis and Gilbert by pressing myself on top of them for some three-way suck face and touchy-feely after-play. When we broke for air, I panted, "Dennis, did your experiment work?"

"Not really, I wanted to get more from what Gil was feeling. It was there only in shadow, not as strong as I hoped."

"If you are still interested in this research, be in the middle next time. I felt both of you climax, almost as strongly as mine."

"Duly noted ol' buddy."

"If you don't mind my two-cent interference, I think the best way to get what you're after is for Gilbert and me to fuck you at the same time, if you can stretch that open?"

For a long moment, Dennis just looked at me. "Huh, I've been fisted. If you guys are willing, I'd like to try that next Christmas. How about same players, different arrangement?"

Gilbert perked right up. "As long as I don't have to get fucked, I'm fine with it. I guess Ray didn't like getting fucked."

I locked on Gilbert's dark green eyes with my baby blues and sincerity came through my voice. "You have no idea what a turbo charged experience you're missing by not being the meat in the sandwich."

Dennis nodded his head in agreement.

Looking from one to the other of us, Gilbert said, "What, what am I missing? Wasn't I here just now?"

"It wasn't what I expected. It didn't hurt or smell bad or feel dirty. Old and new sensations got mixed together in totally amazing ways. It took great sex to a high level."

"You want to explain that so I can understand?"

"I'll try, so as long as I can remember sex has always been about getting my rocks off, period. Getting fucked today was collaboration, giving and receiving, involved with both parts, more of the whole deal."

"What are you talking about?"

"I imagine it was more of a female-like experience. Without all the reproduction responsibility attached, different physiology, and misogyny. Allowing, giving and *getting*, rather than just taking possession ... *understand*, I got both halves of the whole experience?"

Gilbert looked perturbed. "No, Ray, I don't understand what you're saying."

Before I could try again, Dennis spoke up. "Gil, when I fuck it is like I plant my flag in conquest, coming inside another's body comes with unspecified protective responsibilities. But when I get fucked, it is like I willingly give and take, allowing myself to be joined in the most intimate way. Not just in an imperial conquest, but rather like Ray said, in collaboration. It is giving without the primary being taking, but that's included. I suppose you couldn't understand unless you tried it."

Gilbert, visibly defensive, scowled at us. "You two are so full of crap. It's Christmas, let's change the subject?"

I swung my legs around and off the bed to sit on its edge and ended up sitting on the floor. I felt weighed down by all kinds of emotions, just a little from failure to communicate with Gilbert. So much had happened since I went to bed Christmas Eve, looking forward to opening our presents on Christmas morning. I was so eager to see the happiness on Mother's face, when she opened the special gift I went into hock for.

Before I realized it, I was silently crying. Gilbert and Dennis noticed my absence and pulled me back up onto the bed. They held me on both sides and kissed and caressed me, but the sobs wouldn't stop.

"I didn't mean to upset you," Gilbert said with concern.

Dennis chimed in with a smile. "Was sex with us so awful it made you cry, ol' friend?"

Before I could try to speak, Gilbert said, "It was his first time being fucked. I guess he had a problem with it even after all the bullshit he said."

Feeling miserable, I shook my head no and between sobs gurgled, "It wasn't any of that."

"What's the problem?"

Clearing my throat and wiping tears away, I said, "I can't start over with nothing. Mother's health isn't good and now I don't even have a piss pot. No way can I begin again at my age. I'm middle-age, over forty. It's totally hopeless." Then my unmanly tears really started to pour out.

Dennis took my hands in his. "Nobody expects you to do it alone. Gilbert and I know people who know people, and the Red Cross and County Social Services are all going to help you get your life back, maybe even better. I bet in less than a year you won't believe you felt like this, and you will know who your friends are."

Gilbert jumped into the conversation. "Ray does think he has to do everything by himself. He has had trouble accepting my help as little as it was."

Dropping my hand and grabbing my shoulders and giving them a gentle shake, Dennis asked, "Is that true, ol' buddy?"

Forlornly I nodded yes.

Dennis said, "Let me tell you a better after-a-disaster story, okay?"

Through tears I choked out, "Sure. Whatever."

"So, on 9/11 a call went out for first responders to help out. We committed one old fire truck and a crew. I volunteered. I had just finished fire department mandatory one-year probation after training. We expected our destination to be the Pentagon in Washington D.C. because it's closer to here. But at the last minute, we were told they had enough help, but New York City could still use assistance. When we got the word, we were going to New York, several volunteers backed out. Many local preachers and most of the televangelists were proclaiming 9/11 was God's wrath on the United States for not persecuting homosexuals and for giving women reproductive freedoms."

Gilbert spoke up right away. "I remember that they were preaching on TV that New York City was the new Sodom and Gomorrah, and God was going to completely destroy it and California. But wait, what did the Pentagon and field in Pennsylvania do to piss off God?"

Dismissing Gilbert's comments with a wave, Dennis continued. "We easily replaced the scared Bible-thumping volunteers and went to the Big Apple, not knowing what to expect. We heard in the past, New York had been generous sending their first responders to other cities during bad times. Trying to get the smoldering fires out under the World Trade Center disaster site, we met fire crews from as far away as Louisiana, Oklahoma, and even Puerto Rico. They came because New York City had gone to help them during their troubles."

Half in jest, Gilbert asked, "Is it really a Sin City like the preachers say?"

"No, I didn't see any more sin there than we have here, maybe less."

"Hot damn, another myth bites the dust."

"We were surprised how friendly and generous the New Yorkers were. We heard New Yorkers were tough, rude, know-it-all arrogant bastards. Maybe some are, but we were treated kindly and with respect. They brought us food they cooked themselves, and even offered to let us stay in their homes. Hotels big and small let us stay for free, restaurants wouldn't take our money, and overall it was a positive people helping people connection. I made a lot of new friends, fire fighters and cops from there and around the country."

My tears and sobbing stopped as I listened to his story. Then snuggling between Gilbert and Dennis I asked, "Is that the good after the bad you want me to know?"

"No, I've kept in touch with some of those New York City firemen and cops. We exchange e-mails and Christmas cards and have standing invitations to visit each other's homes. When I have asked how New York is doing after the Twin Towers were destroyed, I get the same answer. New York is a more optimistic place since the Towers came down."

"How is that possible, over 3,000 innocent people were killed in the name of some vengeful, hateful God?"

"They say the constant complainers and other malcontents fled the city fearing another attack. The people who remained were willing to handle what came next and to be good neighbors. New York has become a friendlier place to live and work, since the bad element ran away fleeing for their lives."

"I don't know ... my situation looks totally beyond hope from here."

Gilbert perked up and said, "Hey, we're telling you, you can handle this. Dennis and I have seen folks worse off than you come out of tragedy just fine."

"I want to believe you guys, I do."

Looking like he just got a brilliant idea, Gilbert took over the conversation. "I'll tell you a different but similar story. So, I've been a Red Sox baseball fan since a kid, and one thing we Sox fans have in common is we *hate* the New York Yankees. Yankees took El Bambino, Babe Ruth, away from Boston and that was unforgivable. Hate, that is until the Boston Marathon pressure cooker bombings caused human pain and death to innocents. At the start of a big game between New York and Boston, the whole New York Yankees organization came out and stood facing the fans in a sold-out Yankee Stadium and sang "Sweet Caroline." That's the Red Sox theme song. Nobody made a big fuss about it, and the Yankees certainly didn't have to do it. By singing the Red Sox's song, New York let Boston know, 'We are with you, and have been where you are. You too will get beyond being bombed and be stronger from it.'"

Feeling better from uplifting stories, I stuck my foot in my mouth again. "Ugh, well see, fellas ... I wanted to hum "A Bicycle Built for Two," when we were screwing." That's when they punched my upper arms, rolled me over, and tickled me until somehow we morphed back into three-way kissing. First one then the other fuck buddy drifted into sleep.

Concrete thoughts flooded my brain as the others went off to dreamland, *Mother is safe. I am alive and safe sandwiched between the fireman who saved my ass and the hotelier who clothed then fucked it. Life is moving on, and I need to stop dwelling on my Christmas nightmare.* Those thoughts brought up the words and tune to "Sweet Caroline." I sang it softly to myself as I drifted into an overdue deep, dreamless sleep.

About the Author

Peter Melillo was born in New Haven, Connecticut, moved to Tucson, Arizona, at age seven, then moved to New York City at age twenty-five. In 2013, JM Snyder Books published a collection of twelve of his gay war short stories: *For Man and Country*. In total, JM Snyder Books published sixteen short stories by Peter Melillo on line as e-books. In 2018 Querelle Independent published *Fairy Swatter*, six short stories with murder as a side issue. Peter can be reached at peteramelillo@gmail.com.

www.ingramcontent.com/pod-product-compliance
Lightning Source LLC
Chambersburg PA
CBHW022012010726
47494CB00003B/1001